MW00399816

The
Perfect
Swing

The
Perfect
Swing

One woman's search for God

THOMAS LENHART

The Perfect Swing ©2019 Thomas Lenhart

This book is a work of historical fiction. Names, characters, places, institutions, and incidents are either historically factual or the product of the author's imagination and are used fictitiously. Any resemblance to actual events, locales, or persons, living or dead, not in the historical record or the author's history is coincidental.

This book is protected under the U.S. Copyright Act of 1976 and all other applicable international, federal, state, and local laws with all rights reserved. No part of this book may be copied, sold, or used in any other way (other than for educational or review purposes) without express permission from Thomas Lenhart.

FOR THE FAMILY

Present and Future

One generation shall laud thy works to another, and shall declare thy mighty acts. On the glorious splendor of thy majesty, and on thy wondrous works, I will meditate.

Psalm 145:4-5

Then they said to him, "What must we do, to be doing the works of God?" Jesus answered them, "This is the work of God, that you believe in him whom he has sent." So they said to him, "Then what sign do you do, that we may see, and believe you? What work do you perform?"

John 6:28-30

Now in putting everything in subjection to him, he left nothing outside his control. As it is, we do not yet see everything in subjection to him. But we see Jesus, who for a little while was made lower than the angels, crowned with glory and honor because of the suffering of death, so that by the grace of God he might taste death for every one.

Hebrews 2:8-9

Contents

I

CORY

The Grandson

Cory's mother knew something was troubling him. He didn't think it showed on his face or could be heard in the tone of his voice. Sometimes his laugh, coming more quickly than usual or lasting longer, would give it away. This time, though, he thought it was well concealed. Yet from the questioning look she occasionally gave him, Cory could tell she wasn't fooled. She had the uncanny ability to spot things like that. Perhaps it was standard equipment for mothers issued at birth, part of the in and out exchange of new life: the baby came out and this sensitivity, similar to radar yet more certain of its sightings, came in. But she didn't say anything about it as the afternoon wore on. It wasn't her way; it wasn't their way. They had a time for matters like this and a place.

Since Cory was a boy, maybe it had started as early as fifth grade, they had an understanding. It had suddenly just been there, without being discussed or agreed to. They would talk not during the day with its intrusions but at night in the living room when everyone else was upstairs in their bedrooms. They had a set of signals as well. For his mother, it was the book she had been reading on the sofa lying flat across her chest. The act of putting down the book invited him to talk and told him she was ready to listen, all night if necessary, until he was finished. He signaled her something was on his mind when he stood next to the fireplace, it didn't matter if there was a fire in it or not, and picking up the poker iron started to swing it the way he swung a baseball bat. They also had their rules. He could meander or be direct, use faultless logic or be illogical, make sense or talk nonsense. She could interrupt him to ask for more information but could not correct him to make his thinking more rigorous, though, on occasion, she did gently try to redirect it. He could tell her whatever it was he was struggling with, there were no boundaries he had to stay within, and, most important, he could ask her anything. She could choose not to reply, if he had asked how much money they had in the bank she wouldn't have told him, but if she did give an answer, it had to be well-considered and honest, and it always was. They both knew they were talking about the hard things of his life, and there was no benefit from half- truths.

A living room conversation that set the standard for the coming years occurred one evening when Cory was in sixth grade. He was trying to understand why swear words were used and if he should use them. Without hesitation, he asked, "Mother, did you swear when you were growing up?" She was cornered. If she admitted to swearing, she could topple from the heights he had raised her to, and since he had put her there that was probably where he needed her to be, and if she didn't, she would be dishonest, and that was against the rules. Some twenty plus years later he still recalled her answer. "On occasion," was all she said, and all she needed to say. For a brief time, during the school day, while walking down the hallway or taking out a sheet of paper from his desk or waiting to catch a ball, he would imagine his mother as a young girl about his age saying in anger, "damn." But soon that voice faded until he no longer heard it.

As the years went by, the standard didn't change but the subject did. It soon switched from profanity to girls, dating, and sex, and in time moved on to relationships and love, employment, aspirations, and events large and small in the wider world. Some matters, though, were never discussed. Among them were what others did, what politicians said, and what his father thought. This meant they didn't gossip; they didn't discuss politics; and they didn't defer to his father's opinions, however perceptive they might be.

That night Cory and his mother were once again alone in the living room. Everyone else, including Cory's wife, had gone upstairs to bed. He and Meg had come from New York by plane to spend a week with his parents. It felt good to be in their home. One of nine houses on a mile and a half long stretch of country road with the waters of Puget Sound on one side and dense woods on the other, it was peaceful. It also brought needed relief from his work on Wall Street. Since graduating from college seven years earlier, he had acquired a master's degree in economics and found employment in the research department of a dealer in government securities. The work, he was beginning to realize, although punctuated with brief periods of feverish excitement, had little hold on him. He could easily walk away from analyzing numbers and turning them into reports that others paid little attention to. The flight across country, though long, especially with a two hour layover in Chicago, had been uneventful. It was after they had landed, and the plane was taxing to the arrival gate that the trip started to sour. His mother was right: he was troubled.

Picking up the poker out of the stand next to the fireplace, he wrapped his hands around its handle and dropped down into his old batting stance. His mother, watching him ready to connect with an imaginary pitch, smiled. "I noticed something when the plane was coming to a stop at the airport," Cory began. "Those close to the aisle got up to retrieve baggage in the overhead bins, those next to the windows stayed in their seats. Some were standing, some were sitting, but virtually everyone was doing the same thing. They were either turning on their phones, or punching in their numbers, or speaking into them. They didn't lower their voices; they raised them to be heard over everyone else. The thought struck me they were dancing with their phones, dancing a compulsive three-step choreographed by the telecommunications industry, and they were singing as they danced. Phone conversations, once often intimate and always private, had become a loud dancing chorus of discordant singers oblivious to one another. I suddenly found the conformity oppressive and alarming. I was a part of this chorus, whether in the front row or in the back, it didn't matter. I was there—dancing someone else's dance, singing someone else's song.

"Inside the airport on my way to the baggage claim area, I stopped at the restroom. I was washing my hands when I heard someone begin talking in a loud voice that careened off the hard, tiled surfaces of that room. He was urinating with one arm resting on top of the partition between the urinals. In that hand, he held a phone, which he was talking into, while in his other hand he was holding his penis. I wondered what the person he was talking to thought the background noise was. Could that person really have been pleased to know that he, and it certainly could have been she, was listening to him urinate? Though the man at the urinal obviously had no second thoughts about what he was doing, I did. He was making what I at least considered a most private act obscenely public. This couldn't possibly get any worse, I thought. I was wrong.

"The shuttle ride from the airport to the terminal on the far side of town took close to an hour and a half. For that entire time, two women sitting in the rear of the van across the aisle from each other talked loud enough to be heard not only by all of us but by everyone else on the highway, even with their windows rolled up and their radios blaring. It wasn't just that they were so loud; what really annoyed me was that they were so personal. One woman, needing to buy a ticket for the shuttle, asked if she could use a credit card. Going to where she was seated, the driver gave her a cell phone to call his office with the required information for the voucher. She shouted into the phone her name, address, telephone number, and credit card number making, I'm sure, the person she was talking to reel and anyone on the van with a criminal bent salivate. She then turned to the woman across from her and the two proceeded to tell each other and everybody else all about their lives. We could only have escaped this onslaught if we had been beaten into unconsciousness, which became increasingly more appealing as the miles went by. It's hard to imagine what they left out about their children, their work, their marriages, their financial situations, their answers to the country's problems. One woman even told us, right down to the raspberry vinaigrette salad dressing, what she was going to have for dinner the next day. We got it all, I think, except for the pin number to their bank accounts. It's not that the distinction between the very private and the public is fuzzy; it's disappearing altogether."

"I remember last year watching on television a Thanksgiving Day parade," his mother said. "One moment the parade was going by and the next moment we saw a young man in the middle of the street kneeling before a girl who had been walking beside a float. He's asking her to marry him we were told. The proposal in front of a television camera with a nationwide audience looking on seemed to startle her, but she threw her arms around him and kissed him, which we took for a yes. Across America millions celebrated their engagement and wished them well. But I kept wondering what would have happened if she had been undecided about the marriage or didn't even want it? She couldn't have asked for more time to think about it and certainly couldn't have said no on national television. She needed privacy for that and didn't have it. If she had misgivings and he was aware of it, then the proposal in its intent wasn't romantic; it was coercive."

"When you met us at the service station," Cory replied, "I sank into the back seat and didn't say much during the drive home. I had to recover from the pummeling the two women on the van had given me."

"And where were you after you had settled down?"

"Immersed in a daydream. I saw myself first in a restaurant at the airport. Waiting for the meal I had ordered, I took out my phone and, holding it to my ear, said in a loud voice, 'Pete, Cory here. What's happening to the stock market?' Everyone in the restaurant stopped eating. 'Sell all my treasury bonds, you say. The interest payment can't be met. The government is bankrupt.' Next, I was at a crowded departure gate at the airport. The announcement had just been made that all the preparations for flight Number 1973 had been completed, and we would be in the air soon. As we stood in an orderly boarding line, I shouted into my phone, 'Ed, Cory here. I'm told you worked on the plane for flight 1973. Is it ready to go?' I'm silent for a moment as everyone looked at me. 'Missing the stabilizing pin for the vertical lifter of the right wing, you say, but made it through the inspection checklist anyway. You wouldn't get on that plane if your life depended on it.' Then I was riding in the airport shuttle. It was empty except for the two women who had tormented me. In the middle of their verbal barrage, I took out my phone, a wicked gleam in my eyes, and roared, 'Jim, Cory here. Has the lab test for the spots all over my body come back?' The two women instantly stopped talking. I looked heavenward knowing that I had just witnessed a miracle. 'A new strain of the plague, you say, and it's highly contagious.'"

"What do you think is happening?" his mother asked.

"Maybe people today feel so desperately alone they have an insatiable need to be noticed, so they are making their personal lives available for public consumption to be recognized. But there is a consequence when the private becomes public. Dissimulation creeps in, even unintentionally, making one's true self recede, possibly to the point where it's lost altogether."

"No, Cory," his mother said, "I mean what do you think is happening to you?"

He stopped swinging the poker and sat down in a leather chair across from her. Looking away from her searching gaze, Cory was silent for a long moment. Why had those phones in the airplane set him off? Families and friends were just being told the plane had landed safely and needed information about pickup times and meeting places. What did it matter to him if someone wanted to urinate while talking on the phone? It was efficient. Perhaps those two women on the van regularly sang the lead roles in a community opera company. Their voices had been trained to project to the last row of a cavernous auditorium. They might have even lowered their volume and thought they were practically whispering out of consideration for others on the van. He finally said, having grown up sailing, "I'm probably making a squall out of a light breeze."

"That happens. But you don't want to make a light breeze out of a squall. I'd say your daydream was more of a gale. Where is this foul weather coming from?"

He hesitated only a moment before replying, "It's coming from work. I don't see myself spending the rest of my life manipulating numbers. They're too lifeless, and I'm beginning to realize that while I am a capable analyst, I am not exceptional. Something else, though, something much more basic, is off. I don't really care about making money—for someone else or, for that matter, even for myself." He heard the clock on the table chime twelve times. "I want work I'll get up at three o'clock in the morning to do, willingly, eagerly. To figure out what that might be, I think I first have to figure out myself."

"If your grandfather were here, he would say to do that you first have to figure out God."

"Because I'm made in the image of God?"

"That's where he'd have you start, yes."

Cory again picked up the poker. "Maybe I should look at that book Grandfather wrote years ago. It's on a bookshelf at home, but

I've never gotten around to reading it. Doesn't the title have something to do with baseball?"

"It does. The title of the book is *The Perfect Swing*. It is about baseball, although not the baseball you're probably thinking of, and a number of other matters as well," his mother said.

"Gracie, our dog, taught me something last month when we were visiting friends living in the country in upstate New York. We were walking the dogs after dinner. Kodi, a typical Malamute, was looking for work to do. He had picked up a tree limb from the middle of the road and was moving it to one side. Gracie, slender, aerodynamic, and very powerful, especially the legs, was hunting. She was moving off the road into the woods. Suddenly, she had a different idea. Something had forced its way into her mind, an inspiration of some kind, or maybe even a revelation. She lifted her head up, turned herself parallel to the road, and then with all the energy she possessed, all the power, and all the grace, she ran as fast as she could for forty yards, and then came back as fast as she could, and then went again and after forty yards came back a second time. She wasn't running after anything; she wasn't competing against any other dog. She just ran. She ran with complete abandonment, holding absolutely nothing back, and for no other reason than for the absolute sheer delight of running. It was an astonishing sight. That run raises the question I have to find an answer to. What is it that gives me sheer delight?"

"Your grandfather would agree. He, though, would probably say you're missing something else Gracie was teaching you."

"And that is?"

"Gracie not running like that," his mother answered. "She stopped didn't she? Her sheer delight lasted only a moment. Come to know what brings those moments and make sure that you do it, but it's the seemingly endless time between the moments of sheer delight that makes up a life. The good life has the right answer to this in-between time."

"Grandfather in that book of his is going to tell me about God, which is to be expected since he was a preacher and that's what preachers do. But I haven't wanted to hear it. I'm not sure where I am with God. Someone or something undoubtedly is out there. Although astrophysics explains how just about everything appeared, it doesn't know where the first tiniest fraction of a second came from. I'll give God this gap in its knowledge. God was back then, but being here now is what I'm having trouble with. Maybe, though, the problem is not so much God as it is the church. Its history hasn't been that illustrious. In the past, it has all too often either been a part of what was wrong, or it has shown up too late to be much of a part of what was right. The church today is hardly inviting. From what I hear, the faithful are fighting over music, politics, sex, language, and probably a dozen other issues as well. Who needs that?"

His mother was one of those persons who required only a few hours of sleep at night. Cory imagined she savored the stillness of the very early morning. She read, he was sure of that, and most likely thought about what had happened during the day, and being very much his grandfather's daughter, she perhaps prayed. It wouldn't have surprised him if she regularly had a living room conversation with God. He, though, needed his eight hours of sleep, and his mother knew it. Having noticed that he had stopped swinging the poker, she said, "Perhaps it's time for you to turn in. If you might want to look at your grandfather's book this week, it's over there in the bookcase. It's not about a pretentious minister and his belligerent congregation, but revolves around a Greek astronomer, a lady baseball player, and a visionary, who did what most of the men in the church, including the ministers, said couldn't be done, or, to be more exact, couldn't be done by a woman. And, of course, your grandfather is a large part of the book too."

As his mother returned to the book she had been reading, Cory went upstairs. Meg, a light sleeper, stirred when he opened the door to their room. "You've had another one of your conservations with your mother," she said, turning on the light next to the bed. "My mother and I never talk the way you two do. I'm envious."

"She thinks I should read Grandfather's book."

"We're not going anywhere this week that I know of. I like the idea of staying put. We can relax, take an afternoon walk in the woods, and, if the wind picks up, maybe go for a sail."

"Did you ever read Joyce's *Ulysses*?"

"Cory, isn't it a little late to be talking about Irish literature? It's after midnight. But, yes, I did read *Ulysses,* though I doubt you could call a good portion of what I did reading. In some chapters, I wasn't even skimming. I was only turning the pages."

"I turned a lot of pages too, but not all of them. Early in the book, Stephen Dedalus walks on a beach talking to himself for an entire chapter."

"Not a very exciting conversation as I remember," Meg replied, switching off the light.

"Right at the beginning, he says, 'I will see if I can see.' That's worth thinking about. He knows that if he's to find his way as a writer, he must see beneath the surface of what he's looking at. Grandfather's book just might help me improve my depth perception. The surface doesn't tell us what is really happening, or why it is happening, or, and this is a point I'm sure Grandfather makes somewhere in his book, what God is doing in what is happening."

"Good night, Cory."

II

RANDALL

The Grandfather

1

ONE AFTERNOON

Randall agreed with the family. The time had come to sell his parents' condominium. His mother had died and his father, because of his failing health, had been moved to a nursing facility where he was receiving excellent care. Over the past week, he had helped empty and clean the home until all the rooms were bare except for the spare bedroom. Its furniture had been removed, first the twin beds and then the end tables and the bureau. Only his mother's rolltop desk, a secretary he had heard her call it, was left. He thought of her at the desk writing her letters, the letters she had sent him regularly when he was away at college and afterwards when he was living on the West Coast and for a time in Alaska. He pulled out a few of the many small drawers toward the top of the desk. In one of them, there were paper clips and an unsharpened pencil. In another, he found an eraser. At the bottom of the desk, he saw to one side a drawer where his mother most likely had kept her stationery and writing tablets and the letters she wanted to answer. He opened it. Inside there was a large yellow envelope closed with a string wound several times around a circular metal fastener. On one side of the envelope, in his mother's unmistakable handwriting, were the words "for Randall."

He knew nothing about the envelope. It might have been in that drawer for the past twenty years. Maybe his mother had intended to give it to him, but as the months had gone by she had forgotten all about it. But she didn't forget about those kinds of things, especially when it came to her children. No, Randall reasoned, she must have put it there shortly before she died eight years ago. She obviously wanted him to have the envelope. Why, then, hadn't she told him about it? Was this another one of those matters she had worked out with God? He pictured his mother writing his name on the envelope, putting it in the drawer, and saying, "Randall will find this when he needs to." Unwinding the string, he opened the envelope and withdrew two books he had never seen before in their home. Both were prayer books; both were old. *The Book of Common Prayer,* the prayer book of the Episcopal Church, he was familiar with. The other prayer book, *Some Little Prayers,* he was not. Turning to the title page, he saw the author's name, Lucy Rider Meyer. The prayer book had more than a hundred pages, and on each page there was a prayer. Most of the prayers were short, so much of the page was blank. Going quickly through it, he could see that since the author had written only a few of the prayers, the book was a kind of prayer anthology.

Randall, a pastor, wondered if his mother was trying to improve his pastoral prayers. Or was she saying he needed to pray more often? Or was she getting at something else? A ruler once asked Jesus what he needed to do to inherit eternal life. Jesus answered obey the commandments, and when the ruler replied he kept them all, he said, "One thing you still lack." While others moved on to what came next, Jesus' order to sell what he had, give the money to the poor, and follow him, Randall in that passage stayed where he was. In Jesus' words, "One thing you still lack," there was, at least for him, an indictment that was the truth. Every week he stood before people speaking of things that if he did not lack them, he, at the very least, did not have enough of them. Yet he knew that while those words convicted him, they were not meant to turn him away from God. Instead, they were God's way of telling him to come closer. His life of faith and his work as a pastor were, in the end, based not upon what he had but all that he didn't have. It was his deficiency that took him to God in repentance and kept him before God in supplication. Had his mother understood this and decided she wanted to provide him with prayers for his many shortcomings?

Returning to *The Book of Common Prayer*, he noticed writing on the blank page across from the title page. Although the ink had faded, he was still able to make out the words "give me faith." Underneath these words were the name Mattie Welsh and the date March 8, 1908. It occurred to him that since the date had been included and, perhaps more significant, the full date had been used and not just the year, something important must have happened to Mattie Welsh that day.

He turned the envelope upside down, and two photographs fell out. One, to his surprise, was of a young woman in a baseball uniform. She wore pants ending just below the knees, long stockings so her legs were fully covered, and a jacket with the word Clippers in large, block letters across the front. Those pants, he thought, were called bloomers. She was holding a bat. Something about her, other than the way she was dressed, was unusual. It was not her size; she wasn't particularly large or powerful. It was, he decided, her intensity. In her attractive face, he saw the icy stare of one determined to win. She took this game seriously. The other photograph was obviously of the same woman, now a few years older, wearing a plain, dark, full-length skirt slightly flared at the bottom. The top was a matching, long-sleeved jacket with a high collar at the throat showing at the collar and at the edge of the sleeves a bit of a white blouse underneath. In this photograph, she was holding what appeared to be a Bible. He wondered if this, too, might be a uniform.

He thought it reasonable to assume the young woman in the two photographs was either Mattie Welsh or Lucy Rider Meyer. Because of her words in *The Book of Common Prayer,* "give me faith," and the Bible in her hand, assuming it was a Bible, in the photograph, he decided the young woman had to be Mattie Welsh. As he looked at the photographs more closely, he realized his mother might have given him the prayer books for another reason. Maybe she saw them in some way connecting him to Mattie Welsh. But how? And why? Putting the prayer books and the photographs back in the envelope and placing it in the cardboard box filled with other items he wanted to keep, Randall knew he had to become better acquainted with this mysterious young woman who liked to wear uniforms.

2

AFTER VISITING HOURS

Randall stored the cardboard box on the top shelf of his bedroom closet. One evening he quickly went through its contents and coming to the envelope took out the prayer books and the two photographs of Mattie Welsh. Inserting the photographs in *Some Little Prayers,* he carefully placed the prayer book on his bureau. He didn't like clutter, so the bureau top was virtually bare. On it, to one side, was a framed picture of a waterfall his wife had taken and, to the other side, a dolphin made out of cut glass, which he used primarily as a paper weight for the stack of letters and bills needing his attention. The rest of the bureau top was empty, so the prayer book, in the lower right-hand corner, was conspicuous. Randall found himself looking at it daily, in the morning as he was dressing, at night as he was getting ready for bed. Somewhere inside that prayer book might be information about Miss Welsh. Even if there wasn't, the prayers themselves would be worthwhile examining. But he didn't open the prayer book. He was thinking of retiring, and if he did, there would be ample time for it then and for a lot of other reading he wanted to do.

He was ready for retirement. Randall thought George Bernard Shaw had got it right in his introduction to *Man and Superman*: "This is the true joy in life, the being used for a purpose recognized by yourself as a mighty one; the being thoroughly worn out before you are thrown on the scrap heap." The ministry had done all three to him. In it, he had been used for what he believed was a mighty purpose. It had brought him joy, real joy. And most assuredly, it had worn him out. To be more precise, it had been, for the most part, suffering that had worn him out. He had lived, for decades now, in the presence of suffering. Never had he been beyond its reach. Either it had completely overtaken him and he was immersed in it, or it was only a phone call or a conversation or an office visit away. A phone ringing wherever he was, at the church, or in his home, or in a restaurant, or even out of town on vacation, invariably made his stomach tighten. What he was feeling, he had come to realize, was one part fear and two parts dread. Fear, as he used the word, had to do with a possibility. Suffering was to be feared because it could, though it didn't necessarily have to, wound the soul and, if severe enough, wound the soul fatally. Dread had to do with a fact. Something awful had occurred, and it was going to bring to someone a terrible sadness.

Years of experiencing this potent mixture of fear and dread had not hardened him to suffering, making him indifferent to it or causing him to turn away from it. He still felt deeply the pain of others and fully offered himself to them. But now the heartache stayed longer; it never really went away. He likened himself to a river being fed by a stream of tears. The water level kept getting higher. It, though, could not rise indefinitely. At some point, the water would overflow the banks of that dark river. That point hadn't been reached yet, but the water was closer to it than it had ever been before. The deaths, some slow in coming and others very sudden, the abuse and neglect that tore families apart, the inability and more often the unwillingness to forgive that destroyed relationships, the terrible loneliness, the discrimination, the rejection, these sorrows and countless others when added together over the years had literally driven him to his knees, seeking in prayer that peace that passed all understanding. Sometimes he found it; other times he didn't, or at least not enough of it. He was, Randall conceded, thoroughly worn out.

This sadness had undoubtedly tested his faith, at times severely. Repeatedly he had stood mute before the question why. Eventually you will know was all he could finally say, and that, in the end, why was not the question to ask. The question that brought hope and strength was how not why: how do I make my way to the other side of my sorrow where there is new life? Often he struggled with whether these few words were enough for the one desperately searching for answers. Most of the time he knew they were not, and there were those occasions when they were not enough for him.

But his faith had never wavered, largely because of a single moment in his life when he had seen with absolute clarity who he was, when he had beheld his true self. It was a moment he had claimed and tenaciously held onto ever since. This defining moment, ironically, had occurred in a hospital, a place where suffering was often most intense and pervasive.

In his second year at the seminary, he had taken a quarter of what was called clinical pastoral education. Though listed in the catalog as a course of study, it was not a class but an experience that had the power to shape one's eventual ministry and even one's life. The student was placed in a hospital for three months as a chaplain. It was full time, and for most, the responsibilities were all consuming. A new and oftentimes menacing world of the sick and the dying was entered with its own smells and noises, its own relationships, its own silences. If death occurred, the family was brought to the hospital having been told only that the condition had worsened. It was the chaplain who met them and tried to find the words and to display the faith that would steady them as they stared into the face of incalculable loss, and it unflinchingly stared back at them. The three months were demanding and revealing; one learned not what was in a text book but what was in the heart and in the soul. Most emerged from the quarter better able to provide pastoral care in a hospital, where a good portion of their ministry would eventually take place, and with a newly found spiritual toughness coming from knowing themselves and their relationship to God at a more honest and so at a much deeper level. Some dropped out along the way.

A nearby hospital accepted Randall into its short-term student chaplaincy program. The three student chaplains were to work five days a week, and each one of them would stay through the night alone every third night. The days did not overly concern him, there would be, if needed, safety in numbers. But the thought of nights by himself in that huge hospital was daunting. He, only a second-year seminary student, would walk its darkened hallways responsible for the spiritual needs of more than four hundred patients with no one to advise him, or to support him, or, if the needs became excessive, to assist him.

His first night at the hospital he ate a late dinner in the cafeteria and then, after visiting hours were over, took the elevator to the third floor. Down the hall on the left was the nurses' station for the surgical wing. As he walked by, a nurse stopped writing on a chart and looked up at him. He smiled and said hello, assuming it was not necessary to explain why he was there since the name tag on his coat pocket said chaplain and his clerical collar, which he had purchased the week before to wear in the hospital not only to assure others that he was official but to help assure himself as well, declared that he was clergy. She returned the smile and resumed her writing. To her, he was the night chaplain starting to make his calls on all the patients scheduled for surgery the next day. Trained to listen to those anxious about tomorrow's operation, to speak a comforting word, to pray with those who made a habit of prayer and with those who did not yet out of fear would turn to prayer that night, the chaplain had value, and she did not for a moment doubt that he belonged there.

But as he walked down the hall on his way to the first patient he would see doubts about whether he really did belong there seized him. What occurred in the ten seconds it took him to reach that room was not part of an assignment his pastoral supervisor had made; it was not an exercise meant to prepare the student chaplain for his first night at the hospital; it was not in any way planned or anticipated. It just happened. Suddenly he knew that he faced a moment of truth. He could not go into that room, declare to whoever was there that he was the night chaplain, and then try to find something to say, even if it was a prayer, that would help that person be more reconciled to what was coming the next day. To do this was to fulfill a function, and if that was why he was there, to perform a task that needed to be done, then he was a fraud. He could only be in that room with the chaplain name tag on his coat and wearing his clerical collar if he believed in God and, more specifically, in God incarnate in Jesus Christ and was convinced that it was God who wanted him there and had put him there. This belief, he fully understood without even thinking about it, could not be a decision. A decision would be reasoned; it would come out of his mind or out of something he had read or something he had heard. It had to come out of him, out of who he was. It just had to be there, the bedrock, the foundation. As suddenly as this question about belief had assailed him, just as suddenly had the answer come. His heart, or perhaps it was his soul, replied "I do believe," and he knocked on the door of the room.

Later Randall looked upon what happened between the nurses' station and the patient's room as his dark night of the soul. There in that hallway he had entered into doubt, and from the darkness certainty had emerged. If he knew anything at all, it was that this still, small voice within him that had said "I do believe" was there because of God, because of God's grace. That night in the hallway between the nurses' station and the patient's room amounted to, he was convinced, the purest moment of his life, to be constantly returned to and never to be denied.

* * *

Retirement, he was sure, was what he needed. But was it what God wanted? God had called him into the ministry through gentle nudges and an occasional push. One of these pushes came early. Actually it occurred the day after he was born. A name was required for the birth certificate. His parents had already chosen Randall for the first name and had talked about James for the middle name. It seemed to go nicely with Randall. On his way to the hospital that morning, his father, though, thought of another possibility for the middle name. As he drove past their church, it occurred to him Lee might be the name they were looking for. Lee was their pastor's last name. A dramatic, captivating preacher with a sharp mind and a powerful, engaging presence, George Lee had brought him back to the church and through the years had become a close family friend and trusted adviser when guidance was needed. Giving their son his name would recognize his importance to them and might in some way have a bearing upon the person Randall became. Pleased with the suggestion and especially with the reasons for it, his mother wrote on the birth certificate Randall Lee Anderson.

Early in his ministry, Randall noticed that he had a peculiar ability. He could remember names. Once he heard a name, he didn't forget it. A rather natural progression then emerged. Hearing names, he remembered them; remembering them, he used them; and using them, he began to think about his own name, not his last name, as many in his family often did, but his middle name. It, he decided, amounted to more than a decision his parents had made in a hospital room. It, most essentially, was a decision God had made. It was God's mark upon him, put there to point him in his earlier years toward the ministry and to remind him in his later years of this calling, especially during those times when he, because of disappointment or failure, questioned his vocation.

Another push, one that he thought was especially influential, came much later. Instead of being something that happened, it was something that didn't happen. When Randall and his wife, Emily, were in their late twenties, they decided to move to Alaska. He was a banker, and she taught junior high school mathematics. Although content with their work and doing well, they felt they needed to bring more of the unfamiliar, more of the unexpected into their lives. So Randall flew to Anchorage to interview for an attractive position in one of the larger banks in Alaska. "I think we have a place for you," the personnel officer said. "I'll let you know once we work it out." For weeks Randall went to the mailbox expecting to find a letter from the bank. But it never came. Another opportunity in Anchorage, in a small business not related to banking, was offered, and he took it. Randall's new employer, a close friend of the personnel officer at the bank, met with him his first day at work. "I need to tell you before you start with us," he said, "the bank wants to hire you. Your file was set aside, and then for some reason, no one seems to know what it was, the file was overlooked. It was entirely out of character for them. But it happened. You have a position there if you want it." Not pleased with those who had forgotten him and committed to those who had not, Randall replied, "I'll stay with you." The work, though, never really satisfied him, and after three years they moved to Chicago so he could attend seminary. Randall always thought they most likely would have stayed in Alaska, a place of remarkable beauty and opportunity, if he had gone to work for the bank. But he hadn't because the letter never came, and the letter never came because God didn't want it written.

Having been pushed into the ministry by a middle name and a letter not written would he now, in some way that was just as unusual, that was just as unorthodox, be pushed out of the ministry? He was ready for anything, but when it came one Saturday in late fall, it took him completely by surprise.

That day Randall and Emily drove to a picturesque village less than an hour from their home. They took separate vehicles because after eating lunch and spending time in the galleries and the craft stores on Elm Street, they were going in different directions, he into the city to make a hospital call and she back home. They turned down a side street and parked in the public lot, the two vehicles, a pickup truck and a compact car, side by side. The first stop was a nearby restaurant. The hostess seated them in a booth with a friendly smile. "Your waitress, Cindy, will be right over," she said. But Cindy never came, so, after waiting twenty-five minutes, they left. Meandering through the delightful shops lining both sides of the street, they quickly forgot the poor service at the restaurant and the lunch they had missed. In a small gallery displaying the work of local artists, Randall noticed a beautifully crafted wooden clock that made him think of the time. Realizing it was getting late, they hurried back to the parking lot. Turning the corner and walking down their row, Randall stopped suddenly. He saw the truck, but the space beside it was empty. The car was gone. An odd mixture of bewilderment and panic seized him. Quickly he looked around to see if the car might be elsewhere. He even caught himself peering underneath the nearby cars, knowing full well the utter foolishness of what he was doing. The car could only have been in one place, in the space beside the truck, and that space was vacant. He turned toward Emily, who stared in disbelief at the empty space, and said, "It's been stolen." From a nearby phone booth, Randall called the village police department, and within minutes a squad car stopped in front of them. A young police officer got out with a note pad in his hand.

"You've had some trouble?" he said.

"Somebody has taken our car," Emily replied. "I parked it in the lot and before getting out locked all the doors from the inside. Even if I had missed one, my husband always checks to make sure all the buttons are down no matter who's been driving." This habit of Randall's irritated her, but for once she was glad he did it.

"There's no sign it has been forcibly broken into," the officer said looking for glass on the pavement. "Give me the license number and a description of the car." He took down the information and got their last name and address from Randall's driver's license. "An all-points bulletin will be sent out. Probably a teenager has taken it for a ride. He'll get tired of driving it around and leave it somewhere. I think your car will turn up in a day or two." With a reassuring smile, he got into the squad car and drove out of the parking lot.

"How could someone in this large lot with people coming and going all the time take the car?" Randall said more to himself than to Emily. "It would be too risky to open the door from the inside with a wire or to pick the lock. There must be some other explanation, but I don't know what it is. I guess we need to call our insurance agent."

Once the call had been made, they got into the truck. Randall started it and shifted into reverse. Before backing up, he saw the police car enter the lot. It turned down their row and pulled into the space beside them. "I've found your car," the police officer said. "It's on Elm, halfway down the street."

"How could that possibly . . .?" Before Emily finished the sentence, she turned to Randall laughing and said, "That's where we parked it. We were here in the lot, but because it started raining and we didn't have an umbrella, we decided to leave the truck and take the car to Elm Street to be closer to the restaurant. On our way back, we went right past it."

They apologized to the police officer, who seemed to be if not understanding at least forgiving, and thanked him for his kindness and efficiency. Then Randall turned to Emily with a puzzled look on his face. "What's really strange about all this," he said, "is that we both forgot about parking the car on the street. I can see one of us forgetting it, but not both of us."

On his way to the hospital, Randall remembered that all-points bulletin and wondered if Emily was going to make it home without a police car forcing her to the side of the road and an officer, with his gun drawn, telling her to get out of the car with her hands up. Soon, though, his thoughts turned to how unlikely it was that both of them had forgotten where the car was. It just wouldn't have happened. The only explanation, he gradually realized, was that someone else other than the two of them and the police officer had been involved, someone who had the power to make it happen. Here then was his push. Their forgetfulness was not a memory lapse; it was a directive. It was time to retire.

Seeing a traffic light, Randall slowed down, coming to a stop as it turned red. He was alone at the intersection, to the left there was farmland and to the right dense woods with stands of ash and birch, their leaves a brilliant orange and yellow. He remembered John Muir saying he had never seen a discontented tree. These trees, he thought, seemed to be more than content. They were jubilant. A light rain started to fall. Turning on the wipers, Randall heard the low rumbling of distant thunder. Could that possibly be, he asked himself, God laughing?

* * *

Retirement brought a different pace. Gone were the alarm clock, the deadlines needing to be met, the events to attend, the appointments to keep, the phone ringing constantly, the late evening meetings, the sleepless nights because of worry about a precarious situation or a fraying relationship. Randall's days, though, were not entirely his own to fill as he wished. Because they were now homeowners, work needed to be done inside the house and outside. Cleaning, painting, repairing, landscaping, taking care of a garden, cutting and stacking wood to heat the home in winter beat out a new cadence for their lives. They gladly gave themselves to these tasks making sure to set aside time for leisurely meals, relaxed evenings at home, extended outings on their sailboat, and long walks in the nearby forest reserve.

Since the home, at the end of a seldom used country road, was isolated and his relationships within the community were casual, Randall felt like he was living on the periphery of the life around him and welcomed it. Emily Dickinson, he thought, had put it nicely:

I'm nobody! Who are you?
Are you nobody, too!
Then there's a pair of us—don't tell!
They'd banish us, you know.

He liked being nobody and not having to think about being included in or banished from anyone's group, or agenda, or favor.

As winter approached, with its heavier and more frequent rain and lower temperatures, the work load eased considerably. Soon most of the day was spent inside. Eagerly Randall turned to the books he had acquired but never read. At the top of the pile was *Some Little Prayers,* the prayer book his mother had left him. One morning he went through it carefully, page by page. The prayers gave him insight into the religious thinking of the day but told him nothing about Mattie Welsh. He was no closer to knowing who she was, what had made her write in *The Book of Common Prayer* "give me faith," and why his mother had given the prayer books to him. Putting *Some Little Prayers* back on his bureau, he said to himself, Miss Welsh, you are not going to remain a stranger.

Later that day, when Emily returned home from shopping, she found Randall in the living room pacing back and forth. She knew what that meant. He was trying to figure something out and wouldn't let go of it until he did. "Are you close?" she asked.

"To the answer, no. To despair, yes. I don't even know where to begin."

"If you need help, supersleuth is available," Emily said, smiling.

So impressed with her uncanny ability to solve even the most baffling mystery, he had once called her supersleuth. The name had stuck. She liked it, and he had thought it, time and again, fitting. Quickly Randall replied, "I do need her help."

"Her time is short, though. In twenty minutes, she has to get dinner started. What happened?"

Randall told her about finding the envelope in the drawer of his mother's desk and showed her the prayer books and the two photographs. After glancing at them, Emily handed him the prayer books and the photograph of the young woman in a religious dress. Then she began to study the photograph of the young woman in the baseball uniform. A moment later, she said, "I need the magnifying glass in the drawer to the left of the kitchen sink."

Returning with the magnifying glass, he watched her use it to examine the entire photograph thoroughly, and then he saw her concentrate on the uniform, paying particular attention to the stitching on the letters and at the seams. When she was finished, Emily said, "The woman in this photograph is not playing baseball in a Sunday afternoon church league. Her uniform is expensive. The material is a high-quality wool, and the uniform is extremely well made. Whoever is sponsoring her has money, and she is being sponsored by this person to make him or her more money. The woman in the photograph is a professional baseball player."

"I can't even imagine women swinging a bat three-quarters of a century ago. They wore dresses long enough to trip over and a corset that squeezed them into the shape of an hourglass. I don't see how they could breathe in that device let alone run around the bases. The waist was pinched so tightly a man of average size could almost wrap his hand around it. Little girls were laced up like that. I read the other day that . . ."

Emily broke in, "You are wandering again, Randall. That device right now is beside the point. The point is women did play professional baseball at the turn of the century. The photograph establishes that fact. Find out all you can about these women at the library."

"That would be the logical place to start."

"It's not the place to start."

"It isn't?"

"No. You first need to call Uncle Walter."

* * *

That night Randall dialed the number for his mother's younger brother. His booming voice came crashing through the phone after the third ring, "Briggs here."

"Uncle Walter," he said, trying to remember where he had seen the volume button on receiver, "it's Randall."

"Randall," he bellowed, "speak up, I can't hear you."

Randall knew why he didn't think of calling his uncle: it was too hard to talk to him. Because of his uncle's hearing loss and his refusal to wear a hearing aid, he had to yell, and his uncle, partly because he couldn't hear himself, but mostly because he enjoyed being cantankerous, yelled even louder. A telephone call to his uncle was not a conversation. It was a shouting match that he always lost.

Choosing his words carefully to make the call brief, Randall took his uncle through the discovery of the prayer book and the photographs. "Do you know anything about Mattie Walsh?" he asked.

The silence startled Randall. His uncle had never run out of words before. Even more unsettling, though, was his reply, "Your mother told me I would one day get a call about her. I have something for you."

3

NIGHT

It was an easy two hour drive to the small town where his uncle lived. Randall turned off the baseball game and divided his thoughts between the light traffic on the highway and the conversation yesterday evening with his uncle. At the end of the phone call, they had talked about getting together. He had suggested meeting for lunch at a restaurant known for its deli sandwiches and especially its strawberry pie and had even offered to pay for the meal, but Walter had rejected the idea. "Why don't you come here," he had said. "I have just made a nice wild mushroom soup with grated pecorino cheese." He had started cooking after his wife's death three years ago and, to the family's surprise, did reasonably well in the kitchen. The soup undoubtedly would be good, but Randall was sure there was another reason for his uncle's objection to the restaurant. It was too public for what Walter was going to tell him.

Randall didn't need the address for his uncle's home. He remembered the way to the quiet, tree lined street where Walter lived, and once there the house was unmistakable. The unique design, with its jutting vertical sections, set it apart. The other homes, having a horizontal roof line, moved one along a horizontal axis. His uncle's home compelled one to look up. It forced one into a vertical axis. His home broke the pattern; it diverged from the norm. That, Randall thought, aptly described his uncle: he was a divergence. He was a character, brassy and a bit off color. But Randall knew there was much more to his uncle than bluster. He had depth. To see this, one needed only to take a quick look around his living room. On shelves along the walls and stacked high on the end table beside a comfortable chair were books. Walter was a serious reader. History, the physical sciences, the classics, poetry: here was a man who was thoughtful and curious, a man who wanted to learn. During his working years, Walter had been an accountant, content to remain in the town where he had grown up. Yet he clearly had a yearning to go beyond the immediate and the familiar into the past, out into the natural world, and down into the mind and the heart.

After a boisterous greeting and an equally vigorous handshake, his uncle settled into an overstuffed chair, and Randall sat in a nearby sofa. They talked about Randall's retirement and his uncle's latest creations in the kitchen. At one point, as their voices kept getting louder, Randall asked his uncle if he had looked into a hearing aid. "I don't think I need one yet," he answered. Eventually his uncle, glancing at his watch, stood and said, "I'll heat the soup. Lunch will be ready in a minute."

Randall began every meal with a prayer. He knew where the food before him came from: it was there most immediately because of the one who grew it, the one who earned the money to purchase it, the one who prepared it, and ultimately because of the one who provided it. At home and when he and Emily were eating out, they joined hands, and he would say grace. The words, admittedly, were sometimes perfunctory, but the act had great significance for him. It declared, once again, in the privacy of their home and in public, that they were people of faith. But when he was in another's home, not wishing to impose his way upon someone else, this too being an important article of his faith, Randall would offer his prayer of thanksgiving silently. Since his uncle immediately started to eat, he did too, adding to his silent prayer the request that he receive calmly what his uncle was about to say.

"Randall, I can't ease into these things; it's not my nature." His uncle's voice fell, and it softened. Randall, looking intently at him, saw pain in his face. "Mattie Welsh was our sister, that's the way your mother and I decided to think of her, despite the circumstance."

Randall was stunned and completely bewildered. He had never heard anyone in the family ever mention her name. "Despite what circumstance?" he finally said. Suddenly he became acutely aware of himself, of how shocked he was. The distress was there, he realized, not in his voice, that seemed steady, but in his hand, which was underneath the table. His fingers on the outside of his thigh near his knee and his thumbs on the inside were digging into his flesh. He was releasing the grip and then tightening it again with increasing pressure.

"We never knew Mattie." His uncle stopped for a moment, struggling to control his own emotions, and then said, "We knew nothing about her until a day before your grandfather Briggs died. Your mother and I were with him that night at the hospital. When we entered the room, he immediately pointed at the door. I understood that he wanted the door shut, and so closed it behind me. We sat next to the bed and waited. In a low, halting voice, he said that in his home on the shelf of the second floor closet, way at the back, we would find a folder underneath a stack of old bank statements. Inside there would be a journal, two prayer books, and two photos of a young woman. That young woman, he told us with his voice starting to break, was his daughter. She, he was quite sure, had never known he was her father. He had watched Mattie grow up from a distance, helping her mother's family financially, especially when her husband was not working, and had provided the money for Mattie's college education. When Mattie died from influenza in her middle thirties, he had asked her mother for something of hers and was given what that folder contained. He stopped speaking, his strength was gone. The next day he fell into a coma and died."

He looked away from Randall. Staring out the window, his uncle said, mostly to himself, "I have believed all these years that the affair with Mattie's mother destroyed my father. Maybe he entered into that relationship because of unhappiness with my mother or because of emotions he couldn't control. Who really knows why something like that happens? I have always thought that when it ended he wasn't able to forgive himself for what he knew was wrong. The shame he felt, the guilt he couldn't erase wouldn't allow it. I have always thought, too, that the greatest torment he suffered, though, was the agony of never meeting Mattie, never speaking to her, never hearing her call him Father."

"Why didn't you and mother tell us about her?"

"Within every family there are boundaries marking off what can be talked about. If the matter falls within the boundary, it gets discussed. If it's outside, it doesn't."

"You mean within families there are secrets," Randall said.

"Yes," his uncle replied. "Your mother, who could be very persuasive, convinced me Mattie must be our secret. When we first learned about her, your mother said that before we did anything, we needed to pray for God's guidance. I remember saying soon after that ruling, 'I want to do what is right.' Your mother immediately answered, as though something had just fallen into place, 'We don't know what is right, and I don't think we ever will.' For her, it really wasn't that we didn't know; it was that we couldn't know. I then asked her the question she was waiting for, 'Who does know?' She replied, 'Only God.' Her mind was made up. She told me to take the journal, read it through if I wanted to, and afterwards hide it. She would hold onto the prayer books and the photos. Her idea, and I didn't have a better one, was that we should do nothing. Something would happen, she was convinced of that, but it had to unfold in its own way. Why wasn't the family told about Mattie? Your mother would answer that it was because God didn't want anyone in the family to know—until now that is."

Getting up from the table, he went into a bedroom and returned with the journal. Though scuffed and in places marred by deep scratches, it was in relatively good condition. Handing it to me, he said, "These pages tell a remarkable story."

Driving home, Randall thought of his uncle's struggle to understand his father and to forgive him, not a cheap forgiveness that ignored the offense, pretending it didn't matter, but a costly forgiveness knowing full well the wrong committed and the damage it had done. He marveled at his mother's faith. It was not only that she believed; it was that she knew what she believed. Hers was a faith rooted in scripture and worked out in her life. He remembered in Philippians Paul talking about giving up all things to be found in Christ in order to have not one's own righteousness but the righteousness of God that comes from faith. That was precisely what his mother had wanted: the righteousness of God that comes from faith. He thought about Mattie's mother forced, or maybe for reasons of her own quite willing, to live a lie. Yet his musings kept returning to a paradox. Mattie was as far as one could be from them, and yet at the same time, as close as one could get to them. She was so far away because they had never seen her, had never spoken of her, had never known anything about her. But she was also so very close to them because she, as a member of the family, was one of them. The paradox, to some degree, might remain, he told himself, but it was no longer going to be a family secret.

Glancing at the journal on the front seat of the car, Randall had the premonition it was going to reveal far more than Mattie Welsh.

He knew, though he couldn't say why, that the entries on those pages told the story of a life meant, in some strange way, to intersect with his, and that this convergence would take him to a deeper understanding of himself and of God. That record would be, as most everything else was, a means of grace. This, he was beginning to realize, was what his mother had intended.

III

MATTIE

1901–1908

L ooking out the large window of his study, Randall stared at the water with its surging waves and cresting white-caps and the towering fir trees rimming the distant shoreline. He then moved a tall glass of iced tea on the nearby table closer, and after it was in place, took off his shoes and rested his feet on the stool in front of his chair. Comfortably settled in, he turned to what he for the past week had longed to do. He opened Mattie's journal. Flipping through it to get a feel for what was there, it quickly became clear his uncle Walter had used the wrong word. It really wasn't a journal. A journal recorded events happening over a period of time. It set down observations that chronicled a life. Mattie's emphasis, though, was not observation but assessment. In these pages, she was at a particular moment in her life reflecting upon her past, where it had taken her and how it had shaped her. She was looking at where she had been to see who she was becoming.

He returned to the beginning. On the first page, there was a single word. Centered in the middle of the page and capitalized, it obviously was the title Mattie had given to these reflections. Randall found himself looking intently at the word *interstices*. He said it to himself silently and then out loud. It was not a word he could hurry through. With the accent on the second syllable, he had to say it carefully to get the pronunciation right. Here, Randall thought, was a word that called attention to itself. Though he couldn't remember ever using it, he knew *interstice* referred to a small space between things or parts. At some point, Mattie must have decided it would make a fitting title because her writing was coming out of brief times of contemplation between the parts of her life. After one part ended, she was stopping to look back at herself in it before going on to the next part.

Randall, glancing out the window again, saw what appeared to be a thirty-foot sailboat heeled over on a starboard tack. He estimated its speed in the strong wind at close to six knots. It was a glorious sail, but there was danger. The boat was getting closer to shore. Someone on it had better know the depth of the water or the boat would soon be aground. This, he suddenly realized, was what Mattie was doing: she was taking a sounding in these interstices, these in-between times, to determine the depth of her life. He was looking not at a journal but at the soundings—of what? Not of the mind. Not even of the heart. He decided they were the soundings of the soul.

He turned the page and began to read.

Vassar College

POUGHKEEPSIE, NEW YORK
June 1905

Oh! law! What a surprise. It caught me totally unaware. And if I had learned anything after being here four years, it's the importance not of being earnest but of being aware (unless, of course, earnest is a last name, at this all-ladies institution it would have to be a last name, connected with money—then being earnest was not just important, it was decisive). Being aware, that's what put you on top in the classroom—knowing what excited the professor. I lived by the rule that if his voice rose or fell or stopped in midsentence, whatever he was talking about was going to be on the test, and I needed to know it backwards and forwards. Outside the classroom, which was for many of the girls what mattered most, it's what kept you up with the swells and the all-arounds—knowing who was doing what and when and with whom. I had gotten to the point where I didn't miss much, but I missed this altogether. Others were in on it, I'm sure, but, of course, no one was talking.

In my defense, Class Day last Tuesday did take an unprecedented turn. It, and for that matter all of Commencement Week, was usually a highly predictable affair. The weight of tradition made it that way. What happened had happened before going all the way back, I imagine, to the first graduating class some thirty-five years ago. So, when we, the graduating class of '05, filed into the chapel for the afternoon ceremony (we had been chased inside by a pelting rain), I fully expected the next hour and a half to go by pleasantly but uneventfully. And it did, for the first hour and twenty minutes. The customary speeches were made, and we, who had a reputation for being a singing class, appropriately sang a lengthy medley of class songs. All that remained was the Class Day song, which would end the program. I was thinking about whether it was still raining when Prexy, saying something about wanting to recognize someone in our class, asked us to sit down. Good, I said to myself, it's about time Martha is honored for her ability to lead this class. I've seen her enter a room filled with a dozen head-strong girls, each fighting to get her own way, and with humor, kindness, and old-fashioned common sense turn a battlefield into a tea party. Or it could be Margaret. Her mind frightened us. She learned, it seemed, instantly and wanted to learn everything. And everything she did learn, she remembered. With her around, who needed an encyclopedia? Or maybe it's Grace. Whatever part she played, whether it was in a comedy or a tragedy, she pulled you irresistibly into the character. You got way beneath the skin. She is one day going to make a big name for herself on somebody's stage. As I waited for what was coming next, something seemed out of place. Then I realized where it was and what it was. It was on Prexy's face. It was the playful smile that started at the corners of his mouth and spread rapidly across his face before he had said a single word. He, and this was the unprecedented turn, was going to have fun with something or with someone.

He carefully took an object out of a box, studied it for a moment, and then held it up for all to see. It looked to me like a plaque of some kind. "I have a presentation to make," he said, "on behalf of the Board of Trustees. It is being given to a graduating senior who has made an indelible impression on the Board. As she has been in its deliberations, so shall she in this way remain in its and in the school's memory." He didn't need to say another word. I knew who that person was and felt my face turn red. "Let me read to you," he continued, "what is inscribed on this plaque, which is to be hung in the chapel on the wall directly across from the northwest window in the foyer: *The longest baseball hit by a Vassar student landed here. Date: May 4, 1905. Batter: Mattie "Thumper" Welsh.*" Everybody was laughing, those sitting beside me slapped me on the back, some started to chant, "Thumper, Thumper." I smiled meekly, what else could I do, and knew that my face and neck were covered with beat-red blotches making me look like I had a severe case of the measles.

Finally Prexy raised his hand. When it was quiet again, he said, "I am sure everyone at school knows about the broken window. It made the front page of the *Miscellany* and was even a featured article in *The Poughkeepsie Eagle*. But undoubtedly many of our visitors have not heard about the window, and those of you who have don't know the story from our perspective. Here is how we saw it. Imagine that you are a member of the Board of Trustees. You are called to an emergency Board meeting because someone has thrown a baseball through a large window of the chapel. On your way to the meeting, you keep thinking that the chapel is a brand-new building, and it has already been damaged. More than irritated, you arrive angry, ready to demand that the one who broke the window must be punished and must pay for its repair whatever the cost. You can tell from what the other Board members are saying before the meeting begins they feel the way you do. This act must not be dealt with lightly. A statement has to be made that such carelessness, and hopefully it wasn't anything more than that, will not be tolerated.

"Calling the meeting to order, the chairman announces Mattie Welsh broke the window and will be speaking to the Board. She is brought into the room. Miss Welsh, though, is not alone. Five other girls are with her and one of them, Liz Fleming, speaks first. 'We want to tell you how that window was broken,' Miss Fleming says. 'We decided to have hitting practice before dinner to get ready for our next game. The chapel was behind the girls in the field, but it was so far away we didn't pay any attention to it. Several of the girls hit, mostly routine fly balls and grounders, and then it was Mattie's turn. The first pitch came in over the middle of the plate, waist high. She swung, and we all watched that baseball: we saw it rise, it went higher and higher, then it leveled out, and finally it came down through the chapel window. No one moved, no one said a word. We stared at the window stunned because it was broken, yes, but mostly because we had never seen a girl hit a baseball like that before.' The chairman then asks Miss Welsh what she has to say. She simply replies, 'I had never hit a baseball like that before.'

"The matter of the broken window is quickly settled. Since Miss Welsh was neither malicious nor careless, the Board decides the school will pay for a new window. Our business is finished, and we all need to leave for our various places of work, pressing responsibilities await us, but no one goes. 'It's good the girls are playing baseball again,' one Board member says. Another member, who is new to the Board, looks surprised. 'Again,' he says, 'I didn't know Vassar girls had ever played baseball. When did they start and, more to the point, why did they stop?' The others, turning to me, want an answer to that question too. I tell the Board that our first class had its share of ballplayers. As early as 1866, the first year after the school had opened, girls were forming clubs to compete against each other, making Vassar, from what I have read, the first women's college to play baseball. Within ten years, though, the game itself fell into disrepute because players and spectators alike in big cities and in small towns had become so unruly. Parents didn't want their daughters playing a game that bred such vulgar behavior. So by 1876, bats and balls had been put away for good.

"But in our day the game has become respectable again. With a different kind of player now, like Christy Mathewson, who, as I'm sure all of you know, is called in the newspapers 'the Christian gentleman,' baseball today has a wide appeal. So when a group of students came to me a few years ago wanting to play baseball, I was ready to listen. Each class, they said, will organize a team, and these teams will play each other during the spring for the school championship. I liked the idea, their enthusiasm was persuasive, but I wasn't convinced Vassar, with its earlier history, was entirely ready for baseball. So we reached a compromise: the girls could practice at school, but their games had to be played in town.

"Having no further questions about baseball at Vassar, the Board begins to discuss Miss Welsh's hit. Eventually the chairman says, 'I'm of the opinion the broken window is not a misfortune but an accomplishment.' Seeing that we are fully in agreement, he continues, 'The issue before us then is how much of an accomplishment?' The Board asks me to look into this matter. Within the week, I meet with the Director of the Gymnasium and the officers of the Athletic Association. They assure me there is no record of a hit like Miss Welsh's. I make one more inquiry. The manager of the Boston Clippers, the famous bloomer girls baseball team, is a family friend. When I ask him about Miss Welsh's hit, he says, 'We have several girls who could hit a ball that far—if they have a stiff, and I mean a really stiff, wind at their backs. I'd like to have her on my team.'

"At the next Board meeting, it is moved a plaque be hung in the Chapel where the ball came down. Before the vote is taken, one member says, 'I do regret that it was the Chapel window the ball went through and not the window of the maintenance shed.' The chairman responds, 'It seems to me the hit, the broken window, and the Chapel all fit together. The three speak not just of what happened but of God who enabled it to happen. They tell us God has given to Miss Welsh and to all of our girls unusual gifts to be used in the most unusual ways. Before I thought it was only the stained-glass window that was beautiful. But now I see that a window smashed to pieces by a baseball can have its own rare beauty and can make its own witness to God.' A vote is called for, and the motion passes unanimously."

At last, Prexy, putting the plaque back in the box, asked us to sing our Class Day Song. Mercy me! I barely heard the words let alone sang them and not only because I was embarrassed. I was happy. It wasn't the plaque. I didn't really care about the recognition. It was the laughter, the pats on the back, and, most of all, the girls shouting "Thumper, Thumper." I was one of them; I did have my place at Vassar. My first day here I received that eerie greeting: "don't let it get you." Now I can finally say that it didn't get me. Whatever else I knew, as a new graduate of Vassar, I did know that. Hurrah!

* * *

Four years ago, on a warm September afternoon, I stood before Main for the first time. Its domed center four-stories high was flanked on both sides by a long three-story wing that at each end, like the center, was an imposing four-stories high. As I stared at the building, it seemed to be staring back at me, trying to determine if I would measure up to its standards. Not at all sure that I would, I hurried through the front door. I only knew that college was at that moment beginning and that I would be sharing a double on the third floor with another freshman named Kate. These two pieces of information told me nothing about what this place was really like and what my life inside it would become.

I was hardly prepared for Vassar. But how could it have been any different? I grew up in a small town, a tiny dot on a map sixty miles north of Chicago. Life there pretty much moved from one day to the next. Just about everybody knew me. There weren't that many people to begin with, a few thousand at most, and my father was the only doctor in town. It was a case of acquaintance by association. A stranger standing next to me in the check-out line at the grocery store would say, "Oh, I've seen you with your father. You are Dr. Welsh's daughter." I always had friends, many of them since grade school. Back then we chased each other and skipped rocks in the creek, and as the years went by, we played catch in the city park, camped in the woods behind the creek, told each other our secrets, and talked about what it was going to be like when we were grown up. School was easy. So, in my senior year, I began to think about college, and since I liked my life where I was and the way it was, I looked for a school close to home.

Father, though, surprised me. No, he shocked me. He couldn't stop talking about Vassar College in Poughkeepsie, New York. My high school science teacher encouraged me to apply there. "It would be a nice fit," she said. Her interest was obvious: she was an alum. But I didn't understand father's connection to the school. Why was he being such a pill about this? It wasn't his way at all. He'd make a point, and if my brother or I disagreed, we talked about it, if necessary, for hours. He always wanted to hear what we were thinking. But he didn't want to hear, actually he refused to hear, what I was thinking about nearby colleges.

"Why must I go to Vassar?" I asked father one evening after everyone else had left the dinner table.

"You don't have to," he answered. "There are other schools like it you might go to. It's the one I happen to know the most about." He looked away from me. Minutes went by that seemed like hours. Finally, he said, "I think your mother needs to be here."

As mother sat down at the table next to him, he did the unthinkable. He took her hand and held it. They were never affectionate in front of others. I had not seen them kiss, not seen them embrace, even when father had been away for several days at a medical conference, not seen them hold hands. Looking at their hands now clasped tightly together, I felt their love for each other and also, I was sure, their need for the strength, or perhaps it was for the courage, to tell me something they had never wanted to and had thought they would never have to. "After medical school," father began, "we were living in a farming community in Pennsylvania. The people, I'd say, liked us. The number of patients I was seeing increased steadily, though there was another doctor in town. Once they came, they must have been satisfied, for they kept coming back."

"I was busy in the community and in the church we were going to," mother said. "We had good neighbors and friends. We were happy there."

"It was a Monday in early July," father continued. "I remember the day because we had spent the weekend moving into a new house. A man came into my office saying his neighbor's wife was sick. I knew the name as did everyone else. Their farm was the largest in the county, and because of the family's influence, seldom did anything of importance happen in that town without their knowledge and their approval. I left for the home immediately. When I got there, I noticed a hex sign on the house and on the barn as well. I saw its beauty, the precise geometric design and the striking colors, but unfortunately I lost sight of its purpose. The woman, severely flushed and only semiconscious, was gravely ill. After examining her, I prescribed medication, making sure the husband understood the dosage and how often it was to be administered, and assured him I would return the next day. I gave him one more instruction before leaving. The room was sweltering hot. It needed fresh air and ventilation immediately. 'Open the windows now,' I said, 'and keep them open.'

"That night, as we were sitting down to dinner, we heard someone pound on the door. I quickly opened it, not knowing what to expect. It was the woman's husband. He glared at me, angrier, I think, than anyone I had ever seen. 'You had those windows opened and let the evil spirits in. She died because of you.' Shaking his clenched fist at me, he shouted, 'You killed her. If it's the last thing I do, I'm going to make you pay for this.'

"The accusation was preposterous—at least I thought it was; the threat, I realized, was not. Many were too much in the family's debt to resist the pressure they would apply. Even if they did, I couldn't dismiss the obvious: a good number of houses and barns in the county had a hex sign. For some, maybe for most, it was mainly a decoration. But I knew enough of the old belief lingered that it, in the end, would sway their thinking. Within a week, I was seeing fewer patients. Within three months, the door to my office seldom opened, and when it did, most often it was someone wanting a bill paid. I was being shunned. People talked to us; they were polite and some, at times, were even friendly. They just didn't come to me when they needed a doctor."

"We talked about leaving," mother said.

"But then we stopped talking. I had become bitter and started to drink. Before long, I'm ashamed to say, that's all I did. Alone in my office, full of anger and despair, feelings I couldn't control and at that time didn't want to control, I would drink one glass of whiskey after another, one bottle after another."

"The bills went unpaid, and we lost the house," mother said. "Then we lost the marriage. Your father had shut me out of his life. I finally reached a point where I stopped trying to find a way back into it. The rejection had become too painful and belittling. I had to leave, or I would have lost my sanity. We lived apart for more than a year."

"Life without your mother," father said, "was unbearable. Something had to change. It wouldn't be the family that had ruined me. They were getting too much satisfaction from their revenge. It wouldn't be the people. They were too beholden to that family and many of them were too quick to dismiss others. It wouldn't be your mother. She had no reason to change. I had made her life miserable. It took a long time coming, self-pity can be paralyzing, but I eventually saw it had to be me. My thinking in those terrible days had become twisted and wild. But something my mother said when I was growing up forced its way into my mind and once there wouldn't go away. I kept hearing her tell me, 'pride goes before a fall.' She was right. Underneath everything hurtful I had become was my pride. The cause of that woman's death was not evil spirits but a virus. The diagnosis was correct, but that didn't matter. I was beaten. There was nothing I could do about it except admit defeat, which, once I finally realized this, I did. I learned through her family where your mother was. When I found her, I made her two promises: I would never drink again, and we would never again live in a place where there were hex signs."

Evil spirits . . . shunning . . . hopelessness . . . separation. Those awful words that told of misery I couldn't even imagine undid me. They seized me, shook me, held me in their power, and wouldn't let go of me. I became frightened.

"You must not be at the mercy of small-minded people," mother said. "Becoming trapped in the world of their making is death. Their world closes in around you no matter which way you turn squeezing the very life out of you." The sharp edge to her voice, put there from what must have been years of smoldering anger, startled me. "We want the world to open up for you. At a woman's college in the East, it will. Your science teacher stopped by the other day to talk to us about Vassar. Although the school is in the country, it is only an hour away from New York. On the weekends, the girls often go into the city for a lecture, a play, an exhibit at the art museum, a concert. Whatever you might want to study—science, literature, philosophy, mathematics, languages, history, astronomy, religion—is offered. It has an observatory, a lake for boating and skating, a gymnasium with a swimming tank."

"What sets Vassar apart," father said, "is the way it teaches. Some years ago, a new history professor told the students that to learn they needed first to spend their time not with what she called secondary authorities but with the original documents. These records, rather than what the girls read in a book or heard in a lecture, would be the basis for the knowledge they gained and the conclusions they came to. This today is how the students are taught at Vassar: they go to the source and do their own thinking; they don't let others do their thinking for them."

We had never talked about money before. It's not what a child discussed with her parents. But the cost of going to a school so far away began to worry me. They had once been unable to pay their bills. I shuddered at the thought of putting them through something like that again. "It would be dreadfully expensive," I said.

"But not too expensive," father replied. "Your mother has inherited money we will use for your education."

They stopped talking and still holding hands looked at me. They had nearly lost what mattered most to them: their marriage, their income, their good name, their happiness. Father could have ended a broken-down drunkard. Life suddenly seemed very precarious.

"I'll go to Vassar," I said.

* * *

The third floor of Main was deserted. Entering my room, I said, almost out loud, "Home." I crossed the length of the room in ten paces and the width in six. A little small, I thought. The walls were bare, and a worn carpet covered the floor. Each side had a bed, a bureau, a desk, a chair, and a bookcase. A small table was in the middle of the room. My roommate obviously had not yet arrived, so, being right-handed, I claimed the side to the right of the door. I unpacked my trunk, made the bed, and then started to put a few writing supplies in the desk. The top drawer pulled out easily. At once I saw that something had been scratched, or perhaps even carved, into the bottom of the drawer. Looking more closely, I read the words, "don't let it get you." Obviously it was a message from someone who had once stayed in the room. The letters appeared newly made, so it might have been one of the girls from last year. Far more important than who, though, was what: what did "it" mean? Maybe "it" was an impossibly difficult class, or a rotten teacher, or a wretched activity of some kind, or the school itself. Or, a startling thought occurred to me, maybe "it" was an evil spirit.

I finished putting everything away and went looking for my new classmates. As I walked down the hall, I saw a girl coming toward me. She was pretty, tall, and slender. Slender, though, wasn't quite the right word. She wasn't thin, but lean. Fit and moving gracefully, she was an athlete, I decided. I smiled and got ready to introduce myself. She smiled broadly, but not at me. "Oh, Ella, I'm here. I'm really here at Vassar," she gushed, rushing right past me. I turned around and saw a girl who had just come out of her room. "Liz," she cried, "it's sooo good to see you." They excitedly hugged each other and rattled on about being at Vassar together and what a grand time they were going to have. I was practically standing next to them, but they didn't say a word to me. For the love of tripe! They didn't even look at me. I suddenly realized that while I didn't know what "it" was, I did know where "it" was. "It" was right in front of me, staring me in the face. I quickly turned away and hurried downstairs.

Early that evening, I heard an impatient knock on the door. I opened it, and a girl carrying a large satchel plunged in. "You must be Mattie Welsh," she said. "I checked the roommate listing downstairs. I'm Kate Peters, but you can call me Katie, everybody does." Then she announced, without taking a breath, "I'm from Philadelphia. My father is a plant manager for a manufacturing company. My mother and two sisters came here. There's not much about Vassar I don't know. So if you have any questions ask." She all of a sudden stopped, held out her hand, and grinned.

I had never met anyone like her. In some ways, she was little. She was a little plain, a little heavy, a little loud, a little beleaguered. She reminded me of someone who was running after a train and couldn't quite catch up to it. But, as I was soon to learn, in other ways she was big. She had a big heart and also a big mind that big aspirations kept working constantly.

I helped her unpack and arrange her side of the room. Then we began to get to know each other. At one point, Katie asked, "Why Vassar?" I told her it was what my parents wanted. "I'm here," she said, "because it's what the Peters women do, but even if they didn't, I'd come because of Maria Mitchell. She taught astronomy. Mary Whitney, one of her students, has replaced her, but it's because of Maria Mitchell that Vassar is the place for a girl to go who is serious about astronomy."

"You want to become an astronomer?"

"Ever since I discovered Venus when I was 10 years old. I'm going to spend the rest of my life gazing into the heavens."

Normally I wasn't impulsive. My actions usually followed my thoughts. But what she said, for some crazy reason, hit me right where I had been hurt earlier that day, and without thinking, I immediately jumped up and walked to the end of the room. "Instead of gazing into the heavens right now, Katie, I'd like you to gaze at me. Can you see me?"

"Shall I cover one eye or keep both eyes open? Of course, I can see you."

"Then why couldn't Liz Fleming and Ella Butler see me this afternoon in the hall? I was almost standing on top of them."

Katie took off her glasses and began to inspect them. At first I thought they must be broken. Maybe a lens had dropped out, or the frame was cracked. But then I realized that while she was looking at her glasses, she didn't even see them. She was thinking. It was her way of putting her thoughts together. "Mattie," she finally said, "you won't read anything about it in the college catalogue, but according to my sisters, it's as much a part of Vassar as semester examinations and chapel on Sunday. It starts, as you have found out, the day we arrive, and it won't go away until the day we graduate, if it does then."

"For goodness sake, Katie, what is it?"

"Social selection. That's what my sisters call it. It's an inevitable process, they say, that like natural selection separates, but the separation here is not the strong from the weak, but rather the desirable from the undesirable. What was dinner like?"

"It was awkward. In the small town where I grew up, I seldom met anyone new. So I wasn't sure what to talk about."

"That will change once classes begin," Katie said.

"There might be some girls, though, I never talk to. Most of us sat down wherever we could. But others, like Liz Fleming and Ella Butler, seemed to be looking for one another. I don't think they knew each other when they came in, or didn't know each other well, but by the time dinner started, they were all sitting together at the same table. They talked among themselves and ignored the rest of us."

"That's social selection, Mattie. Eventually we are going to be divided into four groups. You saw the swells at dinner. They come from families having money and standing. A small-town girl, whose father is a doctor who can be paid by his patients in chickens and vegetables, will never be one of them. You don't have their breeding or their birthright. They don't work their way up to the top, which is where the swells think they are; it's where they, in their minds, rightfully start. It's what they are born into. They promptly seek each other out and are then only aware of themselves and the all-arounds, who are one rung down. No one knows now who the all-arounds in our class will be. But soon enough they'll emerge, or I should say, they'll be selected. We'll be hearing from them and talking about them endlessly. They'll be the leaders who make things happen. Not only will they be an officer of the class or the drama club or the athletic association, a lead in the hall play, a champion at Field Day, a member of a half dozen societies, they will also make high marks and write volumes of poetry, which we will be frequently reading in the *Miscellany* and other school publications. Before it snows, they'll have the class spirit, and the school song will bring tears to their eyes.

"Beneath them are the grinds. These girls will be forever hunched over a book. But not all will be serious students. Some will read into the early morning hours either because they must not do anything else, one more failed exam and they'll be going home, or because they are so shy or backward or unsure of themselves they can't do anything else. Usually the grinds are ignored and worse than that ridiculed. My sisters tell me it's because they study too much. Learning matters, but it's friends, the class, athletics, parties, having fun that for many of the girls matter most. A grind, to their sensitive noses, begins to smell like the musty pages of an old book. The odor is irritating and also unwelcome because it reminds them that others are going to get the marks they want."

"What's at the bottom?"

"The objectionables. There is something about them, they cling, or they whine, or they grovel, that the other girls can't stand. They don't fit in anywhere. Some never try to and others try too hard."

"Katie, where would you have sat at dinner tonight?"

"Are you asking if I am a swell? That, Mattie Welsh, is neither my birthright nor my temperament. I would have been right beside you."

"In my high school class, no one was really left out. It's horrid to think of anybody being called objectionable or even a grind. Will it . . .," I hesitated, "but then you might be one of the all-arounds."

"That, I assure you, I will not be. Will it bother me to be a grind? Not for a moment." Katie went to the window and looked up into the sky. "I am here to learn all I possibly can about astronomy. I want to fill my mind with astronomical physics, solar spectroscopy, stellar chemistry, planetary evolution." Turning back to me, she said, "After I graduate, I'm going to get a master of arts degree in astronomy and then work at one of the great observatories, maybe the Leander McCormick Observatory in Virginia, the Lick in California, or even the Royal Observatory in England. Why, Mattie, only last February, a senior, Ida Watson, discovered a new star in Perseus. She entered history at that moment. I know that something out there is waiting for me to find it."

"So that you can take your place in history?"

"Just think of having one's name linked to Nicholas Copernicus, Tycho Brahe, Johannes Kepler, Galileo Galilei, William Herschel." Katie stared out the window again. "The girls can call me a grind or anything else they come up with. They're not the ones I'm going to be listening to."

That night I couldn't sleep. I kept seeing myself being stuffed into a box labeled first *grind* and then *objectionable.* As I started to condemn that ghastly selection process and those who were going to subject us to it, I remembered Katie saying something that at the time seemed interesting but not particularly significant. The more I considered it, though, the more important it became. "Katie, are you still awake?" I finally whispered.

"I'm counting stars."

"Isn't it sheep you're supposed to be counting," I said, smiling. "You mentioned a Field Day. What's that about?"

"My older sister, though she wasn't much of an athlete, helped get it started six years ago. At the time, no other girls school in the nation had anything like it. That first year there were different races and jumping events. The girls got soaked—it rained so hard the starter's gun wouldn't fire—but they all had a grand time. It's become an annual event. The hurdles, a fence vault, a basketball toss, a baseball throw, and even the shot put, which my other sister entered the four years she was here but never won, have since been added."

"Will many of the girls come to it?"

"The entire school will be there to compete or to watch and cheer. I expect this year everyone will be talking about Liz Fleming. I read about her in the paper last month. She also is from Philadelphia and, according to the article, is the fastest female runner the city has seen in years. There was an unusual picture of her. She stood on a track at the starting line holding in one hand a basketball and wearing on the other hand a baseball glove. She's what they call a triple terror."

"I think you mean she's a triple threat."

"You're right," Katie replied, giggling. "The article said that of the three sports her favorite is baseball."

"When will Field Day be this year?" I asked.

"It's scheduled for May. In the Peters family, everyone else tries to be an athlete, though without much success. I don't even attempt it. So I'll be a spectator for the next four years. Will you be in any of the events?"

"I'll be sitting on a bench next to you."

We were silent for a moment. Then Katie said, "I'm awfully glad we're together."

"So am I."

Katie, I said to myself before falling asleep, I won't be competing. Not this year at least.

* * *

Rushing into the dining room at lunch the next day, I looked for Katie. She waved and pointed to the empty chair across the table from her. "You're twenty minutes late," she said as I sat down out of breath.

"I've been in the library trying to find pictures of your astronomers."

"Good heavens, why?"

"I had the craziest dream last night. A lot of people were in a huge room with dark wood paneling and a vaulted ceiling. I could see out the windows a field of glittering stars. Somehow the room was suspended in the sky, or it might have been the heavens. A door opened, and everyone stopped talking. You entered with a surprised, actually it was more of a shocked, look on your face. You obviously didn't expect to be there. Two men stepped forward. 'Katie Peters,' one said, 'my name is Nicholas Copernicus, and this is Tycho Brahe. We have been waiting for you.' Then everyone in the room began to clap."

"Did anyone happen to say why I had been brought into the room?"

"I think it had something to do with your discovery that the moon is made of marshmallows." Katie picked up a pea from her plate and threw it at me, almost hitting a girl at the next table. "It's strange I wasn't in my own dream. I'm always in my dreams some-where. It's even stranger I could see all those people who were com-plete strangers so clearly. I could tell how straight their teeth were and which ones needed to trim their beards. Copernicus didn't need to trim his. He didn't have a beard in my dream or in the picture I found of him at the library. How did I know that? Did my mind know something I didn't know, or at least I wasn't aware of knowing, or had it been a lucky guess? Because of the picture of Tycho Brahe,

I'm leaning toward a lucky guess. I read that he lost the tip of his nose in a duel. For the rest of his life, he wore on the end of his nose a piece of gold. Whenever it came loose, he'd glue it back on with wax. In my dream, his nose was like everyone else's. Katie, my mind made up all those people giving them in a split-second different sizes and shapes and features. Mercy me! Just think of the imagination I have when I'm asleep. If I could find a way to make it work like that when I'm awake, why I could write a best-selling novel, or discover the cure for consumption, or eliminate poverty."

"Or measure the universe."

"Maybe my dreams are like your stars. You study the stars. But sometimes do you just look at them?"

"Looking is the best part," Katie said. "When I study them, I'm bringing the stars down to me. When I look at the stars, I'm being taken up to them."

"That's how I feel about my dreams. I don't know where they come from or how they work, but I've figured out that I have dreams mainly to look at them. My dreams take me beyond myself. I think it's the mind's way of telling me there will always be something more, something that is grand and mysterious above me, and around me, and possibly even within me."

"You might say it's God's way of telling you that." Katie got up from the table. "Right now, though, that clock on the wall over there is Vassar's way of telling me I need to leave or I'll be late to my English class."

"So, Katie, college begins."

"That it does, whether we're ready or not."

* * *

Mercy me! I found I really wasn't ready. It wasn't the classes. A few of them were easy and the others I could manage with some effort. It was all that went on outside the classroom. The clubs, the committees, the practices, the performances, the lectures, the concerts, the receptions, the parties, the excursions into the city could, if a girl let them, swallow up practically every waking moment. Girls would sit down in the library with half a dozen books in front of them looking like they were going to study for the rest of the day. But appearances I learned were deceiving. After thirty minutes, they would stuff the books into a bag and rush off to a meeting of the New Jersey Club, or the Floral Society, or the Society of the Granddaughters of Vassar College.

Even more surprising than the number of different organizations they could join—I counted twenty-seven of them—was the number of girls joining one organization. Over four hundred girls belonged to the Athletic Association. Its membership was nearly half the total enrollment. No wonder Field Day had its place on the school calendar. The girls here did like their games.

Katie had her four categories mostly right. There was, though, some overlapping. I knew all-arounds who were secret grinds. They were the last ones in their rooms at night, having been to a play rehearsal, or a choir practice, or a club meeting, and they were also the last ones to bed. Needing far less sleep than the others, they studied until the sun came up. Seldom seen with a book, they were not thought to be bookish, though they were. They weren't deceptive; it's just that they had a much longer day than everyone else. Then there was a category Katie hadn't mentioned. I called it the drifters. These girls, with no thought of where they were going, were happily carried along by whatever was happening at the moment. They wanted to have fun, and because they were good at it, they fit in, and because they were smart enough, they got by.

I was a grind, by choice, I suppose, but really by default. The swells didn't want me. With no talent for the stage, whether it be singing, dancing, or acting, no gift for a foreign language, I wasn't going to win the Greek or the Latin prize, no experience in student government beyond being the secretary of my senior class in high school, a position I was voted into not because my classmates thought I was a leader but because they liked my handwriting, I wasn't in the running for an all-around. I was not a drifter, right from the beginning I knew I was at Vassar to learn. I wasn't an objectionable, or at least I hoped I wasn't. That left only a grind, whether I liked it or not. For the most part, I did, though it could be a solitary, and so at times a lonely life.

But it never was in the evenings. At the end of the day, like so many of the girls in Main, several of us regularly gathered in one of our rooms to drink hot chocolate and talk. We were all grinds. That's what brought us together, and, being the serious students we were, it was also what split us apart. Coming from different backgrounds, possessing different abilities, having different tastes, pursuing different objectives, clinging to different interpretations, embracing different convictions, we seldom agreed about anything. As we in time moved from our classes to people, issues, ideas, and beliefs, our conversations, which at first were courteous and calm, often became heated, not heated enough to stop us from meeting, but hot enough to make the sparks fly. Oh, how we liked to argue—sometimes, I thought, not to get any closer to the truth but just to see who was knowledgeable enough, or clever enough, or forceful enough to come out on top.

Harriett Grooms and Laura May Ocher got into an awful tussle over the new President, Theodore Roosevelt. Harriett's brother had been one of his Rough Riders. "He followed Colonel Roosevelt up San Juan Hill," Harriett told us. "Others fell back under the deadly enemy fire, but the Colonel kept on climbing. They saw that only a fatal bullet would keep him from making it to the top. His courage rallied them, and they fell in right behind him. He was a hero to every man in the regiment."

"He was a warmonger," Laura May snorted. "He got us into the Spanish-American War. He drew up the plans for it, sent the ships to Cuba to ignite it, and pushed President McKinley into it."

"Spain blew up the Maine in Havana Harbor, more than two hundred sailors died," Harriett broke in. "Do you think telling Madrid not to sink any more of our ships would have been the proper response? Spain committed an act of war. When we're fired upon, not just the right response but the only response is to fire back."

"How can you be so sure it was Spain? The Court of Inquiry said nothing about who sank the ship. It concluded only that an underwater mine caused the explosion. You must have gotten your information from Teddy Roosevelt. He thinks that fighting and killing are what make a people strong."

From the war, they went to the President's trust busting. "He's right to break them up," Harriett said, "they're monopolies. Smaller businesses can't compete against them." Laura May countered, "He should let them be. They're making the country rich." Then they fought about the President's interocean canal. "It's wise to put the canal in Panama," Harriett declared. "The cost of building it there will be lower than anywhere else. It's the shortest route." Laura May threw up her hands, "It belongs in Nicaragua. Panama is too unstable politically. Sooner rather than later the country is going to come apart and the canal with it." Next came his foreign policy. "He wants America to stand alongside the most powerful nations of the world as an equal," Harriett insisted, "to protect its own interests and at the same time to serve others." Laura May shot back, "He wants to build an empire that will serve us, by cunning if possible, but where that doesn't work by force. We come first; others are a distant second, if they count at all." Finally they got to the man himself. "He can take what is old and tired and make out of it with daring and willfulness something new," Harriett exclaimed. "He is creative." "No," Laura

May cried, "he's grasping, reckless, and self- absorbed. He's destructive." Around and around they went.

Others also squared off. Helen Icks and Clara Griffen argued about music. They'd take a train into New York City together, but once there they separated. Helen, who when she was not studying could usually be found in her room practicing the violin or on a stage performing with the Vassar Symphony Orchestra, headed for Carnegie Hall to hear The Philharmonic Society of New York or The New York Symphony Orchestra play what she called "the sublime creations" of Bach, Mozart, or Liszt. Clara gravitated to a much different kind of music in hotels and cafes. Her music came not from the various instruments of an orchestra but from a piano. "It seems like only yesterday," she'd say to anyone who would listen, "that father asked me to go with him to Sedalia, Missouri. Others were talking about a new type of music, and he wanted to hear it. Immediately I ran to the hall closet to fetch my coat. He smiled and said that we wouldn't be leaving until tomorrow. The music didn't interest me. Traveling with father did. Before Scott Joplin sat down at the piano, I thought we were just having another glorious trip together. Then he started to play his "Maple Leaf Rag." Before I knew it, the music had taken hold of me and started to shake my body. I could feel it run down to my toes and out to my fingertips. There's nothing in the world like ragtime. I find myself tapping my feet to its beat even when I'm studying."

"There is nothing else in the world like ragtime," Helen said the first time she heard Clara's story, "and thank heavens for that. It has no substance, no brilliance, and I might add the music certainly has no significance. How could it? It came out brothels and saloons."

"How could anyone listen to your stuffy old music," Clara retorted, her voice getting louder. "Its day came and went a long time ago. You can't hold onto what has been. If you try to, you'll be run over by what is going to be." Somewhere she had come across the statement by Heraclitus that permanence is an illusion. This pronouncement had become fixed in her mind. It was, in her thinking, the truth of the human situation, which she managed to bring into most everything she talked about and without fail into everything she argued about. We knew it would be coming in our evening gatherings; we just didn't know when. "Helen, in case no one has told you, we're in a new century. Everything is changing. It always has, and it always will. The "Maple Leaf Rag" is what's here today. Tomorrow it will be something else. But for right now . . ." Clara began to snap her fingers to the syncopated rhythm of ragtime.

"My music is timeless."

"No, it's not. Mozart didn't play Bach. Bach died and was forgotten. Only a few paid any attention to his music for almost a century. If Mendelssohn hadn't revived his work, he would have remained a tiny footnote in a history book. People stopped listening to Mozart soon after he died. His music didn't move them enough. It was too complex and showy for their liking. They moved on to Liszt and Schumann and Wagner, who had their day, but it was only a day. Nothing is timeless."

"It's regrettable," Helen came back, "your taste in music isn't up to your knowledge of the history of music." And so it went.

Mercy me! Alice Scott and Marion Dunsberry fought like cats and dogs. They were on the opposite sides of something we all thought about. At times, it sprang into our thinking, roughly shoving aside whatever else had been there; at other times, it rested quietly, stirring only enough to let us know it had not gone away. It was our destiny, or so we had been told in subtle and in not so subtle ways ever since we could remember. "I can't wait," Alice said. "Tomorrow wouldn't be too soon for me." But another lifetime would be way too soon for Marion.

What set them off was marriage. Alice wanted to get married. It wasn't because she was in love. It was because she was convinced only marriage and the children it produced would make her life complete. One night when she once again began to list the virtues of marriage, Marion stopped her. "Someone has cast a spell on you, Alice. Who is it?"

Alice got up from her chair. "There is a book I'd like to show you. It's in my room." She returned quickly, holding the book tightly in both hands, as though it was her most treasured possession. "When I was packing for school, mother put this book in my truck and told me I had to read it." We all looked at the title, *The Physical Life of Woman: Advice to the Maiden, Wife and Mother*. "It covers intimate questions I had wanted to talk to her about but didn't have the nerve to ask." Alice's face reddened slightly. "I'm timid, and she's distant. The mixture doesn't make for an easy conversation. The book spoke for both of us."

"How do you know it's got the right answers?" Katie asked.

"The author, George Napheys, is a respected doctor. All his findings, he emphasizes, are scientifically valid. Judges, medical school professors, ministers, and the late surgeon general of the United States Army have endorsed it. And my mother, a woman of good common sense and wisdom, endorses it too."

Alice opened the book to a page she had marked with a slip of paper. "Listen to this." She began to read, "'Very carefully prepared statistics show that between the ages of twenty and forty-five years, more unmarried women die than married, and few instances of remarkable longevity in an old maid are known. The celebrated Dr. Hufeland, therefore, in his treatise on *The Art of Prolonging Life*, lays it down as a rule, that to attain a great age, one must be married. As for happiness, those who think they can best attain it outside the gentle yoke of matrimony are quite as wide of the mark.'" Looking at us with a startling intensity, Alice declared, "Dr. Napheys explains that selfishness and loneliness await the woman who chooses not to marry. More often than not, a despair that can end in suicide sets in, robbing her of happiness. He cites the statistic that nearly two-thirds of the women who take their lives are unmarried and in some years the percentage increases to three-fourths. Nothing, he writes, is nobler or more fulfilling for a woman than marriage. It is, as he puts it, her loftiest mission."

A worried look suddenly spread across Alice's face. "I'm caught in an awful dilemma," she said. "Dr. Napheys makes it clear the right time for a woman to marry is between the ages of twenty and twenty-five. These are the years when it's safest to have children. I'm going to be twenty next year, and I am in a school that drives men away. A month can go by before I see a man my own age. There are dances, but we don't dance with men; we dance with one another. Did you see what Jane Smythe wore to the dance last month? She came in bloomers and a coat with a boutonniere. She kept the coat unbuttoned so we wouldn't miss the white shirt and the tie underneath. I don't want a girl dressed as a man; I want a man. To get one, I've got to go elsewhere. But here's the dilemma: if I go to another school, it won't prepare me for marriage the way Vassar can. We do get an education here. To get married at the right time, I need to leave; to have a good marriage I need to stay. I'm stuck."

"I'll be right back," Marion said. She returned holding a pair of scissors. "Alice, I have in my hand the way out of your dilemma. Cut out all the pages in your book about marriage and put them in the waste paper basket. Take the waste paper basket immediately to the trash bin downstairs. Do not, I repeat, do not be tempted to retrieve from the trash bin what is not only a falsehood but an outright lie. It is not the author of your book who is lying, like most everyone else he is just repeating what he's been told all his life, it's society itself. The truth is the moment you say 'I do' to the minister who has just asked if you take this man is the moment you don't." Marion stopped abruptly as though nothing more needed to be said.

"I don't what?" Alice asked.

"You don't have control over your life. And if you don't, you won't be happy." Marion read history all the time, even to relax at the end of the day after she had finished studying. She remembered everything—events, dates, names—and would always bring this knowledge into an argument. "The New York legislature passed a Married Women's Property Act in 1848 giving a married woman the right to dispose of her own property and the earnings it produced. By now, all the other states have passed legislation patterned after the 1848 Act. So a married woman does have some control over her property and earnings. But some control is not full control. There are loopholes in the law, and lawyers have proved themselves skillful at finding them.

"You don't have control over your body. Your husband decides if you are going to have a child. So does your doctor. He's not going to talk to you about contraception. The law won't allow him to. Congress passed in 1873 a law prohibiting the distribution of birth control information and devices through the mail. It is still the law, and it amounts to a national ban on contraception. Is there a single word in that book of yours about contraception?"

"Why should there be?"

"Why shouldn't there be? It's your body; you have the right to determine what happens to it." Marion now was really picking up steam. "You don't have control over your time. If you want to work with the poor, or make scientific discoveries, or manage a business, or play professional baseball, stop thinking about it. It's not going to happen. You've got to be home."

"Do girls play professional baseball?" I asked. I should have waited until Marion was finished. The question would slow her down. But she liked to educate us, I think she considered it her duty, and I wanted to know the answer. I had never heard of a girl being paid money to play baseball.

"Bloomer girls do," Marion replied, her irritation at being

interrupted disappearing quickly. Always the historian, she started at the beginning, "They weren't the first to get paid. Twenty-five years ago, promoters formed two teams, the Blondes and the Brunettes, and put them on the road. They played each other in Philadelphia, New York, and New Orleans. But the girls weren't athletes. People soon tired of the novelty and stopped coming to their games. Although the two teams vanished, the notion of women playing baseball professionally didn't. Fifteen years later, the promoters got it right. They again organized teams, this time, though, the women were skilled. Some could hold their own against anyone, male or female. They wore bloomers and so were soon called bloomer girls. Today it's good baseball, frequently it's very good baseball, and the girls are usually well paid."

"Do they play each other in a league?" I said.

"The girls don't play against other girls. A team enters a town and to much fanfare challenges the men. The crowd that has gathered to enjoy the banter moves over to the ball park and happily pays to see the women humiliated, or at least that's what they think is going to happen. But it seldom does. The games are close, and often the girls win. I once saw Lizzie Arlington pitch. She gave up six hits in four innings and three unearned runs. At the plate, she got two hits off Mike Kilroy, who had pitched for the Baltimore Orioles and the Philadelphia Athletics in the National League. The women that day beat the men 18 to 5." Turning back to Alice, she went on, "You don't have control over . . ."

Even Katie and I had a falling out. For goodness sakes! It was, of all things, about an astronomer. That morning I had to drag myself to my 11:00 Greek class. I hadn't slept at all the night before, maybe I was coming down with something, maybe it was just another one of those wretched sleepless nights I'd been having. The classroom was hot, and my eyelids were getting heavier. As my head started to drop, threatening to hit my desk at any moment, I thought about leaving the room. But I couldn't do that; it would be too embarrassing. It would be even more embarrassing if I got caught sleeping in class. My only hope was to pay closer attention to professor McCurdy. Sitting up straight in my chair, I strained to hear every word she said. Her asides, since they would not be on the exam, usually went right by me. Not that morning, though. I missed nothing. I even heard her comment to Evelyn Cruthers. Evelyn had just made a ridiculous statement about history having it all wrong. Plato, she declared, had not come after Socrates, but before him. Therefore, it was Socrates who had circled Plato, like the planets circling the sun, not the other way around. Smiling, Professor McCurdy said, "Evelyn, you think like Aristarchus." Just how did Aristarchus think? I wondered, as my eyes started to close again. Professor McCurdy then suddenly stopped talking, and the other girls began putting their notebooks away. Class was over. I hurried back to Main for a quick lunch and afterwards went straight to my room to take a nap. I couldn't get to sleep, though. Aristarchus wouldn't let me. He forced his way into my groggy mind and refused to leave. I finally got rid of him when I promised myself I'd find out before the day was over why he had made the professor smile.

After dinner I went to the library. I had assumed Aristarchus was a philosopher. The librarian, to my surprise, directed me to a shelf lined with astronomy books. Not knowing which ones might be helpful, I took all I could carry to a nearby table and dug in. The third book, *Tycho Brahe: A Picture of Scientific Life and Work in the Sixteenth Century* by J. L. E. Dreyer, solved the mystery of the professor's smile. What I read, though, didn't make me smile. I put the book down astonished and disturbed, and staring blankly into space, I began to think. If the other girls in the library had been watching me, motionless and with what must have been a dazed look on my face, they would have thought I had fallen into a trance of some kind, maybe had even been hypnotized. Eventually, it could have been five minutes or fifty-five minutes later, I had lost track of time, I went through the other books. Finding nothing more about Aristarchus, I returned the books to the shelf and went to Helen's room where I knew the girls were meeting that night. I joined them, but hardly listened to what they were talking about. My mind was elsewhere. Clara broke into my thoughts. "Mattie, you haven't said one word. Are you ill?"

"I'm not sick. I'm . . .," I thought for a moment, "engaged. Yes, that's the best way to put it. This evening in the library I got engaged."

"Congratulations!" Alice cried. "Who is he? Forget that. How did he get into the library? Forget that too. Are there any other men in the library?"

"Mercy me! Alice, I didn't get engaged to someone. Rather something, something positively shocking, engaged me. I'm bewildered and perplexed."

"Could we add to that baffled, mystified, and confused?" Laura May asked.

"You could, and you could also add befuddled."

"And what is the cause of this befuddlement?" Katie said.

"Page 167 of J. L. E. Dreyer's book about Tycho Brahe," I answered. "The library let me charge the book out overnight. I've got it with me."

"Is it the whole page?"

"No, it's just this one sentence, 'The Ptolemean system was too complicated, and the new one which that great man Copernicus had proposed, following in the footsteps of Aristarchus of Samos, though there was nothing in it contrary to mathematical principles, was in opposition to those of physics, as the heavy and sluggish earth is unfit to move, and the system is even opposed to the authority of Scripture.'"

"The writing is awful, a sentence like that gives me a splitting headache, but the point Dreyer is making is valid," Katie said. "He is simply saying Copernicus had his critics. Astronomers, because of their physics, didn't like his view of the solar system, which put the sun at its center instead of the earth, and the church, because of Scripture, wasn't happy with it either."

"You're missing the point, Katie." Giving her the book, I underlined with my finger part of the sentence I had just read. "It's right here in front of you. Open your eyes."

"You must be talking about Aristarchus. Why, though, is beyond me. Most astronomy books don't even mention his name."

"They all should. Dreyer says in this sentence Copernicus followed in the footsteps of Aristarchus of Samos. Those footsteps had been made more than seventeen hundred years before Copernicus. Aristarchus had the earth going around the sun. He got it right, and then for seventeen centuries, the world's greatest astronomers got it wrong."

"What does it really matter? We've got it right now."

"But it does really matter. They were wrong back then. How can we be so sure we're right now? Why, of course, that's it."

"What's it?"

"That's why McCurdy smiled in Greek this morning."

"One moment you're talking about Aristarchus and the next McCurdy smiling. Mattie, your mind has snapped."

"No, it hasn't. Evelyn Cruthers made another one of her silly pronouncements in class."

"What was it this time?"

"She informed us that although history says otherwise, Plato actually came before Socrates. The class laughed."

"I would have laughed too."

"McCurdy, though, smiled and told Evelyn that she and Aristarchus thought alike. Earlier, in the library, I figured she smiled because both were willing to appear foolish. But I've just realized that it was not the foolishness of what was said but the irony of what it implied that made her smile. She smiled because we don't really know what we know we know. Those footsteps of Aristarchus, and even those pronouncements of Evelyn Cruthers, force us to keep asking ourselves not only what do we know but also what can we know with absolute certainty."

"Are you saying that everything we know is uncertain?"

"How can you say that it's not?"

Katie gave the book back to me. "That's probably enough of *Tycho Brahe: A Picture of Scientific Life and Work in the Sixteenth Century* for tonight."

"Not quite. Aristarchus raises another question. Why didn't anyone in his day listen to him? Astronomy wasn't standing still then. The Greeks were looking at the stars; they were measuring distances in the heavens; they were proposing brilliant theories for what they saw. Why didn't they pay attention to his brilliant theory? How did Aristarchus offend them?"

"He didn't," Clara said. "I don't think the explanation has anything to do with personalities. It has to do with the mind, with the way the Greek mind worked. Certain ideas that were considered self-evident controlled their thinking. They were held with an unquestioning conviction and were deeply embedded in what the Greeks thought. So they didn't examine them critically. The ideas were just always there. They were not the starting point for what they were thinking, but a given they built their thinking upon. Ideas having that much power were not easily overturned."

"Aren't you talking about a presupposition?" Harriett asked.

"That's exactly what I'm talking about," Clara answered. "A presupposition is the assumption we make before we assume something. It's so basic we aren't even aware it's there most of the time. Yet it is, and it's strong enough to close the mind to whatever opposes it. The Greeks had their presuppositions: knowledge comes not out of experimentation but out of abstract thought; the observed world is only an imperfect reflection of the real world; the circle is the perfect and, therefore, the true form. I'm no astronomer, but I imagine ideas like these went a long ways toward closing the Greek mind to Aristarchus."

"I can close the Greek mind completely with one name," Katie said. "One hundred years before Aristarchus, Aristotle pieced together the universe from the understanding of others. At its center was the earth and revolving around the earth in a nearer sphere were the five known planets, the sun, and the moon and in a more distant sphere the stars. No other system was thought possible. If the earth moved, everything on it would fly off and the stars, as viewed from the earth, would change their position relative to each other at different times of the year. Both did not happen. The earth, therefore, did not move; everything else must move around it. His universe became the given, or to use your word, the presupposition for thinking about astronomy for nearly nineteen hundred years."

"And so Aristarchus's voice wasn't heard. What voices are we not hearing today that we should or we're hearing that we shouldn't?" I asked.

"You put us in a fine predicament," Katie said. "We can't know anything with certainty, and what we think we know is wrong because of faulty presuppositions we know nothing about. What can we poor mortals do?"

"We can keep asking questions."

"Oh, Mattie Welsh, you ask too many questions."

"And, Katie Peters, you want too many answers."

The conversation shifted from Aristarchus to a lecture earlier in the week. Most of us had heard Jane Addams, a leader of the settlement house movement in Chicago, speak about social reform in the city. While the others began to discuss the impact she and women like her were having, Katie and I got ready to leave. We had more reading to do for our morning classes. We said good night and started walking down the hall. Suddenly I stopped. Stuck to the door of Liz Fleming's room was a sign that in large block letters said POSITIVELY ENGAGED. "Katie, you are right," I fumed. "I can't say we don't know anything. We do know with absolute certainty that stupid sign is not about those who are inside the room. It's about us who are outside it. 'Stay out, you are not wanted, you are not good enough.' That's what the sign is saying, and it makes me so angry." As we started down the hall again, I thought about my parents. They were overjoyed I was at Vassar. Here I wouldn't be subjected to the superstitions of small-minded people. But, I said heatedly to myself, there are other ways to be small-minded.

Later that night, Katie said, "You want to question and probe and contemplate to get closer to the truth, Mattie. All this searching is the work of a philosopher. Isn't philosophy something you should be considering?"

"I'll be taking a philosophy course next year. Because of a series of events, a chemist might call them a chain reaction, I'm thinking, though, about something else. It began with a lecture I decided to attend at the very last minute on the speeches of Abraham Lincoln. We were told that Lincoln's ability to move an audience came not only from what he said, but also from the way he said it, from the words he used and how he put those words together. The lecture got me interested in words. Words can heal or hurt, expand or contract, reveal or conceal, open or close, unify or separate, create or destroy. Katie, words have the power to give life and to take life away."

Katie took a Bible from the bookcase. "I know it's here in Isaiah somewhere," she said. "Ah, here it is." She began to read: "'For as the rain cometh down, and the snow from heaven, and returneth not thither, but watereth the earth, and maketh it bring forth and bud, so shall my word be that goeth forth out of my mouth: it shall not return unto me void, but it shall accomplish that which I please.' I think this is saying God agrees with you." Katie smiled, "Maybe I'd better make that you agree with God. What came next?"

"Nellie Bly, who used words and was paid for it. One afternoon in the library, I came across an article about her. Just like the lecture, I could have easily missed it. A magazine I had picked up after finishing a problem for my trigonometry class fell open to a photograph of Elizabeth Cochrane. The name didn't mean anything to me, but I needed to take a break. So, I started to read about her. Several years ago, the *Pittsburgh Dispatch* told women they belonged in the home. She disagreed. She sent the editor of the newspaper a blistering letter scolding him for printing such stupidity. Write something for me he answered back. She sent him an article about divorce. He liked it and hired her as a reporter."

"We're coming soon to Nellie Bly?"

"We're already there. Back then a woman could write for a newspaper, but not under her own name. Maybe it was to protect her from the public."

"Or," Katie said, "maybe it was to prevent her from having her own voice in public."

"Whatever the reason, Elizabeth Cochrane became Nellie Bly. Taking a new name was the least of what she did. To write about child labor, low wages, and dangerous working conditions, she went to work in a factory. To expose incompetence and abuse, she pretended to be insane and got herself committed to an insane asylum. To promote the *New York* World, the newspaper she later worked for, and most likely to make her own name more widely known, she went around the world in the record time of seventy-two days and six hours. She became famous. But it's not her fame I keep thinking about; it's her writing and the money she was paid for what she wrote."

"And from Nellie Bly you went to?"

"My dreams. All of us think about dreams we've had. We can't help it. They can be so real."

"And sometimes so alarming," Katie said.

"It's as though they're trying to tell us something. The other morning while I was brushing my teeth, I had an idea I could have forgotten before I had put my tooth brush away. I could have once again missed it. But once again that didn't happen. If we're looking for the message of a dream, we go to its content, to what has occurred or to what somebody has said. But there in the bathroom with my mouth full of tooth paste, I found myself thinking I needed to look at the form the dream takes. Every dream I've remembered has the same structure. It has always been a story. One event has led to another, and whatever that was has led to something else that makes a point of some kind. Could it be that the truth I'm seeking is to be found in a story? And might it be that at least some part of this truth is itself a story?"

"Truth and story are the same."

"Perhaps, up to a point. I think that's what my dreams are telling me. I put all these near misses together—words, Nellie Bly, and stories—and, Katie, this is what I have decided: I'm supposed to be a writer. I'm supposed to write stories."

"Do you like to write?"

"When I was in fifth grade, our teacher once told us we could either draw a picture or write a story. Everyone else in my class drew a picture. I wrote a story. I liked to draw, but I wanted to write. I remember thinking later maybe I had not made that decision; maybe something had made it for me."

"Or someone."

"You mean God? If it was God, there has been no follow-up. I have written letters, themes in high school, papers for our classes now, but since that day in fifth grade I have never been a writer. That's going to change, though. Putting the right words together in a pleasing way is satisfying. But satisfaction, I beginning to realize, isn't the point. The point is I have to write. Maybe it's the need to create, to bring to life something that comes from me. Whatever the reason, what's important right now is that I get started. I'm keeping a journal. It makes me write every day, and even if the entries are only a line or two, they will eventually become a collection of thoughts, impressions, and experiences that I might be able to use later in my stories. I'm going to take all the literature courses I can. To write, I'm sure I have to read and to read especially the great authors. I'd like to do something else, something we might do together. Before going to bed, we have been talking about a star. Could we do this every other night? One night we might look at a star and the next night at a word we don't know. It'll help me increase my vocabulary."

"My vocabulary also needs increasing." Katie looked at the clock, "But let's start tomorrow night. It's almost one o'clock, and I've got a class at nine. Right now the only word I'm thinking about is bed."

* * *

My parents didn't go to church, and so when I was growing up, except for a time or two with friends, I didn't go either. Although they never talked about God or used God's name, I always felt they believed in God. Father, after all, had said that the righting of their marriage after it had gone so terribly wrong was a miracle. Miracles don't happen by themselves. God makes them happen. It wasn't God they had rejected, but the church. Mother only said that going to church was something they didn't do. She never explained why. It was only much later, after that night when they told me why they wanted me to go to Vassar, that I understood, having once been forced out of the church, they could never go back. The memory was too painful.

I, however, went to church at Vassar. It was not by choice to begin with. Vassar, the school catalogue declared, is a Christian college. Though one need not be a Christian to enroll, all students were required to attend the Sunday morning worship service in the chapel. Mercy me! The service was at first terribly confusing. Words like sin, incarnation, atonement, redemption, salvation were used all the time but never explained or at least not in a way that I could understand. I would find myself standing when I should be sitting or sitting when I should be standing. Never sure of what I was being told or of what I should be doing, my mind, sooner or later, began to wander.

Each Sunday, though, I did come to worship with a request. Aunt Polly, who lived in California, once visited us for a week when I was ten. I overheard her one morning tell my mother I was graced for goodness. The only Grace I knew sat behind me in school and pulled my hair when the teacher wasn't looking. After thinking about what she had said, I figured, mainly because of the tone of her voice, it had something to do with God, and, because it included the word goodness, I probably wasn't in any kind of trouble. Oddly enough, those words didn't leave with Aunt Polly. I held onto them as the years went by. I would be doing something nice for my brother, or a neighbor, or a friend at school and all of a sudden I'd hear Aunt Polly saying I've been graced for goodness. So when the minister began his sermon, I'd silently ask him to talk about grace and what it had to do with goodness. But he never heard me, or at least I don't think he did. Although the preacher was different most Sundays, their sermons were all pretty much the same. In a voice loud enough to rattle the pews or seductive enough to coax a frightened cat out of a tree, they would tell us what we should be thinking, and doing, and particularly what we should not be doing. Eventually they might have moved on to some other matter, they might have even gotten to the subject of grace, but if they did, I missed it. By then my thoughts were elsewhere.

But one Sunday was different. Prexy had finished listing the degrees the preacher had earned. More was coming, I was sure, probably the books he had written and the positions he held on important boards, when the minister suddenly jumped up and said laughing, "Just tell them I'm nuts." Hurrah! This preacher had a sense of humor; he could even laugh at himself. He literally leapt to the podium. "It's true," he said, "I am definitely a nut. It's the family name, spelled with two *t*s. I'm a nut because every day I try to do something or to say something others call nutty. It's my small act of rebellion against the way society is telling me how to behave, which helps me keep my sanity. And, I am nuts," he held up the Bible, "about what's in this book." For the briefest moment, I had a weird picture in my mind. Instead of being in the chapel, we were, of all places, at a party. People were laughing and dancing. Out of the crowd, this man, who spelled his last name with two *t*s, came rushing up to us. "I'm so glad you are here," I heard him say, "there is someone I want you to meet." Then the picture, as abruptly as it had come, was gone. As the preacher began to speak, I realized it wasn't only his energy that made him compelling. It was, most of all, his voice. It beckoned me, not because of the volume, it was a soft voice or the tone, it was slightly guttural, but because of a certain quality it possessed. I quickly ran through several possibilities and stopped at the word joy. Phillip Nutt was joyful. I leaned forward in the pew, my arms on my knees, my hands clasped together. I was ready to listen.

Immediately after the service, I hurried back to my room. On the way, I saw Laura May and Marion in front of me and went past them so quickly Laura May yelled, "Is there a fire somewhere?" Lunch didn't start for another forty-five minutes. So I had just enough time to get as much of the sermon as I could remember into my diary. I began writing:

I love the Psalms. They are filled with faith and with so much life.

They are filled with God. Reading them, I find that the more I know about God the more I really don't know. God, I've come to realize, is most essentially an enigma that we are not meant to decipher, but to welcome and to embrace. The further we go into this enigma not the more knowledge we gain but the more love we encounter, and the word for this love is grace. Psalm 40, especially, opens our eyes to grace. It enables us to see what might be called the two sides of grace. Verse 5 says: "Many, O Lord, my God, are thy wonderful works which thou hast done, and thy thoughts toward us: if I would declare and speak of them, they are more than can be numbered." What we have here is the far side of grace. The psalmist is telling us there is no end to God's love for the world. It is always more than whatever the world's requirements might be. Not even the most fanciful imagination can conceive of its breadth, and of its height, and of its depth. This verse moves endlessly outward. Alongside of it, there is verse 17 that moves relentlessly inward: "But I am poor and needy; yet the Lord thinketh upon me: thou art my help and my deliverer; make no tarrying, O my God." Here is the near side of grace. It doesn't stop until it reaches you and me, and what it declares is that although we are only the tiniest particle next to the immensity of the universe, still we are immensely significant, for we are a thought in the mind of God. In this life, God has a purpose for us that beckons us, and a love for us that is more than what our needs are and more than what our needs will ever be. And when this life on earth ends, God has a place for us and a life for us that will never end.

But because of those final words in verse 17, "make no tarrying, O my God," we're not finished with this Psalm. To the far and near side of grace, which is about space, we have to add another dimension, the dimension of time. We are in God's mind, but we have not yet received all of what God has in mind for us. "Make no tarrying, O my God" also gives to grace a now and then side, what we already have and what we're later going to have, and it makes clear where we are in relation to the present and the future. We are in the gap between the two, between what is and what is yet to be. We are always in this gap, no matter what our age is, no matter what our circumstance in life is, for God always wants us to have more. It is this gap that defines the human condition before God. It is this gap that continuously shapes us: there we are tested and become strong in spirit or weak; there we learn what is inside of ourselves, what we desire, and value, and fear, and claim this knowledge or deny it; there we turn to God or away from God, we turn to faith and grow in it or away from faith and reject it, we turn to a way of life the Bible sets before us or forsake it and take some other way of life.

The psalmist frequently gets personal. What he writes about often comes out of what he has experienced. I'd like to get personal with you for a moment. More than two months ago, I ordered an Acme trout reel from the Sears, Roebuck catalogue. Normally it takes, at most, a week for the company to get the order, two weeks for it to be filled, and another week for it to be delivered. That's a month. When two months had gone by and the order had not come, I thought it might have gotten lost in the mail, or the company had lost it, or the reel had been discontinued. So I wrote a letter last Monday asking Sears, Roebuck to look into the order. But I never mailed it because that day the reel arrived along with a note from the company saying the order had been misplaced, and they were sorry for the delay. I was delighted with the new reel and placed it on a shelf in the garage. I intended to examine it thoroughly that evening and then put it in my tackle box. When I went to get it after dinner, the reel wasn't there. I spent the rest of the evening and a good part of the next day looking for the reel, but I couldn't find it. I began to wonder if the reel had really come, perhaps my mind was playing tricks on me, perhaps I had imagined receiving it in the mail. But if it had not come, I would have mailed my letter to the company on Tuesday at the very latest, and I still had the letter. So, the package must have come. But where was the reel? That was

Tuesday. In the mail on Wednesday, there was a package. I opened it, and inside was the reel I had ordered. Stunned, I sank into the closest chair. The reel had already come, I had lost it, and now it had come again. What in God's wide world was going on? Maybe I was losing my mind; maybe someone was playing a joke on me.? Then suddenly it became clear. There was an explanation for what had happened, the only possible explanation: it was God who was playing a joke on me. It was God's way of saying, "I'm thinking about you. I just wanted you to know that. And, oh yes, I also wanted you to know that I'm a little bit nutty too."

Phillip Nutt was saying I, at this moment, was in two places at the same time. I was, to begin with, in the mind of God. What a nutty idea. But maybe that was the point: it was just nutty enough to be true. If God was thinking about me, then my life must be important to God, important enough to make my life worthwhile. I remembered Aunt Polly's words: I had been graced for goodness. Did she mean that God had already given me something, given it to me when I was a little girl, that will allow me, in some way, to bring goodness into the world? I was also, to use Phillip Nutt's word, in a gap. I was now and apparently will always be somewhere between what God has done for me and will do for me. I had no idea where I should be going in this gap or what I should be doing, but if I understood him correctly, I didn't need to know. It would eventually come to me, in God's time, and in God's way, if I wanted it, worked for it, and, I could hear him say, if I prayed for it.

It was time for lunch. I closed the journal but didn't put it away. Instead I sat there thinking, my fingers running lightly over the cover, my eyes nearly shut. Phillip Nutt, I decided, would have listened to Aristarchus. He, too, was a seeker of the truth. Because he was, he was someone I needed to listen to. That conclusion took me to three questions. First, Phillip Nutt had given me not an ultimatum but an invitation. Could it be that the day will come when I accept it? Second, he, of course, was himself in the gap, an unsettling and probably at times an intimidating place to be, yet he had, I felt sure, found joy there. Could it be that one day I will find joy in the gap too? Third, if, as he says, God is an enigma, could it be that I must always keep the subject of God open; I must always seek to know more about God because there will always be more to know; I must always be ready to be surprised by God who will think and act in enigmatic ways?

I put the diary in the lower drawer of the desk and got up. Lunch had already started. Most likely, though, Katie had saved me a seat beside her. Hurrying down the hall, I suddenly thought of a fourth question. Could it be that I had just been praying?

* * *

That first year Field Day was scheduled for early May. Girls picked the events they wanted to enter, and classes formed teams for the relay race. Several of the girls started in April to train for their events. They wanted to win. But their names weren't mentioned when conversations on the way to class or around the dinner table shifted to Field Day. Instead everyone was talking about Liz Fleming, though she was a freshman and probably no more than two or three of the girls had ever seen her run. One afternoon I overheard Louise Campbell, a junior we all knew because of the poetry she wrote, say to friends that Lucy Fredericks had decided to try the 100-yard dash. "Yes, I saw her name on the list," Clara Burt replied, "but Liz Fleming is also in that race, and she runs like the wind." Mercy me! How did Clara Burt know that? She was a grind who lived in the library. She might have seen through one of its windows an occasional squirrel run to a nearby tree, but I was sure she had never seen Liz Fleming run. The girls would pass Liz Fleming in the hall, stop, turn around, and just watch her walk. We all had our own walking style. There were the slouchers, the marchers, the shufflers, the amblers, the lopers. Liz Fleming was none of these. She was a glider. Her step was light and springy; her stride was fluid, rhythmic, graceful. She, I had to admit, was going to be good. I needed to find out how good.

No one asked me to be part of a relay team, if someone had I would have declined, and I did not put my name down for any of the events. With Katie, I watched Field Day, rooting for Harriett, who had at the last moment entered the fence vault. She gave it her best effort, but being new to the event, didn't place. Later she joined us exhilarated. She had never been in an athletic contest and found, as she said, "the test of one's ability and will to win thrilling."

Liz Fleming easily won the three races she was in. After the last event, the girls lined up to congratulate her, and at dinner that evening they fell all over themselves trying to sit close to her table. They, of course, couldn't be at her table; the seats were reserved for other swells. "Like the wind" swirled around the room throughout the meal. It wasn't just the number of times I heard those words that made me wince, it was the way the girls said them. They didn't think, they believed, which went beyond thinking, she was unbeatable. If anyone had noticed my face, she would have seen on it a lingering smile. It was there not because of what Liz Fleming had done or what one of the girls had said. It was there because of what I knew.

When dinner was over, I started to get up. Katie, who was seated next to me, put her hand on my arm. "Wait a minute," she said. I sat back down, wondering what she wanted to talk about. She gave me a searching look in silence. I knew then Katie had seen me smile. "Mattie Welsh, do you know what I think? I think you have been hiding something from us and next year at Field Day we're going to find out what it is. And there's something else I think. This is Liz Fleming's day, and I think she had better enjoy it because it's the last one she is going to have at this school."

The next year, even before the snow melted, I began to run in the early morning. Though Katie and I were still in Main, we were no longer roommates. In the spring drawing for a double, I had picked Lucy Fredericks. An inside forward on the class hockey team, a good student, and a member and most of the time an officer of more committees and clubs than I could remember, she was an all-around. I didn't see her much; she was always off somewhere doing something or talking to someone until the early morning hours. A sound sleeper, she never heard me when I left to run and returned. Nobody knew what I was doing, until the morning Katie, on her way to the observatory, came out of Main just as I was coming in. She didn't say anything to me other than, "I thought so."

Three days before Field Day, Alice sat down next to me in the library. "You are listed to run three races," she whispered. "Do you think you can run that far?"

"I think I can make it to the finish line in the 50-yard dash and the 100-yard dash. We'll just have to see about the 220-yard run."

No one else seemed at all interested. Either they didn't know who I was, and even though it was my second year there were a good many who didn't, or they didn't care, or they thought I didn't have a chance and were sure that I was going to embarrass myself. The morning of Field Day even Lucy, who would be running in the same three races, didn't say anything to me other than, "See you at the 50-yard dash."

When we lined up for the 50-yard dash, Liz Fleming took the center lane, and I was in an outside lane. As she was getting into position, she glanced at me and then said something that made the girls in the lanes on either side of her laugh. The starting gun went off, and since it was a short distance, I held nothing back. For the first ten yards, we were bunched together with Liz Fleming in the lead. At twenty-five yards, I saw no one in front of me. I had both speed and endurance, and so over a distance of fifty yards the farther

I went, the stronger I felt and the faster I got. I crossed the finish line, Katie told me, two yards ahead of Liz Fleming and at least five yards in front of everyone else. For the 100-yard dash, I again was on the outside with Liz Fleming in the middle. This time she looked warily at me before we crouched down to begin the race. We were both primarily sprinters, but I knew that in the longer distances, I was the more powerful runner. I waited until half way through the race to take the lead and this time finished five yards in front of her. I went to the outside lane for the final race, the 220-yard run. Instead of taking the middle lane, Liz Fleming moved to the lane beside me. I think her strategy now was to stay with me stride for stride, slowing down if I went slower and increasing her pace if I went faster, until the very end of the race when she would pull ahead of me in a final burst of speed. But three quarters of the way through the race, I had worn her out. She couldn't keep up with me the last fifty yards, and the distance between us kept increasing. I beat her by a good ten yards.

Returning to my room after dinner that evening, I found a package in front of the door. I picked it up and went in. On my desk was a note from Lucy: "No one knew you could run like that. Congratulations! Off to play practice. Be back late." I sat down and looked at the package. My name was on the wrapping in large block letters and nothing else. Inside there was a box of Huyler's candies and a card saying, "Please meet me in the second floor parlor of Strong tomorrow at 4:00." That was it. There was nothing about who would be there or why I should go. I had a whole lot of questions and no answers. Completely at a loss, I went upstairs to see Katie.

"You're a celebrity now," she said. "There are going to be girls, some who had completely ignored you before, who will want to be your friend. If the year were 1883 instead of 1903, I would say that the meeting tomorrow might lead to someone getting smashed."

"Smashed?"

"Back then when one girl fancied another, she sent her candy, flowers, flattering notes on exquisite stationary. If the one being sought was caught, the two became inseparable in a Platonic or, according to what my older sister said, in even an amorous relationship, which sometimes, again according to my older sister, included a lot of public hugging and kissing. The one who had done the chasing was told by her friends she was smashed. These attachments had changed somewhat by the time my older sister got to Vassar. In her day, it was usually a younger girl, and most often a freshman, who was doing the pursuing, and the word used to describe her was not smashed but crushed. Since we've been here, I haven't heard of anyone being smashed or crushed, but a whole lot is going on that I, a contented grind, know nothing about."

"Katie, I don't want to be a part of anything like that. What am I going to do?"

"The meeting might be about something else," Katie said. "There is only one way to find out. Be there at 4:00. If it's not what you want, take off running. She'll never catch up with you."

Apprehensive and yet also curious, I entered Strong the next day at 4:00. The door to the parlor was open. No one was in the room except for a girl looking out the window. She had her back to me, so I couldn't see her face. Still I knew right away who she was. Liz Fleming turned around when I came in.

"I didn't mean to disturb you," I said. "I'm supposed to meet someone here."

"I sent you the candy and the note, Miss Welsh." I couldn't hide the confusion I felt and the disbelief. Seeing what must have been a look of absolute astonishment on my face, Liz Fleming quickly explained, "You ran three spectacular races yesterday. I'd like to congratulate you."

"Thank you, Miss Fleming. It was a good day."

"It was far more than that. They were smart races. You used your head as well as your legs. With your speed, that's a combination no one around here is going to beat." Three girls came into the parlor talking about a history test they were studying for. "Let's go to my room," she said. "It's just down the hall."

A positively engaged sign hung on the door. This time, though, it was not there to keep me out of the room, but rather to keep others out while I was inside sitting in a comfortable chair across from my adversary. That's how I saw her. But how did she see me? Before she had ignored me. Now, though, she seemed respectful or was it intrigued? I really had no idea what it was. I had run not to compete in a race, but to beat her, to beat her so convincingly I humiliated her. But she didn't appear to be humiliated or even upset. Instead she was pleasant; actually, she was friendly.

"I'm confused," she said. "Why didn't you run last year?"

"I wanted to watch you run."

"To see if you could beat me," Liz Fleming said.

"Yes."

"I like to win, but that's not the reason I run."

"What other reason is there?" I asked.

"It's what I do. One person plays the piano, another paints. I run." She was silent for a moment and then asked, "How long have you been running?"

"I've never been in a real race before. When I was young, I played tag with my brother and his friends. I was never "it," because no one ever caught me. In school, every once in awhile, we'd see who got to the end of a field or a road first, and I always won. I knew I was fast, that's what everybody told me, but I had no idea how fast."

"In our final race, just before I fell behind, I looked at you. Though we had another fifty yards to run, I could tell you knew the race was over. I saw on your face a smile of triumph. Maybe it was more a smile of conquest. But, and this is what I want you to know, I also saw joy. It was there because running is what you do too." She got up out of her chair and asked me to stand. When I got up, she said, "Please lift your skirt."

I was alarmed. Maybe this meeting was about being smashed or crushed or whatever other word was currently being used. Remembering Katie's remark that I could always leave, I looked at the door. I knew I was faster than Liz Fleming and most likely quicker. I wasn't trapped; I did have a way out. I raised my skirt an inch.

"Above your knees, please." She then lifted her skirt above her knees. "What is the difference between your legs and my legs?"

I had always taken my legs for granted. They were just there. All my life I had seen them, but not once had I really looked at them. Certainly I had never looked at anyone else's legs. "My legs are shorter than yours and thicker."

"Your legs, Miss Welsh, are more muscular than mine. You have the legs of an athlete. Whatever else you may think you are, you are an athlete. It is not what you have made of yourself; it is what you have been given. It is a gift. I hope you will receive this gift, and use it, and, this is what I believe is most important, be thankful for it."

"We have Field Day only once a year. What other races can I run in?"

"I've been thinking about something today," Liz Fleming replied. "It's not a race, but it is about running. The Athletic Association has decided Vassar is going to start playing baseball again. We'll have a tournament next year on Founder's Day, and the classes are now putting together teams to play a few games this year before school is over in June. We need your speed."

"My father gave me a fielder's glove for my birthday last summer. We started to play catch when he got home from work. On the weekends, he hit me fly balls at the school yard."

"We will put you in center field. You'll cover a lot of ground out there and can back up the other fielders. Can you hit?"

"Not very well," I answered. "The best I did when father pitched to me was hit a couple of balls on the ground."

"We'll have you crowd the plate. The pitcher will be so rattled she'll probably either walk you or hit you with a pitch. We'll also teach you a running bunt where you dump the ball down third or push it towards first. You'll be on first base more times than not. A single will get you to third, and a double will bring you home before the batter is half way to second. Our first practice is Saturday at 1:00 in the field next to the Chapel."

"I'll be there."

"If you need a fielder's glove, I have an extra one."

"I do need a glove. I didn't bring mine to school. Thank you." I got up to leave, supper started in twenty minutes. "Miss Fleming, I want to thank you for the candy and for inviting me into your room to talk about, I guess you might say, who I am."

Holding out her hand, she said smiling, "My name is Liz."

I shook it. "I'm Mattie."

* * *

That first Saturday we had batting practice. Liz, who had been made the captain of our team, put me in the outfield. "See how the other girls hit," she told me. Most were awkward—their swings were choppy, and if they hit the ball, it usually didn't go out of the infield—but Liz was different, very different. After one swing, I knew I needed to study her closely: how she held the bat, the way she stood at the plate, what her swing looked like. By the time she had finished, I had figured out what I was going to do when it came my turn to hit. She eventually called me in, and I picked up the bat and walked to the plate. Like her, I put my hands together near the end of the handle, kept the bat close to my body, brought it back behind my right shoulder, and pointed my left shoulder toward the pitcher.

My feet were about six inches from the plate and twelve inches apart. I bent my knees and put my weight on my back foot, slightly turning my hips away from the plate. The position felt surprisingly comfortable, even natural. When the ball was pitched, I rocked back causing my body, arms, and the bat to lift up, and then uncoiling I came forward as I swung.

It was embarrassing! Missing the ball was bad enough, but nearly falling over as I did was beyond words. As I got set at the plate again, determined to do better, Liz, who had been talking to Sylvia Baumann at second base, moved closer to the pitcher, Ruth McKennon. "Watch the ball," she yelled. I managed to hit the next pitch. The ball slowly rolled a few feet toward Ruth and stopped. Liz now was behind Ruth. After hitting two more pitches, one I weakly popped up toward first base and the other I fouled off behind me, Liz asked all the other girls except for Mirah Ester and Lillian Jennings to come watch me. She kept the two of them in the field, though I couldn't imagine why.

"It's that bad," I said. "I might be a good bunter."

"No, Mattie," Liz replied slowly, "it's that good."

"But I haven't hit a ball past the pitcher."

"Your timing is off. When it comes around, and it will, you'll be hitting the ball way past the outfielders."

Ruth threw me another pitch. I swung and missed it. "It's the swing, isn't it," Lydia Howe, the third baseman, said.

"What exactly is it about the swing? Liz asked.

"It's so hard."

"It is hard, but that's not the point. It's fast."

"Her arms aren't that much bigger than ours," Ruth said, "How does she get the bat around so quickly?"

"I've seen a lot of boys hit," Liz answered. "Their arms are twice even three times the size of Mattie's. But their swing doesn't have her speed. It's not in the arms; it's in the wrists. Watch how smoothly she rolls her wrists and how rapidly. She's got extraordinary snap in her wrists."

The next pitch Ruth threw me I did hit. I heard the bat hit the ball. It was the most beautiful sound—it must have like that moment when Clara first heard Scott Joplin play the "Maple Leaf Rag." I stood there motionless, the bat almost wrapped around me, watching the ball go over Mirah's head. As she ran after it, Liz said, "Mattie, I don't think we're going to have you bunt, and you can forget about crowding the plate."

"Beautiful swing, Mattie," Jessie Wallace cried. "You really thumped the ball."

With a gleeful smile, Sylvia, a captivating actress in our school and hall plays, who was known for her dramatic roles, though she preferred comedy, raised her hand. "Silence," she intoned. "Ladies of the Vassar sophomore baseball team I beg you to be still. Miss Wallace, your happy choice of words has transformed this humble playing field into a cathedral."

"It has?" Jessie said.

"Indeed, it has. Ladies, we are not at a baseball practice, we are at a christening. Mattie to your knees." I obediently got down on my knees, and she placed her hand on my head. "Before us all, you are now given a new name and by this name you shall hereafter be called."

"Swing?" Jessie asked, looking down at me.

"No," three of the girls responded in unison, "Thumper."

While my swing might have been talking, my bat wasn't. No one heard a peep out of it in the two games we played before school ended. We beat the freshmen 7 to 5 the following Saturday on Liz's long double with the bases loaded. I struck out twice and popped to the third baseman. Our final game was against the juniors—the seniors had not formed a team, it was too close to graduation for them to think about baseball. Though we scored three runs in the last inning, they won 6 to 5. The best I could do was a slow roller between the pitcher and the third baseman. By the time they had figured out who should field the ball, I was standing on first base. I scored on a single and a throwing error. My speed, as Liz had said, helped the team. But I was beginning to wonder about my hitting.

Liz stopped by my room that night. She sat down and got right to the point. "You need help with your timing, Thumper. A neighbor, Sam Davis, who played outfield in the Eastern League until a shoulder injury ended his career, knows hitting and knows how to teach hitting. I just finished talking to mother and to Mr. Davis. Both think you should spent time in Philadelphia this summer. Come home with me and stay with us for as long as you like. We'll have a grand time together, and Mr. Davis told me he can see you every day before dinner and even after dinner if you'd like. He'll have you knocking the cover off the baseball before you leave."

I spent three weeks with this quiet, unassuming man, who couldn't lift his left arm above his head because of a torn muscle in his shoulder that had never healed properly. He did more than improve my hitting; he turned me into a hitter. Every day he first talked to me about hitting. He kept telling me I needed to watch the ball; to swing only at strikes and, early in the count, only at the pitch I wanted to hit; to choke up on the bat and to shorten my swing when I had two strikes so I could be sure to make contact with the ball; to hit the ball where it was pitched, when it was on the inside of the plate to pull it toward the third base side of the field, when it was on the outside of the plate to hit it toward the first base side of the field. He then would go to the field with a large bag of balls and throw me one ball after another, changing the speed and the location of the pitch. He even threw me a pitch I had never heard of before called a curve. Instead of ending up where it started, it kept moving away from me. I had to watch it carefully because the ball not only curved but dropped as well. When the day came I could consistently hit a concealed curve ball—it was concealed in the sense that the curve was thrown between other pitches so I didn't know when it was coming—I realized I had at last found my timing and my eye.

It was not just what he knew that had brought me to the point where I at times did almost hit the cover off the baseball, or at least that was what it felt like, it was how he taught it. Sam Davis was much more than a ball player. Above all, he was, as Liz had said, a teacher. He never got tired of my questions. He once told me the only bad question was the one I didn't ask. He never got tired of working with me. When I thought I had hit enough pitches, he would say, taking another ball out of his bag, "Let's see what you can do with this one." He never got tired of baseball, itself. He loved the game, loved it passionately, and it was especially this love that made his teaching extraordinary. Baseball for him was fun to play and exciting to watch. But he told me baseball was more than fun and excitement. It was, he insisted, most of all beautiful. It was a beauty he could see when a bat was swung, a ball was picked up off the ground or caught in the air and thrown, a base was slid into and a tag was made. And it was a beauty he could hear. All of its sounds blended together—the bat hitting the ball, the pounding of a glove, the call of the umpire, the chatter of the players, the cheers of the fans and their jeers—produced a symphony that he thought matched anything Bach had ever composed.

The day I left for home, I went to see Sam Davis. "You are the best," I said.

"No, Mattie, you are the best. You learn quickly, have exceptional ability, and work hard. I want you to do as well in the classroom these next two years as you've done here."

"I would rather be swinging a bat than turning the pages of a book."

"Doing one helps you do the other."

"Are you telling me that literature and history and mathematics will make me a better hitter?"

"That is exactly what I am telling you. Mattie, where do you think your power comes from when you hit?"

"According to Liz, it comes from my wrists," I said. "They give me a fast swing."

"Liz is only half right. Where else does your power come from?" He saw me look down at my arms. "It's not your arms; it's your mind. Your mind determines what the pitch is, where it is, and where it is going. The quicker and the more accurately you gather this information and act upon it the better hitter you are going to be."

"So, I need to go to the library to develop my mind."

"And to the chapel. You can develop your mind there, too. That's where you get the mental toughness you need to accept the dark side of baseball. You will get on base most of the time at Vassar. But if you play baseball after college, and I hope you do, most of the time will drop down, at best, to some of the time. With runners on the bases, with the outcome of the game in your hands, most likely you will fail. When you do, you must be strong enough not to think of yourself as a failure. And the day will come," he said, raising his left arm, "when, because of injury or age, you can no longer play the game. On that day you must be strong enough to walk away from it, to put it behind you not in bitterness or despair but in gratitude for all those days you did play it."

"Do you really think I can play baseball after Vassar?" I asked.

"I do, Thumper." Sam Davis had not used that name before. At first it had been Miss Welsh, which soon became Mattie. But now it was Thumper, not, I felt, to be friendly but to confirm by using that nickname what he was going to say next. "You are made to swing a bat and to run. Since baseball is where one does both, I'd say that for some reason you have been made to play baseball. I don't know what that reason is, you'll have to figure that out yourself, but I do know, let me reword that, I do believe one needs to do what one has been made to do."

The next two years we won the Founder's Day Tournament and every other game we played. After the last out had been made in our final game at Vassar, we sat down in the outfield and began to talk. As we relived the good moments when we had played well and those times when we hadn't, it became clear that what we valued most was not the victories but each other. We had become friends. The Saturday afternoon practices, the games, the nights in one another's rooms talking about baseball and whatever else we might have been thinking about had brought us together. We were different, a mixture of swells, all-arounds, grinds, and objectionables, and yet we were, in a more basic way, the same. We were students trying to learn, teammates trying to win, and young women trying to find ourselves.

* * *

Yesterday I received my diploma from Vassar. Hurrah! After the commencement ceremony, I met my family on the lawn outside the chapel where they congratulated me and took my picture with the new Kenwood camera Father had purchased. I then hurried off to the Trustees' luncheon, given in honor of the new graduates. Before going, I asked them to come to my room in Main at 2:30. "I have a surprise for you," I said.

The affair went longer than I had expected. After the concluding remarks, I sprinted back to Main, rushed up the stairs, and burst into my room. I had only a few minutes to get ready, but then I only needed a few minutes. As I was viewing myself in the mirror, I heard a knock on the door. I opened it and basked in the astonished look on their faces. I stood before them in a long sleeve shirt with Clippers across the front and bloomers. "I'm going to play baseball for the Boston Clippers," I said. Mother was speechless; my brother, who probably had never seen a girl in bloomers before, stared at me, his eyes wide open and his mouth, for once, shut; and my father, he did something I had not anticipated, he smiled. It was, I believe, a smile of pride, and of approval, and just possibly of envy.

"But, Mattie," Mother finally said, "we thought you were going to teach English and write your stories. Of all things, baseball. I need to sit down."

"I think we all need to sit down," Father said. After everyone was seated, he asked, "Why baseball, Mattie?"

"Sometimes even I can't believe I'm wearing this uniform. Mercy me! I didn't know women were being paid to play baseball until Marion Dunsberry one night two years ago told me about bloomer girls baseball. At first, I didn't like the idea. A woman, I thought, shouldn't be playing a man's game against men."

"You'll be playing against men?" my brother broke in.

"Yes, we'll be going to cities and towns to play their men's teams. It seemed strange, even wrong, at the time. But playing baseball here, and especially after the three weeks with Sam Davis in Philadelphia, I discovered I was good at it, and I loved it. When our final game was over, I realized coming off the field I was going to miss baseball terribly. I didn't want it to end. I wanted to play more, every day if possible, and to get better. Sam Davis thinks I can play professional baseball and feels I have been given this ability for a reason, for a purpose of some sort. But to get paid to play baseball, to play against men, to pit my skill against theirs? Could I do that? I kept asking myself that question and got nowhere until I saw myself in a rocking chair."

"A rocking chair," Mother blurted out. "Is that what this school has taught you, to make your decisions in a rocking chair?"

"What this school has taught me, Mother, is the need to ask questions. More times than not the right answer follows from the right question. So, I began thinking about what that right question might be. One afternoon, walking back to Main after a philosophy class, it came to me. I pictured myself as an old woman sitting in a rocking chair unable to do anything other than look back upon my life. Nothing could be added to it; nothing could be taken away from it. Seeing myself in that rocking chair, which is where I very well might be one day, I realized there will be two questions I'll be asking myself. Has my life been good? Has it been right? I knew I could say yes to both these questions only if I had at least tried to play professional baseball. I must do this. In the end, it's that simple. The teaching and the writing I can always do later, and because of the baseball, I'll be able to do them better."

No one spoke. They were silent, I felt, not because they didn't know what to say, but because they were hearing my words again, weighing them, ordering them in their own way to make sense out of them. At last Father said, "Mattie, you are adventurous. Perhaps you have always been and I've missed it, or maybe it's something new."

"Me, adventurous? I've never thought of myself that way. But, my goodness, this certainly will be an adventure."

"Will they pay you a lot of money for playing baseball," my brother asked, "and for wearing those bloomers?"

"It depends upon how many people come to watch us play."

"Well, if you sprain an ankle or break a leg, you know where you can get free medical care," Mother said, always the practical member of the family. "What will you do about the winter months?"

"I'll get a job as a salesclerk in a department store or as a secretary. The girls can always find something in Boston until the team starts to play again in the spring."

"I can't wait to tell my friends at school that my sister, Mighty Mattie, is going to be a professional baseball player," my brother exclaimed.

Father was smiling once again. "In light of the attention she received at Class Day, I'd have to say that Mighty Mattie is the perfect name for her."

From Thumper to Mighty Mattie, I thought to myself. I wonder what name I'm going to be called next.

* * *

Looking at the new yearbook this morning, I came across the poem "History of 1905," a light-hearted remembrance of life at Vassar these past four years. I lingered before each scene it portrayed. Yes, that's the way it was, I said to myself smiling. Then I came to the final verse and heard it say to me, that's the way it is.

And now she saw forever end
Her college life, and reverend
She held these days
Whose never-ending light is all our song,
And another faithful daughter
With the love that Vassar taught her
Bids goodbye to Alma Mater,
Ever fair and high and strong.

Goodbye. I began to think about that word. It's what you said when you left someone behind. Of course, I would be doing that. But I also knew when I boarded the train for Boston I would also be leaving something behind. At first I couldn't figure out what it was. But then I realized that it was my innocence, in the sense of being untouched not by sin but by the world. Vassar had kept the world out, it had sheltered me, and the school had made it unnecessary for me to go out into the world, it had provided for me. When I was hungry, it had fed me, the kitchen staff always cooked the meals for me and served them on time, all I had to do was sit down at a table in the dining room and eat; when I was ill, it had nursed me back to health, the doctor was always available day and night, she lived at the school, all I had to do was tell her why I wasn't feeling well and take the medicine she gave me; when I was ignorant, it had taught me, the faculty, every one of them highly educated, was always ready to instruct me, all I had to do was come to class and complete the assignments; when I was bored, it had entertained me, somebody wonderfully talented was always organizing something or running something or performing something, a club meeting or a class play or a concert or a dance, all I had to do was attend and enjoy myself. The school had served me. The world would not. My goodness, if I keeled over in the middle of the street, it would go right by without even slowing down. Why, it wouldn't even see me. I knew that. But beyond the world's indifference, what did I really know about its ways, its demands, its temptations, its dangers?

To ask a larger question, what did I really know about life? I had studied in my literature classes how others had examined life, in my history classes how others had experienced life, in my philosophy classes how others had understood life, in my science classes how others had explained life. I had listened to what they had to say. What, I began to wonder, did I have to say? While they might have their certainties or at least their likelihoods, I, at best, had only my hunches. It was my hunch, as I thought about it, that the starting point for whatever I might come up with was not a lecture I had heard or a book I had read but my grandmother's apple pie.

Grandmother made the best apple pie. One summer when we were visiting my grandparents, I must have been fifteen at the time, I decided to find out how she did it. "Grandmother," I asked, "when are we going to have apple pie for dessert?"

"I'll be making one this afternoon," she answered.

I followed her into the kitchen that afternoon and sat down on a high stool close to the worktable she'd be using. "Why is your apple pie so good? What's the secret?"

"Why, Mattie, there is no secret. It's simply the ingredients I use."

I watched her put sugar, cinnamon, flour, and spices in a large bowl. She mixed them together and then added the apples. "How do you know these are the right ingredients?"

"This is not the first apple pie I have baked."

My grandmother had spoken to me like this for years. She would give me only half an answer to what I had asked and expect me to figure out the rest. It was her way, she had told me when I was a little girl, of improving my ability to think. "You mean that you know just the right ingredients to put in the pie you're baking now from all the baking you have done before."

"What you want to know is usually right in front of you if you will only look for it. That's what I mean," she said.

I was sure this was another one of her half-answers, but I had no idea what the other half might be. Being fifteen, I fully understood the benefit of saying nothing when I was confused. So I just smiled sweetly. She smiled back. Behind my smile was a desire to hide my bewilderment; behind hers, I was sure, was downright stubbornness. She refused to make it easy for me. If I was going to know something, I would, in the end, have to come up with it myself, and I would have to use my mind to do it.

What I came up with now was a comparison. I had a feeling life in a way was like that apple pie of hers. It had its ingredients. Those ingredients were mixed together, and at least some of them were right in front of me in my own life if I would only look for them. I did, and right away I found four. The one I came to first was surprise. A philosopher perhaps or a writer might use instead of surprise the word irony. You expect something to end up one way, in fact you are sure of it, and it fools you; it ends up some other way you've never even dreamed of. Take, for example, Liz Fleming. I expected her always to be Miss Fleming. Yet she became Liz. Mercy me! A foe had turned into a fast friend. She was the one who had told me I was an athlete; the one who had gotten me to play baseball; the one who had seen the way I could swing a bat and made sure, through the help of Sam Davis, I could swing it better. Because of her, I was going to be a professional baseball player. If I questioned the truth of her importance to my life, all I had to do was turn Liz back into Miss Fleming. Where would I be then? I would be taking a train tomorrow to who knows where to teach English.

Liz was irony enough. But there was, I think, another irony, this one at a deeper level. Sam Davis had told me that because of injury or age a baseball player's days were numbered. He was saying, as I understood it, that success eventually leads to failure. Isn't this the sequence we expect: failure in time coming out of success? But I had reached Sam Davis, who because of his teaching would, I hoped, bring me success, only because I had failed. If I had not hit so miserably that first spring, Liz would never have invited me to Philadelphia, and I would never have met him. The expected sequence had been completely turned around: success had come out of failure. This I realized was true not only for me but also for my parents, and it was true for what they valued most. Their successful marriage and our family happiness had come out of their earlier marriage that had failed. My father's thriving medical practice had come out of his earlier medical practice that superstition had ruined.

I noticed in the new yearbook Lucy Salmon, our history professor, had written, "The college woman, like the college man, is master of herself and of her surroundings." She might as well have said that the college woman was successful in all she undertook. Failure, from what I could tell, had no place and no purpose at Vassar or anywhere else; it was shameful, it was to be avoided at all cost. Yet, ironically, might it not be that at least sometimes it was from the very shambles of failure new life comes, that out of its debris a creativity and a power of greater force than ever before emerges? This sequence, if taken to its logical extreme, implied that while death came out of life, the reverse might also be true. Life could come out of death. Katie and I had one night read in Psalm 23 about the valley of the shadow of death. Without question there was in that valley death. But might not life be there as well? Now that would be an irony to top them all, and seeing how surprising life had been at Vassar, I was beginning to think it just might be so.

When I thought about those late-night arguments we used to have, I came to another ingredient of life. Those quarrels, it didn't matter what the girls were fighting about, usually had the same impact on me. As they would heatedly go back and forth about some issue, I would go back and forth with them. I'd find myself agreeing with whoever was doing the arguing, and after the final word had been spoken and the argument was over, I couldn't make up my mind who had won. At first, I thought something might be wrong with me. I was not knowledgeable enough, or insightful enough, or smart enough to see the truth. Gradually, though, I realized that usually the truth was not one-sided. It was more like the onions mother put in her vegetable soup than the carrots. Whatever layer of an onion I might be looking at, there always would be another layer underneath. No matter what had been said about the truth, most of the time there seemed to be more to say. The truth, I was beginning to understand, was complicated because life was complex. This complexity was, I guessed, the second ingredient of life.

The complexity of life worried me. If it made everything murky, how could I expect to know what was right? Maybe sometimes it wouldn't even be a question of what was right, but what was less wrong. Why, I could get caught in a moral dilemma and not be able to find a way out, or at least a way out with a clear conscience. I was troubled by something else. I suspected complexity had a whole lot to do with a subject I didn't know anything about but needed to. I was going into the world knowing nothing about men or, to write the word even made me blush, sex. Sex had been handled in one of two ways: either it had not been talked about, this was the approach my parents and Vassar had taken, or it had been made utterly incomprehensible.

I once confessed to Liz that the thought of being in the bedroom with my husband—if, indeed, I did get married—tied my stomach into knots and gave me a headache. "I'm so ignorant," I said. She was ignorant too. But she had found in a bookstore a popular medical guide for women that promised to explain everything and even had illustrations. I borrowed the book from her that afternoon. After dinner, I quickly finished my assignments for the next day, put an "Engaged" sign on the door of my room, and started to go through it. The title page raised my hopes: *Beautiful Womanhood, Guide to Mental and Physical Development, A Complete Instructor in all the Delicate and Wonderful Matters Pertaining to Women.* The preface raised my hopes even higher. The author, Dr. S. Pancoast, declared, "It is high time some really scientific work should be interposed, in order to render nugatory the prurient and imbecile efforts of medical pretenders who have, of recent years, flooded the country with unreliable literature." Then he made the statement I had been waiting for and was beginning to think I would never hear, "All that is known of a truthful and reliable nature will be found embraced in this volume." All that is known. Finally, I was going to learn what so many had conspired to keep from me. I was to be let in on their secret. But I soon realized it was to remain their secret. The book did describe the female anatomy and even had a short section on the male anatomy. But, my goodness, it used way too many scientific terms, and soon I was hopelessly lost in them. Whatever did the author think I could possibly do with his description of the clitoris:

It consists of two corpora cavernosa; has a glans, prepuce and double fraenulum, but no meatus urinarius. It is situated below the anterior commissure of the labia minor, and is covered by the prepuse. It is attached to the pubic bone of anterior part of the pelvis; and by two crura from the ascending rami of the ischia, to each of which an erector muscle is attached. The corpora cavernaose unite under the symphysis pubis terminating in the glans of the clitoris which reaches beyond the prepuce in the shape of a roundish body of the size of a pea. It is united superiorly to the symphysis pubis by means of a fraenulum, and inferiorly to the labia minora by means of another fraenulum. This portion of the pundendum is richly endowed with nerves and vessels. It becomes erect during coition, and is the principal seat of the thrill or voluptuous sensation in the female.

The book did have illustrations, but they were too technical to be helpful. And it did not, as was promised, tell all that was known. In his discussion of the clitoris, Dr. S. Pancoast spoke of coition and of the thrill or voluptuous sensation in the female. But he did not speak about them. I wanted, make that I needed, clear and complete information about both and was told nothing. Once again.

Frustrated, I put the book aside. Reading it had been a waste of time. But then had it? Not saying anything about sex, I suddenly realized, might be saying a whole lot about it. The author had backed away from sex. Why? He was extremely knowledgeable. It, all at once, occurred to me he was afraid of it. I saw his fear in the section on courtship. Courtship, he warned, was a dangerous time having three stages. It began with the meeting, moved to the first kiss, and ended with the betrothal. The betrothal, he insisted, must be short, otherwise the woman would fall prey to a sexual passion she could not restrain. Sex, he was telling women, was not to be comprehended and controlled. It was way too powerful for that. It instead must be accommodated. The only accommodation available to a woman was a hasty marriage. Once married, she would then listen to and obey her husband. His fear of sex made me afraid—I was so unprepared for what I might find in the world—but I didn't think it was ignorance or obedience I needed.

I realized next a third ingredient of life had something to do with the mind. In a philosophy class, we were required to read parts of William James's book, *The Principles of Psychology*. In his discussion of the mind, he said there was in it a stream of thought that always kept flowing and the thoughts within that stream always kept changing. If a thought returned to that stream, it never came back exactly the way it had been there before. I had one of those recurring thoughts. It had entered my mind the day I first arrived at Vassar four years ago and had never left it. It was always somewhere in that stream, sometimes at the top easy to see and at other times at the bottom out of sight, and it did constantly change as time went by. The five words, though, that had given rise to that thought never changed in my mind. Time could not alter or erase them. These were the words I saw that first day when I opened the drawer to my desk: *don't let it get you.* Within the hour, I had figured out they were telling me I had to find a way to accept the social categorization I was going to be subjected to. If I didn't, it would make my life at Vassar miserable. Having in that first hour already felt the sting of rejection, I took the warning to heart and began to think seriously about those words. My original thought, *hopefully it doesn't get me,* quickly became *it's not going to get me,* which, after Field Day that second year, turned into *it hasn't gotten me.* My friendship with Liz, the "Positively Engaged" sign on her door that no longer applied to me, my friendships with the girls on the baseball team and with other athletes, my enviable standing within the school because of my hitting, my Class Day plaque and the response of the girls to it all convinced me it had not gotten me.

But, as I now thought about those five words, perhaps after all it had. I had always assumed I was being warned about what others might do to me. Maybe I had it backwards. Maybe it was about what I might end up doing to myself. I had changed. The last two years I did like the other grinds, but I didn't spend much time with them. I didn't go to their rooms, didn't sit at their table to eat a meal, didn't attend their evening gatherings. I saw Katie only infrequently, though we were in different dormitories now, and she usually was in the Observatory a good part of the day and the night as well. The desire for acceptance, I should probably make that the need, had made me into a person who, while not consciously excluding others, stood alongside of those who did. I was happily inside rooms having large "Positively Engaged" signs on their doors knowing the signs were there to keep the undesirables out. I had conformed to their ways; it was more than that, I had joined them. *It hadn't gotten me* I boasted. And yet, without seeing what was happening, not even for the briefest moment, it had. I had deceived myself.

This deceit, I knew, was close to the ingredient of life I was trying to name. But deceit wasn't the right word. It was too much centered in me. I needed a word that could apply to life itself as well. I then realized that the word I wanted was illusion. Life could be in part and, if we let it, in its entirety illusory. We didn't see what was there, but what we wanted to or needed to see. This was, to a smaller or larger degree, our failing. But could not illusion also be a property of life? Life just might have its hidden side that was only grudgingly revealed.

Irony, complexity, illusion. Could it be that these three ingredients of life were not static, that they, instead, were gathered up into another ingredient that, in some inexplicable way, encompassed them and shaped them? Because of the fifty-sixth Psalm, I was beginning to think so. After hearing Phillip Nutt preach, I had hoped he would come back to us. Always, though, it was someone else at the Sunday morning chapel service, and when I asked why, I was told he had moved to the Midwest. He was gone, but I could still see him and even feel him, I could feel his playfulness and his energy, and with his sermon in my diary, I could still hear him. He had talked about the Psalms in that sermon, how he had found himself at home in them. I figured that since they had spoken to him, they just might have something to say to me. So, I got into the habit of reading a Psalm a day. I got through all 150 and then read the ones I especially liked a second time. Of all their insights, and there were many, one statement stood out in my mind; one, as William James would say, had become embedded in my stream of thought. It would, I was sure, stay there, constantly changing over time in its implication and yet never changing in its basic meaning. It came from the fifty-sixth Psalm, the lament of one being assaulted by his enemies. In verse nine, the psalmist wrote: "When I cry unto thee, then shall mine enemies turn back: this I know; for God is for me." These simple and yet enormously powerful words said all that in the end needed to be said: God is for me. This love of God, I'm sure Phillip Nutt would make that this grace of God, was the fourth ingredient of life. I had put it last because I had a feeling the other ingredients flowed into and emerged from it. Its rightful position, though, was first.

Just the other day I was a college girl. Mercy me! Tomorrow I'm going to be a bloomer girl.

The Boston Clippers

EVERLY, ILLINOIS
January 1907

I was a rookie—or as Ruthie Montgomery, our cantankerous first baseman, kept reminding me, a yannigan. What more is there to say? A college graduate, I could solve a quadratic equation, explain why the French Revolution had gone wrong, recite the periodic table, converse in French, and repeat Hamlet's "to be or not to be" soliloquy without stumbling once. Yet when it came to playing baseball professionally, I knew nothing. Absolutely nothing. I learned how dumb I was within fifteen minutes of joining the team. That's all it took, fifteen minutes, to make a fool of myself. Actually, foolishness isn't a strong enough word; complete humiliation is closer to it. My face became so red-hot I could have fried an egg on it. Oh, I was a yannigan all right.

We were somewhere outside of Boston. I don't remember the town, but, then, I have forgotten just about all the towns we played in. There were so many they soon all ran together in my mind. The ball field, I do recall, was close to a lake with a sandy beach. Anyone on the team could have easily thrown a baseball into the water from first base. Though it was June, that Saturday morning was windy and cold. Except for the girls practicing for the afternoon game and a man seated rigidly on a nearby bench, no one else was there I could see. Carrying my uniform, mitt, and bat, I headed for the field. The man on the bench, Mr. Roscoe Jenkins, noticed me coming. Carefully putting aside a note pad and pencil, he got up and started toward me. Tall, lean, and somewhere in his forties, he wore a lightweight mackintosh, a navy blue serge suit with a striped four in hand necktie, and a derby hat. Stamped, or maybe I should say stitched, onto his face was a stern expression that declared he was the manager of the team and was to be listened to and heeded if a girl wanted to play for him. Awkwardly he shook my hand and, pointing to what I assumed were the changing rooms for the beach, told me to get into my uniform.

As I walked toward the bath houses, I saw two of the girls leaving the one on the right. I started for it without giving the girls or the bath houses another thought. There was no reason to. Besides, my mind was elsewhere. I was thinking about Mr. Roscoe Jenkins. He, I guessed, would be more of a businessman than a coach. His eye would primarily be on the ticket sales not the game or the girls. I was wondering too about the girls. Would they like me? Would I like them? How good were they, and next to them, how good was I? My emotions also got in the way. With all the excitement, anxiety, loneliness, and even fear I was feeling, it was like my first day at Vassar all over again. So, when I got to the bath house on the right and saw MEN on the door, I stopped for only a second. The other two girls had used this bath house, I told myself. The women's bath house was obviously being cleaned, or it was being repaired. In I went.

At the end of the room and around the corner, I found a spot to change and got undressed. At that moment, someone came in and coughed. I froze. It wasn't a woman's cough. I was in that bath house with a man. He didn't know I was there, but I knew he was. I knew, too, I had to figure out what to do and figure it out fast. I couldn't leave, he was in my way. So I could either stay where I was and pray he didn't come around the corner, or I could try to hide somewhere and hope he didn't see me, or I could tell him I was there and trust he was enough of a gentleman to leave. Then I heard what I thought was the sound of running water. He must be washing his hands. Or he might be—I didn't want to think about what that other possibility might be. Either way, I reasoned, he would be facing a wall. Picking up my clothes, I ducked into a stall, sat down on the toilet seat, lifted my legs, closed my eyes tightly, and slowly began to count from one hundred backwards. When I reached seventeen, though it seemed like I had been to zero and back to one hundred seventeen times, he finished whatever he was doing. I heard the door of the bath house open and then shut. At last. I began to breathe easier. I finished putting on my uniform and hurried to the door, intending to open it slowly so I could see if anyone was outside, but it started to open before my hand was on the doorknob. Someone was outside, and he was coming in. I was caught, exposed. I stepped back and waited. The door swung open, and I saw in front of me another girl from the team. She looked at me, in my Boston Clippers uniform carrying a bundle of clothes, in disbelief and then started to smile. The smile turned into laughter. She laughed so hard her body shook. As it did, her hair moved. That wasn't supposed to happen. Hair doesn't move; it's rooted in the scalp. Unless . . . Suddenly it hit me. It wasn't her hair but a wig, and she was a he. I pushed him aside and bolted out the door. Walking quickly, actually it was more like running, toward the ball field, I all at once realized, to my horror, I had left my bat and mitt in the bath house. I was close to tears.

"Hey."

I heard a voice behind me and turned around. There he was, wearing that stupid wig and a Clippers uniform, with my bat and mitt.

"Did you forget these?"

I grabbed the mitt and bat from him and, without saying a word, stormed off. I wanted to get away from him. The quicker I could, I figured, the less stupid I'd feel.

"Slow down," he said, catching up to me. "You must be Mattie Welsh. We've been told that you're fast and hit a long ball. Welcome to the team. Everyone calls me Slugger."

"You hit a long ball too?" I muttered, not looking at him.

"I'm lucky if I get the ball out of the infield. My name is Gene Harris. That's Gene spelled with a *G*," he added with a grin. "I'm the catcher on this team."

"I can just imagine what you'll be calling me," I replied, ignoring his welcome.

"Oh, we'll have a good time with you all right." He paused a moment. "I've got it. We will begin with Sneak-A-Peek, which, in no time at all, will become Sneaky Peeky, and this, before you know it, will turn into either Sneaky, or Peeky, or maybe even Peekaboo. The possibilities are endless."

"That would be so . . ." I was about to say cruel but wasn't sure that was the right word and not knowing what the right word might be said nothing. Angry at him for making me into a joke and also at myself for being so brainless, I kept looking straight ahead and started to walk faster.

"Now hold on, Mattie. I'm kidding. There's something you have to understand right away. We're always making fun of somebody, and we do it for a good reason. We come to this team wanting something, whether it's to make money, or to see the country, or to get away from home, or to change the way people think, or to play baseball. Some get what they want, some don't. But what we all do get, and we get it right away, is a hard life. Always there is another game to play and, with Roscoe Jenkins the manager, to win; another smelly, noisy train to take; another dreary boarding house to stay in;

another bad meal to eat; another rowdy fan to put up with; another nasty player to watch out for; another aching muscle, or sprained ankle, or bruised shin, or jammed finger to ignore. The kidding loosens us up. It helps us play better and makes life a little easier. You'll get a nickname, just about all of us have one, and it probably will not be too flattering, nicknames are not meant to be, but it will have nothing to do with the men's bath house. Unless, of course . . ."

"Of course, what?"

"You tell the others what happened."

I slowed down and, for the first time, really looked at him. He was a little over six feet, stocky, probably in his early twenties. Because of his nose, which clearly had been broken, maybe because of a collision at home plate, and the long, jagged scar under his lower lip, his face was rugged. But his friendly grin and his thoughtful way of looking at me made me think I also saw in his face kindness. His eyes were blue. They didn't dig into me, searching for a weakness to take advantage of, but instead seemed to respect me; they seemed to greet me. Obviously, I couldn't tell the color of his hair or whether he parted it in the middle or on the side. "You look cute in that wig," I said. "Are there other ravishing beauties like you I should know about?"

"Just Henry Winters, the shortstop. He's the brunette with the deep voice. Women's teams always have at least two or three men, sometimes they're only boys, playing for them. Usually one will be the pitcher. Most of us still wear a wig and bloomers, but that's starting to change. Soon we'll all be in a regular baseball uniform, and when that happens, we'll gladly throw the wigs away."

"Do you fool anyone?"

"Only children under four. The fans know we're out there. They like to see how quickly they can spot us. A few ride us pretty hard, but most, though, have fun with it. It does make the game closer.

Some of the town teams play good baseball. But, then, as you will see, the girls on this team do too."

"Why don't we have a man pitching for us?"

"We don't need one," Gene said. "Nina Clark doesn't have a man's fast ball, but puts her pitch right where she wants to, which, against most hitters, is better than speed. She can make the ball curve to the left and to the right and even throws a spitter."

"Are you saying she . . ." I stopped. I had never said the word spit before and wasn't sure I wanted to start now.

Gene finished the sentence for me. "Spits on the ball? She does facing the outfield and with her glove in front of her face so nobody can see what she's doing. The pitch comes in straight as a string and kind of slow. Then something odd happens that I for the life of me can't figure out. The ball reaches a point where all of a sudden it drops down like it has just fallen off a table. The batter, fooled out of his jockey strap, swings over it." He suddenly turned bright red. "Sorry. I should have said 'fooled out of his socks.'"

"You should have." But I had no idea why. I had never heard of a jockey strap before. I had, however, studied deductive logic in my philosophy class at Vassar. Gene had changed jockey strap to socks, therefore it must be an article of clothing one wore to play baseball. A woman didn't have one, therefore it must be worn only by a man. Suddenly I thought I knew what this strap was and where it went and felt myself getting even redder than Gene. This is silly, I told myself angrily, hoping he had not noticed how embarrassed I was. I am no longer a student; I am a baseball player. "I suppose she's called Spit," I said, emphasizing the word spit.

"What else?" We walked for a moment in silence. Then he said, "Mattie, don't let what happened back there get you down. You're a rookie, and rookies do strange things. Besides, others have done much worse. You went to the wrong bath house. When Nina joined the team, she went to the wrong town. She was to meet us in Oxford,

Massachusetts, but got her states mixed up and went instead to Oxford, Pennsylvania. When we didn't come, she thought it was Roscoe Jenkins' mistake, he had most likely given her the wrong date, and she decided to stay there and wait for the team. Nina finally caught up with us a week late. She got The Speech without even being asked to sit down."

"What speech?"

We had reached the ball field. Mr. Jenkins saw us and picked up the tablet and folders that were on the bench next to him. "The one you are going to get now."

"Miss Welsh," Mr. Jenkins said, pointing to the space he had just cleared, "please be seated here." After I sat down, he cleared his throat and adjusted his tie. "I always tell a new girl the day she arrives the rules of the team. The way we view baseball makes these rules necessary and, I must stress, makes them mandatory. What, may I ask, is baseball?"

"It's a game," I replied. From the frown on Mr. Jenkins' face, or maybe it was a scowl, I knew he wasn't pleased with my answer. But I couldn't take the words back, and even if I could, I didn't know what else to say.

"No, Miss Welsh, baseball is not a game. Nobody today pays money to see a game of baseball. They used to. Once the game itself so bewitched people they didn't care where it was being played—on a field, or in the water, or even on ice—or who was playing. But those days are gone. Some say baseball now is a contest. People will pay money to see one team play another. They want to know which team will prevail. The one that does acquires standing. If the contest is between a men's team and a women's team, baseball turns into a struggle between the sexes. The side that wins this contest gains power. There is truth, though it is only a partial truth, to this understanding. The whole truth, though, is that baseball is a product. People who watch baseball are not spectators, they are consumers.

The Sears, Roebuck Catalogue opens with the heading 'Consumers Guide.' Miss Welsh, our real competition is not another team, but it's what is in that catalogue and the catalogue itself. People can buy from that catalogue anything and virtually everything they want in their homes while stretched out on a sofa sipping lemonade. What the consumer demands is a good product; he insists on getting his money's worth. What makes any team a good product is winning. The three rules of the Boston Clippers Baseball Team come from the letters in the word win. Rule # 1: there will be no whining—that's the *w* in win. Rule #2: there will be no immorality—that's the *i* in win. Rule #3: there will be no nonsense on and off the field—that's the *n* in win. We feel right, we act right, and we think right, and we will win. We win, and we are a product the consumer will buy. It's logic, Miss Welsh, pure and simple logic. These three rules are not a standard we try to attain; they are the code we live by. If, at any time, you decide to live by another code, you will be dismissed from the team. You will play center field and bat seventh. If you hit successfully, you will be placed higher in the batting order. Go into the outfield and catch fly balls. You will be called to the plate when it's your turn to hit."

No whining, no immorality, no nonsense. The three rules did spell win, assuming, of course, the talent was there. I wasn't sure about baseball being a product, though. It seemed to me I needed to keep baseball a game to play it well. As I headed for the outfield, smiling at the girls as I passed them and particularly at the one who needed to shave, I also wondered if I had already broken at least one of the rules. Mr. Jenkins would undoubtedly consider my choice of bath houses nonsense.

* * *

Within a month, I was hitting and had acquired a nickname. The two were not related at first, but then came together in an unexpected way. I was pleased with the hitting. So, too, was Mr. Jenkins. He moved me to the number five position and, when I continued to hit, to the number three position in the batting order. Like the other girls, I choked up on the bat and tried to slap the ball in-between the fielders. If the count, though, was in my favor, I would slide my hands all the way down the bat and take a full swing. Often I would miss the pitch, but then I had another strike coming. When I did connect, I hit the long ball. The long ball not only meant extra bases, it also set up my next time at bat. When I came to the plate again, the infielders would move back. I could then bunt the ball toward third and with my speed make it to first base easily.

I was not pleased, though, with my nickname. Right away the girls called me Vassar. A nickname had meaning. It told a girl she had a place on the team. It told her she belonged. Vassar told me I didn't belong. I was too different—no one else had been to college, only a few had graduated from high school—I was too privileged. Some of the girls might have envied me, most of them probably thought I felt they were beneath me. If anything, I felt I was beneath them. I admired these girls. What Gene had said that first day outside the bath house was true. It was a hard life. But because of their remarkable abilities, their high spirits, their perseverance, and, perhaps most important, their camaraderie, they managed to turn a hard life into a good life. When I got a hit, or stole a base, or scored a run, they cheered and patted me on the back when I came to the bench. But otherwise, except for Gene, they stayed away. I felt excluded but didn't know what to do about it. Gene told me to be patient. They would be calling me something else soon enough. He was right.

One Friday afternoon in late August, we stopped in a town in upstate New York for a game. Mr. Jenkins had hired a band to meet us at the train station. We marched down Main Street with the band in front of us. The horns blared and the drums banged making enough noise to get the attention of those living in down-state New York. In front of the band, the mayor walked beside a magnificent white horse. A large sign draped over both sides of the horse announced in bold, capital letters colored red, white, and blue Baseball Tomorrow Afternoon. We, though, didn't need the fanfare to draw a big crowd. A year ago, the Clippers had beaten the town team 8 to 6, and they wanted revenge.

We stayed at a boarding house Friday night. While most of us returned to our rooms after supper, a few went out. I wrote a letter home and then read until 10:30. We had to be in bed by 11:00. To be up later was, according to Mr. Jenkins, nonsense. I couldn't fall asleep, though. It must have been well past midnight when I heard a door to one of the rooms where the girls were staying open and then close. Someone must be using the bathroom, I thought. I listened for the door to open and close again when whoever it was came back to her room but heard nothing. One of the girls, I realized, had just come in.

Saturday was hot and humid. We dressed for the game in the boarding house, thankful that although the Clipper's blouse was a heavy flannel, the bloomers were made of cotton. Carrying our equipment, we walked to the ball park in ten minutes. It seemed twice as long, though, because of the cranks (that, I quickly learned, was what the players called the fans) we met along the way. They hurled insults, curses, and even rotten tomatoes at us, trying to bully us into thinking we had already lost the game. But it didn't work. We had heard it all before. Besides, as we passed McDonald's Mercantile Store, we saw through the window a barrel filled with nails.

We all were superstitious. Often there was a thin line between getting a hit or striking out, making a good play in the field or committing an error, stealing a base or being thrown out. A little extra help, it was thought, would put us on the right side of that line and keep us there. No one knew if a superstition made any difference, if it convinced the baseball gods to work for us. But then no one knew if it didn't. When I came in from center field, I always touched second base with my right foot. Each time Maggie Watts, the third baseman, stepped into the batter's box, she pulled down the bill of her cap and hitched up her bloomers. Lizzie Connors, the left fielder, tapped her bat on the plate three times before getting ready for the pitch. A superstition was personal. Unless we were desperate, we wouldn't do what another girl did, even if she started to hit .350 instead of her usual .275 after wearing a piece of red ribbon on her blouse. But there was one superstition we all had in common. Seeing, by chance, a handful of nails before a game, no matter where they were, meant victory. It was the way the baseball gods told us they were going to be on our side. We reached the ball park knowing we were going to win.

Unlike many of the ball parks we played in, this one was well cared for. Rocks had been removed from the field, and the field itself, instead of either sloping to one side or dropping down into a gully, was level. The grass was green and had been recently cut; the outfield fence was painted; the foul lines down first and third base and the batter's box were neatly drawn; the stands were clean. Usually the teams sat on benches on either side of the field, but here there were dugouts that would keep us out of the sun when we were at bat. This town embraced its baseball.

Before the teams were finished warming-up, the stands were almost full. By now, I understood why. Many came, as Mr. Jenkins had said, to watch a good baseball game. But some also came to be entertained. Seeing a ball hit out of the park, a third to second to first double play, a single stretched into a double with a head first slide into the bag, a diving one-handed catch of a sinking line drive broke the monotony of their daily lives. Some came looking for hope. A batter finding a way to get on base, a pitcher finding a way to get a batter out inspired them. Some came to see the home team win. They were proud of their team and loyal to it. Some came to make trouble. They didn't like women playing men, it was improper, or women wearing bloomers, they were indecent. Some came because they thought we helped their cause. They wanted more rights for women and more opportunities. They, too, wore bloomers and cheered us even when we made a dumb play in the field or struck out on a bad pitch. Some came to make noise. They drank and became loud. Some came because someone else had brought them. They didn't know anything about baseball beyond the pitcher threw a ball and a batter tried to hit it and were quiet.

Sitting next to Gene before the game started, I noticed he had two mitts, the one he always used and another one almost twice its size. "Where did you get this one?" I asked, picking up the oversized glove.

"I had Spalding's in Boston make it for me."

"It's big enough to catch a basketball."

"It's got to be," Gene said. "For a month now, Nina has been working on a knuckler. Instead of putting her fingers over the ball when she throws it, she digs the tips of fingers into the ball. It's a slow pitch that doesn't spin at all. At first, it didn't do anything. But after she got the mechanics of the pitch right, it began to flutter, and then it started to dance. She can't control it, and even if she could, she doesn't have any idea where it's going—and neither do I. I can usually knock it down with my regular mitt, but I need this one to catch it. We're going to try the knuckler in the game this afternoon when Nina wants to waste a pitch. If she gets it over, no one is going to hit it, and if she doesn't, the batter will be scratching his head wondering what that crazy pitch was and if it's coming again. She'll then be able to sneak her straight one right by him."

We watched the other team complete its warm-up. "They're good," I said.

"To beat them again, Nina will have to be sharp. I haven't seen their pitcher before. He's big and looks mean."

"Isn't that what a pitcher is supposed to look like?"

"It helps. But the other way around works too. On the mound, Nina is the friendliest person in the world. She smiles at the batter and patiently waits for him to get set for the pitch. Before she begins her windup, he is almost sure he hears her say, 'I hope you're enjoying yourself this afternoon.' Then she throws him a spitter. Because it's slow and comes into the plate looking like a watermelon, he swings at it with all his might, and because it is a spitter, he misses it by a foot. Before throwing her next pitch, she smiles at him again. Their pitcher makes a batter nervous; Nina makes him overconfident."

Using a megaphone, the umpire announced who would be pitching and catching for the two teams. "For the Clippers," he cried, "it will be Clark and Harris, and for the Lions Jones and Daily." Then he yelled, "Play ball." At once we saw their pitcher was not only big and mean, he was also fast. Our lead-off batter, Agnes Henshaw, who played second base, struck out on three pitches. She sat down muttering, "I didn't even see the last one." Next up was Helen Miles, the right fielder. Because of her good eye and short swing, she almost always hit the ball somewhere. After working the count to three balls and one strike, she bunted the next pitch toward first. In one graceful motion, the first baseman charged in, fielded the ball with his bare hand, swung his body around, and flipped the ball to first base. The coordination and timing were beautiful. The play had only one flaw. No one was there. The pitcher knew he should have been but got to first base late. By the time the right fielder picked up the ball, Helen was standing on second base. Hitting third, I went to the plate thinking I'd try to slap the pitch into right field. If it went far enough, Helen, with her good speed, would be able to score. But I got under the ball. I hit a weak pop fly that landed in-between the second baseman and the right fielder. Thinking the play would at least be at third, I rounded first and, with my head down and arms pumping, headed for second. I barely heard Emily Moore, the first base coach, cry, "Don't go." Looking up, I saw Helen, flat on the ground, being tagged out by the shortstop. Quickly I got back to first. "What happened to Helen?" I asked Emily.

"The shortstop tripped her. He stuck out his foot when she broke for third."

"Didn't the umpire see him?"

"What do you think?"

"He was watching the right fielder, of course," I said, "or the pretty girl buying a knockwurst sandwich behind third base. We get tripped, held, and pushed all the time, and the umpires never see anything. It makes me sick to my stomach."

"Get sick after the game, Vassar. There are two outs. If Henry hits the ball, go."

Henry didn't hit the ball, and we took the field. After Nina had thrown her first warm-up pitch, the manager of the other team suddenly shouted, "I won't allow this." Jumping up from the bench, he nearly ran to the umpire, who was standing behind the pitcher's mound, and Mr. Jenkins did too. All the Clippers on the field gathered around the three of them. This, I thought to myself, was going to be good. "The catcher's mitt is too big," the manager blared. "He can't use it. It's against the rules."

"And which rule would that be?" Mr. Jenkins said.

"Obviously the one about the size of the players' mitts."

Taking from his pocket *Spaulding's Official Base Ball Guide* and turning to the page he wanted, Mr. Jenkins said, "I believe you are referring to rule number 20. Let me read it to you: *The catcher or first* baseman may wear a glove or mitt of any size, shape or weight. Every other player is restricted to the use of a glove or mitt weighing not over 10 ounces and measuring not over 14 inches around the palm. According to the rule, the catcher's mitt could be twice this size."

"It could," the umpire said. "The mitt is allowed."

Mr. Jenkins, smiling, returned to the bench, and we went back to our positions in the field. After finishing her warm-up pitches, Nina faced their leadoff hitter. She struck him out with a wicked curve ball. The next two batters didn't do any better. One hit a soft fly to Lizzie in left field. The other grounded out to Maggie at third base. Coming off the field, I had the strongest feeling this game was going to be the one that Nina had always hoped she had in her. Each pitch was going to work: it was going to curve or to drop the way it was supposed to and go where she wanted it to. She surprised me, though. As the innings went by, Nina didn't throw her knuckler. When I asked Gene why, he told me she didn't need to. He knew the big mitt made him look silly, but thought it gave us an advantage. It kept the other team looking for something that never came and also kept them busy riding him. Half of their bench yelled repeatedly, "Why does the catcher have that big mitt?" and the other half yelled back, "Because the catcher can't catch." The time they spent making fun of him and the mitt was time they didn't spend thinking about the game.

Their pitcher surprised me, too. We all were an easy out, especially Maggie, who batted ninth. She never hit a single pitch he threw, not even a foul ball. Yet he kept pitching her inside. More than once, the pitch was so far inside, it would have hit her if she hadn't jumped out of the way. Why was he doing this? It didn't make sense. But as I thought about it, perhaps it did. Maggie might have been the one who had come in late the night before. Maybe the two had been out together, and he had wanted something she wouldn't give him. And what he wanted now was to frighten her; it wasn't an exaggeration to make that terrorize her. If the ball did hit her, he'd say the pitch was unintentional; it had slipped out of his hand.

They pushed a run across in the fourth inning, and with a walk and two errors, we got a run in the sixth inning. The score was still tied one to one going into the ninth inning. After working the count to three balls and two strikes, Helen, who led off for us, popped to the first baseman. I was up next. As I was getting my bat, Maggie approached me. Since she had constantly ignored me before, other than asking me to pass the peas at supper, her sudden interest now was another surprise. A mediocre fielder and a poor hitter, she was the weakest player on the team. But because of her strong personality—she had a loud voice, an opinion about everything, and, at times, a biting sense of humor—she did influence the other girls. "Make him look bad." That's all she said. But she didn't have to say anything else. Her eyes said it for her. In them, I saw pain, and humiliation, and anger. I nodded. I didn't like the pitcher either.

The first pitch, a fast ball, came inside. It was meant to move me off the plate so I couldn't hit anything on the outside corner, or at least not hit it hard. But I didn't budge. One ball and no strikes. The count was in my favor. I slid my hands down the bat to the very end, raised my arms and moved them further back from my body so that it was more tightly coiled, and waited for the next pitch. When it came, right down the middle of the plate, I swung at it with all my strength. That pitch, I knew instantly, was going over the left field fence. It was the hit that I had hoped I had in me. I dropped the bat and started to run. I was almost three-quarters of the way down the line when I saw the first base coach put out her hands, not to wave me on or to congratulate me, but to stop me. "Foul ball," the umpire shouted. I groaned. I had missed hitting a home run by the blink of an eye. If I had swung that much later, the time it took my eyes to close and open, the ball would have landed to the right of the foul line and I would have been rounding the bases instead of going back to the batter's box. A nearly perfect swing had accomplished nothing. That glorious swing had not only been useless, it had been detrimental. Because of it, the count was now one ball and one strike. Baseball, as Sam Davis had said, did have its cruel side. I shortened my swing for the next pitch but fouled it off behind the catcher. One ball and two strikes. The next pitch was an inch off the outside corner of the plate. I was tempted to go after it, but at the last moment checked my swing. Two balls and two strikes. Then I was fooled. Instead of the fast ball I was looking for, the pitch was a change-up. It was in the dirt, a terrible pitch, but having started my swing, I couldn't stop it. Strike three. The pitcher had made me look bad. But I heard the girls on the bench cry, "Run." Without looking back, I knew why. The ball had gotten past the catcher. I made it to first base a step ahead of his throw.

I took a big lead off first. From his stretch, the pitcher slowly looked over at me. He looked away and then quickly looked back, thinking he would catch me leaning toward second. He did more than that. He caught me breaking for second. I ran as fast as I could for seven feet and then stopped. The break for second had been a feint. It had been a performance worthy of the award for best actor of the year at Vassar. The pitcher started to throw the ball to second base. Changing his mind, he swung around to throw it to first base. Changing his mind once again, he finally decided not to throw it anywhere. "Balk," the umpire cried. "Runner take second base." Trotting to second, I turned toward the pitcher, who was watching me, his face contorted in anger, and smiled sweetly.

After working the count to three balls and one strike, Henry hit a hard ground ball in between the shortstop and the third baseman. Intending to steal third, I had taken off before the pitch was even thrown. Both the shortstop and the third baseman started for the ball. The shortstop fielded it, the ball was closer to him, and threw it to first base. "The runner at first is out," the umpire shouted.

Pointing at me, he then said, "And the runner on third base is out for interfering with the third baseman while he was attempting to field the ground ball." The umpire was right. If the base runner does not give the fielder the room he needs to make a play, she is out. I was past the shortstop when he went for the ground ball, but nearly ran the third baseman over. I had made the third out; the side was retired. But Mr. Jenkins, walking out onto the field, obviously didn't think so.

"I'd like to ask you a question," he said to the umpire.

"There is no question about the third out. Your base runner clearly interfered with the third baseman, and the Rule Book is clear about interference."

"It most certainly is. And because it is, I would like to ask you which fielder was closer to the ground ball?"

"The shortstop, of course."

"In your judgment, then, it was the shortstop who was going to make the play."

"Yes," the umpire answered. "I would say that."

"Well, then, what you must say is that the base runner on third is safe."

"Now why must I say that?"

"Because of the Rule Book," Mr. Jenkins replied, once again taking *Spaulding's Official Base Ball Guide* out of the pocket of his suit coat, "to be more specific, Rule 56, Section 8." He started to read: *The base runner is out if he fails to avoid a fielder attempting to field a batted ball; provided that if two or more fielders attempt to field a batted ball, and the base runner comes in contact with one or more of them, the umpire shall determine which fielder is entitled to the benefit of this rule, and shall not decide the base runner out for coming in contact with a fielder other than the one the umpire determines to be entitled to field such batted ball.* The interference rule applies in this case to the shortstop, since he was fielding the ball, not to the third baseman."

I returned to third base. We still had life in this inning, but just barely. Ruthie Montgomery came to the plate with two outs. Usually she was a strong hitter, but not today against this pitcher. She was going to strike out, I just knew it, and we weren't going to get another runner on third base. He was too good. I had to do something. Ruthie swung at the first pitch he threw and missed it. Strike one. In his mind, he already had the next two strikes. He only had to throw them. So, he forgot all about me. That gave me an idea. He wasn't throwing out of a stretch. Most pitchers didn't with only a runner on third. The runner wasn't going anywhere. If he tried to steal home, the ball would beat him to the plate. What's more, this runner on third was a girl. But because he wasn't pitching from a stretch, even if he did look over at me, once he started his windup, he couldn't throw to third base. If he did, it would be a balk, and I would walk home. So, by timing it right, I could take a long lead off third base and get a good jump on the pitch. I also had another advantage. Because Ruthie batted right handed, she stood between the catcher and me. To the pitcher, she was a hitter; to the catcher, she was an obstruction. Looking at Maggie on the bench, I made up my mind. The moment the pitcher started his windup, I broke for home. The pitcher never saw me go, and the catcher never saw me coming until it was too late. The pitch was outside, moving the catcher off the plate and away from me. At the last moment, Ruthie realized what I was doing and jumped out of the way. I slid across home plate as the catcher holding the ball in his mitt lunged for me. Everyone was yelling, but I only heard the umpire shout, "Safe."

I have often thought about what happened next. In that moment, everyone seemed to be either arguing with the umpire or cheering—everyone that is except for the pitcher. He had come to the plate furious and was now standing over me. I had made him look bad. Forcing him into a balk at first base was embarrassing, but that was nothing compared to stealing home, especially when that one run would most likely decide who won the game. "You think you're pretty smart," he snarled. Leaning over me so that his face was directly above mine, he spit on me. Then he turned around and walked back to the mound. Stunned and disgusted, I was slowly starting to sit up when I suddenly saw Maggie and Gene run out onto the field going in different directions. Maggie came to me. After helping me to my feet, she dug into the pocket of her bloomers and pulled out a handkerchief.

"It's clean," she said, handing the handkerchief to me.

I wiped the spit off my face and gave it back to her. "Thanks."

"Thank you, Vassar. You got him good."

We then heard a howl coming from the mound. There was Gene on top of the pitcher pounding him with his fists. We stared at them relishing the sight, especially when we saw blood spurting from a gash on the pitcher's face. All too soon, as far as we were concerned, players from their team pulled Gene off him. With his fists still clenched, he angrily walked toward our bench with Mr. Jenkins beside him.

The umpire, who hadn't seen what the pitcher had done to me, ran over to Gene. "I'm ejecting you from this game," he said.

Gene stepped toward him with a cold, menacing look on his face. "You're tossing out the wrong person. That bastard on the mound shouldn't be allowed on a baseball diamond ever again."

"Leave the ball park now. If you don't, your team will forfeit this game." Looking at Mr. Jenkins, he snapped, "That's Rule 60 of *Spaulding's Official Base Ball Guide*."

Gene picked up his bat and oversized catcher's mitt. Looking at his mitt, he said to Mr. Jenkins, "Who's going behind the plate?"

"Henry, and I'll put Mattie at shortstop and Emily Moore out in center field."

"Have Henry use this mitt and tell him Nina's first pitch has got to be a knuckler. Wherever she throws the ball, Henry has to miss it. He has to miss it by a country mile. But it's got to be a good act. Those batters have to think that even though he knows the knuckler's coming and he's got that big mitt, he still can't catch it. They think that, and they'll figure it's coming again. They'll have to. But she doesn't have to use the knuckler again. That one time will set up her other pitches. The way she's throwing, they won't touch her."

And they didn't. The first two batters went down swinging, and the third hit a soft line drive to Maggie at third base for the final out. After the game, it was agreed that Nina's arm, my legs, and Henry's stomach—that's where he had "caught" Nina's knuckler—had won it for us. But as we passed McDonald's Mercantile Store on the way back to the boarding house and saw the nails through the window, we all knew there was another reason. It's what the baseball gods had decreed.

Everyone continued to call me Vassar. That didn't change, but mostly because of Maggie its meaning did. Slapping me playfully on the back, sitting next to me at meals, making me the object of her silly jokes which more times than not had something to do with Vassar, Maggie announced that I belonged. The other girls heard her and, at their own pace, accepted me. They told me I was a teammate, I was one of them, in different ways. But it was the nickname, especially when it was used to needle me, that I found most heartening. Whenever I did something ridiculous, they thought it was great fun to say Vassar with a disbelieving tone of voice and a furrowed brow that turned the nickname into a perplexing question. How could you, a Vassar graduate, have done that?

That perplexing question, though, soon turned into more of a statement. The voice and the look now seemed to be saying you might be smart about some things, but you're really dumb about other things, the things that matter most. For the life of me, I had no idea what the girls were getting at. Finally one day Maggie took me aside and told me their teasing had to do with someone on the team. I thought it odd she had not made that one of the girls on the team and wondered what was coming next. She then said, "I want you to take a test."

"But I haven't studied for it," I protested, smiling.

"Right there is your problem," she replied. "It's what you should have been studying. That you haven't is more baffling to me than Nina's knuckleball. Sometimes, Vassar, you really are dense. Now answer the questions I am going to ask you with either a yes or a no. Does Gene listen to us if we are troubled?"

"Yes."

"Does he advise us if we are confused?"

"Yes."

"Does he comfort us if we are sad?"

"Yes."

"Does he protect us if we are threatened?"

"Yes."

"You've passed the first section of the test with a perfect score. From your answers it's clear Gene wants to keep us from falling. We come now to the second section. Gene wants to keep us from falling. But Gene, himself, has blank for blank. Those two blanks are to be filled in, each one with a single word. What are those two words? Don't ask anyone to help you," Maggie said, starting to walk away, "that would be cheating."

I didn't need anyone to help me. Of all the words I could think of, only two of them explained why the girls kept needling me and why Maggie had given me that test. Gene wanted to keep us from falling. But Gene, himself, had fallen for me. Oh, my! Those, I was sure, were the right words for the two blanks, but had the girls got it right? No man, or for that matter no boy, had ever fallen for me, at least that I had been aware of.

Later that evening, alone in my room, I went to the mirror and, maybe for the first time, looked closely at myself. I was of average height, definitely trim, and after considering my chest, which I evaluated with some curiosity and a little embarrassment, I concluded I was moderately full. I was not pretty, but perhaps I was pleasant looking. My teeth weren't straight; my nose was crooked from a spill I had once taken on my bicycle; my eyes were too far apart; my jaw was too square. Yet, I had a clear complexion, soft brown hair, high cheek bones, and a nice smile. I appeared wholesome. I might be appealing to some men, possibly even to Gene.

I soon found myself thinking about him. Usually it wasn't intentional; he was just there in my mind. We often sat next to each other on the bench, at meals, on the train. When we weren't talking, most of the time we were laughing. I felt at ease with him. More important, I felt I was myself with him. I started to have a strange sensation that was hard to locate and even harder to describe. I only knew it was there because of Gene and it was telling me I had fallen for him.

I wondered what would come next. We had been beside each other but never really close to each other. I imagined Gene putting his arm around me. I saw us holding hands and, some evening, even kissing. I wasn't quite sure how a man and a woman kissed, but figured I'd work that out when it happened. I started to think about that first kiss, what it would feel like, how long it would last. As I did, I remembered the book *Beautiful Womanhood* Liz had given me at Vassar. One sentence had stuck in my mind. When the author was discussing the clitoris, he had written something about it being the center of the thrill or the voluptuous sensation—I couldn't forget those words—in the female. I certainly wasn't looking for that thrill or voluptuous sensation, but a tingle or a flutter, I thought, might be nice.

The next week I had a terrible game. I dropped a fly ball, allowing a run to score, struck out twice, and hit into a game ending double play with the bases loaded. We lost 11 to 9. I ran off the field and grabbing my glove and bat hurried back to the boarding house ahead of everyone else. I went up to my room and closed the door. I wanted to be alone. That's what I told myself, but I knew what I was really doing: I was hiding. That night, Gene told me everyone has a game like that; it's part of playing baseball. Tomorrow would be better. All I needed was a good night's sleep and a little extra batting practice. I nodded. He, of course, was right, but it didn't help.

"Get a sweater," he said, "we're going for a walk."

It was a lovely, late summer evening. Overhead there was a full moon. A cool breeze gently wrapped itself around us, and fireflies lit our way. After stopping for ice cream, we sat on a bench in a nearby park. In the distance, we heard a band playing "In Love with the Man in the Moon."

"What wonderful music. Where's it coming from?" I asked.

"The town square. At dinner I was told there's a concert in the pavilion every other week during the summer."

"The moon is beautiful tonight."

"Are you feeling better now?"

"Much better." Without thinking about what I was doing, I took his hand and, looking up at him, said, "Thank you, Gene."

Moving closer, he put his other hand around mine. We sat there in silence, holding hands. As the band started to play "Only One Girl in the World for Me," I leaned my head against his shoulder. I knew he was going to kiss me. But then he suddenly moved away, saying nothing, not even looking at me. I was devastated. "I don't understand," I said at last. "Have I done something wrong?"

"No, Mattie. You are the one girl in the world for me. But there will never be anything more than this."

"More than what? The two of us holding hands on a park bench? Gene, what are you telling me?"

"I'm telling you I will never get married." He stopped talking. I didn't know what to say and so said nothing. After a moment, he went on, "Part of the reason is I don't want to. I could tell you it's because of my parents' marriage. They have never been happy together. But that doesn't really explain what I feel, or perhaps I should say what I don't feel. Marriage just doesn't appeal to me. I used to think I was odd. But the President convinced me I'm not."

"The President of the United States?"

"Teddy Roosevelt, himself. A couple of years ago, the team was playing a game in Iowa. The town was on his western tour. A huge crowd went to the train station to see him. Our game was over, and I had never heard the President speak, so I joined them. When he came out of his railroad car, some children lifted a sign that said No Race Suicide Here, Teddy! I didn't understand what those words meant until he started talking. He tore into men who weren't getting married and women who weren't having children. The way he saw it, if we didn't stop what we were doing, actually it was what we weren't doing, it was going to ruin the country. Without enough people, and especially the right kind of people, the country would stop growing. We'd become poor and not be able to defend ourselves. But as he blasted away at us, wagging a finger that seemed to be pointed directly at me, I realized it wasn't guilt I was feeling but relief. I was even happy. Other men felt the way I did, and there were enough of us to make the President's blood boil. I wasn't odd after all."

"What is the other part of the reason?" I asked.

"This is not easy to talk about," he said, the faint smile on his face fading. "When I was fifteen, a man nearly beat my older sister to death. For almost a week, we didn't know if she was going to live. I hated seeing her in that hospital bed, her arm and three ribs broken, her face and the upper part of her body covered with terrible bruises. I kept asking why someone would do that to her. But mostly I wanted to know why someone was allowed to do that to her. Why hadn't God protected her? If he had been too busy, why hadn't he sent an angel? Isn't that what angels are supposed to do? If somebody else had been anywhere on that street, she wouldn't have been attacked. I got lots of answers—from my parents, the teachers at school, the minister at the church we went to—but nothing they said helped. I felt awful. I didn't want to eat; I couldn't sleep; I didn't care about anything. She got better, but I got worse. But then, just when I thought I'd never feel right again, I started thinking about a different question. I stopped asking others why it had happened and began to ask myself why wasn't I trying to stop it from happening again? Why wasn't I protecting not my sister, it was too late for that, but some other girl needing . . .?" His voice trailed off.

"Needing an angel," I said.

"I haven't looked at it quite like that before. Maybe you're right, Mattie. Some girl needing an angel. But back then I didn't want to be anyone's angel. All I had ever cared about was playing baseball. So, I forgot about that question; or at least I tried to. But it wouldn't go away. I'd be doing something and all of a sudden there it was. It seemed like sometimes it would tap me on the shoulder, and other times, it would grab hold of me and no matter what I did, it wouldn't let go. I finally said, 'Okay, I'll help out when I get the chance.' But I knew part-time wasn't an answer. I was still trying to run away from that question. Then it dawned on me I wasn't being asked for an answer; I was being given an answer. I could combine what I wanted to do and what I needed to do. I could play girls baseball. I started playing bloomer girls baseball when I was seventeen and won't quit until I'm too old to throw a runner out trying to steal second. When baseball is over, I'll find another way, to use your word, to be an angel to a girl or to a woman who is being mistreated. It could be anything, anything that is except marriage."

We started to walk back to the boarding house. "I've never known anyone like you," I said. I wanted to be close to him, not as an infatuated young woman hoping to be kissed, but as . . . I thought about it for a moment . . . a sister, perhaps. But, no, that wasn't it either. It was something else, something deeper maybe. I couldn't find the word for it, though, and it occurred to me I wasn't even sure what that relationship might actually be. "Is it okay if I take your arm?"

"It's always there whenever you want it."

Neither of us spoke for a while. Then I said, "Do you believe in God?"

"It depends upon which God you are talking about. If you mean the church's God, then I don't. That God is too much like old sourpuss."

"Old sourpuss?"

"That's what we called the grumpy old man who lived down the street from us when I was a little boy. He'd sit in a chair on his front porch and watch us. He didn't have much to say except when we did something he thought was wrong. Then he'd jump up out of that chair, sometimes knocking it over, and start yelling at us. I stayed away from him. When I got older, I stayed away from a God like him. But, Mattie, I know a different God. He wants to take care of us and finds ways, sometimes outrageous ways, to bring us together so we can take care of one another. Not too long ago, when I was trying to make up my mind about God, I happened to read in one of the Psalms that his loving kindness is better than life itself. It's this love and this kindness of God that, more than anything else, I need and, if I'm thinking right, I want. This is the God I believe in. Because of what happened to me, it only makes sense to. Where else could a question that brought me back from the dead have come from?"

"You said God wants to take care of us. Does that mean there are times when God doesn't want to take care of us?"

"It means there are times when God can't take care of us without our help. It's not only what I believe, it's what I know because of my sister. There is evil in this world, Mattie. It is a powerful force that

God is always fighting. But the day is coming when that fight will end. Do you believe in God?"

"Most of the time," I answered. "Right now, I'm where Job once was. After losing everything and then getting it all back and more, he tells God that before he had heard of him, but now he sees him. I keep hearing of God and what's being said about him, but I haven't seen him yet."

"Keep looking. What's strange is that while you think you are looking for him, it's actually the other way around. He's looking for you. What's really strange is that whatever happens, it most likely won't be what you're expecting. He likes surprises."

I'd found that I often did my best thinking when I first got up. What I couldn't figure out the night before would all at once be clear the next morning when I was brushing my teeth or washing my face. Maybe I was freshest then or least distracted. Or possibly it was because my mind had somehow put everything together while I was sleeping. Whatever the explanation might be, that's what happened the morning after Gene and I had talked. I was putting on my shoes when suddenly I realized that what he had said about not wanting to get married made sense. Lots of women weren't getting married. Some couldn't find the right man, but others just didn't want to. If women felt that way, why couldn't men? I remembered Marion Dunsberry, my classmate at Vassar, telling us why she wasn't going to marry. Her list of reasons seemed endless. But the more she talked, the more convinced we became marriage simply didn't interest her. She didn't like the arrangement. Gene obviously didn't either. But there was another side to this. Gene didn't want to marry because something else was more important to him. Although Teddy Roosevelt said the country needed him to marry, God, he believed, had told him he didn't need to marry, and he had decided years ago to listen to God. It then occurred to me Gene was somewhat like a Catholic priest. He was serving God in a way that made marriage, or at least marriage as we normally think of it, impossible, and in doing this dressed like a priest in distinctive clothing. I smiled. It was, indeed, very distinctive clothing. I finished lacing up my shoes, took a quick look at myself in the mirror, and went downstairs for breakfast.

* * *

We'd have a test in our subjects at Vassar three or four times a semester. For the professional baseball player, every game was a test. Mr. Jenkins recorded in a notebook he always carried with him what we did each time we hit or made a play in the field. Numbers didn't lie, he said. Those numbers and the statistics they produced measured how good we were. They gave us our grade for that day, that month, that season. That first summer I batted .310, drove in 30 runs, hit 4 home runs, stole 23 bases, and made 4 errors in the field. I had done well, but at the beginning of the next season, Mr. Jenkins told me I could do better. He wanted me to study the pitcher more closely, to analyze as thoroughly and as precisely as I could what he was throwing, when he was throwing it, and what he did when a runner was on base. By the third inning, he said, I should know not only what the pitcher was thinking, but what he was going to think. This knowledge, which he called anticipation, would boost my numbers at the plate and on the bases. He was right. I batted that the second season .331, drove in 42 runs, hit 7 home runs, stole 27 bases, and made 5 errors in the field.

The numbers didn't lie—I could play professional baseball—but they didn't tell the whole truth. Statistics had nothing to say about how hard it was to get even a passing grade in this game. Stones in the field could make you miss an easy ground ball. A gust of wind could make you misjudge a routine fly ball. The sun could blind you. One moment you'd see the ball and the next you'd have absolutely no idea where it was. All you could do was cover your head with your mitt and hope it didn't hit you. If the grass was wet, you could slip and fall running after a ball; if the field hadn't been cut, you could step into a hole you hadn't seen and twist an ankle or go chasing after a ball that had been hit over your head and not be able to find it.

Stealing a base wasn't simply a matter of running ninety feet and beating the throw to the bag. As the term made perfectly clear, it most basically was a matter of theft. That next base belonged to the other team, and they didn't want you to take it from them. Attempt that, and the player covering the base might spike you sliding into the bag. Or when he made the tag, he might bring his mitt down so hard he knocked you senseless. Or he might miss the throw from the catcher all together and let you catch it.

The pitcher always had the advantage. It was like coming to the plate with one strike, depending upon the pitcher it could be two strikes, already against you. There was the ball itself. Usually there was just one baseball, and at the most only two, for the entire game. The ball was soon lopsided, and by the end of the game, it was soft like mush. There was what the pitcher could do to the ball. He could cut it with his belt buckle, or rub paraffin on it, or scuff it with sandpaper. The pitch would then dart in or out as though it had been yanked about on a string. There was what the pitcher could throw. A duster came close to you, a bean ball came right at you, a screamer came at you so fast you had to swing almost before it was thrown to catch up with it. There was the pitcher who owned you. Although everyone else might be hitting him, this pitcher got you out every time and made you look silly doing it.

My day was coming, the girls kept telling me. That pitcher who would make me wish I had stayed in bed was out there, they said. I hadn't seen him yet and began to think they were wrong. But she was. We didn't play against other girls. The crowd would have been too small. So the pitchers we faced were men. But there was an exception. Midway through the second season, Mr. Jenkins called us together one day after practice. He told us we'd be facing Maud Nelson the following week. She was the best pitcher in bloomer girls baseball, he said. Put a mitt anywhere over the plate and she could hit it with her fast ball, her curve, her drop ball, her change-up nine times out of ten and probably the tenth time as well.

People lined up at the ticket booth an hour before the game started. Maud Nelson was spectacular; we weren't. We all had a weakness at the plate somewhere. The men didn't figure out where it was. Either they weren't smart enough to or didn't feel it was necessary. But Maud Nelson did, and early in the game. Once she had found it, she threw to that spot time and again with her dazzling array of pitches and at speeds we weren't expecting. A few of the girls got on base, two of them even reached second base. I never got out of the batter's box, striking out four times. If I had hit another four times, the outcome wouldn't have been any different. She owned me that afternoon, and I knew it.

After the game, I introduced myself and told Miss Nelson it had been a privilege to bat against her. Blushing slightly, she thanked me. I realized I had embarrassed her, which surprised me more than that sneaky change-up of hers that had me swinging minutes, maybe it was more like hours, before the ball actually got to the plate. She was the best baseball player I had seen, the very best by far, and yet she was humble. I liked that. As we said good-bye, I told her it would be nice to see her again, and added with a smile, but not in a baseball uniform. Her response baffled me. "Oh," she replied, "I think we will meet again." Since she had emphasized the word will, I knew she wasn't being polite. She believed, it might even be accurate to say she was sure, our lives, in some way, were going to converge again. But why? It couldn't have anything to do with baseball. I'd have struck out if she had pitched the ball underhand. And if not baseball, then what?

Something else baffled me that second season. It, though, had nothing to do with playing baseball. We were eating supper together after having won the game that afternoon. I noticed that while everyone else was talking about Nina's pitching and the runs we had scored, Agnes wasn't even looking at us. She obviously was troubled. At last she interrupted Henry, who was telling us about his two hits, one with the bases loaded, and said that someone had stolen ten dollars from her.

"Are you sure?" Gene asked.

"A ten dollar bill was in my purse last night," Agnes replied. "I'm sure of that. It's not there now."

"Did you take your purse to the game?" Ruthie said.

"No. I kept it in a dresser drawer in my room. We're the only ones in the boarding house." She stopped and looked around the table. "One of you is stealing money. Don't do it again. You are going to get caught."

Someone on the team was a thief. I was angry. Stealing was an assault. It hurt like a punch in the stomach. Mostly, though, I was bewildered. How could this possibly be? We were teammates. The good fortune that had come our way and the misfortune had bound us tightly together. We cared for each other; we protected each other; we laughed and cried with each other. I wanted to catch the person who had violated our trust, our friendship. But since I didn't know what to do, other than putting my purse underneath the mattress of my bed, I did nothing. That, though, didn't mean nothing was being done. Something was, which I inadvertently almost became a part of. Four days later, Lizzie and I ran into each other chasing a fly ball. That evening, just before supper, I went to her room. I wanted to make sure she was all right and to see what we could do to avoid future collisions in the outfield. Lizzie, though, wasn't there. As I was leaving, I noticed in an open drawer of the wardrobe underneath her shirt waists a five dollar bill. I was about to take the money and give it back to her at supper when I heard one of the girls downstairs ask where I was. I was needed in the parlor. Expecting Lizzie to return shortly, I left the five dollar bill in the drawer and shut the door to her room.

Late that night I was awakened by a loud knock on my door. Thinking there might be a fire, I bolted from my bed and rushed to the door, nearly tripping over a footstool in the dark. Opening it, I found Mr. Jenkins standing there with a grim look on his face. "I want you in the parlor at once," he said.

"Why?" I asked, afraid someone was seriously sick or hurt or worse.

"You'll find out soon enough. Hurry up now."

Glancing at the clock on the dresser, I saw it was one o'clock. What was so important it couldn't wait until the morning? Still half asleep, I quickly dressed and with the other girls, some of them in their bath robes, went downstairs. After making sure everyone was there, Mr. Jenkins told us to sit down. There weren't enough chairs for all of us, so a few of the girls sat on the floor beside Gene and Henry. Lizzie, though, remained standing. As I looked at Lizzie, it occurred to me I hadn't seen her since the game that afternoon.

"Earlier this week more money was stolen," Lizzie said. "I became so upset when I heard about the theft I called my father. He's a detective on the Boston police force. He told me to mark a five dollar bill, hide it carelessly in my room so a part of it was visible, and when it was missing, use the identifying mark to determine who took it. So, after the game today, with Mr. Jenkins' approval, I made a small circle in black ink in the lower right-hand corner of the five dollar bill he gave me and put it in a drawer I left open. Then I went out, making sure the door to my room was unlocked and most of you saw me leave. When I came back at twelve thirty, the money was gone."

"Lizzie and I will take you, one at a time, to your room," Mr.

Jenkins said. "There we will inspect your belongings. I am sorry we have to invade your privacy like this, but we will soon know who is stealing the money. Stay in the parlor until it is your turn to go. Ruthie, we'll begin with you."

As they started upstairs, Helen suddenly burst into tears. Her body heaving violently, she buried her head in her hands. "I've been taking the money," she cried. "I'm so ashamed of what I've done."

The girls close to her moved away. No one said a word. We didn't need to: the distance we had put between ourselves and Helen spoke for us. All alone, she wept uncontrollably. Finally, she stopped and, lifting her head, looked up at us. Seeing us silently staring at her, she started to sob again. At last, Mr. Jenkins said, "The day you came to us, Helen, I told you the code we live by: no whining, no immorality, no nonsense. As theft is immoral, you have violated this code, which, as I then made clear, brings immediate dismissal. You have also broken the law. Stealing is a crime. I will not report you to the police. I am, however, as of this moment, removing you from the roster of the Boston Clippers baseball team. You may stay the night but will leave us tomorrow morning and not return." He paused, and then added, "Ever."

"Why did you do it, Helen?" Maggie asked.

"What difference does it make why she did it?" Emily cried. "She did it; she robbed us, that's all that matters. If I had my way, she'd be gone tonight."

"Something else does matter," Nina said. "We want our money, Helen. When are you going to give it back to us?"

"Right now," Helen answered.

"You're telling us," Henry said, "you haven't spent any of the money you stole?"

"Not a penny of it," Helen answered. "It's all upstairs in a box in my suitcase."

"How much more were you going to steal before you had enough to get the diamond bracelet or the gold necklace you wanted?" Agnes said.

"I wasn't going to buy anything with that money," Helen replied.

"Then, why, in heavens name," Maggie almost shouted, "did you take it?"

All the color drained from her face, Helen stared at Maggie. Slowly she curled the fingers of each hand into a fist. Then using her hands like a club, she began to beat her legs with increasingly harder blows. Grabbing hold of her hands, Maggie said, "Stop that, Helen, you're hurting yourself."

"It's what I deserve. I never wanted that money. All I wanted was to take it. That's wrong, I know, horribly wrong, but I can't stop myself. I'm too weak." She began to cry. Nina took a handkerchief out of her pocket and bending down put it in her hands. Drying her tears with it, Helen murmured, "I'll get your money now."

All we seemed to talk about the next week was Helen. Some thought she was a thief who had been stealing money and getting away with it for years. One or two were convinced she had taken the money to pay for an operation her mother, or maybe it was her younger brother, needed. They remembered her talking about someone in the family being ill and her father having lost his job. Others felt she was afraid of being dismissed from the team. Her batting average had fallen, and she was making more errors in the field. Unable to find work or a husband, she saw herself living in a tiny, filthy tenement begging for food in the streets. It was this fear of being destitute, they said, that had made her steal. A few believed she had told them the truth. They, however, didn't think she had taken the money because she was weak or, as Mr. Jenkins had declared, immoral. Rather, she had taken it because she was sick. Something wasn't right inside her. She had an impulse of some kind that made her act in a strange and harmful way, and what she needed was not to be banished but help. They couldn't agree, however, on whether the help should come from her family doctor, a mental clinic, like the one at the Boston Dispensary, or God. I, too, thought she needed help. At first, it was because of Helen's tears. I felt sorry for her. But then I remembered William James had written in his *Principles of Psychology* about a disorder he called kleptomania. Apparently some people have an uncontrollable urge to steal. They don't want whatever it is they are stealing; they only want to take it. If they're caught, they return the item immediately. This seemed to fit Helen. I didn't see, though, why I had to choose either a doctor, or a psychologist, or God. Couldn't she get help from all three?

Her body and her emotions needed to mend, and as I thought about it, I realized her soul did too. When she confessed to taking the money, Helen had told us she felt ashamed. Undoubtedly she had also felt guilty, but shame, since it was what she had spoken of, must have been the stronger of the two feelings. Shame, as I understood the word, moved in. Because of the disgrace, she had hurt herself. Guilt moved out. Because of the offense, she had hurt us. To take away the guilt, she needed our forgiveness. Because she was sorry and had given back all the money, most of us, at least to some degree, had forgiven her. But to take away the shame, she needed to forgive herself. How could she do this? I didn't think this forgiveness would come from whatever she might tell herself or, remembering how she with clenched fists had started to strike her body, from however she might punish herself. Neither words nor suffering would be enough. What, then, would be? In Psalm 51, David, after seducing Bathsheba, prayed, "Create in me a clean heart, O God; and renew a right spirit within me." He, I suspected, wanted to be set free not only from the impure thoughts and desires of his heart, but also from the shame those thoughts and desires had put into his heart. This freedom, he knew, required an act of creation; it called for the giving of a new heart. Only God could do this, and it seemed to me, God would only do this if he had forgiven David. Didn't this mean that what David, and what Helen too, needed most of all was God's forgiveness? Forgiven by God, both, with a new heart, could then forgive themselves.

I kept thinking also about how close Lizzie and also Mr. Jenkins had come to catching me. If I had entered Lizzie's room ten seconds earlier, I would have left with that five dollar bill. It would have gone into my pocketbook for safekeeping and stayed there until the next time I saw Lizzie, which, of course, would have been at that late-night meeting in the sitting room. I would have explained why I had the money. What I said would certainly have made sense. But would the others have believed me? They might have, but probably not completely. Most likely there would always have been some doubt in their minds. Before, I thought that if I stayed out of trouble, trouble would stay away from me. But now I knew that wasn't necessarily so. Life, I was beginning to understand, was risky.

Life, I was soon to learn, was also fragile.

* * *

The second season ended in early September. Returning to Boston, I found work in a bookstore around the corner from where I was living. Although I told Mr. Weber, the owner, I would be leaving in May when the Clippers started spring practice, he still hired me for the position of sales clerk. He was happy to, he said, because he liked baseball and baseball players, male and female. Just how much he liked baseball became clear the moment he started to talk excitedly about his team, the Boston Beaneaters, and their prospects for the coming year. Nodding in agreement—I really did want the job—I could hardly keep from laughing. The Beaneaters were awful. The worst team in the National League, having lost more than one hundred games this past season and the previous season as well, they couldn't hit, pitch, or field. Since their shortstop, Abbaticchio, was no longer on the team, they couldn't run either. The best anyone could say about them, except for Mr. Weber, of course, was they had good looking uniforms.

I was glad to be around books again. The store was like a library. On its shelves were the discoveries and inventions of the mind. It was inspiring, and a little humbling, to be in the midst of all that thought. It made me more determined than ever to write a book of my own one day, once, I told myself smiling, I knew something worthwhile to write about. I liked waiting on the customers, helping them find a book they were looking for or might be interested in. Seeing them go through a book and then decide to buy it made me feel I had brought together the writer and the reader. I was more than a sales clerk; I was an important link in the transmission of knowledge. I knew that notion was an exaggeration and laughed at myself for thinking it, but I did believe I was doing more than making money for Mr. Weber.

Evenings and on the weekends, I visited with friends, took leisurely walks, read, and attended concerts and public lectures. One day after another passed by pleasantly. In late October, I was sitting in my room after dinner reading. Suddenly I shivered. The temperature had dropped; several at the store had talked about the possibility of an early snowfall. Taking a heavy blanket from the closet, I wrapped it loosely around myself and settled back into my comfortable, overstuffed rocker. Soon I felt not just warm but, as I thought about it, secure and, most of all, content. Life, I said to myself, was . . . what? A word came to me that I used all the time at Vassar. It sounded odd, and I would never say it now, if I did Maggie and the others would ride me mercilessly, yet it seemed to fit. Life, I began again, was dandy. The very next moment, right after I had said dandy, I heard a soft knock on the door of my room. It was Lydia, the twelve-year-old daughter of the woman who ran the boarding house. She handed me a telegram, explaining it had been delivered earlier that day. I must have missed it when I came in. I thanked her for bringing it up to me and as she was leaving gave her a chocolate from the candy tin I kept in my room.

From the marking on the envelope, I could tell the telegram had been sent from Philadelphia. Immediately I thought of Katie Peters. Through letters and occasional visits, we had again become close. Katie had finished her graduate studies at Vassar and was now in Philadelphia with her family. But, from her most recent letter, I knew she wouldn't be there long. The Leander McCormick Observatory in Charlottesville, Virginia and the Warner Observatory in Rochester, New York had both offered her a job. She preferred the work at Rochester but would probably be going to Charlottesville because of Martin Wentworth. The Wentworths and the Peters had been neighbors since she was eight. Five years older than Katie, Martin had mostly ignored her until last year when they had literally run into each other chasing a balloon in the city park. Obviously that collision had opened his eyes and knocked some sense into his head. Suddenly he saw that the kid down the street with a dirty face and hot temper had somehow grown into a lovely young woman. He called on Katie every day until she left the following week for Poughkeepsie and he for Atlantic City, where he was a surgeon at the City Hospital. The miles separating them didn't slow him down. He wrote her, phoned her, and, whenever he could, visited her. He was chasing her, but she wasn't running very fast. Actually, she was barely moving. Four months later, I received a telegram from Katie announcing they were in love. After that when we got together, she talked constantly about Martin and what he was doing. Astronomy was seldom mentioned unless I brought it up. I quickly tore open the envelope. Maybe they were engaged. I read the first sentence of the telegram and slumped to the floor, barely able to breathe. Crumpling the telegram in my hand, I began to cry. It can't be, I moaned. It just can't be. Then I suddenly stopped. It wasn't. That first sentence said something else. My eyes had played a trick on me or my mind had. Sitting up, I smoothed out the telegram and forced myself to read *Katie killed in terrible train wreck. Funeral Wednesday Nov. 7. Please come if you can. The Peters Family.* I sank to the floor sobbing and remained there late into the night.

Growing up, I had been sheltered from death. As a doctor, father confronted death all the time. Whenever he saw a patient, it must have always been somewhere in his thinking. It had to be. Yet he didn't talk about death at home. I had never seen someone dead, and because no one close to me had died, I had never experienced the feelings and the thoughts death brings. I went to Philadelphia not knowing what to say or how I was supposed to act. I only knew I ached terribly inside. I had just lost my dearest friend. I would never again see her face or hear her voice. Never again. I could barely think those dreadful words, let alone say them.

I learned from the family Katie was going to see Martin in Atlantic City. On Sunday, she boarded a train that left Camden, New Jersey, at one o'clock. At two thirty, a mile from Atlantic City, the train hit something on a drawbridge, nobody knew for sure what, that threw it off the tracks. It hurled forward fifty yards, cutting deep grooves into the ties of the bridge, and then plunged into the water. The train had three cars. The first two cars sank thirty feet beneath the water. As the third car went over the edge, it got caught in the underside of the bridge, which kept its backend out of the water. With the doors between the cars closed, no one in the first two cars could get out. The rear door of the third car was forced open and the windows above the water were broken allowing the passengers able to pull themselves out of the wreckage to escape.

Martin had been waiting for Katie at the terminal in Atlantic City. When he heard the train had derailed, he ran to the bridge and began searching frantically for her. Unable to find her and told she wasn't among those taken to the hospital or to the morgue, he decided she must be in one of the submerged cars. He and the family, who had come to Atlantic City from Philadelphia, had to wait for the two cars to be lifted out of the water. A large crane raised the first car the next day. She wasn't in it. The second car was pulled out of the water the following day using dynamite. She wasn't in it either. They began to think she might have missed the train or had got off before Atlantic City. The hope that she was still alive and the immense relief that brought, however, quickly gave way to the fear that since they had not heard from Katie she might have died in the water. Then, on Thursday, four days after the accident, they were notified a diver had found her body almost completely buried in the muddy bottom of the river. Besides massive bruising, a deep gash in her right leg, and internal bleeding, her left arm had been completely severed from her body. It was a clean cut probably made by the razor sharp edge of a broken piece of glass she was thrown against while going through a window of the car. These injuries, though, were not thought to be the cause of death. Most likely she had drowned.

We went to a large downtown church in Philadelphia for the funeral. The church's massive size—the sanctuary seated nearly a thousand people—and its sublime beauty declared God's presence. The Gothic architecture said in its soaring vertical lines look up in awe, the God of glory is above you. The magnificent organ with its rows of pipes said in the thundering music it produced look up in hope, the God of power is before you. The cross said in its harsh loveliness look up in thanksgiving, the God of compassion is underneath you. The minister said in the words he spoke and especially in the words of Jesus he read from the Gospel of John, "I am the resurrection, and the life: he that believeth in me, though he were dead, yet shall he live; and whosoever liveth and believeth in me shall never die" look up in faith, the God of love is around you. But, as I sat in my pew two rows behind the Peters family, I couldn't look up; I wouldn't look up. My mind wouldn't let me begin to think about how Katie had suffered, but I knew with absolute certainty she had suffered. She had suffered horribly. God hadn't been above her, or before her, or underneath her, or around her when she got on that train in Camden, New Jersey. Didn't God care? Was he even there? Was he anywhere? After the service, barely able to contain my sorrow for all that had been taken away from Katie and from those who had loved her and would have loved her if she had lived and seething with anger at God, I ran out of the church. I couldn't stand being in that building a moment longer with its empty promises, its deceptions, its lies.

Returning to Boston on the train the next day, I came to a decision. I didn't know where the decision would take me or what it might mean for my life. I only knew that it was a decision I had to make and that once made I couldn't change it or revoke it. In that coach car just outside of Hartford, Connecticut, I vowed not to believe in God because someone or something, no matter who or what it was, insisted I must. Maybe God didn't exist. Maybe God existed but didn't pay any attention to us. Maybe God existed and paid attention to us but wasn't strong enough or smart enough to stop bad things from happening to us. I didn't know which one was right, or if the truth was something else, but I made up my mind I was going to find out.

* * *

After the funeral, I started going to work early and staying late to put the shelves in order. I did this not because I was expected to but because I thought I needed to. I needed to keep busy. One morning in late November, I got to the store an hour before it opened. The day before books had arrived from a publisher which were still in their packing crates. Mr. Weber was already at his desk going through a stack of papers. He put in long hours usually at night. Seeing me come in, he set the papers aside and motioned for me to sit down. I hadn't been in that chair in front of his desk since the day I had interviewed for the job. Something was on his mind.

"Miss Welsh," he began, "you are not yourself."

"I know I'm making mistakes. I'm putting books where they don't belong and sometimes get the wrong amount when I add up a bill. I'll do better, I promise."

"Oh no, it's not your work, Miss Welsh. It's not your work at all. It's how long you are working. You are here early and stay late almost every day."

"Isn't that good?" I asked.

"It isn't good for you, not the way you are feeling. I know because I felt that way too, and I must say there are days when I still do. My wife died four years ago. It wasn't sudden like your friend. She had been ill for more than a year, so I was prepared for it, or at least I thought I was. But when the end came, I wasn't. No, I really wasn't at all. Not knowing what else to do and afraid of what I might do, I worked. Other than eat and sleep, that's all I did, every day, all day, and practically all night. But the day came when I realized I wasn't losing my sorrow in my work, I was losing myself. I was vanishing, and if I may say so, I thought that an affront to God. Work helps; it does, Miss Welsh. But it is only a part of the answer and only a small part at that."

I looked down at my hands, folded much more tightly than I had been aware of. My fingers were bright red; my knuckles were white. Oh no, I thought to myself, here it comes. He's going to tell me I needed to believe in God, I needed to receive Jesus, I needed to go to church. I didn't know how much longer I could sit there. I quickly went through the possibilities. I could tell him I heard someone knocking on the door wanting to get in, or I wasn't feeling well, or I had to put those new books on the shelves before the store opened.

"I went to a lecture last night by William James," he went on.

"Maybe you have heard of him. He's been teaching philosophy at Harvard now for more than twenty-five years. He has also written several books, which I'm proud to say we sell here at the store, and is a frequent lecturer. Earlier this year, he spoke at Stanford and has been at Berkeley in California, Edinburgh, and, if I am not mistaken, Vassar. Over the next two weeks, he is giving lectures at the Lowell Institute on what he calls pragmatism. You might find them worthwhile. Indeed, you might find them very worthwhile."

I looked up at him in surprise and also in relief. "Why Mr. Weber," I replied. "I know William James. I should say I know of him. Sections of his *Principles of Psychology* were on the assigned reading list in my philosophy class at Vassar. His analysis of the mind has helped me better understand myself and others as well. He did speak at Vassar on psychology and relaxation but that was several years before I was there. The Lowell Lectures would give me a chance to hear him. What is pragmatism?"

"It's his way of getting at what he thinks is true."

"That's something I need help with."

"In the lecture last night, he talked about the dilemma he sees in philosophy."

"That sounds way too abstract for me."

"That is precisely his point. He is convinced philosophers today, and in this group he includes religious philosophers who talk about God, Love, and Being, are way too abstract for all of us. They have nothing to say about the confusion, the pain, and the ugliness of the real world. In their theories, all this is either ignored or explained away. But all this, he says, won't go away. It's here now for everyone and will continue to be unless and until it is, in some way, examined thoroughly and insightfully. When he told of a man who, in the dead of winter, lost his job and having no way to pay his rent or to feed his wife and six children ended his life by drinking carbolic acid, he got everyone's attention. At one end of the spectrum, rationalism, with its religious pronouncements, offers only a shallow optimism in the face of this evil, those were his exact words, while at the other end, empiricism, with its acceptance of the facts alone, offers only hopelessness. In between the two ends is pragmatism, which, as I understand it, brings religion to the facts and the facts to religion. How it does this is the topic of his lecture tonight."

"I'll be there."

"I would like to, but I probably won't be finished with all of this," Mr. Weber looked at the pile of papers on his desk, "in time to go. Now, Miss Welsh, I believe we both have work to do."

* * *

Wanting a seat in the front row, I arrived at the lecture hall a half hour early. Promptly at seven o'clock, a slender man of medium height, somewhere in his mid-sixties, approached the podium. His hair was short; his beard, which was turning white, was full; his features were sharp and pleasant to look at. His darting blue eyes, I thought, were especially telling. They were searching; they were penetrating. Whatever he was seeing, as his gaze swept the room, he seemed to want to see more of it and to see it more deeply. At the podium, he never stood still; some part of him kept moving, one moment it was his hands, and the next it was head, or his legs, or his whole body. A kind of nervous energy flowed out of him. As he spoke, I quickly sensed his intelligence. He obviously had a keen mind. His subject was a serious matter, so he himself was serious, and yet he was also playful. He liked to have fun. But I soon felt there was another side to him. Mixed into that gaiety was sadness. We seldom saw it and when we did it was only a flicker, but a haunting sorrow was there, I was sure of it.

That night he explained pragmatism and then over the next six lectures examined it from different perspectives. What he did reminded me of a balloon being inflated. As it got air, the balloon expanded. As Professor James gave pragmatism content by relating it first to metaphysics and common sense and then in the later lectures to truth, humanism, and finally religion, it got larger and larger. Now, fully blown up, it seemed huge, but as I was leaving the auditorium after the last lecture, it occurred to me pragmatism really was quite small. It wasn't an end but only a means to an end. It, most basically, just gave us a way, a relatively simple way, to find our own truth. If an explanation fit an experience we were having and the experiences we have already had, if it held all of these experiences together giving us peace of mind, then it was true. But if the fit was at some point lost because something had changed in our lives or something new had been added, then a new truth was needed. Consequently, there was no absolute truth, only truths that appeared and, when they failed to hold in our lives, disappeared.

As these thoughts were running through my mind, I heard someone behind me say, "Miss Welsh." Turning around, I saw Mr. Weber. I had noticed him at two of the earlier lectures, but since he had each time left with several other gentlemen, I hadn't approached him. Coming up to me, he asked if I had enjoyed the lectures.

"Immensely," I replied. "They've been enlightening."

"And timely?"

"And very timely. Pragmatism just might be the answer I've been searching for, although I think Professor James would cringe if he heard me say that. If I understand him, pragmatism isn't an answer; it's a process that keeps moving us closer to the answer that is always beyond us. Actually the answer may not even be there. He would probably add reaching it is not what's important anyway, only trying to is."

"I must admit, Miss Welsh, that is a good part of what bothers me about Professor James' pragmatism. I am not at all ready to say an answer doesn't exist. It does, I am convinced of that, and it always will whether we get to it or not. Truth is not what we make it."

"In his lecture on what pragmatism means, which I think you missed, he mentioned that objection and responded to it. As I remember, he said that it is a matter of where one begins. You start with a fixed general statement and from that height you may or may not reach down to the particulars. If you do, you bring a few of them or some of them into your thinking but never all of them. He, though, begins with all the particulars, in other words with all his experiences, and lifts them up into some kind of a general statement that is not fixed. It may or may not change depending on what he experiences next."

"What makes a person choose one starting point over the other?"

"The mind," I said. "I think these lectures were really about the mind, not the truth."

"As I see it, Miss Welsh, right there is the problem. He makes the truth secondary to the mind. The truth then becomes dependent on how a person thinks or what he wants. But the truth is primary. It comes first, and coming first, it doesn't depend on anything; we depend on it."

"He might, up to a point, agree with you, but I'm not exactly sure why," I replied. "There were times when I didn't fully understand what he was saying, or he was saying too much to take it all in."

"There is something else that troubles me. I heard him say that an idea must have cash value to be true. I am a businessman. When I consider ordering a book for my store, I always ask myself if it has cash value. Will it, to put this another way, make money? Is he suggesting that whatever makes money is true? Or, to take this one step further, is he saying that for something to be true it must make money? Making money is important. It's what keeps this country strong and growing. But it can't be, it's not, that important."

"I don't believe Professor James was saying it is," I answered. "Basically he was telling us truth is what works. To make his point, he used the term cash value because it's what we understand without even thinking about it. We know from our everyday lives cash does have value; we know it does work. A customer wanting to own a book gives us cash. It's only paper or a piece of metal. Yet we take it without asking any questions and at once give him the book. It's now no longer ours but his. An idea that is true has cash value not because it's going to make money but because it's completely reliable. It's going to bring us every time what we want; it's going to accomplish every time what we want to have done."

"I see."

"Mr. Weber, I have a question for you. Right at the end of the lecture tonight he said that we are either tough or tender, or we are a mixture of the two. Whatever we are, he then said, determines what we believe or don't believe. Since this was his concluding point, it has to be important; it has to be very important. Yet I don't remember him discussing these qualities in his earlier lectures. Did he talk about them in his first lecture?"

"It's how he began the first lecture. He said that a person's temperament gives him either a more sentimental or a more cynical outlook on life. Then he moved into a description of what he called the tender-minded and the tough-minded temperaments. Tender-minded people lean toward the intellect and the ideal. They are optimistic, religious, and dogmatic. Tough-minded people want facts, making them skeptical and pessimistic. They, therefore, are not religious. Most people, though, fall somewhere in-between the two. They recognize the importance of both facts and religion. One without the other won't do."

"That gives me something more to think about."

"I am glad you found the lectures beneficial. I must leave now.

I have accounts to look at before the store opens tomorrow. Good night, Miss Welsh."

As I watched him go, I began to think about Mr. Weber. He was tough-minded when it came to the bookstore. Those accounts wouldn't be put away until he had gone through all of them, even if it took him until tomorrow morning. He wanted the facts. Still, I would have to say he was mostly tender-minded. He had to be. How else could he be a Beaneater fan? What was I? I was, I decided, at least one part tender-minded. After all these years, I still heard my aunt say I was graced for goodness. I hadn't put those word in my mind, and I certainly wasn't the one keeping them there. That was somebody else's doing. Maybe it was God. I wasn't ready to rule out that possibility, but, then, maybe it wasn't. I needed facts, and nothing was going to be settled until I had them. Having established that, I had to admit that I was two, or three, or maybe even four parts tough-minded.

Whether tender or tough, my mind at times did astonish me. It could make connections that were startling without being asked to. Abruptly my thinking jumped from God to the discovery of the curve ball. I remembered Nina telling me a fourteen-year-old boy found he could make a clamshell bend when he threw it with a quick twist of his wrist. His name was William Cummings. To the grownups who knew him, he was William or Bill. To his friends, though, he was Candy. If he could make a clam shell curve, Candy reasoned, why not a baseball? His friends laughed at him. Everyone knew a baseball couldn't curve. It would be easier, they said, to make a baseball talk. But Candy thought otherwise. Over the next four years, he practiced throwing a baseball with the same sharp twist of his wrist. It seemed to be curving, but he couldn't be sure. He decided the only way to know was to throw it in a game. The following year he pitched for the Brooklyn Excelsiors. Early that season, the Excelsiors played Harvard College in Cambridge, and Candy was on the mound. He threw the new pitch to the first batter he faced and then to everyone else in the lineup. All of them, one after another, swung at it and missed. After striking out, some walked slowly back to the bench shaking their heads. The ball hadn't come in that fast; it was right there in front of them. How could they have missed it? Others angrily flung their bats to the ground and stomped out of the batters-box. It's wasn't fair, they muttered. The pitcher had covered the ball with a concoction of some kind that had made it change direction. Candy had his proof: the ball did curve. Just as abruptly, my thinking jumped from the curve ball back to God. One, I saw, informed the other. As the curve ball had to be verified, a verification that could only come from its success against an opposing force, so also did God. The difference between the two was the verification had to occur for the curve ball in a game and for God in life, in the beauty and in the terrifying ugliness of life.

* * *

A week later, as I was going to my room after a tiring day at work, Lydia called to me from the kitchen where she was helping her mother get dinner ready. "Miss Welsh, a gentleman is waiting for you in the parlor."

"I hope he hasn't been there long."

"He came a half hour ago. He took a chair in front of the fire, and I gave him a cup of tea."

"Thank you, Lydia. Please tell him I've arrived and will be down in a minute. I want to put my coat and boots away and get a sweater. It's going to snow again tonight."

I wondered if it might be Robert from the bookstore. He said something about stopping by one day after work. Or perhaps it was that rather tall young man with the red hair and quick smile I had met at the last lecture on pragmatism. Going downstairs, I glanced at my watch. It really was too late for someone to be calling. Maybe, though, the gentleman was from out of town. It might be Uncle Edward. He lived in Springfield and had promised to visit the next time he was in Boston. I slowed down and found myself reaching for the banister. It might even be Gene. Entering the parlor, I saw a man standing in front of the fire with his back to me. He didn't need to turn around; I knew instantly who it was.

"Father," I cried, "what a wonderful surprise."

The more we talked about the medical meeting he'd be attending the next day, the attractions of Boston, my last season with the Clippers, my work at the bookstore, the more convinced I became there was something he wasn't telling me. It wasn't what he said. Father had an easy way with words. Flowing out of him like water coming out of a faucet, regardless of the circumstance, they could, and oftentimes did, mask what he was feeling. Instead, it was what I heard—or rather didn't hear. The playfulness was missing, the infectious laughter. Something was wrong. Knowing where depression had once taken him, I was worried.

Well into a description of the new office he would soon be moving into, he paused, trying to remember the exact dimensions of the examining room. It was the moment I had been waiting for. "Forgive me for interrupting, Father," I said. "What's troubling you?"

His body stiffened. He briefly looked away and then turned back to me. "It's your mother. For the past month, she's been despondent, has little or no appetite, and doesn't sleep well. The doctor we consulted in Chicago, Steven Lewis, who is widely recognized for his diagnosis and effective treatment of nervous disorders, is convinced she is suffering from neurasthenia."

"Why haven't you told me?" I said.

"We thought it best not to say anything at this time."

"Because of Katie?"

"Yes. We didn't want to make your life any more difficult than it already is. Also, we at first weren't greatly concerned."

"Now you are?"

"Let's just say we are concerned. With proper care, she will get better."

"Doesn't neurasthenia have something to do with tired nerves?"

"That's what it most basically comes down to. We all have our own unique physical makeup that sets a limit to the amount of nervous stimuli our bodies can effectively process. If this capacity is exceeded because either the limit itself is so low or the number of stimuli is so high, then the nervous energy we have is used up, and the system breaks down. The nerves become, to use your word, tired or exhausted which leads to emotional problems."

"How is Mother being treated?"

"Dr. Lewis has prescribed bed rest; restricted social interaction; massage, which exercises the muscles without actually using them; a protein rich diet; and electrotherapy."

"What is electrotherapy?"

"A low voltage electrical current is passed through the body to stimulate brain cells and nerve fibers."

"You're telling me Mother is being struck by electricity?"

"Not struck, Mattie, but gently injected with a very small and carefully controlled dosage."

"If you are using electricity, why not try Carter's Little Nerve Pills or even Coca-Cola? Coca-Cola is supposed to be an excellent remedy for exhaustion. Its advertisements claim it restores energy, banishes worries, invigorates the mind, brightens the faculties."

"I doubt either would be very useful," father said. "Dr. Lewis's treatment is medically sound, and it is generally considered the best prescription for her condition. It reduces stimulation and increases the body's capacity to be stimulated. The treatment is safe and has been successful."

"When will she recover?"

"It could take up to six months. Dr. Lewis thinks she is beginning to improve, but healing will be slow. So, we must be patient."

"Do you have help at home?"

"Yes. We have employed a nurse, Susan Wheeler, who provides full time care during the week and also the weekend if we need her. We have just learned, though, next Monday Susan will be leaving for her brother's home in Minneapolis. His wife fell and broke her arm. She needs help taking care of their two children and herself. Since they can't afford to bring someone into the home, Susan agreed to come. She will return next month, but until then we have to hire a temporary replacement for her. Before leaving for Boston, I talked to three women who are quite willing to fill in for Susan. It is now a matter of determining which one is best suited for our situation."

"I know a fourth woman who is also quite willing to fill in for Susan."

"Who is that?"

"Your daughter, and I insist you choose her."

"Could you possibly come?"

"I'll be home Sunday," I said, reaching for Father's hand. Mother bedridden and secluded was upsetting enough. The thought, though, of her needing electrotherapy was alarming. After being shocked once when I was five, I knew I had to stay far away from electricity. Now she was being pelted with electricity regularly. "Although we are busy at work, I'm sure Mr. Weber will understand."

"Family always comes first," Mr. Weber told me. The store had just opened, and people were starting to file in. Yet he urged me to leave immediately. His niece, a junior at Boston University, was looking for work over the Christmas vacation and could come in that afternoon if necessary. I decided to stay, however, until the end of the day. When I went to his office to say good-bye, Mr. Weber gave me a gift wrapped in colorful paper held in place by a bright red ribbon. As I started to open the package, I assured him I would be back in January. He hoped I would return but said he wouldn't be surprised if I didn't. Inside was William James's *Principles of Psychology*. He thought the book might give me insight into Mother's condition and suggested I take it with me. He also suggested I pack whatever belongings I left behind into boxes.

"For easier storage," I said.

"For easier transporting," he replied.

"Do you know something I don't?"

"I only know that often things work out in unexpected ways."

"Even for the Beaneaters?"

"Especially for the Beaneaters," Mr. Weber said, laughing.

On the train, I took out of my traveling bag James's *Principles* and, for no particular reason, began to look at his chapter titled, "Association." In the first paragraph, he wrote that analysis, the breaking down of ideas, and synthesis, the bringing together of ideas, were two alternating activities of the mind. You began with one, it led to the other, and it, in turn, brought you back to the one you started with. That observation interested me enough to continue reading. Two pages later, I came to his statement: "The great law of habit itself—that twenty experiences make us recall a thing better than one, that long indulgence in error makes right thinking almost impossible—seems to have no essential foundation in reason. The business of thought is with truth." I read those last words, "The business of thought is with truth," again. Closing the book, I began to think about what Mr. Weber had said, "Often things work out in unexpected ways." It occurred to me he was something other than a pragmatist. For him, truth, in the end, was not things working, but things working out, which was a different notion altogether. What, then, was he: an optimist, a dreamer, a believer? More important, after enough analysis and synthesis to satisfy even Professor James, was his truth the truth? I again opened the book, and seeing that

I was now somewhere in his chapter on hypnotism, I started to wonder if a trance might in some way be used to treat neurasthenia. With these ideas, as Professor James had written, floating by in my stream of thought, I drifted off to sleep. The sharp whistle of the train awakened me with a start. Looking out the window, I saw farmland covered with snow. Set back from the road in a cluster of trees, there was a white house tightly shuttered with a wisp of smoke rising from the chimney and close by an old red barn with a few pieces of machinery next to it. Soon, I would be home. However that statement might be analyzed and synthesized, I said to myself with a smile, it was unquestionably and indisputably the truth.

* * *

I agreed with Dr. Lewis's assessment. Mother was getting better. As the days went by, she was alert and functioning for longer periods of time and increasingly interested in others and in what they were doing. We began to talk, at first about the family and then about the activities important to her: the hospital auxiliary, the community theater group, the lighting of the Christmas tree in the town square, the school's annual Christmas program. Finally the day came when she was well enough to talk about her illness. She told me she knew last summer something was wrong, but not wanting to trouble the family, had kept it to herself. She began to treat herself secretly from the remedies appearing in *The Sears, Roebuck Catalogue*. First, she tried Dr. Worden's Female Pills, a blood purifier and nerve tonic that promised to cure weak muscles, fallen spirits, poor appetite, heart palpitations, swollen feet, back pain, hysteria, rheumatism, partial paralysis, rickets, and shortness of breath. When these pills didn't work, she turned to Dr. Hammond's Nerve and Brain Pills. They guaranteed relief from low spirits, nervousness, weariness, lifelessness, weakness, dizziness, poor memory, shortness of breath, and cold feet. Feeling no better, she moved on to Vin Vitae, the Wine of Life. All who were tired, who couldn't sleep, who were nervous, who didn't want to eat, who were too thin, who were weak were assured this tonic of unmatched potency would settle the blood, the brain, and the nerves and, best of all, would begin to do it immediately. It didn't—not right away, and not later. She even started to wear a 15 cell, 60-gauge current, electric Heidelberg Belt that was supposed to help anyone suffering from any organic disease. Maybe it benefited others, but it didn't benefit her. By now she was feeling so feeble she had to tell Father. Before when he had asked if something was wrong, she had always answered, "don't be silly." This time when he asked, she said, "isn't it obvious." That afternoon he took her to see Dr. Lewis.

Though I now understood the course of Mother's illness, I never did find out its cause. Father insisted the cause was physical. The nerves had simply become tired. They undoubtedly had, but he couldn't tell me what had made them tired. Mother, however, knew. Late one morning, we were alone in the bedroom discussing the dining room table, whether to refinish the one they had or to buy a new one, when she all at once grabbed my hand. Tears started to well up in her eyes. As I looked at her, I not only saw in her face, I felt the pain that was seizing her. It was that deep, that searing.

"What is it, Mother?" I murmured.

As suddenly as she had taken my hand, she released it. Quickly drying her tears, she said, trying to smile, "Oh, it's nothing, Mattie. It's just my nerves acting up again."

I'm convinced Mother wanted to, I should make that Mother needed to, tell me something that morning to be at peace with herself. But she had made up her mind, probably much earlier, to keep whatever it was from me. I let her; I had no right to do otherwise. But ever since that morning, I felt certain the cause of her neurasthenia was not physical. It was emotional. It was regret, or sorrow, or guilt, or shame; it was any one of these emotions, or some of them, or possibly all of them together that had made her ill. But where this emotional state had come from, what had produced it, and what had kept her trapped in it, that I didn't know; that remained her secret.

* * *

The Saturday before Christmas I told Father I'd been thinking about going into the city to see the holiday decorations and to buy gifts for the family. Turning me toward the closet where I kept my winter coat and overshoes, he said, "Go today. Your brother and I can take care of everything, and since your mother is feeling so much better, maybe she'll be able to help. You can make the 9:30 Interurban if you hurry." I caught the streetcar to Elgin with only a minute to spare, and there, after running two blocks to the station, boarded the train for Chicago. Breathing hard, I sank into the first empty seat. Not having a book to read or someone next to me to talk to, I looked out the window as the train gained speed. One farm after another soon appeared followed by long stretches of woods and grassland. Then I suddenly saw in every direction land that had been cleared and divided into sections. Some of the parcels were large; others were much smaller. There was nothing on these lots. With every tree, bush, and stone gone, they looked naked. The sections were all by themselves. Nothing else was close to them or even in sight of them. At first the landscape seemed odd. But after thinking about it, I realized it made perfectly good sense. There were undoubtedly investors, most if not all of them from Chicago, who were betting the land would not be vacant for long. They figured new homes were coming and with them a whole lot of other new buildings that were going to make those sections increase in value many times over. I suddenly had another thought. Maybe this land was actually more of an announcement than a wager. As I stared intently at those barren lots, I heard the city cry, "Whether you want me to or not, I'm coming."

Once in the city, I went directly to The Fair Store on Adams Street. This huge department store's motto Everything for Everybody was clearly a shameless exaggeration. But that day if anybody had asked me, I would have said the slogan was the absolute truth. In less than two hours, I had purchased all my presents and everyone one of them reasonably priced. Glass cases beautifully displaying the merchandise, cheerful salesgirls eager and able to help, Christmas music and stunning decorations throughout the store made the shopping delightful.

After lunch in a busy restaurant on the fourth floor, I set out for Marshall Field's, not to buy anything but to look at everything, or as much of everything as time allowed. Ever since I was a little girl, I loved to wander through the aisles of this grand department store. Its elegance, everything in it was of the finest quality, had made the store unique. Rare, too, was its policy the customer, whatever the circumstance, was always right. Whether there to purchase an item or only to admire it, she came first. She was served, not just waited on. Thinking of the clothing, much of it imported from Europe, I would be seeing, the jewelry, the home furnishings, the sporting equipment, all of it so gloriously splendid, I hurried up State Street.

At State and Madison, I came to an abrupt stop. I couldn't cross Madison. Wagons, streetcars, carriages clogged the street. Standing there at that crowded intersection, unable to move because of the congestion, I took in the city. It ingested it, and as I did, it revealed itself to me. In that moment, I saw the city's beauty in the strikingly bold lines and in the exquisitely fine details of the massive buildings and the towering skyscrapers. I felt the city's energy in the relentless movement on the sidewalks and in the streets; the movement that seemed to come directly at me and with enough force to lift me off my feet and carry me away. I sensed the city's secrets, its dark secrets, in the thief lifting a wallet out of an overcoat pocket, in the little girl begging for money, in the *Closed: Workers on Strike* sign in a store window, in the old woman picking up a cigarette butt off the street, in the office buildings with curtains drawn and behind those curtains doors closed, doors that only a powerful few could open, where decisions about prices to charge, wages to pay were being made that would bring hardship to people hurrying by. There on that street corner I fell under the city's spell, enchanted and at the same time frightened. I shuddered.

The next moment, seeing a gap open in the oncoming traffic, I darted across the street. A small group of people circled a peddler's cart halfway up the next block. Curious, I stopped to look at what he was selling. He had arranged in carefully laid out rows an assortment of delicately carved wooden Christmas ornaments. I picked up one, an angel with the most sublime expression on her face, to inspect it more closely. The design and the workmanship were by anyone's standard exceptional. As I ran my fingers across the perfectly smooth surface of the ornament, someone hit my arm. Looking up, I saw a boy, probably no more than ten years old, racing down the street. "Sorry," he shouted. The collision knocked the ornament from my hand, and it fell to the pavement. The angel didn't appear to be damaged. But when I picked the ornament up, I noticed one of her wings was broken.

The peddler, pointing to a *Do Not Handle* sign in a corner of the cart, said, "I'm going to have to charge you for that ornament."

I hadn't seen the sign. It was too small and needed to be in the middle of the cart. Still I was at fault. "What does it cost?" I asked.

"The ornaments that size sell for $3.75."

I didn't have enough money for the ornament and a train ticket home. Maybe I could pay him the next time I was in Chicago, or send him the money, or go back to The Fair Store and return one of my gifts. But the insistent and I thought the desperate look on his face told me I needed to pay him now. If I didn't, he couldn't be sure I'd ever pay him, and he had a family to feed.

"I would like to buy the ornament," the woman standing next to me said to the peddler, "if, of course, this young lady will allow me to."

I hadn't noticed her before, and glancing at her now, I understood why. There was, maybe intentionally, little of her to see. All of her except for her face had been swallowed up by the full length black coat, the large black bonnet, and the long black gloves she was wearing. I could only tell she was most likely somewhere in her early forties, tall, probably close to six feet, heavyset, and plain. A second look at her face, though, made me quickly change my mind. It wasn't by any means plain. To say it was pleasant or even kindly would have been right and yet also wrong, wrong because those were not strong enough words. Deeply etched into her face were lines that laughter and sorrow, compassion and, I was sure, love had put there. I also saw in that face, especially in the eyes, joy, that contagious joy of Reverend McNutt.

"I couldn't possibly let you do this for me," I replied.

"Oh, but I'm not doing it for you. I am doing it entirely for myself."

"But the ornament is broken. It's worthless."

"That's exactly why I want to buy it."

While keeping his eyes on me, the peddler had moved to the other side of the cart where a man with two small children was looking at the ornaments. I was glad this gave us a chance to talk. She was, I felt, someone I needed to know. "I don't understand," I said.

"Every Christmas I look for something no one wants because it isn't pretty, or it's not the right color, or it doesn't work, or it's out of date, or, as we have here, it's broken. If it's small enough, I put it on my Christmas tree; if it's too large, I find some other place for it in my room where it's conspicuous. One year, it was the Christmas tree itself. Crooked, short, it couldn't have been more than three feet high, and missing half its branches, it was perfect. I gave the man who sold me the tree twice the amount he was asking for it."

"So the object itself isn't important, only its condition is."

"The object is important because of its condition. The object is a symbol. A symbol is said to be something that stands for something else, but I like to think that it speaks for something else. Whenever I look at the object that has been thrown away, I hear God say, "This is the one I have come for."

"The one who has been thrown away, the one nobody else wants."

"Precisely."

"You can buy the ornament on one condition," I said.

"And that is?"

"I can buy you a cup of hot chocolate."

"That's a condition I'll gladly accept. My name is Emma Lloyd."

"It's very nice to meet you, Mrs. Lloyd," I said, shaking her hand. "I'm Mattie Welsh."

"Actually, it's Miss Lloyd, though to most people I'm Sister Emma."

Her name intrigued me. I wondered if "Sister" was the title a religious order used. Maybe, though, it was just how others saw her. I was even more intrigued when we went to a nearby restaurant and removed our coats before sitting down. Underneath her long black coat was a long black dress. She did take off her gloves but kept the plain black bonnet on. The only other color, and against the black it was quite striking, was a large white collar, small white cuffs, and the white muslin ties that held her bonnet in place. "Please excuse me for being so forward," I said, "but you seem to be wearing a uniform of some kind."

"This, Miss Welsh, is the dress of a Methodist Episcopal

Deaconess. We're women; we dress alike; we're single; we all, in one way or another, are involved in city missionary work; and we all have attended the Chicago Training School for City, Home and Foreign Missions started more than twenty years ago by two remarkable individuals, Lucy Meyer and her husband, Josiah Meyer. By now, there must be more than two hundred of us scattered throughout the city. I'll be happy to tell you about the Training School and our Deaconess Order but first, Miss Welsh, I want to know something about you. I have been doing all the talking."

We were drawn to each other. Though we lived in two different worlds, our lives overlapped at two crucial points, one in the past, the other in the present, that brought us together. At the time, the connection appeared to be just a coincidence, so I didn't attach much significance to it. But later, when I looked back on it, I began to think it might, in some way, have been arranged.

As I was telling Sister Emma—that was what she had asked me to call her—about my four years at Vassar, she beamed. "Why I graduated from Smith College in Northampton, Massachusetts, the class of '86," she exclaimed. "I was a member of the debating society. In my senior year, if I remember correctly, we competed against Vassar and won."

We had both graduated from a women's college in the East. That was one point of overlap. But there was another point that was much stronger, especially since it was happening right now, and a whole lot more surprising. When I told her I played baseball professionally, I thought that since she was obviously religious, she, like many others, might think I shouldn't be wearing bloomers and competing against men. Instead, if we had not been in a restaurant, I think she would have cheered. She might have even danced. But since we were, she, with almost as much exuberance, gushed, "How wonderful. I love baseball. The skill, the speed, the daring are absolutely thrilling. Then there's the strategy of the game. It's tremendously challenging. Should a pitch be thrown high or low? Should a batter hit away or bunt? Should the outfielders move back or in, to the left or to the right? Should a base runner steal or stay where he is? Should a pitcher remain in the game or be relieved? If you get it right, you win. If you don't, you lose. I adore the Chicago Cubs. I know I shouldn't. They are not always, or probably not even most of the time, godly men. They use bad language, bait the umpires, and get into brawls during the game and sometimes after it's over. But they are so exciting. This year they won the pennant by seventeen games and beat Detroit in the World Series. I went to six of the regular season games and two of the World Series games and have already set money aside to buy a ticket for the opening game next season. Miss Welsh, you must tell me how you hit a curve ball. What is the secret to stealing second base? Do you always take the pitch when you have a count of three balls and no strikes? Do you think it is wise to steal third base when there are two outs? Oh, there is so much I want to know."

That afternoon we never did get to the Chicago Training School or to Sister Emma's Deaconesses. We were still talking about baseball when I realized it was time to leave for home. As we were about to say good-bye, I had an absurd idea. Maybe I should become a Deaconess. Imagining myself dressed in black and white and carrying a Bible, which I assumed all the Deaconesses did while they worked, I almost laughed. But the thought, I had to admit, did have a certain appeal, a certain logic. Among these women, who were Deaconesses because of God and for the sake of God, I would find God. If I didn't, then I would have not someone else's truth but my truth. I would know God doesn't exist. William James would approve. It would be consistent with his pragmatism. From the particular, my experience, would come the general statement, the conclusion I reached based upon my experience. He would be pleased. I didn't think Mr. Weber would be, though. "Sister Emma," I said, "I'd like to hear more about the Deaconesses. Would there be a time when we could visit again?"

"Certainly, Miss Welsh. I teach church history at the Training School. Why don't we meet there next Friday. Any time in the morning will be fine. It's located at Fiftieth Street and Indiana Avenue. I'm sure our principal, Mrs. Meyer, will also be available if you might like to talk to her as well. I'll tell her you are coming."

Going home on the train, I kept thinking about Sister Emma. She was different; no, I needed a stronger word, she was strange, but, I had to admit, in a most wonderful way. I remembered reading somewhere in the New Testament, maybe it was in the first letter to the Corinthians, something about the foolishness of God. Buying my broken angel to hang on a Christmas tree that this year might be missing all of its branches was foolishness. I could hear Sister Emma happily saying that's exactly what it was. But she wasn't a fool. She understood something, or at least thought she did, and believed in it so deeply and had given herself to it so fully that this truth of hers, whatever it was, had remade her. A word came into my mind that had been discussed in a religion class at Vassar. It meant to be set apart. It described a person who stood outside the world and yet, almost paradoxically, was still in it, was still in it with a whole new way of thinking, and seeing, and living. Could it be that this word described Sister Emma? Could it be that she was holy?

At supper that evening, Father asked me about my day in the city. I mentioned the train ride in, the shopping, and the nice lunch I'd had at The Fair Store. "Now Mattie," he said, "I know you are saving the best for last. Tell me all about Marshall Field's. What stunning necklace did you see that you absolutely must have? Or was it a dress?"

"I didn't get to Marshall Field's," I answered.

He looked surprised but didn't ask for an explanation. Instead, he began to talk about Mother's improvement. He was so eager to relate his day with her I decided not to say anything more about Chicago until later that evening. After we had finished eating, Father returned to his paper, and I picked up the book I had been reading. But without even opening it, I put the book down. The time had come, and I hoped the words would also. "Father," I said, "I need to tell you what kept me from Marshall Field's."

"I didn't think anything could."

"Neither did I," I said, remembering the day, I was probably seven at the time, when Father told me we couldn't go to Marshall Field's even though the store was only half a block away. I sank to the pavement right there in the middle of State Street and cried.

"What was it?"

"An angel with a broken wing."

I told him about dropping the ornament and the woman dressed in black wanting to buy it. When I said she bought something every Christmas that others threw away because it spoke to her of God's love for the rejected, Father asked, "Were her cuffs and collar and the ties of her bonnet white?"

"Why yes, they were," I replied, surprised, actually I was astonished, by the question.

"She must have been a Deaconess worker."

"That's exactly what she was. What do you know about them?"

"I only know what one of my patients told me the other day. His niece was arrested for shoplifting. Her husband left her, and she is trying to raise their two children on her own. She worked at a factory but because of sickness lost her job. There was no money for shoes the children needed, so she stole them. She was caught and sentenced to ninety days in jail. That first afternoon a young woman dressed in black with white cuffs, collar, and bonnet ties appeared. Stopping at each cell, she talked to the women. Some laughed at her, some even cursed her, but others gratefully welcomed her. She listened, his niece realized, not in judgment but in love; promised to help however she could; and, if there was no objection, read from her Bible and prayed. 'That,' one of the women in her cell said, 'is a Deaconess. She's here all the time. Her name is Sister Ruth, and she's my guardian angel.' Sister Ruth also became his niece's guardian angel. Because of her, she waked away from that jail with hope. Her children, who had been well cared for in the Methodist Deaconess Orphanage in Lake Bluff, were waiting for her; Sister Ruth had found her a new job that was better than the one she had before; and at Sister Ruth's gentle insistence, she no longer saw herself as a criminal but as one God loved."

"What would you say, Father, if I told you I am thinking about becoming a Deaconess?"

He looked away for a moment. I knew what was going through his mind. I didn't go to church; I didn't talk about God; and I didn't particularly like the color black. When he looked back at me, he was smiling. "Mattie, I didn't expect this. But then you certainly are one to do the unexpected. I guess that's who you are. Your mother is getting better, and we heard today Miss Wheeler will be returning in two weeks. I do have a question, though. Is Katie's death in some way connected to this new direction your life might take?"

"Yes, it is," I answered.

I didn't say anything more, and fortunately father respected my silence. If pressed, I wouldn't have told him the whole truth, that I intended to keep to myself, and a half truth would have been misleading. He'd have probably thought I had seen a vision of some kind or had heard a voice in the middle of the night. Thoughts like that would have turned me into someone I definitely wasn't. He only said, "I've found that when I'm trying to make up my mind about something, the better informed I am, the better my decision is."

"Next Friday I'm going to the Deaconess Training School. I will be seeing Sister Emma."

"She teaches there?"

"Yes. I will also be talking to the principal, Lucy Meyer, who started the School with her husband."

"Meyer . . . Where have I heard that name before? Oh, I remember now. Last week I was wandering through a bookstore and in the section reserved for books about science I came across the title *Real Fairy Folks.* Wondering what it was doing on that shelf, I looked more closely. The two subtitles *Fairy Land of Chemistry* and *Explorations in the World of Atoms,* the one rather bizarre and the other commonplace, intrigued me. I quickly went through the book, which introduces children to both the marvels and the complexities of the physical world and liked what I saw. The facts were all there, and the writing was" Father paused, "I'd say the writing was clever, imagine using fairies to educate the young, and playful. The author's last name was Meyer, and I think the first name was Lucy. Most likely, though, she is not your Mrs. Meyer."

"From what Sister Emma said about her, I think she most likely is."

"If she is, then it is not only her book that's unusual. While religion and science are battling each other, she's teaching both. In our day, I'd say that's remarkable."

"That's the word Sister Emma used to describe her."

* * *

At the corner of Fiftieth Street and Indiana Avenue, there were two large brick buildings. Standing next to each other and having the same dimensions, they looked alike, though there were some minor architectural differences. Over the front door of the building bordering fiftieth Street was the sign *Chicago Training School for City, Home and Foreign Missions.* Impressed by their size—they were five stories high and had to be close to three hundred feet long and one hundred feet wide—I found myself wondering how they got there.

Had the school built them, or had they been built earlier by someone else? Maybe they had once been apartment buildings or possibly the business offices of a large company. I had another question, a better one. Since the school had started with nothing, how did it get there? Where had the students come from, the teachers, the administrators? Where had the money come from? Somewhat awed by these structures and, to use Sister Emma's word, by the success and the significance they symbolized, I entered the building fronting fiftieth Street. A friendly receptionist took me to Sister Emma's office on the second floor. It was small and sparsely furnished with a desk, two straight-back wooden chairs, and an oblong table that was piled high with books. Along one wall there was a large bookcase holding pamphlets, files, books, and stacks of papers.

"Good morning, Miss Welsh," Sister Emma said. "I trust you had a good Christmas."

"Oh, we did. Mother had been bedridden for several months but is now much improved. She was able to stay downstairs with us for most of Christmas day. Although there were many wonderful gifts under the tree, that was the best present of all. How was your Christmas, Sister Emma?"

"It was lovely. I live in a Deaconess Home with a dozen other women. We opened presents, sang Christmas carols, and had a splendid meal together. I must say, though, my greatest joy this Christmas has been your angel with her broken wing. She blesses me each time I look at her. Now, as I look at you here, I am blessed once more. We are so glad you have come. When I told Mrs. Meyer you'd be visiting us, she suggested I talk to you about the Training School and she'll cover the history of our Deaconess Order. After she's finished why don't you return to my office so we can discuss any thoughts you might have. We do hope you will then join us for the noonday meal. Is this arrangement satisfactory?"

"It is most satisfactory. Thank you."

"Let's sit in the parlor. It's more comfortable there, and since the girls are gone because of the Christmas break, we won't be disturbed."

Quite unexpectedly, she began her account of the Training School not with God but with the two men Mrs. Meyer has loved. Because of the first, Mrs. Meyer could not do what she had wanted to, and because of the second, she later could. The first was a young physician she had met while studying to become a doctor herself at the Woman's Medical School in Philadelphia. They were soon engaged and planned to marry after she had completed her studies and then serve together as medical missionaries overseas. But during the winter of her second year, her fiancé suddenly died of cholera. She left medical school heartbroken and didn't return.

Instead, she worked for the Freedman's Aid Society, the Troy Conference Academy, and eventually McKendree College where she taught chemistry. A teacher and deeply religious by nature, she organized at one point a Sunday school class and, dissatisfied with the material available, started to write Bible lessons for her students. Seeing this as a way to earn extra money, Mrs. Meyer submitted these lessons to Sunday school periodicals. As the lessons appeared in these publications with increasing frequency, she attracted attention. Churches and conventions invited her to speak. The body responsible for sending representatives to the World's Sunday School Convention in London elected her one of its delegates. The Illinois State Sunday School Association asked her to be its Field Secretary, a post she gladly accepted, though it meant resigning her position at McKendree College.

Now thirty-one, Mrs. Meyer once again knew where her life was headed. Or at least she thought she did. The next four years, as the Association's Field Secretary, she traveled almost continuously throughout Illinois addressing gatherings large and small, demonstrating teaching methods, conducting Sunday school classes. As she talked and listened, she realized a growing number of women, especially young women, were looking for ways to serve God. But they didn't know the Bible, or the history of the church, or its doctrine, and they lacked the necessary practical skills. The desire and oftentimes the passion were there, but the competency wasn't. The answer to this dilemma was, at least to her, obvious and urgent. These women needed a training school, and they needed it now. The idea took hold of her, and no matter how large the obstacle or how adamant the objection, it wouldn't let go.

She put committees together in the Methodist Episcopal Church to consider the idea and even got them to pass resolutions endorsing it. But nothing happened. The uphill climb was thought to be too steep: it had never been done before, it was too costly, it would never be able to attract enough students. Then there was a thunderstorm in Lake Bluff, Illinois. That day, in late August 1885, the Woman's Foreign Missionary Society of the Methodist Episcopal Church celebrated its anniversary in the town's auditorium. After the final speech, almost everyone hurriedly collected their belongings and headed for the nearest exit. Among their number were many who were supposed to stay for a further review of Mrs. Meyer's proposed training school. But it rained so hard, they couldn't leave the building. Rather sheepishly, they, along with others who were either curious or just had nothing else to do, joined those who had remained for the committee meeting. A tiny group, that by itself would have been insignificant, unexpectedly became a large and meaningful body. Once again Mrs. Meyer pressed for authorization to open a training school in Chicago, attempting in her presentation to answer objections, particularly the thorny issue of how the property would be paid for. A nickel fund, she told the committee, would easily take care of that concern. In the Methodist Episcopal Church, there were a million women. If each one gave five cents not once a month, not once a year, but once in a lifetime for the purchase of the building,

$50,000 would be raised, double the amount needed. Though the plan appeared flawless, she saw the committee was not persuaded.

The featured speaker at the anniversary celebration had been Dr. William Butler, a widely recognized authority on foreign missions. Earlier that day, Mrs. Meyer had talked to him at length about the training school and had asked him to stay for the committee meeting. She now called on him, not knowing what he would say, if anything. Moving to the front of the committee, he hesitated for a moment and then began, "I assure you, friends, your missionaries in foreign fields need training before they go. I cannot find words to express the desire of my heart that this plan shall go through. You could well afford to establish the school and pay all the expense yourselves. It would save you money in the end in the increased efficiency of your workers." As heads nodded in approval, she felt the objective had at last been reached, and it had . . . almost. It was moved and seconded that the school be opened in the fall. The motion passed.

But the question of salaries remained. Mrs. Meyer knew that money could not come from the students. It had already been agreed there would be no tuition, and since the girls would work in the home, making a housekeeper unnecessary, there would also be no charge for lodging. Their only expense would be meals, amounting to $2.50 to $3.00 a week. Instead, she looked to churches and to individual church members for help. But no money had been forthcoming. Realizing time was running out, she told the committee at its next meeting she would not take a salary for a year and would make extensive use of guest lecturers who also would not be paid. Though surprised, even startled, by this proposal—the idea of a woman who had been earning a handsome salary volunteering to build a school, in effect, out of thin air was almost comical—the committee was at last satisfied enough to authorize her to secure an appropriate building at once. The committee, however, was still

Thomas Lenhart

skeptical, for its approval contained the clause that she undertook this task at her own risk.

Behind this proposal was neither faith nor foolishness, the conclusion many of the committee members had come to, but the second man Mrs. Meyer has loved. The two met one evening in a Chicago restaurant. Dining alone at nearby tables, they shyly smiled at each other and exchanged a few words. As she was leaving, he gave her his card and asked if he might call on her. She wrote down her address on a piece of paper and, trusting that she wasn't being too forward, gave it to him. This chance meeting turned into friendship, and then into love. On May 21, 1885, at the age of thirty-six, she married Josiah Shelley Meyer, also thirty-six. He had attended Bryant and Stratton Commercial College in Philadelphia, been a bookkeeper in New York City and Chicago, and was at the time of their wedding the assistant secretary of the Young Men's Christian Association in Chicago. The two were different, as different as Maude Nelson's fastball was from Nina Clark's knuckler. She was a dreamer, an idealist filled with glorious plans, impetuous at times, constantly in motion, always ready to set aside a time-honored understanding for a new and deeper truth; he was practical, liked figures and the intricacies of contractual agreements, moved at a slower and more measured pace, rejected all modern notions that threatened to displace established truth. Although there were spats, at times heated spats, the two, as they labored together, were, however, much more capable and much wiser because of these differences. The work one couldn't do, the other could. She saw the building; he got it built.

They immediately started searching for a home for the Training School. A narrow, three-story residence located at 19 Park Avenue on the west side of the city looked like a possibility. The rental agent gave them the key to the home so they could inspect it, but by mistake sent them to 21 Park Avenue. Of course, with that key, they couldn't unlock the front door. Mr. Meyer took out several of his own keys and began trying one after another. To their surprise, he eventually came to one that worked. The door opened, and they started to enter. They were even more surprised when they saw the home was furnished. As they looked around and then at each other not knowing what to think or to do, they heard a woman cry, "Why they are coming right in." Hastily they retreated, closed the front door, and rang the bell. When the woman opened the door, they quickly apologized for the intrusion and explained what had happened. Relieved, she told them the home they were looking for was next door. Both thought it would be quite suitable, at least for that first year, and although the $50 a month rent, given their meager resources, appeared to be far more than they could afford, they took it.

Now all they needed were students. Hundreds of letters and thousands of circulars were sent out describing the Training School and urging especially young women to apply. When the school opened October 25th, four students started two years of training. Classes in the Bible, church history, and medical practices and lectures on subjects ranging from the theory of domestic industry to social and family relations were in the morning. The afternoons were set aside for study and housework and twice a week for home visitations. Saturday afternoon the girls taught children in an Industrial School everyday skills like cooking and sewing. Sunday they taught a Sunday school class in one of the nearby churches.

Soon more girls joined them raising the number to twelve, but then this growth abruptly stopped. A barrier of some kind had apparently been reached. A way beyond it had to be found for the school to continue. Although prayers for additional pupils became more earnest and frequent, nothing changed until the Meyers realized it was not more students or money they needed but more faith. Everything came down not to numbers but to size. How big was their God? Was he big enough to bring the Training School to life and, more than this, to keep it alive? And if so, did they trust him enough to do it? He was, of that they were sure, and they did. They made a decision that before had seemed too risky: girls would be accepted who could not pay for their meals. At once new students came, so many that by the end of the school year the house was completely full, and with them enough money, in small and large donations, to establish a Students' Aid Fund that could be drawn upon as needed to meet uncovered expenses.

With more girls wanting to attend the Training School the next year and no place to put them, it was clear another home was necessary. There was, however, nothing suitable for rent. So, in the late spring of 1886, the Meyers decided to purchase a lot and to build a house on it large enough for at least fifty students. After a lengthy search, they found a piece of property at the corner of Ohio Street and Dearborn Avenue that was exactly what they were looking for. The neighborhood was pleasant; the Loop, the city's central business district, was close by; and the streetcar lines that could take the girls practically anywhere they wanted to go were within easy walking distance. Only one obstacle stood in the way: the $25,000 it was going to cost to build the home.

Money had often been a worry. A bill would come in for gas, or water, or printing, or postage, or groceries and the school account would be empty. But God had always provided, though sometimes in a most unlikely way. There was for instance the bitterly cold winter day Mrs. Meyer went to see a woman about an admissions matter. She lived on the south side of the city several miles from the school. After a long ride on a frigid streetcar and a fifteen minute walk through the snow, Mrs. Meyer discovered the woman wasn't home. Dreading the return trip and angry at God for all this time she had wasted, she started back. As she got on the streetcar, Mrs. Meyer saw a gentleman she knew and sat down beside him. He asked about the school and was particularly interested in the monthly expenses.

When she couldn't give him the precise amounts, he laughed, saying it was fortunate she wasn't the treasurer, but then quickly added he did want to help and promised to send the school a few stamps. An envelope with his name on it arrived the next day containing not stamps but a check for $100.

At the end of the year, after all of the bills had been paid, there was $1,000 in the school's account. This balance was a beginning. A lot more money, though, was needed, and it was clear most of the ministers and their churches were not going to help. Many churches couldn't because they, too, were looking for money either to make themselves more attractive where they were or to move with the people into more appealing neighborhoods farther away from the center of the city. Those churches that could help didn't want to. Their aid was going elsewhere. Although they never said so, training women, and especially training them to be leaders, for any kind of work outside the home was not a high enough priority and, without question, for some it wasn't a priority at all. Instead, support then and in the years ahead came mostly from wealthy individuals. When the school received three gifts totaling $6,000 and a $1,250 contribution from the Woman's Home Missionary Society work on the new home began. Progress, though, was agonizingly slow. Because of the rioting at Haymarket Square in May nothing happened quickly. That protest of working conditions, which had turned violent leaving two dead and close to a hundred wounded, had virtually shut down the building trades. The new school year scheduled to begin in October had to be moved back to November and then again to December. Finally, the home opened on December 8th, and classes began without any knobs on the doors, paint on the walls, or furniture in most of the rooms. Hammering and sawing continued for weeks, and everywhere there was the smell of new paint. Finally, the home was completed and formally dedicated in February. Coming primarily from small towns, fifty students from eighteen states were enrolled in the school that year, and at the end of the following year, twenty-seven graduates became home missionaries and twenty-four graduates missionaries overseas, serving in India, China, Korea, Japan, South America, Africa, and Jamaica.

Although it was thought to be a long-term solution for the school, the new home within a few short years was inadequate. As the city rapidly grew, often in unanticipated and oppressive ways, the church's need for workers grew along with it. With many more opportunities now available, the number of girls wanting to attend the school sharply increased. As the enrollment rose, the home on Dearborn Avenue quickly ran out of space. Faced with overcrowding, which made it necessary to rent outside rooms for the new students, the Meyers once again began to talk about expanding. Chicago Methodists, though, weren't listening. But New York Methodists were. They wanted the school in New York and to get it there promised results that far exceeded what had been accomplished in Chicago.

One day Mr. Meyer had an unexpected caller. A wealthy banker, Norman Wait Harris, founder of the Harris Trust and Savings Bank, stopped by his office. Leaving soon for Europe, he wanted Mr. Meyer to know he was thinking of making a sizable donation to the Training School and after his return would speak to him again about the gift. When Mr. Meyer replied the school would most likely be in New York by then, Mr. Harris asked that nothing be decided until he got back. After listening to Mr. Meyer talk about the New York Methodists, how aggressive they had become, how attractive their offer was, Mr. Harris had another request. He asked Mr. Meyer to find land in Chicago that would fully satisfy all the school's requirements. Three days after his return, Mr. Harris bought the land Mr. Meyer had chosen, the lot at fiftieth Street and Indiana Avenue, and immediately offered to give it to the school if the Meyers agreed to build on the property a 120-room structure costing at least $30,000.

They accepted the proposal. The money was raised, with considerable help from Mr. Harris, and the school moved across the city into its new home the following year. Within five years, it was too small. So Mr. Harris paid for the construction of a second building adjacent to it, providing space for another 130 students. With the additional rooms, the school continued to grow until the enrollment reached 250 students, the home's maximum capacity. Since then, because of the space limitation, the number hasn't increased, and although students have left the school because of graduation or for personal reasons, with many more girls wanting to enroll, it hasn't declined.

From the beginning, the school's mission has been to train. This it has always done. But through the years, in unexpected ways, its mission has expanded because of what might be called unplanned for possibilities, though the school would probably prefer the word responsibilities. Take for example the evening Mrs. Dickinson, an office assistant, was working late preparing a report for Mrs. Meyer. She heard a faint noise. At first she couldn't place where it was coming from and then realized it sounded like someone tapping on the front door. Puzzled and somewhat irritated that the visitor didn't have enough sense to knock, she went to the front door and opened it. When she did, she chastised herself for being so judgmental. Standing there was a little boy, about five years old, who shyly looked up at her. Mrs. Dickinson waited for him to say something. When he didn't, she noticed a woman at the bottom of the stairs and asked if the child was hers. The woman shook her head. Late that morning, the woman explained, she had noticed the boy enter the waiting room of the Northwestern Railroad Station where she worked. He sat down on a bench and seemed to be expecting someone. But the hours went by and no one came. Thinking that he must be hungry, she bought him a sandwich. As she was giving it to him, she saw that he had a tag around his neck. Nothing was on it except the name and address of the Training School. At the end of the day, the boy was still there. Since she lived nearby, she decided to drop him off at the school on her way home.

After making several inquiries at the train station the next day, Mr. Meyer learned a man in a small town in Illinois, no one knew exactly where, had put his son on the train saying someone would meet him in Chicago. His wife had died and the boy was being sent to school there. What could the Training School do? They couldn't send the boy back. They didn't know where he had come from, and even if they did, his father clearly didn't want him. They couldn't send the boy away, that, they were sure, God didn't want. They could possibly find a home for him. Several other children had been cared for in this way. But when the next unwanted child was sent to the school, or the one after that, would they be able to locate families for them? Fearing the answer would be no, Mr. and Mrs. Meyer decided what they needed was not a different home for each child but one home for all the children. When told about the boy in the waiting room of the train station with a tag around his neck, a woman of considerable means, given to helping others, agreed. If the school could find the right home, she would pay the rent. A cottage of suitable size became available in Lake Bluff, to the north of the city. It was secured, and a dozen children moved in under the care of a housekeeper from the training school. A short time later the school was given an entire city block in Lake Bluff, which soon became the site of a three story building large enough for fifty children.

Under the able guidance of its administrator, Lucy Judson, a graduate of the Training School, the children's home stood on its own. Behind it, though, and thirty-eight other institutions were Mr. and Mrs. Meyers and the Training School. Look back far enough into the history of twelve deaconess homes, four children's homes, seven schools, one rest home, ten hospitals, three orphanages, and two homes for the elderly and there in some key capacity—receiving property, raising money, erecting buildings, organizing and supervising personnel, formulating policy, providing skilled and dedicated staff—was the training school. Repeatedly the school faced the question of how much it should take on, particularly since much of what it was considering far exceeded the scope of a training school. In reaching a decision, it was so often guided by the words of Abner to the Israelites "Now then do it" this statement in 2 Samuel 3:18 became the school motto. It was an article of faith the school lived by. Time and again the school did it.

In some ways, the school over the years has changed. New courses, like social and family relationships and child psychology, were being offered. Some of the older courses had been dropped. Admission standards were higher. The course work had become more demanding. Because the school was now important nationally, Mrs. Meyers was frequently absent for days and weeks at a time attending meetings and conferences all across the country. But in other ways the school has remained the same. The curriculum hasn't changed. It still has both an academic and a practical emphasis. Alongside of courses on the Bible, church history, theology, and doctrine, there were classes in nursing, hygiene, citizenship, and the practice of evangelistic visitation the students had to take. Each week, time continued to be spent in the classroom and outside of it on the city's streets visiting people wherever they were, in their homes, in asylums, in prisons. Resident teachers and volunteer lecturers—ministers; physicians; instructors from the University of Chicago, Garrett Biblical Institute, and Hull House—still did the teaching. A student still needed to complete successfully two years of study and field work to receive a diploma. An integral part of that study continued to be, especially in Mrs. Meyer's and her classes, the thorough and critical examination of ideas and explanations old and new.

Glancing at the small alarm clock on the corner of her desk, Sister Emma exclaimed, "It's eleven o'clock. Forgive me, Miss Welsh, for going on like this. Mrs. Meyer has been expecting you for the past half hour. She knows, though, that when I start talking about the Training School, I do find it hard to stop. Her office is at the end of the hall on your right. If there is anything you would like to discuss, I'll be here when your visit is over."

I knocked softly on Mrs. Meyer's closed office door. There was no answer. Not sure if I should wait or return to Sister Emma's office, I decided to try once more and knocked again, this time more forcefully. A voice inside, sounding faint and even distant, as though it were coming from the far end of a tunnel, told me to enter. Opening the door, I was immediately struck by how big the room was. It made Sister Emma's office look like a closet. But then, I told myself, because of all the books, newspapers, pamphlets, and papers it contained and all of the furniture, it had to be much larger. There were enough desks, tables, and chairs for two people. It suddenly occurred to me there probably were two people in the office. Most likely Mrs. Meyer had an assistant, a stenographer perhaps or maybe a personal secretary, who routinely worked right alongside of her. Behind one of the desks sat Mrs. Meyer, who seemed to be staring at the wall in front of her. Since there was absolutely nothing on that wall but white paint, I decided she must be praying, or contemplating a passage from the Bible, or possibly even receiving a vision of some sort. I certainly didn't want to interrupt her, but she had told me to come in.

"Excuse me," I said, "I'm Mattie Welsh."

Though she turned toward the door and looked at me, I had the feeling she really wanted to go back to the wall. Not knowing what I should do, I just stood there and waited for her to speak. After pursing her lips, sitting up straighter in her chair, and looking slowly away from me and then back again, she finally said, "Sister Emma tells me you graduated from Vassar. At some point, I imagine you took a course or two in religious studies. In the classroom or in your reading, did you ever come across George Berman Foster?"

"I don't remember the name."

Taking a book from her desk and holding it up so that I could see it, Mrs. Meyer continued, "He teaches theology at the University of Chicago. Two years ago, he wrote this highly contentious book, which I have just purchased. It's titled *The Finality of the Christian Religion*. While waiting for you, I started reading the introductory chapter and found myself pulled into a statement he makes." She put the book down and thumbed through several pages until she found the one she wanted. After adjusting her glasses, she read: *Our mode-philosophy preaches to us that there is nothing static, nothing fixed, nothing final, but that mutation and process characterize all that is; nay, that it belongs to the very nature of the "absolute" to grow. Can Christianity, then, be final? Thus it has come about that our religion, with a Master and a message which claim to be the same yesterday, today, and forever, is summoned before the judgment seat of a progressive humanity.* Is this, Miss Welsh, what you are thinking?"

This was exactly what I was thinking, except it wasn't a progressive humanity that was bringing Christianity before the judgment seat. It was what I was doing. But I couldn't tell Mrs. Meyer that. She'd ask me to leave. She might even usher me out of the building herself. I needed to attend this school, and in that moment, I knew precisely why. The school and beyond it the Deaconess Order were going to be for me the judgment seat. Knowing, though, I had to say something, I replied, "I need to read the book. Until I do, I can't determine what his position is and if it has validity."

"Your response, then, Miss Welsh, is that we must first let him speak."

"Yes,"

"I like that. Indeed, I like that very much." Rising, she welcomed me with a warm smile and a firm handshake. Then pointing to a chair in front of her desk, she said, "Now do sit down. We're not here to talk about theology but these people called Deaconesses."

As she put Professor Foster's book to one side and straightened the papers in front of her, I looked closely at Mrs. Meyer. The strands of gray in her light brown hair and the lines across her forehead and beside her blue-gray eyes suggested she was probably in her late fifties. Of medium height and slender, she had a high, receding forehead, a pale complexion, drooping eyelids, and sharp features, particularly her nose and chin. At the corners of her mouth there were what my mother called smile lines. She had a sense of humor; she liked to laugh. The intensity deeply etched into her face, however, and her controlled and penetrating gaze spoke of one who was serious most of the time, of one who knew there was work to do and was not going to let anything stop her from getting it done. What I saw was appealing, but it was what I didn't see and yet sensed was there on the inside—the depth, the inner strength, the searching mind, the compassion—that was most compelling. There was something else that drew me to her. She emitted a force of some kind, perhaps it was a more of a presence, that I couldn't begin to describe. I only knew it was there, and I knew it was powerful.

Mrs. Meyer began with an unexpected question. She asked if I read Greek and seemed pleased when I told her I had taken an introductory course in Greek at Vassar. "Deaconess comes from the Greek word *Diakonos*."

"Doesn't *Diakonos* mean service?"

"Prompt and helpful service, yes. A Deaconess has essentially always been one who serves." She then asked me a second question, "Miss Welsh, do you know what women are created for?"

"Helping," I said.

"That's right," she replied. We're told in the second chapter of Genesis God made for Adam a helper. Women are made to be helpers. In the Old Testament, seen not as individuals with their own rights and responsibilities but as an appendage of their husbands, they helped in the family but not outside of it. Jesus changed this. They had their own place in his life and then, to an increasing degree, in the life of the early church. According to Romans 16:1, the first helper to be called a *Diakonos* was Phoebe. *Diakonos* in our English Bible is translated servant, though most authorities today think Deaconess is a more faithful rendering of that Greek word. But even if servant is the correct term, there is ample historical evidence an Order of Deaconesses did exist in the church in the second century. Commissioned for service by a laying on of hands, they at first primarily cared for the poor. In time, their duties were enlarged to include the instruction of new converts, the visitation of believers imprisoned for their faith, and, eventually, the regular and systematic visitation of non-believers to bring them to Christ and into the church. The Order grew, until at one point a large church in Constantinople was utilizing forty Deaconesses, but primarily because of the spread of monasticism, it gradually declined and then disappeared altogether in the Western Church in the sixth century and in the Eastern Church in the twelfth century.

"The Order, however, reappeared in Kaiserwerth, Germany in the nineteenth century, largely because of the efforts of Theodore Fliedner, a Protestant pastor who believed it to be Biblical and women to be uniquely equipped to serve. He started in his home a refuge for discharged female convicts and in a garden outbuilding a knitting school for little children. Although bitter opposition to this work came from many parts of the Church, there arose from this modest beginning reformatories, orphanages, lunatic asylums, training schools, and hospitals, and today there are affiliated Deaconess houses operating in Italy, England, Asia Minor, Syria, and Northern Africa. A woman wanting to become a Kaiserwerth Deaconess first had to complete a probationary period lasting from three months to three years, and then she committed herself to at least five years of service. Instead of a salary, she was given shelter, food, a blue uniform, pocket-money for incidentals, and a home to live in when she could no longer serve because of illness or old age. Because the Order was able to sustain itself financially, it was never under the Church's direct control. Holding this independence dear and, when necessary, more than willing to fight for it, the Order saw itself not as a department within the Church but as an extension of it.

"In 1849, Pastor Fliedner sent two Deaconesses to Pittsburgh, Pennsylvania to establish the Order here in America. Although this effort was unsuccessful, the Evangelical Lutheran Church in Philadelphia soon started its own Order, devoted largely to nursing, which continues to flourish. Today the Episcopal Church has deaconesses serving primarily on the East Coast, and our Methodist Episcopal Church, which formally approved the Order at its 1888 General Conference, has a Deaconess Home in more than a dozen cities across the country."

Not with pride but, to use her words, in wonder at what God has wrought, Mrs. Meyer next turned to the Chicago Deaconesses. The Deaconess Order in the Methodist Episcopal Church started right here in the Training School, she told me. In 1887, as the school neared the close of its second year, there was talk about continuing the students' city missionary work through the summer. The need was obvious, and if the girls stayed at the school, they wouldn't have to pay for lodging, food, or carfare. The idea had its appeal, and it had an implication that was even more enticing. If the girls did stay at the school and if they did the missionary work in the city, then for all practical purposes the school would be a Deaconess Home for those months and the girls, not in name, of course, but certainly in effect, would be Deaconesses. Of the fifteen students attending the school, eight chose to remain in the city. That summer they visited struggling families, offered prayer in desperate situations, took wayward children to Sunday school, and brought to the sick and the dying comfort, hope, and love.

At the end of the summer, six of these girls either returned to the Training School for another year of study or left the city to serve the Church elsewhere. But two of them were determined to continue their work in Chicago. If what we did during the summer had merit, they kept saying, it must be maintained, it must be increased. Lives depended on it; souls depended on it. Their voices were heard. Convinced the question before the Training School was not, as one member of the Executive Committee succinctly put it, "dare we go on?" but rather "dare we do anything but go on?" it was agreed the school must support the two girls.

A Deaconess Home Committee was formed to provide them with housing. Because there was no room for the girls in the Training School, a flat two blocks away, large enough for a dozen girls, was rented for them. Though it was leased, and when they moved in, it had only two beds, four chairs, and a lamp, the flat was, the Committee insisted, an independent Deaconess Home. In the coming months, the number in the flat steadily grew as other girls learned of the home missionary work in Chicago, largely through articles in the Training School's monthly publication, *The Message*, and felt themselves drawn to it. When the number reached twelve, the decision was made to move the girls out of the flat into a larger and more permanent residence, one that was owned, not rented. The house they wanted was right next door to the Training School. Since it wouldn't be available for another year, the girls were temporarily placed in an annex that was built for them in the school's back yard.

When they did move into the house next door it had become by that time an officially designated Deaconess Home, and the girls, licensed and set apart by the Church in a consecration service, had officially become Deaconesses. To identify, to protect, and to maintain equality among themselves and to save money, they wore a black blouse and skirt with a white collar and cuffs and a black outer coat with a small black hat held in place by white streamers that tied underneath the chin. Their hair was plain, and to reduce the likelihood of being robbed, they wore no jewelry except a collar-pin. Instead of being paid a salary, they received room, board, carfare, and $8 a month for personal expenses. They were single, lived in a community, and belonged to a sisterhood. Though they had committed themselves to serving the needy of the city for the sake of Jesus, they were not bound by a vow, and as they felt directed by God or by their own desires, they could leave the Order at any time.

As the Order grew over the years, it retained these basic features, though there were two significant, and in a sense opposing, changes. In time, the Order, in Chicago and elsewhere, became regulated by requirements established by the Church at the national level. These rules made the Order more rigid. The *Doctrines and Discipline of the Methodist Episcopal Church* clearly stated who could and could not be a Deaconess. To become a licensed Deaconess, one had to be single; over twenty-three; in good health; and recommended by the church one attended. Also one had to complete two years of probationary service, which could be satisfied by enrollment in a training school or work in a hospital; pass the course of study prescribed by the Bishops; meet to the satisfaction of the Conference Board the religious requirements of a Deaconess; commit to at least one year of service beyond the training period; and wear the approved dress of a Deaconess.

But the Order also became more flexible, not in who the Deaconess was but in what she did. In the beginning, most often she either visited in the home or worked as a nurse in a hospital. In recent years, however, because the *Discipline* declared that she could perform whatever Christian labor suited her abilities, she could be a secretary, religious or secular teacher, superintendent of a religious or secular school, writer, housekeeper, prison worker, field worker, or bookkeeper. The list didn't stop here, which made it clear she had now received the Church's blessing to do whatever needed to be done. Mrs. Meyer then quickly added that whatever it was, it had to be done for Jesus' sake. That, she emphasized, with her index finger pointed directly at me, hadn't changed and it never would.

"Could she even be a baseball player?" I asked.

"Indeed, she could," Mrs. Meyer replied, smiling. She even started to laugh. "I've heard that a woman who plays baseball professionally wears bloomers. A Deaconess in bloomers. Now that's a sight I would like to see, and one that I think would be most appropriate . . . on a baseball diamond, of course." Looking at a note on her desk, she then said, "I'm expected at a meeting shortly. I'm sure Sister Emma will be able to answer questions you might have. If you are considering attending the Training School, we do hope you will come."

"Since meeting Sister Emma, I have been thinking seriously about enrolling," I replied and worried that thinking wasn't a strong enough word, quickly added, "and praying about it too. What I have seen this morning and learned has definitely helped me make up my mind. It is what I want to do."

"Wonderful. With your permission, I'd like to call the Administration Office at Vassar to confirm your graduation from the college and to receive its recommendation for your admittance here."

"Please do make that call."

"Now off you go. Sister Emma is waiting for you."

Before knocking on her door, I paused. I had just realized there was something Mrs. Meyer hadn't asked me. Perhaps, I reasoned, I shouldn't say anything about it to Sister Emma right away. If I did, I might be telling her more about myself than I wanted her, at least at this point, to know. I decided to mention it at the end of our talk. Put it there, I told myself, and it might appear to be nothing more than a mere afterthought.

"Well, Miss Welsh, what do you have for me?" Sister Emma asked, as I entered her office.

"It seems to me," I said, sitting down in a chair in front of her desk, "the Training School and especially the Deaconesses resemble bloomer girls baseball."

"I don't see the connection. We don't do anything with a bat or ball."

"Oh, it's not what you do that is similar. It's where you do it."

"Where is that?"

"In a man's world."

"Do continue, Miss Welsh."

"Not all, to be sure, but a good many men who play baseball don't like women entering this world of theirs. It makes them so angry they open this world of theirs up to us and practically beg us to come in."

"So they can beat you."

"Not just beat us but humiliate us so we leave their world and never come back. Do men in the church treat you like this?"

"Some certainly have, particularly at the beginning. When the girls first put on the black dress, they immediately attacked Mrs. Meyer. It was not just wrong, they said, it was immoral for her to take a young girl out of the home and put her on the city's streets. A girl, if she must, might be in a shop making dresses, or in a school teaching, or in a hospital taking care of the sick, or even, if her circumstances were particularly unkind to her, in a faraway country serving God. But to be dressed in black holding the hand of an unmarried mother, or visiting a thief in jail, or weeping alongside of a young father whose wife had just died, or playing hide and seek with a little boy who could hardly speak English, that must not be tolerated. Allow that and it wouldn't be long before those 'hen preachers'—that's what they were calling the girls at ministerial conferences—pushed the men right out of their pulpits. Don't let that dress fool you, they went on. It's wasn't as unassuming as it looked. It was a uniform that declared to those who wore it and to those who didn't that they belonged to a sisterhood that was held together by perpetual vows and answered only to itself, a sisterhood that ultimately was making its way to Rome and aimed to take the Church along with it. Don't be fooled by their sacrificial service either. They weren't saints because they weren't getting paid for what they did but cheap labor, and cheap labor meant lower wages for everyone else."

"Why that's like a pitcher throwing his fast ball right at you. Did Mrs. Meyer strike back?"

"Like someone who had been hit by a fast ball. She wrote volumes; she spoke whenever, and wherever, and to whomever she could; she prayed; and, in one instance that really was pretty silly, she even laughed," Sister Emma said, laughing herself.

"What was so funny?"

"After time had proved her critics wrong, they dreamed up a new charge. They saw that the girls were making calls only in the afternoon. Here these girls were supposed to be servants of the Church, they bellowed, and yet they were working just three hours a day. Sleeping late and having long, leisurely breakfasts and equally long lunches was not an efficient use of time and reflected badly upon the Church. Such inefficiency was indefensible. Considering this latest attack nonsense, Mrs. Meyer at first ignored it. But Mr. Meyer felt it had to be addressed. Efficiency, he pointed out, was what the business world now demanded. It wouldn't do to have people, especially important people who might be interested in helping the school or the Deaconesses, thinking they were wasting time.

"Mrs. Meyer reluctantly agreed. At first annoyed, she then brightened. Giving all the Deaconesses a diary, she instructed them to record everything they did each day leaving out nothing, not even the smallest detail. After a month, she collected the diaries and put their entries in several issues of *The Message* and the *Deaconess*

Advocate. In this way, readers, including critical ministers, learned Deaconesses spent huge amounts of time collecting and preparing material for the many classes they organized and often taught; gathering old clothing for needy families; selecting appropriate institutions for the ill and making sure they got there and were comfortably settled in; finding wheel chairs for invalids; arranging funeral services; making plans for people who were too sick, or too frightened, or too despondent to make those plans for themselves. At the end of one of the articles, she wrote—and this is where she laughed—if a Deaconess's usefulness was to be judged by the amount of time she spent making calls in the afternoon, then it was only right to judge a pastor's usefulness by the amount of time he spent in the pulpit."

"I imagine that silenced them."

"Not entirely, though they did begin to speak in lower voices. They, however, were not the only ones talking. Through the years, there have been many other ordeals or, as Mrs. Meyer prefers to call them, tests. Some have turned out favorably; others have not, like the Jane Addams predicament."

"I heard her speak at Vassar. We all found her inspiring."

"She once asked to teach a course at the Training School. Because she is so stimulating, Mrs. Meyer put her in a classroom full of second-year students. After three years with us, she was given a seat on the Board of Trustees. Her first Board meeting, though, was dreadful. At the time, the churches were angrily denouncing Hull House. They thought the decision to remove religious instruction from its curriculum a sacrilege. One member of the Board called Hull house a profane organization and insisted that Miss Addams, the leader of the settlement house, should not be on the Board of Trustees. Others backed him. Mrs. Meyer knew she couldn't oppose these members. It would have been too costly. She needed their guidance and support to resolve other, weightier matters. Bitterly disappointed and embarrassed beyond words, she did what was for her the unthinkable: she asked Miss Addams to resign from the Board."

"Did she continue to teach at the training school?"

"Yes, Mrs. Meyer made sure of that. Eventually she did leave, but only because Miss Adams became so busy at Hull House there wasn't enough time for us.

"Another terrible test, though I think tribulation is the better word here, has come not from the men of the Church but from the women. To use one of my grandmother's favorite expressions, some have always looked upon our Order as a plum ripe for the picking. Mrs. Meyer has fought them off, and I do mean fought, for years now, especially the Woman's Home Missionary Society, which would swallow us up whole if given the chance. Some time ago, the bishops of the church, determined to restore order, placed the Deaconesses under their direct jurisdiction. Very little has changed, though. The misunderstandings, the quarreling, the rancor have not only continued, they have intensified. Mr. and Mrs. Meyer have talked about forming a general board from the bishops, the Church at large, and the competing groups which would oversee the Order. Something like this might help. But given the ill will is so pervasive and so long-standing, I am not too hopeful."

"Have all these trials slowed Mrs. Meyer down?"

"Slowed her down? No, I would say they have sped her up. She has been hurt, oftentimes very deeply hurt, but she keeps pushing relentlessly ahead. Something else, however, did slow her down; actually, it almost stopped her. Unexpectedly, she became ill about fifteen years ago. At first, she didn't tell anyone about her condition, but then the pain became so acute she couldn't eat or even stand for any length of time and so was forced to see a doctor. He diagnosed a stomach ailment and prescribed bed rest and a restricted diet. Over the next two years, she gradually improved, but then the condition returned, this time with greater severity, making surgery necessary.

Again there was a slow recovery followed by renewed and more intense suffering. A second operation was performed, which seems to have been more successful. But she is still not well and most likely never will be. Mrs. Meyer, though, remains an indefatigable worker, who has been likened to a toy top that keeps on spinning. She is always ready to write the next article, to compose the next song, to read the next book, to prepare the next lecture, and, indeed, to fight the next battle, even if she has to do it from her bed, which sometimes she's had to."

"Do you think she has ever wanted to stop?" I said, realizing at once this was a question I had no right to ask. I wanted somehow to retract those words, but Sister Emma seemed quite willing, even eager, to answer the question.

"I don't think that is the right question to ask," she replied, without any hesitation and with such conviction I felt sure it was a possibility she had considered before. "The right question, I believe, is could she have ever stopped? Can she stop now?"

"Don't we always have that choice?"

"We do, but she doesn't."

"You are saying she is different from us?"

"That, Miss Welsh, is exactly what I am saying. Of the many hymns Mrs. Meyer has written, I think there is one in particular that helps us to understand her, to understand who she is. In the fourth verse of the hymn she titled "He Was Not Willing," Mrs. Meyer says, 'He was not willing that any should perish. As his follower, can I live longer at ease with a soul going downward, lost for the lack of the help I might give?' These are not words of compassion; they are words of compulsion. There is a difference between the two. The compassionate act is one we decide to commit. The compulsive act is one we have to commit. Deep within Mrs. Meyer there is a compulsion to save the soul going downward. That compulsion is not there because she wants it. It's not going away if she doesn't want it. It's been put within her, and it's been put there for a very specific purpose: it is there to guide her, to inspire her, to strengthen her, to move her. If she attempts to turn away from that compulsion, it will only become stronger and more insistent until she has to turn back to it. Having said this, there is another question we must ask. Why does she have this compulsion? The answer, I am convinced, is found in Matthew 22:14, 'Many are called but few are chosen.' She is one of the chosen." After pausing for a moment, Sister Emma said, "Do you have another question for me?"

"Is Mr. Meyer still working at the YMCA?"

"Before that first year ended, he was so busy here and there was so much more for him to do he left the YMCA and became superintendent of the Training School. While Mrs. Meyer frequently has been away, often for an extended period of time, either attending a conference or needing rest to regain her health, he has always been here, day in and day out, with his friendly words of encouragement, his sound judgment, and his strong faith. He has been a rock we all have stood upon through the years."

"I have only one more question. Why did you come to the training school?"

"I came here because of a funeral," Sister Emma said.

Immediately I thought of Katie. "A funeral?"

"Actually, it was two funerals. I grew up in Chicago two blocks away from the church we attended. Nothing I heard at the Centenary Methodist Episcopal Church really interested me including the announcement one Sunday morning a new pastor, Reverend Hiram W. Thomas, was coming. Being fourteen and happiest when we were leaving the church, I didn't pay much attention to him either, although I did notice that as the months went by it became harder to find an open pew and that people were always talking about him. I picked up some liked what he was saying and others, not as many but they were louder, didn't. I noticed, too, his Sunday sermon was regularly appearing in the Monday newspaper, though I never read it. A year went by and nothing much changed except I was a little older and maybe a little more curious about what was going on around me. So, when Father said at supper one evening he had done it again, I listened to find out who had done what. Who turned out to be Reverend Thomas and what he had done was speak at the funeral of Mamie Stevens. I began to listen very closely when Father explained she had been shot by her enraged husband for infidelity. Reverend Thomas was not the officiating minister but had been asked to say a few words. Though they were few, those words were more than enough to stir up another controversy. When I asked why people were upset, Father told me I could read exactly what he had said in the afternoon newspaper. Right after supper, I grabbed the newspaper from the table next to Father's chair and hurried to my room. His words, though not eloquent, in some strange, inexplicable way, stirred something inside of me, especially what he said at the beginning. I still remember reading, 'It is my misfortune that I cannot keep from thinking. My thoughts give me trouble, and sometimes give my friends trouble. I am troubled here today.' I remember also what troubled him. He didn't understand how the Church could say the woman, who had no time to prepare for death, was going to hell forever, while the man who had killed her, if he repented before his execution, is going to heaven.

"The next Sunday everyone at church was talking about that funeral and also an earlier one. Because the deceased at the earlier funeral had been a notorious billiards player, other ministers had refused to help the family. But not Reverend Thomas. He told the family he'd be glad to take care of the service, which upset many in the church he was serving at the time. Even more upsetting, though, was his statement at the funeral that while God loved everyone, apparently the Church did not, which so disturbed him that he sometimes felt he should labor outside the Church so he could draw closer to the homes and to the hearts of the people. While others were distressed by his thoughts at these two funerals, I, at the age of fifteen, was attracted to them, to the importance of thinking for myself, of questioning and probing, of coming nearer to the homes and to the hearts of others."

"Was Reverend Thomas in trouble?"

"Very serious trouble. A movement, led mostly by incensed ministers, was underway either to silence him or to remove him from the ministry. Told he must stop making these statements against the Church and its doctrine, he became even more outspoken. No longer willing to tolerate this obstinacy, the conference tried him for false and harmful teaching, declared him guilty, and expelled him from the Methodist Episcopal Church. We heard the last sermon he gave at Centenary. Fortunately, we arrived early, for well before the service started there was nowhere to sit or to stand. The main floor was full and so were the galleries, the aisles, the vestibule, and even the steps outside the church. Clearly and forcefully, he spoke of what he could not accept: the inspiration of scripture in its entirety, the transference of man's sin to Christ on the cross, the impossibility of repentance and forgiveness in the life beyond death. He concluded the sermon with the statement he had to be mentally and spiritually free. His final words, which I have never forgotten, were, 'It would be better to die in poverty wearing the crown of liberty than to live in a palace and be in chains.' After finishing college and my graduate studies, I returned to Chicago and one day heard of a woman who had established a training school for women. It was said she thought for herself, questioned and probed, and had found a way to enter into the homes and into the hearts of the people. I came here to find out if it was true. It was, and so I decided to become what she was."

"A Deaconess."

"Yes. Are you hungry?"

"I am," I replied.

"Let's then be on our way." As we were leaving her office, Sister Emma stopped in front of a shelf lined with books. Pointing to one with a worn cover, she said, "Here is a collection of Reverend Thomas's sermons. Although I don't agree with everything he said, I return to them frequently. Because of his deep faith and compassion, he was probably closer to God than most, and so is someone I need to keep listening to."

After quickly making a mental note of the title, I said, thinking this was the right time to raise the question Mrs. Meyer had failed to ask, "Oh, Sister Emma, there is something else. I hope you don't mind."

"Of course not."

"Mrs. Meyer said I will probably be accepted here if the report from Vassar is favorable."

"I'm very glad to hear that."

"I'm surprised, though, she didn't ask me if I felt called to serve God or even if I believed in God."

"I would be surprised if she did," Sister Emma replied. "Girls come here for all kinds of reasons and some of them have nothing to do with God. It is not what is said at the beginning of the training that matters, but what is believed at the end. More to the point, though, Mrs. Meyer knows full well she is not the one who needs to hear the answers to these questions."

"If she doesn't need to, then who does?"

"You do."

When we entered the dining room, Mrs. Meyer was already seated at a table. She waved us over and even before I sat down said, "Thumper, I have just heard about the longest ball ever hit at Vassar. Apparently every freshman girl is expected to know where it landed and how far it traveled in feet and inches, though no one is absolutely sure where you stood. The principal, Mrs. Kendrick, told me it's something they've been having fun with ever since you graduated. She also assured me you were an excellent student and a person of exemplary character. Therefore, Miss Welsh, I am very pleased to say that you are officially admitted to the training school."

"How wonderful," I said, my face so flushed from embarrassment and, I had to admit, excitement I was sure it was by now glowing. "I will come."

"When would you like to enroll?"

"As soon as possible."

"The winter session begins a week from Wednesday," Sister Emma said.

"May I start then?" I asked.

"Yes, you may," Mrs. Meyer answered. "The girls will be returning Monday and Tuesday."

"I'll be here Monday afternoon."

"Do you know what you would like to do after you complete your training?" Sister Emma asked.

"I would like to become a Deaconess," I answered.

* * *

Leaving the training school, I first stopped at a nearby bookstore and purchased Reverend Thomas's sermons and Professor Foster's *The Finality Of The Christian Religion*, promising myself I would finish both by the end of the following week. I then got on the street car going to the train station. Some of the people close to me were talking, others were looking out a window, a few were reading. While they all appeared to be content, it struck me many of them, perhaps all of them, were in some way hiding from something. Apparently that was what we did. Mother, I was sure, was hiding; I certainly was; even God was, at least from me . . . that was, I reminded myself, if there is a God.

The Chicago Training School

Those nine days before I left for the Training School were hectic. I wrote Mr. Jenkins to tell him I was entering a religious training school and consequently had to resign from the Clipper baseball team. I wrote Mr. Weber to ask him to ship my belongings home. I thanked him for being kind and understanding, and at one point in the letter I assured him the Beaneaters were going to be the pride of Boston this coming season. I wanted to write Gene but didn't have his address. Occasionally I found myself thinking we might meet before leaving but would be reminded of something I needed to do and start to scold myself for such idle daydreaming. I packed for school, spent time with the family, and by reading late into the night finished Reverend Thomas's sermons and Professor Foster's book on Christianity.

That reading, I had told myself when I first got home, was just another chore I had to take care of. I could do it whenever and however I wanted to. If I had to, because there wasn't enough time or the writing was too dry, I could quickly flip through the books, stopping occasionally to pick up a particularly good illustration or maybe even a tidy summary statement that in a few sentences would tell me all I really needed to know. But instead of taking hold of those books and using them as I pleased, they began to take hold of me. I felt myself being pulled into their pages, at first with a mounting curiosity and then out of the conviction that they contained ideas I needed to hear and, what was much more important, I needed to respond to. One of the books I didn't like; the other I did. Both, though, had the same effect on me. They did what I had told myself I would not let happen; they turned me toward God. The turn was only a degree or two, but it was enough that in unguarded moments during the day or in the stillness of the night when I couldn't sleep, I began to ask a new question. I began to hear myself saying where are you God?

Foster's *The Finality of the Christian Religion* was disturbing. At the end of the book, all I was left with was myself. With the precision of a skilled surgeon, he had cut away the Bible and the Church and dumped them into the trash can. The Bible could not be trusted because no one knew where it had come from or how it had been altered over time. The Church, since it was not the exclusive vessel of God's revelation, had no right to require its members to live by its rules and by its pronouncements and, therefore, was not to be obeyed. Jesus was not divine; truth was not absolute; miracles did not occur; faith was not to be relied upon to determine what was of God and could be said about God.

With the trash bin now so full the lid wouldn't close, he moved from rejection to approval. What he approved of completely and enthusiastically was the individual. The personality and the experience of the individual were what could be relied on. The mind and the conscience of the individual were what determined truth and morality. He put the individual at the center of everything that existed, which is to say he put me at the center. Instead of immediately realizing this statement expressed exactly where I was placing myself and why I would be at the Training School in less than a week, I laughed at the idea and tossed the book into my trash can.

But after I stopped laughing, I began to question my strange response to George B. Foster, my very strange response indeed, given my insistence that God prove himself to me. After a moment's reflection, however, I understood that it, at least in part, had come out of my astronomy class at Vassar. I had seen that if it had been a huge mistake for so many great thinkers to put the earth at the center of the universe for all those centuries, it would be a colossal mistake to put myself there now. Neither I nor anyone else nor anything else belonged there—dare I say it?—only God did. But I also knew there had been another reason for my response. I was unwilling to throw away what was of God, including the Bible, the Church, the divinity of Christ, a truth that was absolute, miracles, and faith that surpassed reason. To do this would have been to throw away Pastor McNutt, Sister Emma, Mr. and Mrs. Meyer, and Hiram W. Thomas, which was unthinkable. In each, there was a beauty that unquestionably emerged from what was in this world, but some place within me—could it have been my soul?—was saying, and I wasn't about to deny it, that something so pure, so lovely could not possibly be of this world. After another moment of reflection, I suddenly realized in total wonderment that here I was defending God. What was happening to me?

The second book was somewhat like the first. In *Life and Sermons of Dr. H. W. Thomas*, orthodoxy was questioned and portions of it rejected, controversial ideas that some in the church thought not only wrong but heretical were proposed, and the Church itself was sharply criticized. But the book's impact upon me was far different. Instead of offending me, I found it compelling and even comforting. Because of what was said and, perhaps even more important, because of who said it, I began to catch myself, as I went through the day, thinking about God. That's not usually where my thoughts had started out. I had been thinking about something I wanted to say to Father, or to pack, or to tell Gene if I saw him again, but that's where they had somehow ended up. Could it be, I had to ask myself, that I was beginning to have God on my mind?

I found Dr. Thomas's sermon on the atonement particularly moving, moving in the sense of drawing God closer to me, or was it the other way around? Dr. Thomas dismissed the traditional explanation of Jesus' death on the cross, which he called the commercial view of the atonement. According to this understanding, the penalty for man's sin was transferred to Jesus. But how could this possibly be? he said. Making Jesus guilty, when he was blameless, was not only unjust but also, to use his word, illogical. Guilt was personal. It arose out of the individual's conscience, out of the individual's awareness of having sinned, and once it did take hold, it stayed with that individual until forgiveness was granted and restitution was made. Given this fact, it did not in any way logically follow that guilt could be passed from one person to another. To claim that it did was irrational.

After searching for what was rational, he finally realized where the problem lay. The direction wasn't right. What happened in the atonement was not man moving to a wrathful God who needed to be appeased, but God moving to a sinful man who needed to have his heart cleansed. The question, therefore, was not what would satisfy an angry God but rather how could God break into the unyielding heart? How could that heart be filled with enough sorrow for sin that righteousness was the consequence? The answer was love. "Love," Dr. Thomas said, "breaks the heart of stone." But, he went on, what was crucial to understand was that it was a particular kind of love: it was a love that suffered that melted the heart and purified it. This kind of love, the love of God that suffered death upon a cross, opened the sinful heart to God, who, because he loved this much, could be, in return, trusted, and believed, and loved.

The day Dr. Thomas understood the atonement this way he became so overwhelmed with joy he wept uncontrollably. He saw that God, who in his mind had always been distant and forbidding, loved him and loved the world. God, he now knew, was his Father who held him in a love that was even more tender than his mother's, and in this knowledge, Dr. Thomas knew himself to be forgiven by God. And there was more that day: he felt welling up within himself a tenderness for all mankind and a willingness to do anything God asked of him, no matter how difficult it might be or how much he might have to suffer because of it.

Suffering did come. There was so much of it and it cut so deeply, I couldn't help wondering if he might have been less willing to serve God had he known the heartache that awaited him. Removal from the Church didn't happen overnight. He endured suspicion, harsh criticism, and eventually unrestrained attack for more than five years. However wrenching that ordeal was, though, it hardly compared to what he suffered at home. Six of his seven children died in early childhood. The death of his sixth child, seven-year-old Lollie, was especially wrenching. The entire family had been ill for several weeks. Bedridden, Dr. Thomas asked that Lollie, who was feeling better, be brought to him. As she was leaving after a brief visit, she blew him a kiss, saying "a kiss papa." These were the last words he heard her speak. Suddenly the fever returned, and falling into a coma, she never regained consciousness. Although his fever was gone, he didn't have the strength to leave his bed and so was unable to see his daughter either before or after she died.

Lollie's death might have broken Dr. Thomas. It was that tragic and, I would also say, that cruel. But it didn't. Instead, her death made him more devout. In a letter he wrote to the Philosophical Society of Chicago after the death, Dr. Thomas spoke of Lollie cradled now in God's love and of the coming day when they would all be together again. Then he said that having been so long in the valley of sorrow, he had come to love its charms and had found in its darkness comfort. Having spent some time myself in the valley of sorrow because of Katie's death, I knew it was not a charming place. A tormenting place, a suffocating place, a shattering place, yes; but a charming place, never. To say that wandering alone and lost in the darkness brought comfort was like saying learning of my parents' separation had brought me happiness.

Where did these statements come from? I could think of only two possibilities: either a disturbed mind, which he did not have, or faith, an extraordinary faith. He closed the letter by saying that with his health restored, the time had come to take up the cause of Christ again, trusting that his suffering had brought him closer to the heart and to the needs of a suffering world. How did he get this faith that kept him from being overwhelmed by suffering and yet at the same time took him more fully into its grasp? Even more to the point, how did he, in the valley of the sorrow where he had been and where he was going, keep this faith? Was it constant or did it become stronger or weaker depending upon the day and the circumstance? If the day did come when he lost it altogether, could he ever regain it?

As I finished packing Sunday evening, I realized that along with my clothes and books I was also taking with me to the Training School all these questions. Would I find the answers there? I'll have to wait and see, I told myself. Then I began to smile. It had suddenly occurred to me that much of faith might be about waiting and seeing. If so, did that mean while I didn't really have faith was I, nevertheless, about to act faithfully? I seemed to have wandered into a contradiction. Would I in the days ahead be able to make my way out of it? Again I said, this time out loud, my smile widening, "I will just have to wait and see."

* * *

At Vassar in a history class I learned people, especially powerful and influential people, made history. This understanding gave me a way to approach the history of my own life, which I found myself looking at with increasing frequency during that first year at the Training School. I could see more clearly how my life had unfolded and why it had unfolded in a particular way if I concentrated upon those people who had influenced me. Soon, though, I became convinced people were not enough to explain the person I had become. A missing ingredient, I quickly realized, was event. Time and again it had been an event, a rather unremarkable event at that, that had brought someone into my life who had made something different, most often something entirely new, happen. A high school science class had brought into my life a teacher who had turned me toward Vassar; a foot race, actually three footraces, had brought into my life Liz Fleming who had introduced me to baseball; stealing home, which humiliated a bully on the mound, had brought into my life Maggie Watts who had made sure I was never again an outsider and who had opened my eyes to Gene, who became my first love; a wooden angel with a broken wing had brought into my life Sister Emma who had ushered me into, of all places, a religious training school.

Event delineated and sharpened, which is to say event clarified. I imagine Sister Emma, though, would tell me event did more than that: it revealed. I could just hear her saying, with her finger pointed at me, "Mattie, those events were arranged. Why, they were the work of God. They, my child, were God's providence."

Toward the end of my first year at the training school, providence, if that's what it was, entered my life again. Except for one annoyance, I was pleased with the school and its curriculum; I was content. I admired the teachers, and since I was always eager to learn something new, I enjoyed, for the most part, my classes. Visiting complete strangers in their homes, which we regularly did in pairs at least twice a week, was initially intimidating at best. I never knew what might be on the other side of that front door. Squalor, rage, illness, violence, loneliness, abandonment, despair were all real possibilities. It seemed like I had so little to give: a tract and a prayer, and if they were not wanted, then all I could do was smile, offer a kind word, and occasionally promise financial help which I knew would be, regardless of the circumstance, inadequate. Eventually, though, these visits became easier. Sometimes a need was met, or a problem was solved, or a wound was healed. Those other times, when this did not happen, the smile, the kind word, the financial assistance were, with few exceptions, gladly received.

I also liked being religious. Worship was uplifting, especially the singing and the praying. It seemed like we were always singing. Much of the music had power. It could move me to tears, to gratitude, even to reverence. Often I would catch myself at odd times humming one of the songs the girls sang with such devotion. Without being aware of it, they had obviously entered into, or should I say had snuck into, my stream of thought. Most definitely, we were always praying: after our meals, at the end of our classes, before our home visits, after our home visits, during our evening prayer meetings, at Sunday morning worship, and at any other time of the day or the night when a pressing need arose or an important matter had to be settled. We prayed so often on our knees I was sure that getting down to them and up from them was making my thighs stronger than ever.

But there was that one exception. There was, to borrow from Paul in 2 Corinthians, that one thorn in my side. The girls irritated me. It wasn't that they were unpleasant. Far from it. It was that they were from the very first day too pleasant, too kind, too friendly, too helpful, too cheerful, too pious. No tempers flared, no cross words were spoken, no wills clashed, and, what was most noticeable, no doubts or uneasiness about anything or anyone were raised. After Vassar and bloomer girls baseball, I believed that wherever there were people there would inevitably be discord. But here there was only harmony. I thought that Mrs. Meyer, whether it was intentional or not, was behind this strange, and I would even say eerie, serenity. Because of her piety and her forceful presence, both of which were felt even when she was absent, a standard of behavior had been set that the girls either tried to live up to or dared not deviate from. I, though, became increasingly convinced that appearances could not only be deceiving but were.

A day in early December proved me right. Once again, what happened in itself was not unusual. It was just another talk by another minister. Yet that talk turned out to be anything but ordinary. It was an event. It brought into our lives C. L. Goodell, D.D. with what was for many a shocking message. He told us it was a terrible thing for us to become Deaconesses and at some later time awaken to the truth that we have made a mistake. If we would be happy anywhere else, we must go there now; if we would be happy doing anything else, we must do it now. We should stay here only if we were willing to give what we have, all of what we have, to the task of saving lost souls. He ended by telling us about a missionary who was tied to a stake in five and a half feet of water. As the tide came in, the water rose above her neck and then above her mouth. Just before it covered her nose, she did not curse her executioners in anger or plead with them for her life. Rather, she declared her faith in Jesus and begged them to accept him as their Savior. If these would not have been your final words, he said after a long pause, you must not become a Deaconess.

Normally the halls at night were busy. Students were either coming or going, or they were in clusters talking to one another. But that night they were deserted. In various rooms behind closed doors, girls had gathered to discuss what was by now called "the address." Laura Aldrich and Eliza Campbell, who shared the room next to ours, had asked my roommate, Ellie Tyler, and me to stop by for a cup of tea. We all wanted to be Deaconesses and so were in the same classes and often ate together. Our conversations were sometimes personal; we talked about what we liked or didn't like. But they were always superficial. They never revealed what lay underneath. They never divulged who we really were on the inside. But tonight was different. Entering the room, I immediately knew that Laura was deeply troubled. The dazzling smile that made her otherwise ordinary features absolutely beautiful was gone. In its place was a tormented look I had never seen before. Even before we sat down, she blurted out, "I shouldn't be here. If I were about to drown on that stake, I know I wouldn't be thinking about Jesus. What am I going to do?"

Putting her arms around Laura, Ellie said, "Right here is exactly where you should be. If any of us would be thinking about Jesus on that stake or anywhere else, it would be you. Why, if someone is just trying to figure out what trolley car to take downtown, you'll find a way to bring Jesus into the conversation."

After we were all seated and the tea had been poured, Eliza said what I had been thinking, "Laura, you are the best student in the school. Your hand is up first when a question is asked in class; you get the top grade on the tests; your voice is the loudest, and the sweetest I might add, when we sing; you visit the most homes, pass out the most tracts, and bring the most people to Jesus. Just think of all you do for the sake of Jesus."

"But that's just it," Laura replied, barely above a whisper, "I don't do it for the sake of Jesus." She stopped. Wiping away a tear that had rolled down her cheek, she at last said in an even softer voice, "I do it for Daniel's sake."

"Who is Daniel?" I asked.

"He's the man I was going to marry. The wedding was to be in August three years ago, and if it had not been for Fort Flagler, I would now be where I belong, not here but on a farm in northern Wisconsin taking care of my husband and our children." Her voice trailed off.

"Fort Flagler on Marrowstone Island in Washington?" Eliza asked.

"That's the one, Eliza. I'm surprised you know about it," Laura said.

"My brother has been there since he joined the army last year. When he was home for Christmas, he couldn't stop talking about the fort and its huge guns."

"Did he say anything about Private Everett Frazee?"

"He did mention Private Frazee has been the only fatality since the fort opened. But he didn't tell us how he died other than to say it had been an accident."

"Daniel was in Everett's Company at the fort. They spent time together hiking in the woods on the island and fishing in the inlet. One morning their Company was sent to the firing range for small-arms practice. Everett was assigned the task of marking where the shots hit the target and sending the results to a scorer at the other end of the range. A corporal, seeing that Everett was standing too close to the target, told him several times to move away. Unaware of the danger, the men at the firing line continued to shoot. Then suddenly a red flag appeared, the signal that all firing must stop immediately. Everett had been hit in the chest with a rifle ball. Taken at once to the post hospital, he died there five hours later. An investigation of the death concluded it was accidental.

"Daniel was on the firing line that morning. He accepted the outcome of the investigation to begin with. Something, though, started to bother him, an uneasiness that instead of eventually going away only got worse. He eventually realized it wasn't a word or an action that had been tormenting him but a sound. He remembered that just before the red flag went up, he had heard a rifle fire, just one rifle fire, and that rifle, he was convinced, had been his. He had shot Everett Frazee. He had killed him.

"Those terrible words turned him into a different person. Before, he had believed, like the psalmist, that the Lord had made each new day and had rejoiced and been glad in it, but now that joy and gladness were gone. Guilt had taken their place, a guilt that consumed him, a guilt that squeezed the very life out of him. The army, his family, the minister of his church told him and the good Lord knows I kept telling him he could not be sure he had fired the last shot, and if he had, he could not be sure the last shot had killed Everett Frazee. Even if it had, he had not been the one at fault. Everett Frazee had been. He had stood too close to the target. But Daniel didn't listen to us. He broke off our engagement, gave up his dream of farming, and withdrew more deeply into a silent and impenetrable world of melancholy until the Daniel I loved was gone.

"He shut me out of his life. If I can't live with myself, he told me, I can't live with you. But I couldn't shut him out of mine. I couldn't shut him out of my heart. What he was feeling was not only wrong, but, according to our minister, it was sinful. Sin, he said, was anything that kept us from God and others. That was what his guilt was doing. It was as though his guilt had put Daniel in a dungeon. The walls were so thick and the door was so securely locked he couldn't get out and we couldn't get in. Our only hope was God. I went to church; I read the Bible; I prayed. At the time, it seemed like that was all I was doing. But nothing happened. God wasn't listening. I had to do something more to get his attention. Nothing seemed to be more difficult, and therefore more deserving, than being a Deaconess on the worst streets of Chicago. So I came here with the intention of becoming not just a good Deaconess, but the best Deaconess ever to put on the bonnet with white ties."

"Better than Mrs. Meyer?" Ellie asked.

"Yes," Laura answered, "even better than Mrs. Meyer. I have to be, because if I am, then maybe God will give me what I keep asking him for every day. Maybe he will free Daniel from his guilt and bring him back to life and to me."

"Laura, I came here for the same reason you did. I wanted to get someone's attention." Eliza said. "But it wasn't God's I was after; it was my father's."

"Is your father a Methodist minister?" Ellie asked. "My cousin talks about the minister of her church constantly. His last name is Campbell. She says he is the best preacher she's ever heard."

"That can't be my father," Eliza replied, "because my last name isn't Campbell. It's Cutler. Campbell is my mother's maiden name, which I have been using now for the last three years."

"Cutler is a familiar name," I said, "especially Arnold Cutler, the philanthropist, who is from all I have heard one of the most generous benefactors of the City. Is he your father?"

"Yes, though it makes me ill to admit it. He hasn't given away all that money to improve the City, although he's very happy that's what people think. He's done it to hide his crimes. When I was younger, I thought he was just vulgar. We had way too much of everything, while so many had way too little. That gap increasingly upset me, but he gloried in it. His display of wealth—the huge home we lived in on North Lake Shore Drive, the fine clothes we wore, the frightfully expensive restaurants we regularly ate in, the exotic trips we took—was shameful and nauseating.

"But the day came when my disgust turned into loathing. Following graduation from college, I worked for the Chicago Tribune as a secretary and on occasion as a reporter and lived at home. After supper one evening, I was the last to leave the table. As I got up from my chair, I noticed a folded piece of paper on the floor where Father had been sitting. At some point during the meal, it had fallen out of his pocket. I picked it up and, not really thinking about what I was doing, unfolded the paper and looked at the note scrawled on it. I still remember exactly what it said: 'My dear Arnold, your contribution has been gratefully received. Be assured your business interests will not be interfered with this year.' When I saw who had written the note, I understood exactly what those words meant. It had come from Michael Kenna, known to his confederates as Hinky-Dink, the senior Alderman of the first ward. The money he had gratefully received purchased his support on the City Council. What didn't go into his bank account went into the bank accounts of judges and police officials who closed their eyes to the prostitution and gambling that thrived in the Levee District. Father had bought protection from Hinky-Dink. He had to because on those streets he was selling sex in his brothels and taking money from spendthrifts at his gaming tables. By the end of the week, I had moved out of the house, and by the end of the month, I had changed my last name to Campbell.

"I knew I was in the presence of evil. Appalled and also frightened, I put as much distance between myself and Father as I possibly could. But I also needed to be close to Father to oppose this evil. Evil is cunning. It can enter into our thoughts, into our actions in devious ways that we are not even aware of. I had to be careful. Whatever I did, it had to be righteous and pure. It had to be of God. So I decided to become a Deaconess, and to confront my father and the vice he was profiting from, I decided to become a Deaconess in the Levee District."

"Hinky-Dink will be sorry to see you coming," I said.

"That's what I was counting on," Eliza replied.

"What you were counting on," Ellie said. "You aren't now?"

"No. I don't think goodness is enough. We help just a few and for most of those few for only awhile. Evil might be slowed down, but it certainly doesn't retreat or disappear. A fundamental change of some kind is needed, not just in the life of an individual, but in the way we live our lives."

"You've been reading Walter Rauschenbusch," Ellie said.

"Who is Walter Rauschenbush?" I asked.

"He's a Baptist minister," Ellie replied, "who for eleven years was pastor of a church in Hell's Kitchen, one of the poorest sections of New York City. In a very controversial book he has just written, he makes a number of harsh statements about society and the Church."

"I have read *Christianity and the Social Crisis*," Eliza said. "Actually I have read it twice, and when my exams are over, I'm going to read it a third time. He says in that book competition has corrupted business and the government, and it threatens the Church. If the Church can't Christianize commerce, he is convinced commerce can and will commercialize the Church. It will then serve mammon, not Christ. Competition in society, he insists, must give way to cooperation, and the emphasis in the Church on evangelizing the individual must give way to elevating humanity. A social mission, a prophetic voice, a call for the Kingdom of God are what is needed. I think he is right. Not bringing in the wayward but bringing in the Kingdom so God's will is done on earth as it is in heaven is the way, the only way, evil is to be bested, if it is to be bested at all.

"I will be leaving the Training School at the end of this term. I'll go back to the newspaper to investigate and write about the social issues the city faces today. If I am not allowed to, either because I am a woman, or because I am not a good enough reporter, I won't be discouraged, though, for there is something else I am going to do. When I was at college, I played the viola and sang. Performance, though, doesn't excite me; composition does. I've written songs and intend to write many more and will do whatever it takes to get them published and into the Church. The songs are not about coming to Jesus, but, as Micah 6:8 puts it, they are about 'doing justly, loving mercy, and walking humbly with our God.'"

We were silent for a moment, and then Ellie said, "The two of you came here because you wanted to do something. I came because

I saw something." She paused and looked down at her hands. We didn't know what might be coming next, if anything. Finally she looked up, apparently having made a decision of some kind, and continued, "I have never told anyone about this. I have been afraid to."

"You don't have to tell us, Ellie," I said.

"I want to and probably need to. I just hope you won't think I'm strange." Again she hesitated, but this time only briefly. "It actually wasn't something I saw, but someone. I saw Jesus."

"You had a vision of Jesus," Laura exclaimed.

"Visions," Ellie replied.

I hadn't expected anything like this. How could I? No one in a class, a sermon, a conversation of any kind had ever even said the word vision, let alone talked about having one, and in the religious books I had read, no one had ever written about a vision or visions either. It wasn't anywhere in the church's thinking, or at least the churches I knew anything about, that I was aware of. There was no place for it. While we could be emotional, most of all we were reasonable. Confess our sins, receive Jesus, commit our life to him, and we were saved. This progression was so reasonable it could be expressed in an equation. Moreover, our faith was systematic. We met Jesus in worship, in the Sacraments of Baptism and the Lord's Supper, in scripture, in preaching, in prayer. These meeting places were all part of a system that was also so reasonable it, too, could be factored into that equation. We, though, did not meet Jesus in a vision. A vision was too much like an apparition to be reasonable and way too unpredictable to be part of a system. It didn't fit into that equation. If added to it, the equation couldn't be solved.

Although the other girls were stunned as well, they recovered much more quickly than I did. Almost at once, they began to ask Ellie questions. How many times did you see Jesus? "Twice." What did he look like? "I didn't see his features, only the love on his face."

What was he wearing? "A robe." Did he say anything to you? "Not that I could hear." Did he come at a special time? "No."

"Why, Ellie, did he come?" Eliza asked, the most important question of all.

"The first time was a complete mystery, but maybe not the second time. When he first appeared, I couldn't be certain it was Jesus or that the vision had even happened. I might have imagined it, or it might have been a daydream of some sort. Even if I had been sure it was Jesus, he didn't tell me what he wanted me to do. So I did nothing. That, I believe, was why he appeared the second time. He has work for me to do but, for the life of me, I can't figure out what it is. That's what brought me to the Training School. If I am going to discover anywhere what that assignment is, most likely it's going to be here."

Visions got me thinking. Since they apparently were so puzzling, they had to be the work of the Holy Spirit. For, as John 3:8 says, the Spirit is like the wind. You can hear it, but you can't know where it's coming from or where it's going. The Spirit then must be like Nina's knuckleball. When she threw it, the ball could go up or down, in or out. Nobody, and that included Nina, knew where that pitch was headed. A huge mitt was needed to catch her knuckleball. I began to wonder how large a mitt might be needed to catch the Holy Spirit.

"Mattie," Laura said, "you're suddenly quiet. Have you also had a vision?"

"No, but I'd sure like to. It would give me the answer I'm looking for. Laura, you are here because you want God to do something for you. Eliza, you are going to leave because you want to do something for God. Ellie, you've come because you believe God wants you to do something. God, for all of you, is very real. But God isn't, or at least isn't yet, real for me. My closest friend was killed in a horrible train accident. Her death made no sense to me if there is a God and could easily be explained if there isn't. The train she was on simply went off the tracks. I need to know if God exists. Because of a little wooden angel with a broken wing, I met Sister Emma. She told me about the Training School and the work of the Deaconesses. What she said and what I was looking for fit together nicely. I needed to find a way to search for the truth about God. What better way could there be than to live among those who have already found that truth for themselves? No one at home or at the school knows why I'm really here, though I think Sister Emma suspects I have come for some other reason than wanting to help needy people for Jesus' sake."

"I think we're right back where we started from," Ellie said, smiling. "What are we going to do about Reverend C. L. Goodell and his stake with the tide coming in?"

"Nothing," Laura replied. "We can't possibly know what we would say unless we're actually on that stake of his."

"I think Sister Emma would agree," I said. "Have you noticed the vase on the top shelf of her bookcase?"

"Every time I look at it, I wonder if she will ever try to grow something in that dirt," Eliza said.

"That's not dirt, at least it's not to Sister Emma. She told me it's soil and that it's there to remind her why she's at the Training School. She's here not to make sure we say something in a particular circumstance but to help us become the good soil in Jesus' story about the sowing of the seed so we can hear and respond to what God is saying to us. Since that's reason enough for her to be here, I think it's more than reason enough for us."

"I do too," Ellie said. "But, Mattie, if you're not even sure God exists, why do you want to become the good soil?"

"Because I want to believe God exists."

"Although it's what you want, Mattie," Laura said, "can you, since you have this doubt, become the good soil?"

"She can," Eliza replied, "because it's what God wants too."

" You're saying the good soil is really about grace," Ellie said.

"It and everything else, yes," Eliza replied.

Having morning classes to prepare for, Ellie and I got up to leave. Before going, we all hugged one another. Without a word being spoken, we knew those embraces were a promise not to tell anyone what we had said and also an acknowledgment that because of what we did say, we were now bound together. The other girls, I'm sure, would have added we were now bound together before God.

Back in our room, Ellie, sitting down in the nearest chair, exclaimed, "God was there; I could feel him."

"I just thought the heat had been turned up too high."

"Oh, Mattie, God is not going to tap you on the shoulder and say, 'Let me introduce myself.' He's way too sneaky for that. He's not there where you think he should be, and then all of a sudden there he is where you're sure he won't be. You can't ever know what God is going to do next. You've just got to be ready for him."

"I'm trying to do that, Ellie," I said, thinking once again of Nina's knuckleball.

"I'm awfully glad I told everyone all about myself."

"I'm happy I did too"

Although I hadn't. That night, because of Reverend C. L. Goodell, I looked not only into the hearts of the other girls but also into mine. I had glanced at what was there before, but maybe because I was too timid, or too unprepared, or too unsure of myself and of what was happening I had then shut my eyes to it. I had covered it up. Their willingness to disclose what they had been keeping from everyone else gave me the courage to uncover what I had been keeping from myself. I opened my eyes to it and there it was, not for all to see, I wasn't ready for that, but for me to see and to lose myself in, and, at the same time, to find myself in. I was in love—and it wasn't with Jesus.

* * *

It began, I suppose, last spring. Although the University of Chicago was within easy walking distance of the training school, I hadn't paid much attention to it. Then one lovely Saturday morning Sister Emma asked if I might like to go there for a track meet. Since I had nothing else planned and the idea of a college track meet intrigued me, I gladly accepted. When we arrived, however, I saw at once that the athletes were too young to be in college. Sister Emma explained they were in high school, but, she emphasized, this was not by any means an ordinary high school track meet. There was nothing else like it west of the Ohio River. More than seventy-five high schools had come to the meet from Illinois, Indiana, Ohio, Missouri, Minnesota, Nebraska, and Kentucky.

"My goodness," I said. "It's wonderful the University does this. Organizing and running a competition of this size must take an enormous amount of time, effort, and, I imagine, money."

"The University doesn't do it." Pointing to a muscular young man on the infield of the track, Sister Emma replied, "He does."

"Who is that?"

"That, Mattie, is Amos Alonzo Stagg."

"Well, then, it's wonderful he's doing this for the high schools."

"He isn't. He's doing it for himself. Mr. Stagg is the University's football coach. Every spring he brings the track teams here so he can determine which athletes are strong enough and fast enough to play for him, and then during the summer he recruits them for his football team. He is very successful at what he does. Although the school opened just fifteen years ago, the University of Chicago today is one of the most powerful football teams in the nation. It went undefeated two years ago, scoring in ten games 245 points while the opposing teams combined scored a total of 5 points, and it lost only one game last year. The season this fall opens against Indiana University. Why don't we see it together."

"I'd love to, Sister Emma. I' ve read about football but have never gone to a game. Over the summer, I'll review the rules and try to find out what a team does to beat its opponent, the formations it uses, the plays it runs."

Because of illness in the family, Sister Emma wasn't able to attend the game, and the girls I asked to go with me either were too busy or weren't interested. Not wanting to miss it, I went alone. Getting there just before the game started, I saw that the only available seating was in the far corner of the stands. Going about half way up, I sat down right next to the steps. Twenty minutes into the game, I noticed a tall, heavyset man, who was probably in his late twenties, coming up the steps. Before sitting down three rows in front of me, he glanced at me and smiled. His face was familiar. I had seen him before, but at first couldn't recall where. Then it suddenly came to me. An instructor in the sociology department at the University of Chicago, he had given a lecture last winter at the Training School on urban growth and social displacement. Afterward, I had asked him a question about the market on Maxwell Street. He seemed pleased with my interest and said that he had been studying the developments in that area for some time. As he talked, I was struck by how much he knew and how eager he was to share it. Could he have possibly remembered me after all these months? Even though the game was thrilling—it was a stunning mixture of speed, power, skill, and teamwork—I often caught myself looking at him. He interested me for two reasons—well, actually for three. To begin with, because of his sharp, penetrating features that projected both strength and intelligence tempered, I thought, by kindness, by decency, he was definitely good-looking. Then there was the back of his hand. On it there was a very noticeable scar. Obviously that part of the hand had been burned somehow. Most fascinating, though, was his indifference. He didn't seem to care if Chicago won or lost. He had been late for the game, perhaps because he had decided to come only at the last minute or he had simply not wanted to see all of it, and when Chicago made a touchdown and everyone else got up to cheer, he remained seated.

The game moved along quickly. It was well played, and Chicago was comfortably ahead. I was thoroughly enjoying myself. It was one of those moments when everything seemed to be right with the world. But it was only for a moment. Out of the corner of my eye, I all at once noticed at the end of the field a man knock a woman down, grab her purse, and start to run. Instantly, I charged down the steps and ran after him. Within seventy-five yards, I had nearly caught up to him. But he suddenly surged ahead. Afraid he might get away, I threw myself at him, completely leaving my feet. I caught him around the waist and wrestled him to the ground. At the beginning, I was on top of him, but being stronger than I, he rolled me over onto my back. I saw his fingers curl into a fist and, pulling his arm back, he was about to hit me. Then I hear him yell in pain. Someone had pulled him off me and, throwing him to the ground, had his knee in his back. "Move," he said to the man, "and I will break it." What it referred to was unclear, maybe his back, or his arm, or quite possibly his neck, but the man was not about to ask. He lay perfectly still until the police came five minutes later.

The girls at the Training School would have said I have a guardian angel. I was happy, though, to see that the person who had rescued me was not an angel but the sociology instructor. Turning to me, after the man had been taken into custody, he asked, "Are you all right?"

"I'm fine, thanks to you."

"When you left the stands, I followed you, but you outran me. I didn't know a woman could run so fast. I have made a few flying tackles myself but none like yours. If Coach Stagg had seen you, he'd have you in a Chicago uniform. My name is Samuel Bingham."

"I know. You gave a lecture at the Training School," I said.

"If I remember correctly, you asked a question about Maxwell Street."

"I did."

"Please tell me your name so I can give it to Coach Stagg the next time I see him."

"Mattie Welsh," I replied smiling.

"Miss Welsh, you do have the most unusual abilities. I would like to find out more about them, but I have to go. A meeting I arranged will be starting without me if I don't hurry."

Once more, I found myself looking at his back. It would be nice, I thought, if I could get him to turn around and to stay put for a while. But how was that going to happen? He probably wouldn't be coming to the Training School again, and I certainly couldn't attend one of his classes. But there was another football game, and when I checked the schedule, I saw that it was three weeks away. That was more than enough time for him to have forgotten me. He had classes to teach and more meetings to attend. He might have someone he was interested in. He might even have a wife and children. I did, however, go to the game, and since Sister Emma didn't say anything about it, I was there alone. Again, I sat at the far end of the field. Ten, fifteen, twenty minutes went by, and just when I was sure he wasn't coming, I saw him start up the steps. He passed one row after another until he stood in front of the one I was in. Waving, he asked if he might sit next to me. Not wanting to appear too forward, I smiled, nodded yes, and then continued to watch the game.

"I'm surprised you are here, Miss Welsh," he said, after play had been stopped for a time-out.

"Why, Mr. Bingham, it's a beautiful Saturday afternoon, and I do like football," I replied.

"No, I mean I'm surprised you are here in the stands and not on the field. Didn't you get Coach Stagg's call?"

"The telephone at the Training School hasn't been working. Maybe it'll be repaired in time for the next game."

Laughing, he said, "Have you recovered from your brawl with that thief?"

"It left some bruises, but I'm fine now. I'm somewhat used to being restrained, but not quite like that."

"You've been assaulted before?"

"That's one way to put it. I've played baseball against men, and they were not always, shall I say, polite."

"You played bloomer girls baseball?"

"Yes."

"I saw one of their games," he said. "The girls were good, and with your speed and agility, I imagine you were among the best. The men were hardly chivalrous, and when they fell behind, some of them became mean. I guess, though, the game can turn nasty no matter who plays it. My sister told me her college has banned baseball because the administration thinks the game corrupts the girls. They say it makes them obnoxious competitors who bear no resemblance to the refined young ladies the school is supposed to be sending out into the world."

"What college is this?"

"Vassar."

"That's where I went to school."

"You played baseball there?"

"I did."

"She's upset she can't play baseball and is really upset she missed by only a few years playing baseball with girls who had exceptional skills, especially one who hit a ball through the window of the chapel. That ball, according to my sister, would have not only gone over the fence at a major league field, it would have gone over the bleachers. My sister said her name was Maggie. I don't remember the last name."

"Where did you play football?"

"Here. I was the center on the school's first team. Just twelve students came out for football when the University opened, and there were only a half dozen of us at many of the practices. We were so new to the game Coach Stagg had to play to make us competitive. Even with him, we won only one game. But we got better. The next year we won six games and the year after that eleven of the nineteen games we played. That third year we went to San Francisco in December to play Leland Stanford Junior University. Each school had a different reason for a game requiring more than six thousand miles of round-trip travel: Leland Stanford wanted to make money, Chicago wanted the publicity. On the way there, I got this." He took off his coat, although it was a cold, windy day, and rolled up his shirt sleeve, revealing the scar I had seen before. "We went west in a private railroad car. When it had been offered to Coach Stagg, he immediately accepted the car without seeing it. When the newspapers described the car, they wrote about its elegant furnishings also without seeing it. When we did see it, we were speechless, not because the car was so grand, but because it was so awful. It was a condemned Pullman car with flat wheels, peeling paint, and sides and a roof that either bulged or sagged depending upon what part of it you were looking at. Late at night, going up the Rocky Mountains, the car caught on fire. A coal stove had become too hot. Fighting the fire with axes and water, we finally put it out but not before I had badly burned my hand and arm. They were still tender when the new season began in the fall, so I didn't play football my senior year."

"Were you disappointed?"

"Not really. I most likely would have been sitting up here in the stands that last year anyway. I had always liked football because it was a game. Winning wasn't the point. Playing hard, improving, being a team was. But I realized, particularly because of the trip to California, football here was becoming much more than a game. We had to play as many games as possible, and we had to win all those games for the sake of the University. A winning football team advertised the school and made it money. Football was becoming a business. I didn't want to be a part of it then. I don't want to be a part of it now."

"Is that why you come late to the games and sit while everyone else is on their feet cheering?" I asked.

"Yes. It accomplishes nothing, I know, but these tiny acts of protest are important to me. What I saw coming did happen and much quicker than I had expected. Turning football into a product was expensive."

"I imagine equipment, travel, and recruiting did cost a lot of money."

"The cost had nothing to do with money, Miss Welsh. That the University either had or could get. It had to do with the school itself. It became smaller. It shrank. To get the best talent, the school waived admission requirements. Top prospects enrolled with poor grades, without having taken the necessary college preparatory classes, even without having graduated from high school. To keep these players eligible, the school suspended its academic standards. Class loads were lightened, courses were made easier, exams were made less demanding, particularly if a test had been failed and needed to be retaken. It was costly for the players too. They became smaller. They shrank. Training year-round took away their time; coming to the University not to learn but to play football took away their opportunity to be well educated; enduring long, grueling practice sessions and being under enormous pressure to win took away their enjoyment; being punched, gouged, kicked after a tackle or in a pile-on, being rammed into by a wedge of opposing players took away their health. This kind of football had its greatest success in 1905."

"Wasn't that the year Chicago went undefeated?"

"Not only undefeated, but, with the exception of one game, unscored upon. When Chicago beat Michigan the final game of the season, the school celebrated with bonfires and parades for three days. But there was a dark underside to that achievement. One had only to look at its spectacular quarterback, Walter Eckersall, to see it. Weighing just 136 pounds, he wasn't hard to bring down. Almost anybody on the field could do that. But because he was so fast and shifty, only a few could catch up with him and even fewer grab hold of him. Eckersall, however, should never have been at the University. He didn't have the grades in high school to be admitted. Once here, right from the beginning, he missed so many classes and failed so many tests he should not have been allowed to stay. But the school instead of expelling him honored him. During the half-time of his final game, it gave him a gold watch to thank him for his contribution to the University.

"Not everyone, though, applauded the accomplishments of the football team. Many faculty members denounced the violence of the game, especially the mass tackling, and the disgrace in the classroom. Two days after the Michigan game, a motion was made at the University Senate, the school's highest academic legislative body, to abolish football. The chairman of my department, Albion Small, and other supporters of Coach Stagg countered with a more moderate motion. Allow the game to continue, they said, but end its abuses. From the intense discussions that followed over the next several weeks two proposals emerged: suspend football or reform it."

"Which did you want?" I asked.

"To get it right, I thought the program had to be taken apart and then put back together in a new way, in a better way. So, I favored suspension. But the reformers prevailed. The University Senate voted to accept the proposals of the conference's governing body aimed at making the game safer and the players better students.

There have been changes. A student now can play football at the University no more than three years and only after his first year has been successfully completed. To enter the University, he must satisfy its admission requirements, and to be eligible to play, he must take a full course load."

"But you are still worried."

"Yes. The faculty has turned to other matters, and I'm afraid they won't get back to football any time soon, if they ever do. Left to itself, the program will go back to its old ways. I don't think football at the University of Chicago will ever be just a game again."

He then asked me about bloomer girls baseball. By the time I had finished describing the team and some of the precarious situations I had found myself in, the football game was over. Since the crowd had cheered almost constantly, we knew Chicago had won but had to ask the person in front of us what the final score was. When he told us 56 to 0, we looked at each other in complete surprise.

"We missed a whole lot of long runs," Mr. Bingham said.

"And a whole lot of touchdowns," I added.

"The final game of the season is two weeks from now. I intend to be here, Miss Welch."

"That also is my intention, though I do plan to come thirty minutes late."

Walking back to the training school, I thought about the game. Although it had lasted more than two hours, why had we never really seen it? Was it because even when we had been looking at it, we had only seen each other? I was also thinking about Gene. Why hadn't I told Mr. Bingham about him? Of all my teammates, he was the one I had been closest to and a large part of the reason, other than the game itself, why I had loved playing baseball. I was also thinking about a new feeling I had that didn't seem to be going away. Where exactly did it come from, my chest, my stomach, or possibly my heart? What did it mean? Most important, did Mr. Bingham have this feeling too?

Two weeks later the weather had turned cold and damp. Leaving the Training School for the University, I tightened the scarf around my neck and dug my hands deeper into the pockets of the winter coat I was wearing. Overhead the clouds were dark and heavy. Snow was coming; hopefully, though, it would hold off at least until the game was over. When I reached the field, I looked at my watch. Play had started twenty minutes ago. I could hear Mr. Bingham saying I was right on time. Looking up in the stands at our spot, I saw he was already there. Even before I sat down, he said, "You did it."

"Oh my, what have I done now?"

"You hit that ball at Vassar. Last week, I started to think the name of the girl who broke the chapel window might have been Mattie, not Maggie. The other night I called my sister. She said, as every student in the school knows, the name on the commemorative plaque in the chapel is Mattie Welsh. Why didn't you tell me?"

"You didn't ask."

"Did I need to?"

"Yes."

"You're way too modest, Miss Welsh," he said.

"It's not modesty," I replied, "it's guilt. That ball went through a very expensive window. If the school had not been so forgiving, I would be paying for its repair the rest of my life. I'd like to forget all about it."

"Others certainly don't want to. That hit of yours has made you famous, at least in Poughkeepsie, New York."

"Mr. Bingham, you are embarrassing me," I said, tapping him lightly on the arm. I began to watch what was happening on the field. The other team had the ball close to their end zone. On the next play, the quarterback threw the ball in a perfect spiral to one of his players, who caught it on the fifty yard line and then ran an additional fifteen yards before being tackled.

"Is that throw legal?" I asked.

"The forward pass has been allowed since last year."

"Why doesn't Chicago use it?"

"No one on the team can throw the ball decently."

"The other team is small," I said, "and it doesn't have many players."

"But it's fast and deceptive, and it is also inventive. A few years ago, the coach had a piece of elastic sewn inside a player's jersey. When he was given the ball at a critical point in the game, he put it under his shirt, where it was held in place by the elastic band, and jogged down the field. The other team didn't even look at him. A few yards from the goal line he stopped, took the ball out of his jersey, and then went into the end zone for a touchdown. The team, though, has used the hidden ball play only once. The coach has decided it isn't the right way to win a game."

"What team is this?"

"The Carlisle Indians," Mr. Bingham answered.

"I have never heard of that college before. Where is it?"

"It's in Carlisle, Pennsylvania. You probably haven't heard of it because it's not a college, but a trade school."

"Only Indians go there?" I said.

"Yes. It was started by an army officer, Henry Pratt, in the late 1870s. While others thought Indians should be put on a reservation and kept there, he believed they needed to be assimilated into society. He felt if they were properly educated and trained, Indians could live among us and do well. At his insistence, the government eventually agreed to establish the industrial school he wanted at an unused military post. The school since then has thrived and so has its football team. At first, Lieutenant Pratt, at that time the superintendent of the school, was opposed to football because of the injuries. The students, though, were adamant. So he finally agreed to start a program. There were, however, two conditions: they could not punch other players, if they did they would all be called savages, and within four years, they must be the best team in the nation. They accepted the conditions and have complied with them fully. They are today a formidable football team."

"And they are going to get even better," the person sitting on the other side of Mr. Bingham said. He was an older gentleman with a weather-beaten face and a friendly smile.

"Why is that?" Mr. Bingham asked, turning toward him.

"Because of the player sitting at the end of the bench."

"He is wide" I said. "If that girth can be turned into muscle, he will be hard to stop."

"Not him," the man replied, "the player beside him."

"The wiry one? If you look at him sideways, he almost disappears," Mr. Bingham said.

"That's the one, all right. My nephew lives in Carlisle. One afternoon this past spring, he was doing some outside maintenance work at the Industrial School. The track team was practicing at that time. He noticed some of the boys working on the high jump. One called out he was setting the bar at five feet nine inches, an inch above the school record. They made several attempts, but no one came close to clearing the bar at that height. A boy who had been watching them asked if he might try. He went right over the bar, which was impressive. After all, it was a new school record. But what was even more impressive was he had gone over the bar wearing overalls. My nephew said that the coach immediately put him on the track team, and at the last meet of the season, he set several more school records.

"This fall he decided to play football. The coach, though, didn't want his newly discovered track star to get hurt. But the boy was persistent. The coach knew he had to find a way to discourage him. So he gave him the ball one day at practice and told him to run at the defensive team. He figured once the boy had been knocked to the ground and piled on, he would realize he was too small for football and go back to track. With no one to block for him, he ran at the defense and with his speed and deceptive movements went right through the entire team. When he ran at them a second time and again they were unable to bring him down, the coach gave him a uniform, but has kept him on the bench until he puts on more weight. My nephew insists when that time comes, and he is sure it will, he will be one of the best to have ever played the game."

"What's his name?" Mr. Bingham asked.

"Jim Thorpe," the man answered.

This time we did watch the game. Carlisle was clearly the better team that afternoon. Chicago appeared sluggish compared to their quickness and cunning. "They win," Mr. Bingham said, "because they play smart football."

"I can see that," I replied. "They must have a smart coach."

"They have a very smart coach. Glenn Warner is affectionately called 'Pop' by those who know him. But those who know about him, about the way he plays football, have another name for him. They call him 'The Old Fox.'"

"He relies on the forward pass."

"He does. But that is only part of what he is doing. Have you noticed the way Chicago's backfield is lined up on offense?"

"I have. It's symmetrical, maybe a better word is balanced. One player is right behind the center and behind him are three players in a tight, even formation."

"That's right."

"Carlisle, though, is using an asymmetrical formation. The backfield is on a diagonal to one side, and the center, instead of handing the ball off to start the play, passes it through his legs to one of the players a good distance behind him. Their players have more room to run at the beginning of the play. They can start one way and suddenly go another. That unbalanced formation confuses Chicago even before the play begins. Not sure where the play is going, they don't know where to position themselves, which makes them hesitant, and hesitation makes them slow to respond to what is coming at them. Carlisle on every play they run has the advantage. That advantage is not just smart, it's cunning. It wins football games."

"Have you ever thought about coaching football, Miss Welsh?"

"Enough of your foolishness, Mr. Bingham," I said, hitting him once more on the arm, this time a little harder than before. As he smiled at me, I suddenly wondered if that punch, though it really had only been a playful tap, had in some mysterious way made us intimate. Because of it had we just now stepped into a new world of our own, a secret world that only the two of us would inhabit? That strange feeling within me began to stir again. If I had to name that feeling, I was beginning to realize I would call it desire; I would call it longing.

During the breaks in the game, especially between the two halves, we got to know each other better. I told him about Vassar and the Training School and then about wanting to become a Deaconess. After I was finished, he began to talk about his year at Newton Theological Institution. He went there after graduating from Chicago to become a Baptist preacher. Eventually, though, he ran into a wall he couldn't get past. I thought the issue must have been God, or the church, or a doctrine of some kind. I was more than a little surprised when he said the problem had been Jesus, and still was.

"The more I studied," he said, "the shiftier he became. He'd start off in one direction then suddenly be headed in the opposite direction. He would be strong, driving out the money changers, calming the storm, raising the dead, then all at once be weak, hiding, running away, and, one could argue, in the end giving up. He'd be smart, perhaps an even better word is shrewd, outwitting his adversaries with answers to their questions that reduced them to silence, then be dull, a better word here might be mindless, healing on the Sabbath, sending pigs over a cliff, having nothing to say in his own defense before others who would determine his fate. He would be compassionate, healing the sick, then be merciless, leaving others who were even sicker behind while he went elsewhere for a new round of healing. He was successful, attracting great crowds of adoring followers who wanted to make him king, then a failure, driving away everyone until he was all alone, dead on a cross, and then buried in another's tomb. I never knew where he was going next."

At that moment, a time-out ended, and Carlisle got into its asymmetrical formation, ready to begin another play. We watched it start to the left and then sharply veer to the right. The player with the ball gained twenty yards before being tackled. "Jesus would fit right into the Carlisle backfield," Mr. Bingham said, laughing. "'The Old Fox' would have him carrying the ball all the time."

"Since he was for me more a question than an answer," Mr. Bingham went on, "I decided to leave Newton and become a teacher. I returned to Chicago and got a graduate degree in sociology. The University then offered me a teaching position in its sociology department. I divide my time between the classroom and research, which Chicago not only expects of its instructors but requires."

"What do you research?" I asked.

"Social groups interest me, their institutions and their behavior, particularly their religious behavior."

"Is that why you know so much about the Carlisle Indian Industrial School?"

"I have looked into the school and its history, initially because of its football team and then because of the progressive and I would also say the courageous thinking of the people who have made it successful."

Carlisle won the game 18 to 4. No one around us got up to leave. Most likely the others remained seated because they were still feeling the sting of defeat. It was Chicago's first and, since this was the final game, only loss of the season. I didn't move because I was thinking Samuel was going to vanish. We would part, and he would become nothing more to me than a memory and I wanted more than that. Neither of us spoke for a long moment, and then Samuel put his hand on mine, which wasn't that romantic since we were both wearing heavy gloves, and said, "There are no more Saturday afternoon games. Miss, Welsh, I'd like to see you again."

"I would like to see you too." I paused, and then added, "But I must insist on two conditions."

"They are?"

"First, you must not come to the Training School. A Deaconess license is issued only to girls who are single. I don't want anyone to wonder how involved we are or might become. If this is acceptable, then the second condition is you must call me Mattie."

"I promise, Mattie, I will stay at least two blocks away from the Training School."

"You had better make it three."

"Three it is. Now I do have a condition of my own."

"Which is?"

"You must call me Samuel."

"That, Samuel, I promise to do."

Usually I had no trouble sleeping. But that Saturday night after the football game I did. I kept thinking about the afternoon, what we talked about, what it felt like to be next to him, what it felt like to have his hand on mine, and what it might have felt like if we had not been wearing gloves. I thought about how considerate, how intelligent, how principled he was. I thought about how much I admired him and, what was probably even more important, how much I felt attracted to him. Something within me or even possibly beyond me was pulling me toward him. I didn't know what it was, or where it was coming from, or why it had so much power over me. I only knew it was there.

Most of all, though, I thought about what we had not said but, I felt sure, had both understood. We were two people headed in different directions, he toward a career in the University, I toward a religious order that required of its members a celibate life. But we liked each other, maybe even more than liked each other, and were willing to see what the future held for us. Maybe something would come out of our time together, maybe something wouldn't. It was out of our hands. But if it was out of our hands, in whose hands was it? Was it in God's hands? I quickly rejected this thought. But I couldn't deny the unlikely chain of events that had brought us to where we now were. Because Sister Emma had taken me to the spring track meet, I knew the University had a football team. Because I went to the first football game even though Sister Emma wasn't able to, and because I sat in the far end of the stands, I saw Samuel. Because he had given a lecture at the Training School, and because I had asked him a question after it was over, I was interested in him. Because a thief had run off with a woman's purse, and because I ran after him and Samuel ran after me, I met him. Because I now have a mysterious feeling somewhere inside of me and apparently he does too, we are going to spend more time together. I had to admit these were a lot of becauses coincidence had to explain. If coincidence couldn't, then what could? Several hours had by now gone by and my mind had finally worn itself out. Too tired to rearrange my covers, I closed my eyes and at once fell asleep.

* * *

We began seeing each other Saturday and sometimes Sunday afternoon. At first, we met at the University. Cobb Hall always had an empty classroom. We'd first eat sandwiches Samuel brought, and then I would study while he prepared a lecture for one of his classes. Occasionally we went to the reading room of the library, which I liked because sitting across from each other, he would put his foot next to mine underneath the table. Usually we ended the day at the Bartlett Gymnasium where we played basketball. A few others would be there, but since it was a large room with several baskets on the walls, we'd have a hoop to ourselves. While guarding each other, we would see who could make the most baskets. I was at a real disadvantage, which I kept telling Samuel about and he, with an impish smile, kept ignoring. He had played three years of varsity basketball in high school and had even been the captain of his team when he was a senior. I, though, had probably shot the ball no more than a dozen times in my entire life and am quite sure I had never once made a basket. So, although I could defend tenaciously, I didn't have much offense. We, nonetheless, had great fun chasing after each other, running after the ball when my shots went astray, which they almost always did, and, of course, teasing one another. Nothing, however, compared to the afternoon we collided. Dribbling the ball, he darted toward me and I, at the same time, lunged toward him. Neither one of us stopped. As the ball bounced away, he first grabbed me, to hold me up, and then drawing me to himself, held me in his arms. As I put my arms around him, he kissed me. That was my first kiss, there in the gymnasium of the University of Chicago while others around us were shooting baskets.

Before long, we were also spending time in the nearby city parks. Jackson Park on the lakefront was delightful. When the snow wasn't too deep, I'd take Samuel's arm, and we would stroll down its walkway at the edge of the water. A sign at the entrance to the park gave directions to the golf course. Whenever we saw it, we always talked about playing golf in the spring and who would have the lower score. I insisted I would, although I had never swung a golf club, because I could swing a bat. He never found my reasoning very convincing. His only comment was "just because you can jump that doesn't mean you will be a champion high jumper."

Our favorite park, though, was White City, only a dozen blocks south of the Training School. The South Avenue Rapid Transit took us there in minutes. Its lovely gardens and walking paths were just the beginning of the park's seemingly endless attractions. There was a ballroom large enough for a thousand dancers, a restaurant that could seat over two thousand customers, a wild animal show, a flying airship, a scenic railway, a shoot-the-chutes ride, a Chicago Fire exhibit. We decided to see and do it all.

It took five trips to the park to work our way down our list until only the dance floor was left. It wasn't at the bottom of our list by chance. We had put it there intentionally not because we didn't want to dance, we did, but because we didn't know how to dance. Samuel had never danced before. Although I had danced with my father, I had been four at the time and he had done all the dancing. But we were not going to be deterred. What we didn't know we could learn. We studied carefully those who did know, the hundreds of couples on the dance floor. We drew a diagram of their movements on a paper napkin Samuel had taken from a nearby table and discussed those movements and memorized them. Subscribing to the axiom there is no substitute for experience, we stepped onto the dance floor and waited for the music to begin. When it did, while looking at the floor, we awkwardly moved our feet, trying to duplicate the steps on the napkin. Before the second dance started, Samuel suggested we look up and let the music move us. This helped, and by the end of the third dance we were doing much better, although he still did at times step on my toes and I more than once swung to the left when I should have been swinging to the right. We laughed at our mistakes and at ourselves, which made our dancing, if it could be called that, all the more wonderful. During our last dance of the day, as I held

Samuel tightly, I looked up at him and said, "I'm happy" and then unexpectedly said to myself "and joyful."

As we were leaving the park, Samuel said, "Mattie, you are so quiet. Is something troubling you?"

"No. I'm just thinking."

"About what?"

"Is there a difference between happiness and joy?"

"Now that is a question for a theologian," he replied. Since he didn't say anything else, I thought that was his answer. But he then seemed distracted. It was as though he had left me. This had happened before, actually it had happened several time before, so I knew what he was doing. He was trying to work something out in his mind; he was putting thoughts together in different ways in an effort to understand something, to clarify something. I knew he would come back to me when he had the answer he had been searching for. He did. "I think," he said, "one is happy when something feels good. One, however, is joyful when something feels right. Happiness is about satisfying one's desires; joy is about satisfying God."

"Can one be both happy and joyful?"

"If what one wants is also what God wants."

"Do the two feel the same?" I asked.

"Happiness makes one glad; joy, because one is necessarily in God's will, brings one peace. There is a difference between feeling glad and feeling at peace, a big difference, I think."

At that moment a stray dog crossed the sidewalk in front of us. As we watched it go down a side street, Samuel began to tell me about his cousin's dog. I thought the story an annoying digression but, to be kind, I appeared interested. Apparently the dog roamed during the day, forcing his cousin, who was a farmer, to go looking for him at night. Since he knew the dog loved to run free on the farm, his cousin didn't want to put him inside a fence. But he couldn't figure out how to bring him home when it got dark. He tried calling his name, ringing a bell, blowing a whistle, but nothing worked. Almost out of desperation, for by now his cousin dreaded the thought of spending his evenings searching for the dog, he finally had an idea. In the morning, he fixed the dog a special breakfast and at night an extra special dinner. The next day, when it started to get dark, the dog was at the front door wanting to come in. "Food," Samuel said, "had brought him home. Now that's what I call a clever solution."

A thought struck me with enough force I shivered. When Samuel asked if I would like his coat, I shook my head and said I instead wanted to take his arm. As we walked on, I considered what had just occurred to me. Perhaps I wasn't the only one doing the hunting. Maybe God had been hunting me all along and was using love to bring me home to him. After all, wasn't there in 1st John 4 the statement that love is of God, and all who love are born of God and know God, for God is love? I found myself saying, "You, God, are the clever one."

* * *

I didn't know Samuel as well as I thought I did.

During supper one evening midway into the winter session of my second year at the Training School, the girls were talking about home visits they had recently made. Martha, a first-year student, told us about helping a five-year-old make a snowman. Then Ellie, my roommate, said, "This afternoon I was visiting families in the Halsted neighborhood. Who do you think I saw coming out of a one story wooden shack on Fourteenth Place?"

"I give up, Ellie," Laura said, "who?"

"Do you remember the young sociology instructor from the University of Chicago who talked to us last spring about immigrants?"

"The one with the broad shoulders and the dreamy blue eyes," Hazel, a high-spirited girl studying to become a nurse, said. "I spent most of my time during that lecture looking at him rather than thinking about what he was saying. I've forgotten his name."

"It's Mr. Bingham," Ellie responded, "Samuel Bingham. He came up the street toward me, so I introduced myself. After we had talked about the increasing congestion on Halsted, I asked him if he knew someone in that shack, thinking if there was a need of some kind maybe I could help. He said no, and then realizing I was probably wondering why he had been there, he added that was where he lived."

"He lives on Fourteenth Place off Halsted?" I said, so surprised I dropped my fork onto my plate, startling everyone including myself.

"In between a kosher meat market and a tobacco shop with display signs written in Hebrew," Ellie replied.

I had always assumed Samuel lived near the University. It surprised me, even troubled me, he had never said anything about a shack in a rundown Jewish neighborhood. While I was hardly ready for this information, I was totally unprepared for what came next.

"Now I remember where I've run across his name before," Laura said. "Samuel Bingham has been writing those radical articles in the newspaper about taking power away from the wealthy and giving it to the people. Apparently he has made enemies in high places. They are claiming he is a socialist and for the sake of the city must be silenced. He says he is a Fabian socialist and for the future of the city, he must be heard."

I had to defend Samuel. I had to tell the girls what he stood for, what he meant to me. But what could I say? The truth was there right in front of me, and I couldn't change it or make it go away. At that moment, I didn't know who he was. But I did know that tomorrow I was going to find out.

The next afternoon, instead of making my assigned home visits, I went to the University. A cheerful young woman in the Administration Office told me Mr. Bingham was teaching his last class of the day in room 17 of Cobb Hall. Better run along, she added with a friendly smile, he'll be finished in another three minutes. I got there just as the students were leaving the classroom. Gathering up the papers he had used for his lecture, Samuel didn't see me come in. When I was almost close enough to touch him, he looked up.

"We're not supposed to meet until next Saturday," he said, a worried look on his face. "Mattie, is something wrong?"

"That remains to be seen," I answered. "We need to talk."

"There is a meeting I should attend that's scheduled to begin in ten minutes."

"You didn't say it's a meeting you must attend. Perhaps I didn't make myself clear. We need to talk right now."

"Sit down," he said, pulling out two chairs from the first row. "I often stay here after the class is over. The room isn't used again until four o'clock. Now tell me, Mattie, what happened."

"Last night at dinner the girls talked about a Samuel Bingham I don't know."

"What don't you know about me?"

"Is your home a dilapidated shack off Halsted Street?"

"Yes."

"Why do you live there? Is that all you can afford? Or do you like living between a meat market and a tobacco shop in a dirty, shabby, disease-ridden neighborhood filled with newly arrived Jewish immigrants?"

"Where I live has nothing to do with money. To teach sociology at the University, I have to do research. Since sociology is about people, I need to get as close to them as I can. At first, like other sociologists, I used interviews, surveys, and statistical reports to reduce the distance between myself and those I was studying. But I soon realized these approaches had only limited worth. The information was always incomplete; it was sometimes inaccurate; and it was too often biased toward a desired outcome. I saw I could only know the people, I could only know who they really are, if I lived among them, in the midst of them, not as an observer for a month or two, but as a neighbor. So, in what you call my shack, I became one of them, and when I did, they became people I admired; they became my friends. So, I live on Fourteenth Place both because I need to, it's necessary if I'm going to keep my job, and because I want to."

"Why did you keep this from me?"

"I didn't. You have never asked me where I live."

"Didn't you think I would be interested?"

"I'm sure you would be. But it has never fit into anything we've been discussing, and I didn't want to bring it up."

"Why not?"

"Because I felt that if I did, I'd be talking too much about myself. Maybe, though, I need to reconsider that."

"Maybe you do."

"Is there anything else," he asked.

"Yes, there is. The girls who have the time and the inclination to read a newspaper say you are a socialist or a Fabian socialist, they're not sure which, who wants to reorganize society. Are you, as apparently powerful people are claiming, a dangerous radical intent upon overturning the social order?"

"No."

"Is that all you are going to say?"

"There is more, Mattie, a whole lot more I want to say. But this you must understand, and you must understand it right from the beginning: no matter what others may be accusing me of, I am not dangerous, and I am not trying to overturn anything."

"What then are you trying to do?" I asked.

"I am trying to be just."

"As in justice?"

"Yes."

"That's not very helpful, Samuel. I'm not even sure what justice means."

"Justice exists, Mattie, when people, all people, receive their due. Whatever else their due might imply, it means that everyone has a rightful claim to all that is needed for a decent life. That's not what we have today. Too many have not only too little but nothing at all. Their lives are not decent; they are miserable. Misery breeds at one extreme violence and at the other indifference. I reject both. I don't want to overthrow the existing structures; I don't want to keep them the same. I want to reform them. I want to cleanse them and to rebuild them not to meet the needs of a privileged few but to meet the needs of the people.

"A professor in the sociology department at the University, Charles Zeublin, has mentioned a small British association he belongs to called the Fabian Society. They are socialists wanting a redistribution of land, capital, and income. But like the Roman general Fabius Maximus who refused to meet the Carthaginian army on the battlefield, they have no desire to fight those who oppose them. They are not pugnacious, but as one of their more notable members, George Bernard Shaw, has said, they are pertinacious. They keep on debating, writing essays, giving lectures, distributing tracts to inform, to educate, to persuade. I like what they are doing. So, while I have not in any official way joined them, I have, at least in the newspapers, declared myself to be one of them.

"I, like them, keep on writing and speaking. Admittedly, my words are strong, and they unquestionably can anger those who disagree with me, but are they radical? The answer to that depends upon where one stands. I want workers to be paid more, to work fewer hours, to have a voice that is heard when decisions are made about the work they do. I want women to vote and the sick, whether they can pay for it or not, to be under a doctor's care. I want children to be educated. I don't want slums, or poverty, or child labor, or an unsafe and unclean workplace. I don't want monopolies where there is no competition or an unregulated marketplace where there is only competition. I don't want only private property or only government ownership but a mixture of the two. I don't want to be governed by the market and by those who control the market. I want, as Daniel Webster once said on the Senate floor, "a people's government, made for the people, made by the people, and answerable to the people." The businessman, like Marshall Field who pays his clerks a pittance and fires anyone who talks to a labor union official, finds these statements offensive. Without hesitation, he says I am a radical. But those who believe that in this country everyone has the right, the unalienable right, to life, liberty, and the pursuit of happiness might say I am anything but a radical; actually, they might say I am a model citizen."

"Are you finished now?" I asked.

"Almost. Breeding also distresses me."

"The breeding of livestock?"

"No. Of humans."

"You oppose eugenics."

"Whenever and wherever I can," Samuel replied. "Injustice makes me angry. The notion that we improve society by increasing the fit and eliminating the unfit makes me livid. Eugenics is wrong; the purpose, the arrogance, the prejudice, even the science that supports it are all wrong."

"Not everyone agrees with you. Articles in the magazines I've looked at approve of it; professional societies endorse it; colleges teach it. At Vassar, I heard about eugenics one semester in both my biology and modern literature classes. The biology professor lectured for most of a class period on Francis Galton."

"Eugenics was his idea," Samuel said.

"And also his term, which, if I remember correctly, he took from the Greek word meaning well-bred. We had to read his book *Hereditary Genius*—that's where he talked about improving the race through judicious marriages—and his article in *Macmillan's Magazine* calling for a state sponsored competition to determine which families had the most distinguished children. He wanted their children to marry one another and to increase the probability of this happening, he thought they should to be married in Westminster Abbey and be awarded a grant from the state after they had children of their own."

"What did you read in your literature class?"

"*Man and Superman.*"

"That, I'm sorry to say, is by George Bernard Shaw."

"Who is one of your more illustrious Fabian Socialists. In that play, he is telling us we're no match for the complexities we face. Left to ourselves, we are going to come apart and won't be able to put ourselves back together again. Our only hope is someone who is one of us and yet is more than any one of us, someone who is made this way by Galton's judicious breeding. Some of the girls in the class were trouble by the implications of the play, but I don't recall anyone, including the instructor, dismissing it."

"One of Galton's most vocal supporters teaches here," Samuel said.

"At the University of Chicago?"

"Yes. Professor Charles Davenport insists epilepsy, insanity, alcoholism, pauperism, criminality, and feeblemindedness can all be passed from parent to offspring. He is also convinced national groups have definite characteristics. Italians are inherently criminals and have a tendency toward violence; Serbians and Greeks are slovenly; Hebrews are thieves. Consequently he endorses a eugenics not of accretion but of negation. He wants to prevent the unfit from entering the country, and if they are already here, from reproducing, if necessary by state administered sterilization."

"That is already happening," I said. "We were told in the lecture on Galton the Aliens Act of 1905 keeps steerage passengers who are ill or destitute out of the country and an increasing number of states have marriage laws making it illegal for the mentally disturbed to marry."

"To judge one person fit and another not is contemptible. The first ones to vanish would be the people I live among. With their strange language and even stranger dress and customs and often without any kind of formal education and little or no access to health care, my neighbors are thought to be ignorant, unsightly, and sickly, and, therefore, to have little worth. Even the settlement houses don't take them as they are but try to make them as quickly as possible into one of us. But with their spirit, their willingness to work hard, their desire to better themselves, their wisdom, their eagerness to help one another, they are to be respected and emulated, not disposed of. We are not to restrict or to discard, but to love. We are to love our neighbor as ourselves. Our neighbor, and I will declare this as long as the heart within me keeps pumping and the blood keeps flowing, is not the person who lives next door or down the street, but the person, whoever he may be or she may be, who needs our love."

"And that is everyone."

"Yes, Mattie, that is everyone. Now I am finished. You know it all. Here I am: a dreamer, an idealist, a crusader, a believer, and, to be entirely forthcoming, a romantic, who is hopelessly in love with a beautiful and remarkably talented and kind young lady, who will soon enter a religious order that will require her to remain single and celibate. What are you going to do with me?"

"Stand up," I said.

"Is that your answer?" Samuel asked, as we both stood.

"Yes," I replied, throwing my arms around him and kissing him. Still holding him tightly, I then said, "Just so I won't be accused of being unforthcoming, Samuel Bingham, I love you."

Leaving Cobb Hall, I suddenly caught myself reciting lines from a poem by Robert Browning I had once memorized but had not gone back to for years: *The lark's on the wing; / The snail's on the thorn; / God's in His heaven— / All's right with the world.* All was right with the world: Samuel loved me; graduation was approaching; God was coming closer. But I was wrong.

* * *

Entering the dining room that evening, I saw Laura eating by herself. I joined her, and as we talked, I smelled an unmistakable fragrance. She was wearing perfume. Perfume wasn't forbidden, but no one in the school, teachers or students, ever used it. We wanted to be clean, but for obvious reasons, we didn't want to be scented. Why did she? When she missed her classes the next two days, I went to her room in the late afternoon to offer her my notes but she wasn't there. Where was she? I intended to speak to her that night, but with Mrs. Meyer's New Testament exam to study for, I ran out of time. The following evening, because of an unusually long visit with a young mother caring for a child with a high temperature, I came late to supper. As I sat down at the table where the girls were eating, I could tell something was wrong. "It's Laura," I said.

"She's gone," Ellie replied.

"She's missing?"

"No, she has left the training school," Marjory said. Lively and bright, with red hair and freckles, Marjory was a new student who had been assigned to Laura's room after Eliza had withdrawn at the end of last semester.

"When did she leave?" I asked.

"This afternoon," Ellie said. "Marjory has just started to tell us what happened."

"I came into our room after lunch to get a book and found Laura packing," Marjory said. "When I asked her where she was going, she told me she had found something else she wanted to do and had arranged to live with a friend in Roger's Park and work in the city. I then watched her carefully put, not one or two but many, and I mean many, bottles of perfume and toilet water, bracelets, necklaces, rings, and what looked like very expensive clothing, including silk lingerie, into two large trunks."

"How did she get these things?" I asked.

"Last fall," Ellie said, "Laura told me she had received a large inheritance from her grandmother. With all that money, she can buy whatever she wants and obviously has."

"Maybe she did buy them, and maybe she didn't," Marjorie said. "Having that money doesn't mean she didn't steal them."

"But that doesn't make sense," Ellie replied.

"No, it doesn't," Marjorie agreed, "but it's still true."

"I'd like to know why she changed her mind about becoming a Deaconess," I said. "She was going to be a better Deaconess than Mrs. Meyer to save Daniel, to save him from himself."

"I can tell you why," Marjory replied. "She has been seduced."

"Oh no," Ellie exclaimed, in alarm, "by whom?"

"Not whom," Marjory said, "but what. She has been seduced by the city."

"The city. How can that possibly be? There is so much ugliness here," Ellie said.

"But there is also so much beauty. Beauty is never inert. It attracts, and holds, and moves the one who sees it. I think Laura, whether gradually or all at once, has seen the beauty, the captivating beauty, of the city, its soaring skyscrapers, its magnificent department stores filled with fountains, and freshly cut flowers, and endless aisles displaying the most exquisite and alluring wares, its elegant mansions on Lake Shore Drive, and has succumbed to it all. It has put within her, to use a phrase from Theodore Dreiser's novel *Sister Carrie*, 'the drag of desire.' Those two trunks filled not with what she needs but with what she wants explain why she is no longer with us. She desires things and the kind of life that goes along with those things. Serving God, self-denial, putting others first have little or nothing to do with this new world she has entered. She has put herself first. Pleasure, amusement, comfort, even titillation are what she values and shopping is what she spends most of her time doing or at least thinking about doing."

"Why do you say titillation?" Ellie asked.

"Because of the lingerie she bought . . . or stole," Marjory answered. "All that can be said about what we wear is that it's serviceable. But the frilly things I saw Laura put into one of her trunks were not just pretty, they were suggestive."

"You mean they were erotic?" I said.

"Yes, Mattie, that's exactly what I mean," Marjory replied. "Seeing them in the store, owning them, wearing them could have easily filled her mind with fantasies that excite her. It's an impulse she may be ashamed of, but is, nonetheless, drawn to and, if the truth be told, likes, maybe even craves."

"You really think she might be a thief," Ellie said.

"If she isn't now, according to my father, she could easily become one. He was working at Siegel Cooper as a store detective when he got sick three years ago. Realizing he wasn't going to recover, Father told me over several weeks what he felt I needed to know about the world. Although those lessons could begin anywhere, they always ended at the department store. The store had been good to him, but he didn't like what was happening there. Increasingly shoppers were being told by the advertising, the displays, the promotions, the special sales, the smiling clerks who were so eager to be of assistance that whatever they had come to buy, it wasn't enough; they had to buy more. People in growing numbers believed this. They returned to the store so often, it seemed like they had never left it. Most but not all paid for what they got. Shoplifting had become a real problem. The most frequent thieves, he said, were women who had money. Often their husbands were men of position and influence. When these women were caught, and a good many of them were, all kinds of foolish reasons were given for their behavior: they were only doing what others did, or they couldn't help themselves, or they didn't know what they were doing, or since the store was so large and there were so many other shoppers, the little bit they had taken wasn't exactly stealing. Some call the department store a dreamworld, he said, but it also is a world of broken dreams. If its temptations are not resisted, its wiles are not rejected, it is likely to take us where we don't want to go. It's likely to take Laura where she doesn't want to go."

"Let's hope that doesn't happen," I said.

"I think we had better pray that doesn't happen," Ellie added.

* * *

Laura's departure—a theologian might call it her fall from grace—was bad enough. But worse was coming. The following Wednesday I was in jail. It was not just another jail, but as William Stead had written in his shocking book *If Christ Came to Chicago,* it was the worst jail in the city. He called the cells of this police station at the corner of Harrison and Pacific underground cages and said that they were filled nightly with hundreds of the foulest creatures, male and female, who prowled the streets of the vice district. That's precisely where I was. I was in a cage with a half dozen women who drank, smoked, cursed, yelled obscenities, and laughed uproariously, and when they had run out of liquor and cigarettes and had tired of their vulgar jokes, they either sank into a troubled silence or, apparently to amuse themselves and to annoy everyone else, they began to shriek. It was a frightening and disgusting place. But I was neither frightened nor disgusted, not because I didn't hear the bedlam, I did, it was impossible not to, but because I was too angry at what had put me into that cage to be bothered by it.

My descent into this hell started Monday afternoon. After visiting several families on the city's South Side, all of them facing bills they couldn't pay, I got on the streetcar that stopped two blocks from the Training School. As I sat down, I happened to look at the empty seat across the aisle. On it was a discarded afternoon edition of the *Daily Journal*. Spread across the front page, taking up three columns, was a photograph of a young man with a swollen, lifeless face. Curious and with a sense of foreboding, I picked up the paper and began to read the article under the heading, "Family Home Scene of Fiendish Attempt to Wreak Revenge for Activity Against Reds." When I finally looked up from the paper, after reading everything in it about the vicious attack, I saw that the streetcar had gone past my stop. Sitting in the station on the other side of the tracks, waiting for the streetcar that would take me back to the Training School, I started thinking about that assault. Much of what I had read was upsetting. One detail in particular disturbed me. The assailant was unknown. The paper said nothing about him other than he was a murderous stranger. The victim, however, was known to virtually everyone, from the highest levels of society to the very lowest. He was George Shippy, the Chief of Police.

The *Daily Journal* reported the entire statement Chief Shippy had given to the city's newspapers. He opened his account of the attack with a point he obviously wanted to emphasize. The city had to understand the assault was anticipated. He didn't know who would try to kill him or when, but because of a premonition, he did know the attempt would be made. So, he was always ready for it or, to use his words, he was always "on guard." That morning at approximately nine o'clock the front doorbell of his home rang. Opening the door, he saw standing in front of him a man, about twenty-six years old, who was Sicilian or perhaps Armenian. The man said that he had a letter for Chief Shippy and drew from the pocket of his coat an envelope. Certain the expected moment had come, the man was not there to deliver a letter but to take his life, he immediately grabbed his arm. They fought, but being stronger, he overpowered him. Restraining him, he told his wife to see if the man had a gun in his pocket. His wife cried out he did. Take it, he instructed her. The man suddenly broke loose from him and pulling out of an inside pocket of his coat a huge knife, twelve to fourteen inches long, he swung it at him, cutting his arm. He drew his own gun and fired it at the man, intending to wound him, but missed. His son, shouting "Papa, I will help you," started to come down the stairs. The man yanked the gun out of his wife's hands and pointing it at his son, shot him in the chest. He then shot to kill, putting a bullet into the man's head and another into his heart.

The *Daily Journal* provided additional information about Chief Shippy's wound and offered a reason for the attack. In his struggle with the intruder, the paper reported, Chief Shippy had been stabbed in the back beneath the right shoulder. A gash like this, the reader was led to believe, was a serious injury. As the headline above the paper's lead article declared, the motive for the confrontation was revenge. Emma Goldman, an anarchist who was called in the newspapers "The Queen of the Reds," had not been allowed to speak in the city. Irate, the attacker assaulted the person he thought was responsible for the ruling. That person, because he was the senior officer on the police force, was Chief Shippy.

The streetcar came, and this time I got off at my stop. On the corner across the street from the station was a newsstand. Whether I was forty-five minutes or an hour late for supper wouldn't make much difference. So, before starting back to the Training School, I stopped there, not to buy a newspaper but to look at what the other papers had put on their front page about the attack. The *Daily News* called the assailant an assassin and reported he might have been the leader of a group planning to kill other city officials. The *Chicago Evening American* ran a gruesome photograph of the dead attacker showing clearly the bullet holes in his head and chest. In the accompanying story, it claimed the assassin—there was that word again—lived on the West Side, had been chosen at an anarchists' meeting for the assault by lot, and had closely followed Chief Shippy for well over a week before shooting him.

It occurred to me that beyond the obvious—a man died, another man shot him, the shooting took place in the home of the Chief of Police—I really didn't know what happened. Since they used the word assassin, the newspapers, however, apparently thought they did. But were they right? Didn't that word assassin convict a man without giving him the chance to speak for himself, or in this case, since he was already dead, someone else the chance to speak for him?

Chief Shippy's statement made me uneasy. I wasn't sure he wrote it. If he was badly hurt, how could he? Maybe someone else wrote it for him. If so, how accurate was that person's information and how willing was he to be truthful? There was something else about the statement that was even more troubling. By his own admission, Chief Shippy was the assailant. I couldn't see how the man at the front door threatened Chief Shippy. He only said that he had a letter for him. Surely that wasn't alarming. He didn't have a weapon in his hand, just an envelope. He didn't lunge at Chief Shippy. Unprovoked, Chief Shippy lunged at him. Instead of an assassin, didn't that make the man at the front door a victim of a willful assault?

I had all these questions and very few, if any, answers. I was confused and worried. Words like assassination and anarchy could inflame the city. More was coming. I didn't know what it would be, but I had a strong feeling it wasn't going to be good.

The papers Tuesday morning said that the man Chief Shippy killed was a Jew named Lazarus Averbuch, a newly arrived immigrant from Russia who had been staying with his sister Olga in an apartment on Washburne Avenue. This new information alarmed me. The address given was very close to where Samuel lived. Many in the city did not like his neighborhood. Their anti-Semitism was already strong, and the assassination attempt, I should say the alleged assassination attempt, would make this bigotry even stronger. Believing the area to be infested with anarchists plotting to overthrow the government, these people could easily turn violent. Samuel could just as easily find himself in the middle of an escalating situation that ended tragically.

We had arranged to meet that afternoon at the University after his last class. I did see Samuel then but only briefly. He had to take another instructor's class the next hour and after it was over attend a departmental meeting. So we had only a few minutes to ourselves. Noticing the worried look on my face, he asked what was wrong. Nothing, I replied, except for Chief Shippy's shooting, anarchy, anti-Semitism, and your home on Fourteenth Place. Getting no response to this outburst, I became more upset. He seemed to be completely oblivious to what I was feeling. Exasperated—how could one who was so smart be so stupid when it came to women and, more to the point, when it came to me—I then called him a blockhead. As I searched for something else to call him, preferably a word that had head in it, he said, with the most beguiling smile, that he undoubtedly was also a knucklehead. That smile did me in. Suddenly I threw my arms around him and in a thin voice barely above a whisper said that I was frightened. After holding me tightly, oblivious now to students and teachers going by and to whatever they might be thinking about us, he suggested we meet at the Maxwell Street Settlement tomorrow in the early afternoon. We'd find there at least some of the answers we were both looking for.

I left, but before I got halfway down the hall, I hurried back, catching him just before he went into the classroom. A question had occurred to me that elsewhere might have been thought foolish but wasn't in this city where the most notable constant appeared to be change. Was the Maxwell Street Settlement still on Maxwell Street? Samuel shook his head. No, he said, it was now on South Clinton Street. When I asked if that was the street on the far side of Jefferson close to the eastern edge of the Jewish ghetto, he replied yes and then added, again with an irresistible smile, that while ghetto was a word sociologists were fond of using, those who lived there preferred the word neighborhood.

Wednesday afternoon, before entering the Settlement, we went to a nearby cafe, and over a hot cup of tea and putterkuchen, a wonderful Lithuanian raisin and cinnamon sweet bun, Samuel told me about, to use his words, this cornerstone institution. When he said cornerstone institution, I found myself thinking now that's a sociologist speaking. He can use a term like that but I can't say ghetto? That wasn't quite fair. But at that point fairness wasn't the issue, understanding was. So I looked attentively at him with only a slight smile on my face, which he completely ignored. Fifteen years ago, he said, two young college graduates, Jacob Abt and Jesse Lowenhaupt, having seen the need for a community center, opened their home on Maxwell Street to the neighborhood. Soon there were cooking and sewing classes, a night school, several boys and girls clubs, musical presentations, plays, dances, and parties. More space was eventually needed making the move to the larger building on South Clinton Street necessary. Today the Settlement was where people of all ages came to learn, to socialize, to perform, to receive aid, and to discuss and find solutions to the problems they were facing. It was also, I was now convinced, where we needed to be.

I wasn't ready for what I found there. I had expected most everyone to be talking about the shooting. I had thought I would hear raised voices declaring Lazarus Averbuch's innocence and lamenting his death. I was sure there would be at least someone questioning

Chief Shippy's statement, someone condemning the newspapers' inflammatory articles, someone demanding justice. But there was nothing. It appeared to be just another busy afternoon at the Settlement. How could this possibly be? Certainly they knew about the shooting. Maybe they thought it didn't have anything to do with them. But it obviously did.

I looked at Samuel for help. He, though, simply shook his head. Clearly he didn't understand what was happening here either. Then I saw him start to scan the room. When he came to an older woman of medium height with dark hair tinged with white, he stopped. Taking my arm, he walked toward her. She's the person we need to talk to, he told me. He introduced me to Miriam Kittle, the volunteer assistant to Miss Heller, the Head Resident of the Settlement. Samuel's neighbor and close friend, she knew those it served intimately. I lost no time asking her if the shooting concerned the people of the community.

"Of course, it does," she answered. "There is an obvious logic here that we can't escape. Since people don't like foreigners, Jews, and anarchists; since Lazarus Averbuch was an immigrant, Jewish, and, according to what the newspapers and the police keep telling us, an anarchist; and since he lived among us, it necessarily follows that these people, or at least some of them, now driven into a frenzy by the gruesome photographs, the wild statements of the newspapers, the groundless accusations of the police could at any moment turn on us as the police already have. It has happened elsewhere— many of our neighbors have come from Russia where they were brutally persecuted during pogroms that brought destruction and death to their families and friends—and it could happen here. Concern, though, isn't really what we are feeling. That's way too mild a word. One is concerned about overcooking the meat for dinner or not wearing a warm enough coat on a cold winter day. When it comes to what an individual or, worse yet, a crowd enraged by bigotry and hatred can do, fear is a much better word. We are afraid; some, especially those who have been through a Russian pogrom, are terrified."

"The police have turned against you?" I asked.

"A lot more of them are here than usual, and they haven't come to protect us. The death of Lazarus Averbuch isn't being investigated. The police have already made up their minds about him. He intended to overthrow the government and so got what he deserved. He probably had an accomplice to help him do it. They want to find whoever that person is and put him in jail for the rest of his life if possible. But Lazarus Averbuch and his accomplice, if there is one, are just two apples in a barrel full of rotten apples. They are after the whole barrel, Miss Welsh."

"That barrel," I said, "is anarchy."

"It is. After Chief Shippy made his statement, the commander of the city's first police division announced all the anarchists in Chicago were going to be either arrested or booted out of the city with a strong enough kick to the derriere to keep them from coming back. These were not idle words. Three thousand officers were at once put on alert, and since then it has felt like all three thousand have been digging into our community trying to unearth anyone who talks like, or even looks like, or, for that matter, even smells like an anarchist. We've heard two men living here were arrested because one had a note from the other saying 'the game is up, you've got to get out of town quickly.' A young man was taken to jail yesterday for no other reason than he was a friend of Lazarus Averbuch and hasn't been released. A frantic search for a woman thought to have assisted Mr. Averbuch finally ended when the police found her at work."

"Why didn't they go there first?" I asked.

"They should have. But then they are the police. They immediately took her into custody, and at the police station, to use her word, sweated her all afternoon, learning nothing, because she had nothing to tell them. The police can be mean. I don't think they are mean spirited because it's their nature. Anarchy makes them mean spirited. Last night there was a public viewing of Mr. Averbuch at the morgue. A reporter for one of the city's newspapers stayed in the room the entire evening watching who came and how they reacted to the corpse. He later said when the police saw the body, many of them mocked it, some made rude gestures toward it, one even struck it in the face."

"What I'm hearing you say about the community, Mrs. Kittle, and what I'm seeing at the Settlement don't seem to go together. The people here don't appear to be aware of the threat to them. It's as though they've separated themselves from the shooting and its consequences for the community."

"You're wrong, Miss Welsh, and, at same time, you're right. To think they are unaware of the shooting is wrong. To think they have separated themselves from it is right. But you are missing something."

"What?" I asked.

"Six words," Mrs. Kittle said.

I thought for a moment and then suddenly knew what they were. "The people have separated themselves from the shooting and its consequences for the sake of the community."

"Yes, for the sake of the community."

"But why?" Samuel asked.

"Because at this point," Mrs. Kittle replied, "they really don't know what else to do. Nobody has given them any kind of direction. Leaders here on the West Side and elsewhere in the city are silent, and the Jewish newspapers have nothing helpful to contribute. Left to themselves, they've decided if they don't stir the pot, maybe it won't boil over. The few who do speak out say, and mind you they say it very quietly, that Mr. Averbuch was the unwitting tool of an outside agitator or that he had gone mad because of the deprivation he and his family had suffered in a Russian pogrom. Both explanations have the same purpose. They attribute the assassination attempt to something other than Mr. Averbuch being a Jew in our community, which, in turn, frees us from the accusation that we breed anarchy."

Mrs. Kittle then offered us refreshments, which we, not wanting to overindulge, declined. At the front door, we thanked her for her time and the information she had so graciously given us. Just before we turned to go, she took my hand and said, "Do pray for us. The coming days are so uncertain."

"I will," I replied.

Once outside, I began to ask myself one question after another. Would I get down on my knees to pray for them? If I did, how many times on my knees should I pray for them? Would once be enough, or twice, or a dozen times? Why really did I agree to pray for them, whether it be on my knees, or sitting, or standing? Was it to be polite, or to say what is expected of someone in a religious training school, or to offer them the only help I could give and that, I knew, was God's help? None of these questions, though, was answered. Something else had made its way into my mind that pushed them all to the rear. I was troubled by what Mrs. Kittle had told us.

"Your friend certainly is informative," I said, taking Samuel's arm as we started to walk down South Clinton Street, "maybe too informative."

"Why do you say that, Mattie? I don't see how we can ever have too much information."

"When it comes to your welfare, a little ignorance, I'm beginning to realize, is comforting."

Samuel was silent for a moment. I knew he was trying to think of a response that would convince me he'd be safe. He then said, "Who, Miss Welsh, almost every day, enters squalid neighborhoods? Who walks down dark and deserted streets oftentimes alone? Who goes into homes of complete strangers not knowing what abuse, or disease, or unholy condition might be there? Who does this?"

"I do," I finally answered.

"As you do this, again I remind you, almost every day, are you overly worried about your safety?"

"No, not overly worried."

"Then you need not at this or any other time be overly worried about mine. While the neighborhood I live in might need renovation here and there, the streets I walk down and the homes I enter are filled with friends and acquaintances. Do you agree?"

"I agree, Mr. Bingham."

"But I still see anxiety on your face, Miss Welsh,"

"It's irritation, Samuel, not anxiety. Maybe it's even anger. Nothing is being done for Lazarus Avenbuch."

"What can be done for him now?"

"His name can be cleared. The contempt his family is being subjected to can be stopped. Their shame can be removed. He didn't want to overthrow the government. He didn't go to Chief Shippy's home intending to murder him."

"So Chief Shippy is not telling the truth," Samuel said.

"No, he is not."

"Very few agree with you."

"There should be many more."

Suddenly we heard what sounded like a boy screaming. We rushed around the corner and saw two teenagers kicking a much younger boy, who was writhing on the pavement with his arms around his head and his body curled up into a ball trying to protect himself. Each time they kicked him, they yelled, "Your father is a filthy Jew anarchist." Seeing us, they started to run. No one else was there except for a policeman standing on the far corner. Glancing quickly at him, I was stunned. He stayed on that corner. He hadn't stopped the assault, and now he was letting the boys go. I had a choice to make: I could either chase after the teenagers or help the boy on the sidewalk. I wanted to catch those bullies, but after more than a year at the Training School, I knew what I had to do. As the boy slowly sat up, I realized that because of his heavy clothing he was not seriously hurt. Out of the corner of my eye, I saw Samuel hurrying over to the policeman and heard him say, "Didn't you see that?"

"See what?" the policeman replied.

Samuel angrily pushed him in the direction the teenagers had fled. The policeman grabbed Samuel, and the two of them started to fight, each one trying to force the other to the pavement. Though the policeman was a large man, I could tell he was no match for Samuel's strength and quickness. Also aware of this, he, to my horror, reached for the club attached to his belt. I raced across the street, and just as he was about to bring it down on Samuel's head, I dove at him. He fell to the sidewalk with me on top of him. Looking up at me just above him and at Samuel now standing over him, he growled, "You two are under arrest."

"For what?" I cried, moving to one side so he could get up.

"For attacking a police officer."

"There was no attack," I said, now seething with anger. "He wanted you to do your duty. I wanted to stop you from bashing his head in."

"And for being anarchists and, if that will not put you away, then accomplices of anarchists," he added, with a sickening smirk on his repulsive face.

Soon we were being crammed into a patrol wagon headed for the Harrison Street Police Station, our arms placed in irons to keep us subdued. I needed those restraints. Without them, I would have busted out of that wagon the first time it stopped and taking Samuel with me vanished long before anyone had started to look for us. That would have put us in more trouble, but at that moment I wouldn't have cared. It was all wrong: a boy beaten because of his family's religion and their politics, a policeman who abetted the assault, a man killed and then maligned for something he had not done, a community terrorized by bigotry. Where was righteousness; where was justice; where was God?

I spent the night in that awful jail with only my degenerate—to be kind, perhaps I should make that my eccentric—cellmates for company. The other girls might have thought confinement in the Harrison Street Police Station a blessing. It would have given them an extraordinary, they might have even said a miraculous, opportunity to tell these women about Jesus and to pray for them. The thought of talking to my cellmates about Jesus, though, never entered my mind. That required faith I did not have and that night I doubted I would ever have. The world appeared to me so hostile and oppressive, and though Jesus wasn't of it, he was nowhere in it that I could see.

The next morning, after a breakfast of moldy bread and luke-warm tea, I lay down, hoping to rest. Feelings I didn't know what to do with, questions I couldn't begin to answer had kept me awake all night. The moment I closed my eyes, I heard someone scream, "Oh, my God." I opened my eyes but didn't look around. The cry was so shrill, it was so piercing, I told myself it was just another shriek and again closed my eyes. But when that voice said, "It's you, Mattie." I sat up at once and saw Elsie Fisher, a second year student at the Training School, standing on the other side of the bars. Her promi-nent blue eyes fixed on me seemed to be larger than basketballs.

I quickly explained I had been arrested because of a run-in with a nasty police officer. Make that run-into I thought to myself, smil-ing for the first time in what seemed like ages, and I would have a fairly accurate statement of what happened. Elsie, who had come to the police station to visit the prisoners, especially the younger girls charged with solicitation, said that since the lost had now been found the Training School needed to be notified immediately. Stu-dents and staff had apparently been searching for me everywhere they could think of. Of course, no one had thought to look for me in a cell in the worst jail in the city. As she was leaving, I asked her to also tell the University of Chicago one of their sociology instructors was here too.

When the Training School and the University heard we had been detained—that's the word both schools used; I would have used locked up—they acted quickly. Calls were made to influential people, who, in turn, made calls to ranking officers in the police department. Before noon, we had been briefly interrogated, the charges had been dropped, and we had been released from custody with the assurance the conduct of the offending police officer would be looked into.

I returned to the Training School knowing Mrs. Meyer was waiting for me. I knew, too, she was angry. But I didn't know how angry. Walking down the hallway to her office, I wondered if she was angry enough to place me on probation or even to expel me from the school. Entering her office, I saw her sitting behind her desk. Looking at her—her face stern, her back rigid—I decided I was going to be expelled. I sat down and waited. She looked at me for the longest moment, saying nothing, and then asked me to tell her what happened. I described the beating, the policeman's behavior, and my response to him, leaving nothing out including Samuel's involvement in the incident, stopping short, however, of telling her how important he was to me, although she probably already knew. Again she was silent, for an even longer moment. I'll be home before the day is over, I said to myself. Then I thought I saw the look on her face soften. Nodding her head, probably more in resignation than anything else, she told me I was truly an original. No one else at the Training School had ever been a professional athlete; no one had ever spent a night in jail; no one had ever spent a night in jail with a man, not the same cell, not even I could have managed that, she said, but the same jail.

She then went to a bookcase and took from one of its lower

shelves a small, well-worn book. The binding was loose and in one place torn and the cover was ragged at the edges. "This is *The Book of Common Prayer* the Episcopal Church uses. A friend gave it to me when I was going through a particularly difficult time, and now I would like to give it to you. I hope you find it helpful."

As she put it in my hand and for the briefest moment placed her hand on top of mine, as though she was blessing both the book and me, I was so stunned I could only stammer, "Thank you. I'm sure it will."

"There is something else," she said. "Before going to bed tonight, I want you to read Galatians, chapter 5, verses 1-6. That's all, Miss Welsh." As I got up, she raised her hand, "Oh, and do try to stay out of jail from now on." I left with the impression she had just dismissed me with a benediction. Without question, those words were an admonishment, but I also felt they were her way of saying, especially with that raised hand of hers, "Go in peace."

Right after dinner I went to my room and started to look at the reading from Galatians. The letter was written to churches that were beginning to turn away from Jesus. Members were being circumcised which, because they were now bound to the law, separated them from Jesus. The law couldn't bring them righteousness, it couldn't save them, and having fallen from his grace, Jesus couldn't save them either. Those verses were important, but I knew they were not what Mrs. Meyer wanted me to think about. They merely provided background for what came next in that passage, for what she felt I needed to hear: "For in Jesus Christ neither circumcision availeth anything, nor uncircumcision; but faith which worketh by love."

I slowly closed the Bible, and sitting still, I stared at it for the longest time. In that silence, I began to see with increasing certainty that the meaning of all its 1,056 pages had just been reduced to those five words: "faith which worketh by love." Here was the understanding Mrs. Meyer believed I had to confront, to experience, to practice, and, most of all, to live. I added with a smile, it was also the understanding that would keep me out of jail; though, on second thought, I could see where it might put me in jail. I said those words out loud: faith working through love. Perhaps I did have the capacity to love. After all, my aunt had once said I have been graced for goodness. But according to Paul, whatever my capacity might be, it would never be enough without faith, for faith would take me where I didn't want to go but needed to and would give me what I didn't possess but needed to have. Faith working through love: those words set before me that question I had to answer and still couldn't: Is God real?

I put the Bible aside and picked up the prayer book. Listed in the Table of Contents were services for various occasions, a catechism, scripture readings, prayers, and the complete Psalter. After thinking about how best to use the prayer book, I decided to read a Psalm every morning right after breakfast and to follow it with one of the prayers. It seemed like a good way to begin the day. It would also be, I told myself, a good way to end this, perhaps I should say, peculiar day. I opened the Psalter at page 368. There, toward the bottom of the page, was the thirty-sixth Psalm. The first verse immediately got my attention: "My heart showeth me the wickedness of the ungodly: that there is no fear of God before his eyes." That was the perfect word for that horrible policeman, I thought, and for all those people who disliked Jews and wanted to harm them just because they were Jewish, and for anyone who wanted to hurt Samuel. They were wicked. The next three verses provided more choice words for these people and others like them. Their sin was abominable; their speech was unrighteous and full of deceit; they imagined mischief upon their beds; they did not abhor anything that was evil. "Yes," I shouted to the empty room, "and they all should be struck down."

Expecting to read next that they were doomed, I wasn't prepared for verse 5, "Thy mercy, O Lord, reacheth unto the heavens; and thy faithfulness unto the clouds," and was even less prepared for verse 6, "Thy righteousness standeth like the strong mountains; thy judgments are like the great deep." The following verses, to my dismay, spoke of God's protection, his generosity, his loving-kindness. The jump from verse 4 to verse 6, the abrupt shift from wickedness to God's righteousness, offended me. God couldn't be righteous when there was so much wickedness in the world. But what I rejected the psalmist had not only affirmed but proclaimed. How could he do that? To answer that question, I knew I had to read in-between the lines, or, in this case, in-between the verses. What wasn't mentioned but was there, of course, was faith. I put down the prayer book and then, after a somewhat heated debate with myself, I cried, again to the empty room, "Why not? I have nothing to lose, and, who knows, maybe something to gain." Instead of turning next to someone else's prayer, as I had planned, I went to the blank page at the beginning of the prayer book and wrote my own prayer. It said, "Give me faith." To remind myself, or what would probably be the case, to convince myself later that I had written those words, I put below them my name and the date, March 8, 1908.

Over the next several days, police officials made it clear they no longer thought Lazarus Averbuch was part of a conspiracy. He meant to assassinate Chief Shippy, who killed him in self-defense and was, therefore, innocent of all wrongdoing. Additional inquiries would be made, but whatever information did turn up would be, in all likelihood, inconsequential. The department now had to direct its efforts toward other matters requiring its attention.

The official position was generally accepted throughout the city, even within the Jewish community. There was, however, a dissenting voice. Five days after the shooting, the *Jewish Courier*, an influential Yiddish newspaper, denounced those who blamed Jews for the actions of a demented individual. Two days later an article in the same paper made an altogether different statement that changed the thinking of many. An editor of the *Courier*, Peter Boyarsky, declared Lazarus Averbuch innocent. Far from defending himself, Chief Shippy had shot to kill without cause. He was a murderer. Lazarus Averbuch, he wrote, was condemned not because he was guilty, but because he gave an anti-Semitic government a way to condemn Jews.

Other voices were soon heard. Leon Zolotkoff, a prominent Jewish journalist and at the time an assistant district attorney, questioned the accuracy of Chief Shippy's statement. He wrote in the *Courier* it was quite possible Lazarus Averbuch went to Chief Shippy's home unarmed. Later his skepticism became even more pointed. In an article appearing under the heading "Tide Turns and Shippy is Now on Defensive," the *Daily Socialist* quoted him at length. Mr. Zolotkoff began his remarks, the newspaper reported, by saying Lazarus Averbuch wouldn't have carried a knife; it wasn't characteristic of his race. He then asserted the young man had gone to the home not to assassinate the Chief but to ask him for a favor. After expressing his surprise that it had taken a strong, well-trained policeman seven shots to bring down a frail nineteen-year-old boy, Mr. Zolotkoff concluded his comments with the statement that although he didn't know everything, he did know somebody was lying.

A judge, who asked that his name be withheld, told the *Courier* in an interview he, too, was convinced Lazarus Averbuch did not intend to murder Chief Shippy. Samuel said most everyone thought the judge was Julian Mack, a powerful Jewish politician, who had attended Lazarus Averbuch's funeral. Worried that something important, whether intentionally or unintentionally, had been missed, Emil Hirsh, the rabbi of Sinai Temple, one of the wealthiest Jewish congregations in the city, wanted the police to look more thoroughly into the shooting. He told the *Inter Ocean*, a daily newspaper, "West Side Jews are much worked up over the situation, inclining to the belief Averbuch went to the chief's house with no evil design. I sympathize with them in the position they have taken in demanding a full investigation."

A number of affluent Jews, who had formed a committee to defend Lazarus Averbuch, acquired the services of a well-known pathologist from Rush Medical College, Dr. Ludwig Hekteon. Because of their influence, Dr. Hekteon was allowed to reexamine the body. According to *The Chicago Tribune*, two bullet holes, one on the left side of the body between the fourth and fifth ribs and the other on the right side at the collarbone, had particularly interested him. From their location, he deduced Lazarus Averbuch had been shot from above. That finding was inconsistent with Chief Shippy's statement that he and his driver had both shot the intruder who was standing between them, which was, for these men and for others as well, further indication that Chief Shippy could not be trusted.

I thought the police would reopen their investigation and once they did expected them to find evidence that would convict Chief Shippy of taking Lazarus Averbuch's life. Samuel disagreed. The voices weren't loud enough, he said, and they had come way too late. In the first days after the shooting, those wretched articles in the city's newspapers and their grotesque photographs had turned hearts to stone. It had already been decided: Lazarus Averbuch deserved to die. Nothing was going to change that verdict at this point short of a full confession by Chief Shippy, which he didn't think would be coming any time soon.

Even his neighbors were silent. No speeches were being made; no demands were being insisted upon; no financial or political pressure was being applied. Afraid of pushing too hard, they were not pushing at all. Instead, they, like most everyone else, were now looking to the approaching inquest, ready to accept and to comply with whatever decision it reached about the death of Lazarus Averbuch.

The hearing was a trial of sorts. It did not consider the guilt or innocence of Chief Shippy but rather the truth of his statement.

Its purpose was twofold: to determine the cause of death and, based upon that finding, the need for a full trial. Acting as judge, the coroner presided over the inquest, decided which witnesses could be called, and ruled on what questions could be asked and who could ask them. After giving their testimony, witnesses could not be cross-examined. Ultimately the way the coroner and the six person jury answered two questions would determine the verdict they reached. They needed to decide what happened in the home of Chief Shippy the morning of the shooting and why Lazarus Averbuch went there. Since the Shippy family and their driver were the only witnesses to the shooting and the deceased the only one who knew the reason for the encounter, the outcome of the inquest was never really in doubt.

I had to take a test on the letters of Paul the morning of the inquest. So I didn't go to it with Samuel and was unable to see him that afternoon because of several families I needed to visit. The next day after breakfast I hurried over to the University hoping to find him in his office before his first class began. He was at his desk staring at an envelope.

"I'm glad you're here, Mattie," he said. "You need to know I'm going to mail this letter today."

"Why do I need to know that?" I replied, feeling my stomach tighten.

"Because the University might not appreciate it. I'm sending the letter to the *Chicago Tribune*."

"It's about yesterday's inquest?"

"Yes. The jury said what Shippy did was acceptable. But what he, and the police, and the newspapers, and the city did was not acceptable. It was deplorable. Yesterday reeks. People aren't going to smell the stink, or if they do, they aren't going to say a word about it. They're just glad it's over. But it can't be, because if it is, we have just sunk deeper into mire that is one day going to bury us. The coroner was Shippy's man right from the beginning. If he didn't like a question, he threw it out; if he didn't want someone to speak, he didn't recognize him; if he didn't want an issue like the illegal arrests or the sweatbox interrogations addressed, he didn't consider it. He didn't even consider the charge of anarchy, which was telling. If Lazarus Averbuch was not an anarchist, and no one claimed that he was, then he had no reason to attack Shippy. If there was no reason for the attack, then there wasn't one, which made Shippy's self-defense argument indefensible. I kept waiting for someone to say something, to say anything, about this omission. When no one did, I understood why. A deal had been made. I didn't know what it was, but I did know what it meant. Somebody was hiding something.

"The verdict was even worse than the hearing. Making Lazarus Averbuch a political assassin will bring more suffering. In the statement his sister made to the *Daily Courier*, Olga spoke of her wounded and broken heart and asked the city for justice. Because of the finding, her heart will never be healed, and instead of justice, there will only be more injustice. Anti-Semitism and the offenses it incites will escalate. The perception that the West Side teams with anarchy will harden. The exploitation of the poor immigrant, and especially the poor immigrant Jew, will increase. The right to equal protection under the law, particularly when it is the police who break the law, will recede, if it is not taken away altogether."

"Is this what you have put in your letter?"

"Yes, but in stronger language." Samuel paused for a moment and then said, "The head of the Sociology Department has made it clear he doesn't want me writing letters to the newspaper. My views might antagonize contributors to the University, which, he emphasized, must not happen. Others have received a similar order and ignored it. They are now teaching elsewhere."

"So you have been sitting here asking yourself whether your convictions or your teaching comes first."

"Actually, Mattie, I've been sitting here reminding myself I answered that question a long time ago."

The following week I went to Samuel's office. The door was open, but this time I didn't see him at his desk. I went in, quickly looked around, and then, feeling my legs beginning to buckle, sank into the nearest chair. He wasn't there and neither were his books and his papers and file folders that had been neatly piled on top of a table and the shelves of a nearby bookcase. Even his pens and pencils were gone. It was as if he had never been in the room before. I instantly felt myself being squeezed by a heart-rending sadness so powerful I couldn't think or move; I was barely able to breathe. Sitting in that chair, my hands folded in my lap, I stared not at the wall in front of me but at the terrible void within me. After what seemed like a lifetime, I left the room. There was someone I needed to talk to, though I knew exactly what she was going to tell me. I went to the secretary of the Sociology Department and asked if Samuel Bingham might be in. Looking up, she said, with a courteous smile, that he was no longer employed by the University and immediately returned to her work, as though it was of vital importance and should have been completed hours ago. I went back to the Training School, my steps so unsteady passersby must have thought I had been drinking, and was told a nice young man had left a message for me. Opening it, I read: "I shouldn't be here. That was our agreement. But after spending the night together in the same jail for the same crime, I imagine everyone at the Training School knows about us including the man who delivers the groceries to the kitchen. We have to talk, and I thought this was the quickest way to reach you. The University didn't appreciate my letter. I have been dismissed. Something better will turn up soon. I'll come by late tomorrow afternoon. Samuel."

Slowly I folded the message, and then carefully folded it again, and then once again. As I kept making the note smaller, maybe hoping that if it disappeared altogether what it said would vanish also, questions rushed in and out of my thoughts. Where will Samuel live? Where will he teach? Where will he get enough money to buy groceries and to pay the rent? Where will we meet? Unlike these questions that came and went, one, the really big one, forced its way into my mind and once there wouldn't leave. Where was God in all of this?

Frightened by my worry and despair—the possibility of a breakdown of some sort occurred to me—I stuffed the message into my pocket and hurried upstairs to a familiar office. After catching my breath, I knocked on the door. She's got to be here, I said to myself, she's got to be. I was so relieved when I was told to come in, I caught myself saying alleluia, a word I was sure I had never used before and thought I never would. Sister Emma was standing next to a window overlooking the grounds of the Training School. Maybe she had been stretching her legs, or pacing the floor, or looking out the window, or going to get a volume on church history out of the bookcase. What she had been doing wasn't important. She could have been standing on her head for all I cared. All that mattered was that she was there. I ran to her, and throwing my arms around her, began to sob. The tears just kept coming, I couldn't slow them down and didn't want to, and as they did, she held me tighter. When I finally stopped, after drying my eyes and blowing my nose with a tissue she gave me, I asked if she might have a few minutes to talk. Gently squeezing my hand, she said that she had the rest of the day and, if that wasn't enough, all night as well.

I told this saintly woman everything. The words rushed out of me like a river in flood. I told her about my mother and her breakdown. I told her I didn't look anything like my father. My skin color, facial features, and bone structure were completely different, which for years had made me wonder if I was his child. Since I couldn't very well ask my parents if I had come from them, I couldn't stop thinking that someone else might be my father and, in some strange way, had always been looking for him. I told her about being an out-sider at Vassar, about the pain of not belonging because my family didn't have enough money and a high enough social standing, until my strong legs and quick wrists rescued me from that fate. I told her about my love for Samuel and the desires I had when we were together, desires that would make other girls at the Training School recoil in shame. I told her about Katie's death and because of it, my rejection of God.

"I'm a fraud. I told you and Mrs. Meyer and anyone else who asked I wanted to come here to serve God. That's a lie. I came to see if the God of the preacher's sermon, the God of the Church, is real."

"What have you decided?"

"Since the world is in a shambles and God, as far as I can tell, is nowhere in sight, I'd say God is either hiding or isn't there at all. Hiding is a good possibility. It's what most everyone does. It's certainly what I am doing. At the top of that list, though, at least according to the Psalm I read last week, is God. Defeated in battle and convinced he has been rejected by God, the psalmist cries out in Psalm 89, 'How long, Lord? Will You hide forever?' Maybe that's what God is doing, but right now not there at all seems to be more likely."

"What's happened, Mattie?"

"A murder, a beating, and a dismissal."

"Lazarus Averbuch, the Jewish boy, and Samuel?"

"Yes."

"Samuel lost his job at the University because of his letter in the *Tribune*?"

"He was thrown out the front door because of it, and, I imagine, told not to return even by the back door."

Sister Emma looked away from me. I noticed that one arm was folded across her body and the other arm, resting upon it, was raised in such a way that her thumb supported her chin and her index finger ran rapidly back and forth across her upper lip. She was undoubtedly deep in thought or in prayer; in all likelihood, she was immersed in both. Suddenly that finger stopped, the arm fell to her side, and, having at last made up her mind about what to do next, she said, "I'm going to tell you something, and then I want to give you an assignment, actually two assignments. Mattie Welsh, you are not a fraud, and you did not lie when you said that you wanted to serve God. The writer of Hebrews, in chapter 4, verse 13, says: 'All things are naked and opened unto the eyes of him with whom we have to do.' We all have to do with God. In our own way and for our own reasons, and I cannot stress here strongly enough that it is meant to be and it has to be in our own way and for our own reasons, we all have to and we all will sooner or later say yes to God, or no to God, or maybe to God. It's a decision a great many run away from, but eventually it catches up with them. It always does. You have done just the opposite. You have run toward it, legs churning, arms pumping. That's not what a fraud does; no, Mattie, that's what a fool does. To give up what you love and are so extraordinarily good at is in the eyes of the world utter foolishness. But in the eyes of God, this foolishness is holy. Like Mrs. Meyer, who gave up everything to do what the world said couldn't be done, you are a holy fool. And your foolishness does have a purpose. It's, paradoxically, to serve the one whose existence you right now doubt. You are a person who, not by reason, or by persuasion, or by inspiration but by nature, serves. Where has that come from? If you didn't put it there, and you didn't, then who did? Now here are your assignments. I'd like you to read the ninth chapter of John tonight and again tomorrow morning."

"Is there something I should be especially looking for in those verses?"

"That's exactly what I want you to be asking yourself when you read that chapter. The other assignment is a visit I would like you to make tomorrow afternoon. There is someone I want you to see."

"And who would that be?"

"Me. Why don't you come here right after lunch. We'll talk about your reading and where you are with God."

"At this moment, I don't think I'm anywhere with God. I guess I, most of all, feel lost."

"Oddly enough, that's a good place to be. You have to know you are lost before you can be found. Is there anything else you would like to talk about?"

"Tomorrow will be soon enough. Perhaps I should do the reading first."

"It will be helpful."

"Thank you, Sister Emma," I said, feeling myself close to tears, "you are a dear friend."

"That's just what I was going to tell you, Mattie. You had better freshen up now. It will soon be time for supper."

I ate quickly. Marjory, who was sitting next to me, said, "I could have been better competition if you had told me we were racing." Without waiting for me to reply, she went on, the playful look on her face turning into an impish grin, "What is the rush, Miss Welsh? Might it be that you have a rendezvous with a certain young man named Samuel?"

"If you must know, I'm meeting John."

"This is becoming interesting. Do tell me about him. What has he done to merit your attention?"

"Among other things, he has written a gospel."

"Oh, that John. How disappointing. I had hoped something would slip out that we girls could gossip about behind your back. I must say, though, we are doing quite nicely with that heinous crime you committed. Your sentence keeps increasing by the hour. Right now, we have you behind bars for five days, sleeping on the floor, eating nothing but stale bread and moldy cheese that a mouse wouldn't touch. Just this morning, one of the girls asked me if it was true the policeman you tackled had a two block head start. No, it's not, I replied, horror stricken that anyone might believe a fabrication like that. It was a three block lead, I told her. Before lunch, another classmate felt I needed to know that the bystander who pulled you off that hapless police officer just as you were ready to give him the licking of his life was Amos Alonzo Stagg, the University of Chicago's football coach. According to her, the rising star from Carlisle we're beginning to hear about, Jim Thorpe, has been keeping Coach Stagg from a good night's sleep. He didn't think anyone on the team was fast enough to catch him. Having seen what is now known throughout these halls as THE CHASE from beginning to end, he dropped to his knees and begged you to play defensive halfback for Chicago in the fall. Again, I felt it was my duty to set the record straight. I informed her Coach Stagg didn't see you stopping Jim Thorpe but, with the ball tucked securely underneath your arm, beheld you outrunning him. What Coach Stagg doesn't realize, though, is you won't be so fleet of foot in your Deaconess dress."

"That may be," I said, laughing, "but I'll always be fleet enough to outrun you."

"I wouldn't be so sure about that. After all, I was the twenty-yard dash champion of my third grade class."

"Marjorie, you do lift my spirits. Although I'd love to hear more about all the races you won in elementary school and be inspired by the records you set there and undoubtedly still hold, I unfortunately must go. John is waiting."

"If, in a moment of indiscretion, I tell the other girls about him, please forgive me if I neglect to mention the part about the gospel."

That evening, after completing my other assignments, I turned to the ninth chapter of John. It was the familiar passage about Jesus giving sight to a man blind since birth. The passage itself was certainly clear enough. Because of Jesus, the man was able to see. His neighbors asked how this happened, and the man said Jesus healed him. Then they and later the Pharisees argued about whether Jesus was of God. Some said he was, otherwise he couldn't have given the man sight. Others insisted he wasn't because the healing, which occurred on the Sabbath, broke the law. When the man was asked what he thought, first he replied that Jesus was a prophet, and then, as the controversy intensified, he answered he only knew for sure that before he was blind and now he saw. When Jesus later told him he was the Son of God, the man, believing Jesus, worshiped him.

The conflict between Jesus and those who opposed him was also clear. Jesus said the man was blind so all could see when he was healed the glory of God. His opponents said he was blind because of sin. What happened was for Jesus more important than when it happened because he put something above the law. When it happened was for his opponents more important than what happened because they put nothing above the law. What wasn't clear, though, was how any of this had significance for me. But the next morning when I read the passage again, I understood the reason for Sister Emma's assignment.

Entering Sister Emma's office that afternoon, I saw that two chairs had been placed next to a table covered with a beautifully embroidered linen table scarf. On a silver serving tray, there was a pot of tea and beside it a plate of freshly baked oatmeal cookies. After pouring us both a cup of an especially fragrant tea—Sister Emma called it mandarin spice—and offering me the cookies, insisting that I take at least two, Sister Emma said, "Well, Mattie, did you find it?"

"The first time through that passage I didn't. After ruling out the healing, the argument, and the rejection of Jesus, I went to bed, having convinced myself I'd see it in the morning. I awoke at six o'clock. Unable to go back to sleep and not wanting to get up, I started to run through that passage in my mind. As I did, it occurred to me I wasn't getting the right answer because I wasn't asking the right question. I realized I should be asking not what those verses might be but where they might be. I reasoned that since I couldn't find them in the foreground, they had to be somewhere in the background. This thought got me out of bed in a hurry. Still in my nightgown, I started digging into the details of the chapter that didn't seem to be that important."

"What did you unearth?"

"Your verses, I think. They are about another rejection. The neighbors not only won't listen to the man defend Jesus, they, in the words of verse 34, cast him out. Isn't that rejection something like the frontier practice of tarring and feathering a scoundrel and running him out of town?"

"That may be a bit extreme, but it is a picturesque way of putting it. Why are they so harsh?"

"Verse 34 says it's because he has made the neighbors angry. Blind since birth, the man is obviously sinful and, therefore, has no right to instruct them. Yet here he is telling them how they are to view Jesus. This they will not tolerate. He has crossed a line, and, none too gently, they're sending him back where he belongs."

"Can the neighbors get beyond their anger?"

"And become neighborly? I don't think so. They won't hear anything he is saying. Their minds are closed."

"What closes the mind?"

"I asked myself that question at Vassar after being told the Greek astronomer Aristarchus had the earth and the other planets going around the sun. He got it right, but no one listened to him for seventeen hundred years."

"What did you decide?" Sister Emma said.

"I felt it had a lot to do with what is presupposed."

"What we have already assumed before we make an assumption."

"Yes. I promised myself at Vassar I wouldn't let my presuppositions get in the way of hearing the truth."

"Have you kept your promise?"

It suddenly occurred to me I had never considered that question before. I had been looking for God but hadn't looked within myself to see where my conclusions about God were coming from. Had I already made up my mind about God? Had it been made up since that horrible night when I learned of Katie's death? If it had been, did that mean I had come to the Training School not to decide about God but to confirm a decision that had already been made? "I'm not sure," I finally answered. "Did you have me read the passage because you think I'm not giving God a chance?"

"Perhaps not enough of a chance. Set aside some time to listen to yourself. You might be surprised by what you hear. There is, though, another reason for the passage. Why do the neighbors believe sin causes the man's blindness?"

"It's what they are told they have to believe."

"That's one explanation, but I think there is another. They believe it because they want to. It makes life rational, faith orderly, and God predictable in a world that would otherwise be, or at least appear to be, chaotic, and random, and, I would add, frightening." Picking up a Bible from a nearby table and after finding the passage she was looking for, Sister Emma said, "Belief in Deuteronomy, chapter 28, becomes, in effect, a formula that fixes and foretells what God will do." She then began to read, *And it shall come to pass, if thou shalt hearken diligently unto the voice of the LORD thy God, to observe and to do all His commandments which I command thee this day, that the LORD thy God will set thee on high above all nations of the earth: blessed shall be the fruit of thy body, and the fruit of thy ground, and the fruit of thy cattle, and the flocks of thy sheep. But it shall come to pass, if thou wilt not hearken unto the voice of the LORD thy God, to observe to do all his commandments and his statutes: cursed shalt thou be in the city, and cursed shalt thou be in the field, cursed shalt thou be when thou comest in, and cursed shalt thou be when thou goest out. The LORD shall smite thee in the knees, and in the legs, with a sore botch that cannot be healed from the sole of thy foot unto the top of thy head. All these curses shall pursue you and overtake you till thou be destroyed; because you hearkenedst not unto the voice of the LORD thy God.* There is no ambivalence here. God is watching, and depending upon what he sees, one's health and, more than that, one's life will be either blessed or cursed."

"That formula, though, is missing in other parts of the Old Testament."

"It is. There is Job who is without flaw but has everything—his health, his family, all his possessions—taken from him. When he demands an explanation, God instead of answering subjects him to a grueling interrogation that leaves him speechless. Humbled and reduced to silence, he realizes, however, that he, ironically, has been blessed. Before he had only heard of God, but now, because of this confrontation, belittling though it has been, he has seen God."

"And," I added, "all he has lost is returned twofold."

"That part of the encounter, at least for me, misses the point. It once again makes belief a formula. Good behavior—his repentance in dust and ashes for reproving God—brings material blessings. To say that the one produces the other restrains God and to restrain God in this or in any other way is to govern God. But God cannot be governed. God governs. God enters not into an equation but into a relationship with Job, a relationship that is intimate, disruptive, and stormy."

"Some of the Psalms are about a relationship like this," I said.

"Of them all, and there are quite a few, Psalm 44 is the most explicit. It basically is an indictment of God. In the past, God had brought the people victory in battle, but now they are being defeated and plundered by the enemy. Like Job, the psalmist wants to know why. Since the people are faithful, the law is being obeyed, the religious obligations are being observed, God, he concludes, is at fault. Maybe God has forgotten the people, or is sleeping, or is hiding. He pleads with God for deliverance, although given the tone of this last section of the Psalm it is more of a demand than a plea. If God had responded, the psalmist would have included his reply. Since he didn't, God is evidently not only forgetful, or asleep, or hidden, he is also silent."

"Doesn't Isaiah say something about God hiding?" I asked.

"You are probably thinking of chapter 45, verse 15 where he says, 'Truly you are a God that hides yourself, O God of Israel,'" Sister Emma answered. "I remember the words and where they are in Isaiah because of Blaise Pascal, a seventeenth century French mathematician, who over several years, particularly after a deep and profound spiritual experience, gave serious thought to God and to the life of faith. After he died, family and friends collected the thoughts that he had written down, over seven hundred of them, and published them in a volume titled *Pensees*, which means in French opinion or notion. A few months ago, I was making my way through that list and came upon the statement that since there are many religions, God must be hidden. Any religion that does not acknowledge this is false. Pascal then said, with much satisfaction I felt, that his religion did and quoted the verse from Isaiah."

"When Isaiah says God hides does he mean God withdraws?"

"No. God is always in the middle of what is happening. But when what we want to be happening or think should be happening isn't, we lose sight of God. He is not where we think he should be. He is not doing what we think needs to be done. So we say he is hiding. He's not, and we would know that if we looked for him in the right places. But we don't know where those right places are. We can't know where those right places are. We also read in Isaiah, chapter 55 if I remember correctly, his thoughts are not our thoughts; his ways are not our ways."

"We think he isn't there, but he really is. We think he's there, but he really isn't. Haven't we moved from God hiding to a hidden God?"

"We have."

"What does a hidden God do to faith?"

"I can tell you what he has done to my faith."

"And that is?"

"He has put my faith into a formula."

"Why, Sister Emma, I thought you didn't like formulas."

"I don't when God is in them."

"He's not in yours?"

"No, I am." As Sister Emma said this, she undid two buttons in the jacket she wore and started to fumble with something fastened to the inside of it. Finally able to release what I could now see was a safety pin, she removed from the jacket a small piece of white fabric and gave it to me. On it was the letter N followed by the number 4 and then the letter W.

"Faith is equal to N4W?" I asked, looking at the strip of cloth.

"I have come to think it is."

"I have never had any trouble with mathematics, until now that is."

"Let me solve that equation for you. N, which is taken from Psalm 73, stands for nevertheless. That psalm speaks of an injustice. The wicked prosper while the psalmist, who is blameless, suffers. Before the Psalm ends, though, the scales are righted by half. The wrongdoers receive their due, they will be brought down, but nothing is said about the psalmist being lifted up. He is shattered. Where is God's steadfast love? Where is his unwavering faithfulness? Where is his goodness? The psalmist finds himself, in his dismay, faced with a choice. Should he turn away from God or remain turned toward God? Should he go or, although he has more than enough reason to leave, after all God is the transgressor here, should he stay? He makes his choice with the first word of verse 23: 'Nevertheless,' he writes, 'nevertheless I am continually with you: you hold me by my right hand.' So often, especially living and laboring for God here in this constantly brutal city, this is a choice I have to make and, not because of what I see but despite what I see, I time and again make it with this word nevertheless. Nevertheless I have believed, and will now believe, and will always believe. Faith is what we choose; it's a decision we make again and again."

"And the 4 W?"

"Actually it's the 4Ws. The first W is for worship. The psalmist says, 'Let us worship and bow down; let us kneel before the Lord our maker. We are the people of his pasture and the sheep of his hand.' Then he says, 'Harden not you heart as in the days of temptation in the wilderness.' I worship because it is what I am made to do. Worship, of course, is what I give to God. It, however, is also what I do for myself. I worship so my heart does not harden. The hardened heart shuts God out. What is most alarming, the hardened heart does this unknowingly. It happens, and one is not even aware it is happening. The second W is for wait. At times I can be somewhat impetuous, which has, I'm sure, a great deal to do with being impatient. God goes by his own clock, which can, depending on the circumstance, run a whole lot slower than mine. I need to keep reminding myself of what Isaiah says, 'They that wait upon the Lord shall renew their strength; they shall mount up with wings as eagles; they shall run, and not be weary, walk and not faint.' The third W is for watch. Jesus tells the Pharisees to discern, a better word perhaps is the one that runs through all of scripture, he tells the Pharisees to behold the signs of the times. That admonition is for me also. As best as I can, I must continually behold the movement, the work, of God in the world in these times. The fourth W is for . . ."

Thinking of the verse from Ephesians I had read just the other day, I interrupted Sister Emma in midsentence. "I know that one," I blurted out. "Paul writes in the second chapter of Ephesians, 'We are his workmanship, created in Christ Jesus for good works.' The fourth W is for work."

"It is."

Thinking about her formula, I looked away from Sister Emma. Suddenly something occurred to me. "You are to wait, but at the same time you are also to work," I said, turning back to her. "You are to watch, that is you are to keep your eyes open and take in what you see, but at the same time, to keep yourself going in situations that appear hopeless, you are to close your eyes and shut out what you see. Your formula has its contradictions."

"Contradiction is a word you can use. I prefer, though, to say the formula has its tensions. Faith pulls you in different directions. This is certainly what we hear in the concluding verse of Psalm 40, 'I am poor and needy. Yet the Lord thinks of me, my help and my deliverer. Do not tarry, O my God.' In the statement 'the Lord thinks of me' offset by the plea 'do not tarry,' there is the tension between having and waiting. Faith puts you in-between the two, and there in the middle you feel drawn to each, to the certainty of the one and to the uncertainty of the other."

"Looking at you, Sister Emma, I see another tension. On the outside, your dress is plain, but on the inside, with that secret code pinned to your jacket, it is intricate. I'd say faith has put you somewhere between the simplicity of the one and the complexity of the other, and you go back and forth between the two."

"I do. I must admit when I'm at one, I tend to minimize, at least initially, the importance of the other. Actually, though, that secret code, which by the way is no longer very secret since you know what it is, is there to lessen, and on my best days to eliminate, a tension. It tells me what I must do to make the person I appear to be consistent with the person I profess to be."

"To close that gap you need to know yourself well."

"Thanks to Miss Hanson, my fourth grade teacher, that's something I've thought about ever since I was a little girl. I remember her telling us one day to put our reading books away and to pay close attention to what she was going to say. She's going to tell us, I said to myself, that someone was ill, or she was leaving the school to get married, or we were getting an extra week of vacation because of the leak in the roof. But I was wrong. Instead she said that we will at some time begin to ask ourselves who we are, and when that happens, she wanted us to have these three answers ready. We are members of our family; we are either a girl or a boy; and we are children of God. Through the years, I have held onto those answers. They are important, but I've come to realize they are not for me what is most important. When I ask myself now who I am, I answer I am a person of faith. It is faith that defines me, or perhaps I should say it is faith that defines me when I am being true to myself."

"Faith, then, above everything else. A lot in that everything else beckons," I said, thinking of Samuel holding me in his arms and of the crowd cheering as I slid safely across home plate with the game winning run. "How do you resist all those pleasures?"

"I hear his cry."

"Whose cry?"

"Jesus'. Beaten, spat upon, mocked, nailed to a cross, Jesus accuses God of forsaking him and, in horrible pain, wants to know why. No explanation is given. Though he is all alone and dying, God is silent. A sponge filled with vinegar is lifted to him on a reed. Then he, as Mark writes in his gospel, 'cries with a loud voice' and dies."

"That cry brings the death to you?"

"No, it takes me to the death. In that ninth hour, I'm always standing behind everyone else; the sight is too gruesome for me to bear and too repugnant. I also stay back because I don't feel worthy enough to come any closer. Since it is dark and I am so far away, I can hardly make out the cross and the form on it. But I do hear the cry. Arising out of the greatest agony and the deepest love, it bursts into my heart, into my soul. My sin is its cause and so also are my forgiveness, my redemption, my eternal salvation. That cry accuses me and finds me guilty, while, at the same time, it releases me from my guilt and brings me joy. Because of it, I am reconciled with God; I am born anew not of the flesh but of the Spirit; I am counted as being righteous before God; I am given purpose and so my life has meaning; I am blessed with a peace that passes all understanding."

"Where does belief like this come from?"

"A better question might be where does the decision to believe like this come from? Most believe because they have made up their minds to believe."

"But not everyone?" I said.

"A few, I would include Mrs. Meyer among them, are, to use a word I dislike but feel is most appropriate here, predestined to believe. They don't choose; rather they have been chosen, chosen for a particular purpose. It is not belief they struggle with, that they already have, it is obedience."

"What causes the others to decide for God?"

"That decision has two parts. God has decided for them. That part comes first and is foremost. When Jesus talks about a shepherd leaving ninety-nine sheep to find the one that is missing, he is saying God searches for those who don't believe even if they have not asked him to or don't want him to. Pascal writes in *Pensees* God inclines their hearts. I like his word inclines. He prepares their hearts, he predisposes their hearts to receive him. He does this, to use a word I also like, by wooing them."

"Their response to being wooed is the second part of belief?"

"It is. They accept God's advances because they are persuaded to. It makes sense to attribute the world they live in—its beauty, its complexity, its diversity—to God. Who else or what else could have designed all the pieces, made them, put them together, got them going, and keeps them going? When everything else ends, it makes sense when they consider the end of their own lives to turn to God, who does not end, to find in him an everlasting life. It makes sense, at least it does to Pascal, to wager God exists. If he does, the bet is won; if he doesn't, it is still won because believing in God makes life better. It becomes more honorable and kinder."

"Lizzie Connors, who played left field on our baseball team, once told me her father sold life insurance. After listening to him talk about its benefits, she decided it made sense to believe in God because faith was a good insurance policy. It would be there if she needed it, and if she did, the payout would be far greater than the cost."

"They also accept God's advances because they need to. When something good happens, they want to, and more than this, they need to give thanks. Thanksgiving for the blessing moves them to God who has blessed them and to belief in him and in his goodness. Or, and this is what most often occurs, this need is felt when something bad happens, whether it is something they have done or it is something that is done to them. The one brings guilt, the other sorrow. Whichever it is, they need to be set free from their torment. When deliverance doesn't come through their efforts or the efforts of others, they look to God for peace." Sister Emma paused for a moment and then said, "Do you remember what happens when Jesus is in the home of Simon, the Pharisee?"

"A sinful woman comes in. Simon wants her to leave, but Jesus doesn't."

"I think about that woman. Because of her many sins, she knows how corrosive and greedy sin is. Sin, to use the wording from the fourth chapter of Genesis, lies at her door and desires her. Her response to Jesus is a measure of how much she fears sin. She bathes Jesus' feet with her tears, kisses them, and anoints them with oil. The fear is so consuming she doesn't stop kissing his feet."

"Reason and need take those who don't believe to God," I said. "Is there anything else?"

"Indeed, there is, and because, from what I can tell, it reveals

God most fully, I'm convinced it is the most compelling. They submit to the advances of God, they fall into his outstretched arms, because they want to. Wooing is most successful when there is intimacy, when there is an intimate encounter with the one being wooed. So God fits what he does into their longings, into what they, at a very particular moment, are looking for, are hoping for, are striving for. If the fit is intense and unique enough, if it is endearing enough, then, through this experience, he is recognized for who he is, a God of love, and believed in."

"But they might think that an experience like this is a coincidence."

"They might. What they believe or don't believe is up to them. God gives them the freedom to accept him or to reject him. Faith is . . ."

Sister Emma put out her hand the way a conductor does when he's trying to get a desired response from his orchestra. By now I knew the response she was looking for. "A choice," I said, smiling.

"Faith is about choosing. It is also about naming. It is about putting the name of God to what you have experienced. No matter how absorbing the encounter might have been, this naming frequently occurs after, sometimes long after, it has happened, usually because something else has happened."

"I have never had an experience like this, an experience that I would put God's name to either at the time or later. God seems to be wooing everyone else in this school except me. What's wrong with me, Sister Emma?"

"Nothing, my child," Sister Emma said, gently placing her hand on top of mine, "absolutely nothing. Are you entirely sure that experience hasn't already happened? Perhaps it has, and you aren't willing to leap over Lessing's ditch."

"Did you say ditch?"

"I did. Gotthold Lessing, an 18th century German philosopher, said there was a ditch, actually he called it an ugly and broad ditch, between event and what could be known about God. It was a ditch he couldn't cross no matter how often he, to use his words, 'tried to make that leap.' The ditch was too wide. That was his problem. Your problem might be something else. You might be looking for a place where there is no ditch. But whenever you go from the finite to the infinite, from the temporal to the eternal, there will always be a ditch and you are always going to have to leap over it, unless, of course, you think the infinite is infinitesimally small and the eternal is infinitesimally short. Did you study geometry in school?"

More than a little surprised—what did geometry have to do with jumping over a ditch?—I managed to say, "Why, yes. I was in the tenth grade. Mr. Crawford was my teacher."

"Did you like it?"

"It was one of my favorite classes. I thought the proofs with their logic and precision were elegant. Two triangles are similar if their corresponding sides are in proportion and their corresponding angles are congruent. That's true for all the triangles that have been drawn and all that will be drawn. I think that's beautiful."

"And because you do, I think that appreciation reveals what you are looking for. My guess is you want a proof of God that has the logic and precision of your geometry proofs. But that kind of proof isn't possible. If it were, you wouldn't have faith, and it is faith that opens our minds to God. Instead of proof, what you need is a willingness to leap, and once you do leap, once you are on the other side, then events, small and large, will happen that will turn your willingness, either gradually or all at once, into conviction. The Bible, the testimony of others, the Church at its best, the experiences you have can fill in part of that ditch, but only part of it. You still have to leap."

At that moment, after softly knocking on the office door, Mrs. Meyer entered and said, "I'm sorry to interrupt you. Sister Emma,

I've just become aware of a situation that requires our attention. Please come to my office as soon as possible."

After Mrs. Meyer left, Sister Emma briefly looked at me without saying anything. She sat up in her chair, and the expression on her face hardened. I sensed that she was about to tell me something I might not want to hear. "Mattie," she began, "you will be graduating in little more than a month. Although your academic record and field work have been exemplary, I don't, at this point, expect you to become a Deaconess. You clearly have a servant's heart, but as you have been telling me, you do not have, or at least do not have yet, a heart for Jesus. A Deaconess must have both. As she has been before, decade after decade, so a Deaconess is now defined by the words she lives by, 'for Jesus' sake.' I need you to promise me you will not enter the Deaconess Order unless you can live by these words."

"I won't, I promise."

"Good. Mrs. Meyer is waiting for me, and I imagine there is some place you need to be."

Samuel had said in his note he wanted to see me that afternoon. Maybe he was already downstairs in the sitting room. I put on my coat, and then, suddenly struck by how uncertain my life had become, I turned to Sister Emma. Aware, I imagine, of how vulnerable I was feeling, she put her arms around me and held me tightly. As I started to thank her for her kindness, for her wisdom, without which I would have been altogether lost, she held me more tightly. Looking at her after she had let me go, I was sure I saw tears in her eyes. I hoped, maybe even for the briefest moment I prayed, they were not there because I was a disappointment to her.

* * *

Samuel was in the sitting room. I longed to sink into his arms, but this kind of intimacy, of course, was not permitted in the Training

School. We sat at a proper distance from each other, our voices were low, our emotions were, at least on the surface, restrained. Anyone looking at us would think we were just two people having a conversation about the weather. It wasn't the weather we were discussing, though.

At the very least, I expected him to be upset. After all, he had just lost his classroom, his sociology department, his university, and in addition to these losses, his livelihood. But instead of being distressed, he was relaxed. He was even cheerful. I was greatly relieved and also curious. How had he turned something bad, I should make that rotten, into something good?

He began by saying he had spent the better part of the morning sitting on a bench in Washington Park examining his life. It had been the perfect place to consider what he had done, what he wanted, and what he was going to do. Taking his time, he had looked at each matter thoroughly. When he had finished, pleased with where his thoughts had taken him, he had left the park at peace with himself and the University.

"I have no regrets. That letter was going to the newspaper no matter what the reaction to it might have been," he said. "That was what I thought and was where I stood. To dilute my convictions, to compromise them, particularly at the expense of the disadvantaged and the oppressed, was something I could not and I would not do."

"That answers what you did. What do you want?"

"I know and have known for some time now I want to be wherever you are, Mattie, today, tomorrow, and always."

"I don't know where I'll be. Sister Emma says I can't be a Deaconess."

"She doesn't think you are good enough?"

"She doesn't think I'm religious enough, and she's right. I'm not. At times, and this is one of them, I don't think I'm religious at all. Who knows where I'll be in another month."

"Wherever it is," he said, looking intently at me, "I'll be there with you, that is, if you will have me."

"I will. Oh yes, Samuel, I will, of that, and right now maybe only that, I am absolutely certain." I paused, as I suddenly realized the significance of what we had just told each other. For the briefest moment I placed my hand on his, and as I did, it occurred to me I was not only the first student to have been a professional athlete and to have spent a night in jail, I should make that, as Mrs. Meyer did, a night in jail with a man, I was also reasonably sure I was the first to have been proposed to in the sitting room of the Training School. Having accepted the proposal, I then asked what any girl in my circumstance needed to know. "What are you going to do?"

"I will probably teach wherever we are part-time."

"Probably. Don't you want to teach?"

"Not as much as I'd like to enter politics one day at the municipal or maybe the county level," Samuel replied. "I'd have more of a voice there than in the classroom. Right now, though, I'm going to write a novel."

"A novel. You've never said anything about writing a book."

"I've never wanted to before."

"Where did this idea come from? Don't tell me it came from God."

"It didn't, Mattie. It came from *Mary North*."

"Who is she?" I asked.

"*Mary North* isn't a woman," Samuel replied. "Well, actually she is."

"Samuel, either she is or she isn't. She can't be both."

"But she is. *Mary North* is the title of a book and is also the name of the woman the book is about."

"I've never heard of the book or the woman. Who is the author?"

"Mrs. Meyer."

"Mrs. Meyer," I almost shouted, "that can't be." Maybe even

more shocked by this outburst than Samuel, I immediately lowered my voice. "Some are still saying good Methodists aren't even supposed to read novels. To write one would be in their eyes sinful and, I would imagine, in the eyes of many other faithful churchgoers highly suspect. I had no idea she had done something so bold. But knowing her as I do, I'm not surprised. She is, especially when it comes to the Training School and her beloved Deaconesses, daring, perhaps I should now make that very daring."

"Mrs. Meyer wrote *Mary North* five years ago. When she asked me to become an occasional lecturer, I felt I needed to know more about her. So I read the book. It's a good story that is well written, thoughtfully put together, and honest. In it hard questions are raised and many but not all of them are answered. It's about a naive young woman the city devours. Alone and wretched, she would have died if a Deaconess, Sister Elizabeth, had not befriended her and through her care brought her back to life. The story, though, is really only incidental. It's a means to an end, not the end itself. Mrs. Meyer is primarily using it to write about the city, its power to diminish and to destroy, and about the Deaconesses, who they are and what they are doing to rescue those the city has struck down and left for dead. This morning when I woke up thinking I should be a writer, I also knew what I wanted to write about. People need to understand my neighborhood, what is good about it, what isn't, and why. I've used sociology to examine where I live, and now, like Mrs. Meyer, I want to draw upon the drama and especially the suspense of a story to make what I have found much livelier and much more compelling."

"It will be a novel then with loss and gain and lots of romance?"

"Yes. I might need your help with the romance, though."

"I'll be happy to give it," I said. Glancing at the clock on the wall, I saw that supper would be served in ten minutes. "It's late, Samuel. I have to get ready for the evening meal." We rose and then did something that was unheard of. Without even looking around to see who might be watching, we kissed. We kissed right there in the downstairs parlor. Anyone from a student, to an instructor, to Mrs. Meyer, to even a Methodist bishop could have walked in on us, but we weren't thinking about that. The kiss was brief. We both knew, though, it had lasted long enough to seal the giving of ourselves to each other for a lifetime.

After Samuel left, as I entered my room to put my coat away and get a sweater, I suddenly knew I needed to ask him something. I rushed downstairs, flung the front door open, and ran down the street until I caught up with him.

"What is it, Mattie?" he asked, concern in his voice.

"It's really nothing," I said, breathing so hard I had difficulty getting the words out.

"Since it can't wait until the weekend, it's got to be a whole lot more than nothing."

"It is, though I'm not sure why. For some reason, which at this moment is somewhat of a mystery to me, I have to know what you meant when you said Mrs. Meyer's book is honest."

"I did choose that word carefully. It's honest because what she writes about is real, at points it is brutally real. The story opens glorifying the faith of a child, which is so often today idealized because it is thought to soften the heart and to stir the emotions of the unbelieving. But this faith, before the onslaught of what I'm sure Mrs. Meyer would call evil, doesn't hold up. It is replaced by a faith that does. It is more resilient, more enduring, and, therefore, is, at least in her mind, closer to the faith God intends for us to have."

After squeezing his hand, I ran back to the school. I was late for supper, but a plate had been set aside for me. As I ate, I heard the girls around me talking, their voices rising and falling depending upon who was speaking, but I didn't listen to them. Instead I kept thinking about Mrs. Meyer's book and what she had to say about faith. After supper I checked the book out of the school library and going directly to my room, I started to read about Mary North. I went to bed that night, but unable to sleep, I threw on some clothes and hurried down to the library where I continued reading until I finished the book at six o'clock in the morning.

Samuel was right; it was honest. Mary North's faith as a child was extraordinary. She went to church every Sunday with her mother and ate caraway seeds during the sermon to stay awake. By the time she was ten, she knew Jesus had died to atone for the sins of the world. Knowing, though, was not enough. For her sins to be forgiven, she had to be converted. Mary longed for this blessing; she fervently prayed for it. When she was thirteen, she attended a revival meeting at the church. After his sermon, the preacher left the pulpit, and walking up and down the aisle, he said over and over again, "Come poor sinner. Come to the altar." Mary came, and as she sank to her knees at the altar railing and gave herself to Jesus, she felt his love sweep over her. Returning to her pew radiant, she told her mother, in a hushed voice, "I do love Him." Now converted, she unfailingly prayed, worshiped, and read the Bible, a chapter every day Monday through Saturday and three chapters on Sunday.

A year later, her mother, who had suffered for years with a failing heart, knew she was dying. Calling Mary into her room, she made her promise she would always remember God is good. Mary kissed her, and then her mother, extremely weak and tired, fell asleep. Looking at her, Mary heard the ticking of the old alarm clock on the dresser. It said so clearly she wondered why she had never noticed it before, "God is good. God is good." After her mother's death, Mary at times felt the world around her was full of her mother, especially when she was walking in the woods. The wind whispered, "Pray always," and the brook, like the old clock, murmured, "God is good."

Mary graduated from high school and then began to prepare for college. But a ruthless young man, a cunning scoundrel, had other plans for her. He seduced her with false promises, lies, and a staged wedding. Believing herself to be married, Mary soon realized to her horror she wasn't. Clinging to her belief God is good, she blamed herself for her plight. She fled to Chicago certain? God in his mercy had provided a way for her to escape humiliation and shame. But there her torment only intensified. Her life, caught in the maelstrom of the poverty, the inequity, the indifference of the city, contracted until everything was gone: her money, her health, her self-worth, her hope. Those words, God is good, were repeated, but as Mary sank deeper into despair, she couldn't say them with conviction, and the day came when she stopped saying them altogether. She no longer went to church; she no longer read the Bible. She still did pray, though now only out of habit. Her prayers were flat. There was no faith in them, no expectation in them. When God didn't give her what she asked for, she didn't even bother to ask why.

Having nothing to live for, Mary wanted to die. But Sister Elizabeth wouldn't let her. Taken to the Deaconess Home, she slowly began to mend. At first Mary had insisted she shouldn't be there. "I'm an outcast," she said. "I'm lost. I will go now. Oh, let me go." Sister Elizabeth, though, would have none of this. Having learned from Mary how she had been deceived, she told her and kept telling her neither God nor anyone at the Home blamed her for what she had done, and she must not blame herself. She had been the victim of a wicked scheme, and it was wrong for her to think that she had sinned and that God was punishing her.

"Oh, it is shocking," Sister Elizabeth said, "how people misunderstand our Heavenly Father." Her statement took Mary to one of those hard questions Samuel had spoken of. "Then why did he let it happen, Sister?" she asked. "I was praying about it all the time—all the time till it came to me on the train the kind of a woman I was, and I didn't dare to pray any more. Oh I can't understand why God did it." Sister Elizabeth answered God didn't do it, the devil did. But her explanation was not good enough for Mary. She said, "But God permitted it. Why did he permit it when I asked for his help?" Sister Elizabeth's response took me completely by surprise. She said, which meant that Mrs. Meyer also said, that she didn't know why.

I was stunned. I couldn't remember the last time I had heard someone in the Church admit to not having an answer to something so critical. It wasn't just a hard question. It was, I thought, the hardest question one could ask, and precisely because it was, it simply had to be answered. To leave it unanswered not only put God's goodness in doubt but his existence. But Sister Elizabeth didn't see it that way. What she did know was that God, loving both her and Mary, had sent her to Mary to love, and knowing that was enough for her.

This exchange left me with a question of my own. Did God permit Mary's suffering or was he unable to prevent it, and if he couldn't stop it from happening, what then did that say about God? There was another question I had that was even more pressing. Did the blessing of God's love outweigh the agony of suffering that couldn't be satisfactorily understood or explained? It did for Sister Elizabeth and, therefore, for Mrs. Meyer as well. But did it for me? Or perhaps I should say would it for me if I ever did experience that blessing and experience it so powerfully that, like Sister Elizabeth, I was certain of it?

The remainder of the story chronicled Mary's recovery. Her health and vigor returned and, largely because of Sister Elizabeth's love for her, so did her trust in God. Her life acquired new purpose. With the help of Sister Elizabeth, she established a School for Trained Helpers that prepared young women, like herself, for employment as skilled housekeepers. The words God is good appeared just once after she arrived at the Deaconess Home and the meaning had changed. God was good only in the sense that he brought good out of evil. God now was said to be love. Stephen, the fine young man Mary fell in love with, declared on the last page, "Love is God. For

God is love. His love is the great, glorious, heavenly stream—ours is the tiny rill. But it is all love. And all God."

Closing the book, I began to think about what Mrs. Meyer, at least in part, had been doing. In the story, she had contrasted God is love with God is good to show the difference between the two and the significance of that difference. God is good made life sweet. Suffering wasn't supposed to happen. When it did, the one who suffered, feeling deceived and alone, was ill equipped to move beyond it. God is love, however, made life sweet after it had soured. Suffering was going to happen. When it did, the one who suffered, being informed and not alone, was able to rise above it. While God is good set suffering aside, God is love overcame suffering.

I also thought about why I had read the book. It hadn't been a choice I had made. It had been a compulsion. Why had I felt this way? Was it because something within me or beyond me had known I too was hearing the clock on the dresser say "God is good"? Perhaps an even better question was why had I needed to read it right away? Why not next month, or next year? Was it because time was running out at the Training School?

* * *

In the early afternoon a week before graduation, the second-year students gathered around the large bulletin board outside the administrative office. The names of the girls who would be graduating and the girls who had chosen to become Deaconesses were to be posted at two o'clock. I stood behind the other girls and looked for Sister Emma. She wasn't there. Then at 1:57 she burst through the front door gasping for air. It sounded like, and from the perspiration rolling down her face it also looked like, she had run all the way from the Loop. Catching her breath, she politely moved through the girls, saying as she went, "please do excuse me," until she stood directly in front of the bulletin board. At exactly two o'clock, Mrs. Meyer's secretary emerged from the office holding two sheets of paper in one hand and several thumb tacks in the other. She pinned the two lists to the board, smiled at us, and returned to the office. I watched Sister Emma go at once to the list of Deaconesses. She kept staring at the names, and since she had her back to me, I couldn't tell what she might be thinking. Then she turned around with a huge smile on her face. Rushing over to me, she threw her arms around me and lifted me right off my feet.

"What happened?" she said.

"I laughed at the devil."

"You must tell me all about it."

"I can be in your office in an hour," I replied, wanting to give her time to rest. She probably had not run like that for a while, most likely for quite a while.

"I'll be waiting for you."

An hour later I was in Sister Emma's office sipping tea and eating gingerbread cookies. The visit was delightful. We laughed and cried, not tears of sadness as before but of joy. At her insistence, I did most of the talking. She wanted to hear it all from beginning to end. "Don't leave anything out," Sister Emma said. So I didn't.

"Three weeks ago I went to see a family I had been visiting for almost a year, Lydia and Willie Lane and their two small children, Mary and Bobbie. They lived in a tiny, one story house a few blocks this side of Forty-Seventh and Halsted Street. The house had only two rooms. They slept in one room and cooked and ate in the other. The toilet was outside, and a public bathhouse was used for bathing. The day I visited I immediately saw the little space they did have in the house had disappeared. Lydia's brother, his wife, and their daughter were now living with them. Six days ago the family had gone to Waukegan to visit an elderly aunt they hadn't seen for years.

Returning three days later, they couldn't find their house. The lot was there, but nothing was on it."

"It had been moved? Sister Emma asked."

"No, it had been stolen."

"I've never heard of such a thing," Sister Emma said.

"Neither had the police. When Lydia's brother reported the theft, they didn't believe him. Since the police weren't going to do anything about it, I decided I would. There were too many people in the Lane's home. The other family had to leave, but they had nowhere else to go. They had searched for the house on the streets close to where they lived but couldn't find it and their neighbors hadn't seen it either. Realizing the family had all but given up and knowing how harmful overcrowding was, I not only told them I was going to look for their home, I promised to find it.

"I needed a description of the house. They said that it was small, had a pitched roof, and was painted white. Since at least a quarter of the houses in the city looked like that, I asked for other identifying features, but they couldn't think of anything. If I didn't know what the home looked like, I obviously couldn't find it. I, too, was about ready to give up when their little girl Lucy, who couldn't have been more than four, said she wanted to show me her dolly in the bedroom. Going into the other room, we sat on the bed. She took a doll from underneath the covers and gave it to me. As I held it, she leaned close to me and whispered, 'There is a little hole at the bottom of the house. I had my friend Chester, he's twelve years old, make it for me so a bunny could come inside when it's cold at night. You won't tell my daddy will you?' I shook my head and then asked if the hole was in the front of the house, and she nodded yes.

"Over the next week, starting at the lot, I went out twenty blocks in every direction. I scoured neighborhoods, went up and down alleys, tramped through backyards, but I couldn't find the house. There were so many streets, so many homes, so few hours in the day.

It was, I knew, hopeless. That night, however, because of the foolish promise I had made, I told myself I would look again Monday. But if I didn't find the home by four o'clock, I was through. Knowing I needed help, I turned to God. I took the prayer book Mrs. Meyer had given me down from the shelf above my desk and read the 130th psalm and read it again. Using those opening words of the psalmist because I felt they described exactly where I was at that moment, I then prayed, 'Out of the depths have I cried unto thee, O Lord. Hear my voice.' I asked the Lord to direct my steps, to open my eyes, to take me by the hand and to lead me to that house. Remembering the words I had written on the first page of the prayer book, I also asked the Lord to give me faith.

"Monday I went out thirty blocks to the southwest. Although I kept searching until 4:30, I still didn't find the home. That's it, I said to myself, I quit. I turned around and headed back to the school. I had gone no more than three blocks when I heard a sound that made me stop so suddenly I tripped over my feet and almost fell to the pavement. I knew with absolute certainty what had made that sound. It had come from a bat hitting a baseball flawlessly. The speed of the swing, the swing itself, and the point of impact were perfect. I had heard that sound only once before. It was that day at Vassar when I had hit a baseball through the window of the chapel.

"I started to run toward where the sound had come from. Turning down a cross street, I saw a dozen children playing baseball on a vacant lot. A girl, she was probably eleven or twelve years old, was rounding third base and heading home while the outfielder was still chasing the ball. As I watched her cross home plate, her face, actually her entire body, glowing, I happened to glance to my right and noticed a side street I had not seen before. The second house from the corner on the left-hand side of the street was small, had a pitched roof, and was painted white. There was a For Sale sign in the front yard. From the sidewalk, I looked for a hole at the bottom of the house that would be large enough for a rabbit to go through. It wasn't there. Slowly, with a heavy heart, I started to turn away. My energy was gone; my resolve was gone; my hope was gone; what little faith I had was gone. It was at this very moment, when I was sure I had nothing left, it suddenly occurred to me Lucy had said it was a little hole. I all at once realized she might not have been talking about a live rabbit. Moving closer, I began to look for a hole a small stuffed bunny could fit through. I found it on the other side of the front door partly hidden by a pile of leaves. I had found the house.

"I could have swooned, or shouted, or sung, or danced. But I didn't. Instead I laughed. From somewhere deep within me, somewhere I hadn't even known was there, laughter came pouring out. It wasn't something I thought about doing or even particularly wanted to do. It was something I just did. And I knew why."

"You were laughing at the devil."

"I was. But that was odd. I had never talked about the devil. I couldn't even remember the last time I had used the word. Maybe I had never used it before. Evil existed, I was sure of that, but I had always thought of it as a force not a creature. Yet I knew that was exactly what I was doing. And I knew I was laughing not because it was funny, but because I was overjoyed. He had lost this time. He might not the next time, but he did this time.

"I at once went to the Lane's home, running all the way, and pounded on the front door. Frightened by the noise I was making, Lydia instead of opening the door made sure it was securely locked. Once satisfied the person on the other side of the door couldn't get in, she cried, 'Who's there?' When I shouted, 'Mattie,' Lydia unlocked the door and threw it open. Seeing the look on my face, she grabbed both my hands and with tears running down her cheeks said over and over again, 'Oh, Mattie, Oh, Mattie.' I then did something in this sublime moment of joy I was beginning to think might never happen. I thanked God. I had thanked God before, of course. But that thanksgiving was different. Those prayers had come halfheartedly from a wondering mind responding to what it had been instructed to do. This prayer, though, rose from the same mysterious place the laughter had come from and was offered not because it was what I was expected to say, but because it was what I wanted to say, it was what I needed to say. The prayer, I later realized, was a part of the joy. The one proceeded naturally, to put it more accurately perhaps, it proceeded necessarily from the other.

"I told Lydia's brother where the house was, and he immediately left for the police station. After saying good-bye, I started to walk back to the Training School. Although I would again be late for supper, which by now was probably expected, I didn't hurry. I had too much to think about. A perfect swing had made a sound that had taken me to a vacant lot and from there I had been led to a side street where I had found the house. All of this had been too tightly woven together to be a coincidence. Someone had done the weaving. Since I knew, at last, who the weaver was, I had a new question to answer. What was I going to do with what I now knew? I began to think about Paul. After his conversion, he went into Arabia before beginning his ministry. He withdrew from the world. I decided I needed to do that too. I made up my mind not to tell anyone what had happened. I first wanted to live with what I had experienced: to savor it, to give thanks for it, and, most important, to ask the one responsible for it what he wanted me to do."

"That was a wise decision, Mattie. How long did this withdrawal last?"

"It ended at one o'clock this afternoon when I asked Mrs. Meyer's secretary to add my name to the Deaconess list."

"You are sure?"

"About God? I am, Sister Emma. I too was found on that side street. While God can be bewildering, exasperating, and even at times infuriating, I also know, because I've experienced his love, I have experienced his love in a very personal and in a very profound way, God is good. I had better make that God is eventually good. I understand now that wanting to know why it can take God so long to be good is futile. That's a question I'm never going to be able to answer. So I have stopped asking it."

"The question, though, shouldn't be discarded. Rejection doesn't release us from it, understanding does."

"Understanding the suffering of innocents?"

"No, understanding what causes the suffering of innocents."

"Wouldn't that be evil?"

"It would be," Sister Emma answered. "One could go on forever, and many do, about evil. But all I really need to know about evil is in two passages. Paul says in Romans 8:22 the creation groans and travails in pain and in 2nd Corinthians 5:18-19 God was in Christ reconciling the world to himself and has committed to us the ministry of reconciliation. Those two statements take me across Lessing's ditch: the world is in pain, it is fallen, and God is redeeming it. God wants our help, more than this he requires our help, and as we are willing, he gives us the grace to be helpful. We, however, are always going to meet at times a subtle, at other times a blatant resistance that ultimately is not of this world. 'We wrestle not against flesh and blood,' Paul writes in the sixth chapter of Ephesians, 'but against principalities, against powers, against the rulers of the darkness of this world.'"

"And when we win one of those wrestling matches, we sometimes laugh at those principalities and powers," I said.

"We sometimes do."

"Sister Emma, the fifth chapter of 2nd Corinthians, along with that passage from Romans, takes you to the other side of Lessing's ditch. I think the fourth chapter of 2nd Corinthians is going to keep me there. In that chapter, Paul says we have this treasure in earthen vessels to show that the power belongs to God and not to us. We are troubled on every side, he writes, but not distressed, persecuted but not forsaken, always bearing in our bodies Jesus' death that his life may be manifest in our bodies."

"What is Paul telling you?"

"We don't do something for Jesus to get something from him. Doing something to receive something is the way business works. Labor is given to an employer in exchange for money. Money is given to a store in exchange for a product it provides. In business there is this exchange. But in the life of faith there is no exchange; there is instead obedience."

"You are right, and also wrong." Sister Emma paused for such a long time I thought she might have forgotten I was there. Then, with a satisfied look on her face, she said, "Do you like riddles?"

This was another one of her questions I wasn't ready for. We had been talking about an exchange, now she was asking me about riddles. I didn't know what one had to do with the other, although I was sure she did. I did know, however, how I felt about riddles. "Oh, I do. My father used to tell me riddles all the time when I was a little girl. I can still remember some of them. Here's one, Sister Emma. What's the highest building in the city?"

"Isn't it the Railway Exchange Building on Michigan Avenue? I believe it's seventeen stories high."

"No, it's not. The highest building in the city is the library because it has the most stories."

"Of course it is," Sister Emma said, laughing. "Now, Mattie, I have a riddle for you. What exchange is made that releases you and yet at the same time binds you?"

Shaking my head, I replied, "I don't know."

"You'll want to solve this one. The answer will make several matters of faith fall into place. You are going to have to figure the riddle out on your own, though."

"But, Sister Emma, my father always told me the answer."

"That's what fathers do. Teachers, however, sometimes don't, and this happens to be one of those times."

"Because you want me to go deeper into the subtleties of faith?"

"Because I want you to go deeper into the mystery of faith," Sister Emma said. "To get there on your own, I do have one rule. You cannot use a study aid of any kind."

"I can use only the Bible."

"And prayer, yes. I will, however, give you a hint. The answer you are looking for won't be where you think it is."

"It won't be in a familiar place."

"Mattie, you have already moved closer to the solution."

"But," I said, groaning, "I still have a long way to go."

* * *

Commencement week began the first Thursday of May with the Class Day exercises. Carrying roses, daises, violets, poppies, and morning glories, we paraded around the May Pole looking like a huge bouquet of beautiful spring flowers. Family and friends gathered Friday for an evening meal and a reception. I invited my family and Samuel, of course. They all came including Mother, who had recovered from her illness and for close to a year now had not suffered a relapse. Although I had told them about Samuel, they had never met him, and they didn't know how serious we were or even if we could be serious because of the commitment I was making. I expected the evening to be somewhat awkward at first. Perhaps it was, but once we sat down and began to eat and to talk the uneasiness vanished. My family was as warm and welcoming as Samuel was endearing. Although the word wasn't spoken, there was love at our table. I heard it said in the thoughts we exchanged, the stories we told, the laughter we shared. As I silently thanked God for my family, which I felt now included Samuel, I remembered the words on the last page of *Mary North*: "His love is the great, glorious, heavenly stream—ours is the tiny rill." Ours, to be sure, was only a tiny rill, I said to myself, but because it came out of that heavenly stream, the water in it was holy.

We attended a prayer service led by Mrs. Meyer Saturday night and Sunday heard the baccalaureate address in the morning and the annual sermon in the afternoon. The faculty entertained us Monday evening with readings from John Wesley Holland's *A Singular Life*. Tuesday we graduated. That afternoon, in a deeply moving costuming service, Mrs. Meyer put the bonnet of a Deaconess on my head, and as she tied the ribbons to keep it in place, she softly prayed, "Continue to use this child of yours in extraordinary ways." I wondered what those words from this saintly woman might mean for my life. Did she want it or expect it to take an unusual turn at some point, a turn that I would not even foresee? At Saint James Methodist Episcopal Church that evening, fifty-nine graduates received their diplomas from Mrs. Meyer. I, however, received more than a diploma. My brother surprised me. After the ceremony, he gave me a graduation gift, saying he thought I would like it. I did. Mrs. Meyer's latest book, *Some Little Prayers*, couldn't have been more fitting. I would keep returning to it, I knew, no matter what the coming years brought.

The training was over, and yet I knew it had just begun.

A Deaconess

CHICAGO, ILLINOIS
December 1908

At the end of the month, after being licensed a Deaconess by the Rock River Conference Board of Deaconess, I moved into the Deaconess Home on Erie Street. Built in 1906, the house was practically brand-new. It was a lovely place to live with attractively furnished rooms, an inviting parlor, a library, and a large dining room that could easily be converted into a classroom or a lecture hall. We were a sisterhood in that home, which is not to say life was idyllic. Bring thirty-one women together, especially those who had been raised and educated differently and have much different temperaments, and there will be disagreements, another word for them might be squabbles, that occasionally were upsetting. But with the help of our house superintendent, Ida Jordan, a gentle soul admired for her kindness and insight, they were usually resolved and when they couldn't be, because there was something else more important to settle, they were set aside.

My days were spread over four institutional churches of the

Methodist Episcopal Church. While the traditional church moved away from the tenement districts of the city, the institutional church went deeper into them, not waiting for the people to come to them, as the traditional church did, but seeking the people wherever they were. When I first talked to the pastor of the Halsted Street Church, he told me they faced almost insurmountable obstacles. Only one person in twenty-six, he said, was born in this country and most everyone was transient, living mostly in boarding houses or apartment buildings. Go from one neighborhood to another and a different nationality resided there, a different language was spoken, a different religion was practiced, a different ethical standard was enforced, a different set of social customs was embraced. These differences had erected barriers between the people, and these barriers, in turn, had instilled in them deeply held prejudices that were extremely hard to overcome.

Barriers and prejudices, though, were only part of what the church confronted. It also had to compete with the pleasures of the city: the dime museum, the dance hall, the beer garden, the nickelodeon, the amusement park with its roller coaster, dancing pavilion, roller skating, vaudeville acts, tunnel of love. Our purpose here, he emphasized, was to lead men and women, boys and girls to Christ, but because of all these divisions and attractions the only way to do that was to address first their immediate needs and desires. This necessity had forced them to see, as they had declared in a statement of self-understanding, that the ministry of the Halsted Street Church was as wide as human life and as deep as human need.

In all four churches, I regularly spent a third of my time visiting families experiencing a hardship of some kind, most frequently unemployment, illness, or death, and the other two-thirds directing their women's athletic and fitness programs. That I was in a gymnasium refereeing a basketball game or leading calisthenics most of the week satisfied both the pastors and the women, though for different reasons. The pastors figured it was what I was best suited for. The women, especially the younger women, thought it was where I belonged, not because of any ability I had, but because it was where they wanted to be. Competitive games and exercise had become hugely popular. The Whitely Exerciser was an unmistakable sign of the times. Easily installed indoors, the Exerciser, consisting of pulleys, an elastic cord, a foot attachment, and screw eyes, promised to make women stronger, healthier, smarter, and comelier. The assured outcome was practically irresistible, especially when it required little effort and guaranteed a more successful effort on a playing field. The Whitely Company couldn't make enough Exercisers to keep up with the demand for the device from women of all ages.

The wealthy had their Chicago Women's Athletic Club for competition and exercise. The city's parks with their golf courses, tennis courts, archery ranges, horseshoe pits, and baseball diamonds welcomed those of lesser means. The poor, though, had nowhere to go. The clubs were only for the elite, and the parks were beyond their reach. The public transportation was too costly; their clothes, threadbare, plain, and soiled, were too embarrassing; the police, eager to detain them for vagrancy, were too threatening. So they came in increasing numbers to our gymnasiums.

Life was good, and I felt blessed, but I also felt life wasn't quite good enough. Something was missing. To my surprise, because I was sure those days were behind me, I found myself thinking about baseball. Maybe, I told myself, I was getting caught up in the Chicago Cubs frenzy. With cold bats and key players injured, the Cubs had languished in third place during the first half of the season. But that started to change in late August. Once again healthy, they began to win behind solid pitching and the best infield in baseball. It was not their hitting and fielding that made Joe Tinker at shortstop, Johnny Evers at second, and Frank Chance, the manager, at first better than everyone else, it was their intelligence and teamwork. Time and again their double plays—from Tinker to Evers to Chance—were spectacular. Hope turned to expectation on August 30th when the Cubs beat the league leading New York Giants at home, their eighth win in a row. For fifteen minutes after the final out had been made, fans in the stadium threw thousands of rented seat cushions onto the field and standing-room only fans joyously threw them back. The Cubs, who had won the World Series the year before, were in the pennant race once again, and the fans were giddy with excitement.

I was too. But I soon realized I wanted to do more than follow others who were playing baseball, no matter how good they were and how gripping the pennant race had become. I longed to play baseball myself. So on a gorgeous Saturday morning in early September, I went to Lincoln Park carrying my mitt and bat in one hand and my baseball shoes in the other. Soon I came across a group of young men, most of them were in their early twenties, getting ready to take the field for what had to be the first inning of a baseball game. Since there were only eight men on the team, I asked the pitcher, who had just finished his warm-up throws, if I could be their ninth player.

"I am a faithful Methodist, Sister," he said courteously, "and have the greatest admiration for a Deaconess. There probably isn't any place you wouldn't go, but there is one place you can't go."

"Where is that?"

"Onto a baseball diamond where men are playing. You are a woman. A woman doesn't play baseball against men. You are wearing a skirt and a bonnet. You are not dressed properly. And there is the obvious. You are not good enough. Everyone here is talented; most of us have played in college. You couldn't even catch my fast ball."

"I can do better than that," I said. "I'll hit your fast ball."

He, and most everyone else who had heard my challenge, smiled; a few began to laugh. Wanting, I'm sure, to get rid of me and eager to begin their game, he, without another word, walked out to the mound, and his catcher, in full protective gear, went behind home plate.

"I'll make you two promises," he said. "The ball will not hit you, that's the first promise, and you will not hit it, that's the second."

"We'll see if you keep your promises," I replied, my knees slightly bent, my weight on my back foot, my bat held high, "particularly the second one."

He wound up, and the ball came in straight and fast. I swung not as hard as I could but with enough speed to send a scorching line drive out into center field."

"You can open your eyes now, Sister," he said.

"I never closed them."

"Well, then, that was a lucky swing."

"Let's find out if it was, and while we're at it, why don't we make this interesting. Throw me another pitch. If I swing and miss, I'll leave and never come back. But if I don't miss, I'm your new right fielder."

He nodded. I thought he would try to make me swing at a bad pitch and was right. The first one came in high. I let it go by and the next one, which was low and outside. The third pitch was right over the middle of the plate waist high, where all my power was concentrated, and with an almost perfect swing, I hit it into the trees beyond left field. After gallantly bowing, he called his team onto the field, and then, looking at me, he pointed to right field with an expression on his face that I felt was somewhere between amusement and disbelief.

As the days cooled and the leaves began to turn color, I knew the men would soon be playing football. Our Saturday games that I was enjoying so much were coming to an end. I didn't like the thought of putting my mitt and bat away until spring. It was like saying good-bye to two old friends. But then after reading an article in the newspaper, I began to think I might not have to. The article traced the rise and eventual fall of roller skating in the city. Several of the deserted skating rinks had been converted into indoor baseball diamonds, and a winter league had been formed. The rules had been modified and a larger ball was being used to accommodate the inside play. The league was open-ended. No team that wanted to participate would be turned away. It immediately occurred to me a team could be organized from the four churches I was serving. Telling myself I was not being self-serving since the men would benefit from the camaraderie and the physical activity and the churches from the increased collaboration, I took the idea to the pastors for their approval. They were in favor of it until they realized I planned to coach the team and even intended to play on it. Their yes then became an immutable no. When I asked why, they only said that there wouldn't be enough interest. I thought about adding, "because I am a woman," but didn't. There was nothing to be gained from fighting a battle that had already been lost. So, with what I hoped was a gracious smile, I thanked them for considering the suggestion and didn't mention the winter league again.

Although baseball wasn't over for the Cubs, who were now in a heated three team race for the pennant, it was for me. I was sure of that. But I was wrong. In early October, on a Friday, I received a letter from a Clarence Tucker of St. Louis, Missouri. Mr. Tucker first introduced himself. He was an industrialist who, after the death of his wife, had just retired from business at fifty-three to devote himself to his two greatest passions, baseball and the social and economic advancement of women. The two converged for him in the management of a bloomer girls baseball team, which he was currently forming.

He then wrote about the team. It would consist entirely of women who had played organized baseball and were competitors of proven ability. After training the last two weeks in May, the team would tour the country from the Midwest to the East Coast beginning June 1st and ending September 15th. The women would be paid a salary. The amount received would not to be based on the gate receipts but be a fixed amount agreed to by the player and the management in a binding contract that both parties would sign before the season started.

He closed the letter with a proposal. Maud Nelson, a close friend of his, had told him that because of my ability—having done nothing but strike out the day I faced her, I read those words again in astonishment—and my experience as a professional baseball player, he needed me on the team. Others, she had said, were a possibility, but I, for some reason that I couldn't begin to comprehend, was a necessity. He, therefore, wanted me to be both the team's center fielder and its hitting and fielding coach. He asked if we could meet October 15th at the Deaconess Home at four o'clock. He would bring with him a contract that he felt I would find most satisfactory. An answer to the proposal at that time would be helpful since my decision would determine what his recruiting needs will be.

I immediately wrote Mr. Tucker saying the 15th was fine. Besieged by questions I couldn't answer—What did I want to do? What should I do? What could I do?—I, however, was not fine. I didn't know where I was going to end up, but I did know where I needed to start, where I had to start. I had to talk to Sister Emma. Because of volleyball games and an extended exercise session at the Lincoln Street Church, I didn't get to the Training School until Saturday in the late afternoon. As I entered the school, Sister Emma was leaving to have supper with a friend and then to attend a concert at Orchestra Hall. Seeing that I was struggling with something, she suggested, to my surprise, that we go to the Cubs game Sunday. When I reminded her tomorrow was the Sabbath and we were supposed to be in church, she quoted Jesus' statement about the Sabbath being made for man, not man for the Sabbath. That pronouncement, she declared with a reassuring smile, also applied to women.

Then she asked if I realized the game tomorrow against the Pittsburgh Pirates might determine who won the pennant. If the Pirates prevailed, they did. If the Cubs prevailed and the Giants lost to the Boston Braves, we did. It was our civic duty, she said, to be at that game. Our boys needed us there. How could we possibly disappoint them? Before she could say anything else, I held up my hands in mock surrender and told her I was in complete agreement. While acknowledging my capitulation, she added that the game after all was the ideal place for us to meet. We'd see these two marvelous teams battle for a championship and also watch the play of possibly the best hitting infielder in the history of baseball Honus Wagner, the Pirates' shortstop, who was leading the league in batting average, hits, doubles, triples, total bases, runs batted in, runs produced, and stolen bases and was second in the league in runs scored and home runs. In-between the innings, we'd talk and have more than enough time to think about what was being said. Now completely convinced it was the very best idea we'd ever had, we agreed to meet at the main gate half an hour before the game started.

More than thirty thousand fans, thought to be a new attendance record for baseball, watched the Cubs win 5-2. Although they lost their early lead to the Pirates in the sixth inning, the Cubs, undoubtedly the better team that day, quickly regained it and then with strong relief pitching from Mordecai "Three Fingers" Brown held onto to it for the remainder of the game. It wasn't difficult to see what came next for them. Either the pennant was theirs, or they would have to play the Giants for it. What came next for me, though, wasn't clear at all.

That afternoon we talked about playing baseball almost as much as we watched baseball being played. After telling Sister Emma about the bloomer girls offer, I asked her if a Deaconess could play professional baseball. "The General Deaconess Board won't allow it," she replied. "Earlier this year the Board informed Mrs. Meyer she could no longer wear the Deaconess dress because she is married. I was in the administrative office talking to her secretary, Miss James, when she returned from that Board meeting in Boston. Entering the school, travel weary and disheveled, she went directly to Miss James. Giving her the bonnet she had proudly worn for twenty years, Mrs. Meyer said, 'Take it. I shall never wear it again.' Those words broke my heart. If a rule couldn't be set aside for the one who had founded the Order, it certainly can't be for you. A Deaconess has to be connected to the sisterhood and overseen by a supervisory agency. Touring the country with a baseball team would make that impossible."

"Would it be awful," I then asked, "if I fulfilled less than a year of the three year commitment?"

"Some, especially the Board, would not be pleased. The vow for them, unless there is a health problem or a moral lapse, is binding. Others, and I am among them, look at that vow differently. We are being forced, not by the church but by the world the church is called to labor in, to see that vow, and a whole lot more, differently. I must admit my eyes have recently been opened by the thinking of Henry Adams."

"Didn't he write a lengthy history of the United States?"

"Exhaustive may be a better word. It's a highly regarded nine volume study of the nation during the years Thomas Jefferson and James Madison were President."

"I remember my history instructor at Vassar felt that being the grandson of John Quincy Adams and the great-grandson of John Adams had given him unusual insight into the forces shaping the nation at that time."

"I believe his privileged education and his solid grasp of history have given him a unique understanding of the forces shaping our country at this time. These forces are what his new book, *The Education of Henry Adams*, is about. Only a few copies of the book have been published. Apparently only family and close friends have seen it. My cousin Laurence isn't one of those friends, but his brother-in-law, a state senator, is. He was given the book and passed it on to Laurence, who, in turn, kindly gave it to me. I'm thankful he did. It is superb. The point Henry Adams makes is these forces now are not just formidable, they are frightening. We have set loose within our world prosperity, power, and speed never before achieved, and they all are out of control. We don't know where they are taking us, and wherever it is, we don't know how we are going to get there. We stand before these forces ignorant and, consequently, ill-prepared. Our education, no matter what it has been, can, therefore, only mislead us; it is, in a word, useless."

"Isn't this conclusion a bit extreme?"

"It is. But from it comes the undeniable and also the inescapable fact that we are in the midst of something new that is of massive scale and is occurring at an unprecedented rate and in unprecedented ways. It has made us, as Henry Adams writes, irritable, nervous, querulous, unreasonable, and afraid."

"Why, he's telling us Nemo's dreams are about to come true."

"Nemo?" Sister Emma said, "I'm not acquainted with the gentleman."

"Nemo, Sister Emma, is not a gentleman. He is a little boy on the Sunday comic page of the *New York Herald* who in the weekly episodes has fantastic dreams filled with fabulous buildings, mysterious people, and gigantic creatures. It is a wonderland that beckons, glitters, and, at times, crushes. In his adventures, Nemo falls through the air thrashing about wildly, or he drowns, or he is impaled. The Clippers would stop in New York at least three or four times a season. Whenever we were there, I'd always get the Sunday *Herald* to find out what was happening to Nemo in his latest dream."

"Out of control in a wonderland with a dark, rapacious side, that, I would say, is pretty much where we are today. Just think of what has happened in this wonderland of ours this year. President Roosevelt sent sixteen battleships on a forty-three thousand mile voyage around the world. Six automobiles from four countries raced from New York City to Paris. The Singer Manufacturing Company built in the Manhattan financial district a skyscraper forty-seven stories high. Wilbur Wright flew an airplane with a passenger for more than an hour before he landed. The Ford Motor Company promised to cut the cost of a five passenger family automobile in half. Dr. Simon Flexner of the Rockefeller Institute wrote that the day was soon coming when a healthy organ will replace one that is diseased. Those who understand how a telephone works spoke of a not too distant future when we will carry the telephone in our hats or in our pockets and be able to use it wherever we are.

"The world is changing; it is expanding. With so many more possibilities, it is becoming larger. But as the skyscraper, the airplane, the automobile, the telephone draw people closer together, it is at the same time becoming smaller. As it becomes smaller, the differences between us—what we have, what we look like, what we think, what we believe—become sharper and as they do, the world becomes more perilous. To have anything to say, to have anything to offer, in this new day, the church also has to change and to change in unprecedented new ways. Thankfully, it has already started to. Do you know Reverend Camden Cobern?"

"I only know of him."

"Always well dressed and neatly groomed, he, in almost every respect, looks appropriately ministerial. I did say almost, however, because there is a glaring discrepancy in his appearance that is shocking, and I am sure to a good many, it is disturbing. He always wears a cross, not underneath his shirt but outside his shirt, or his vest, or his suit coat. Ten years ago, maybe even five years ago, it wouldn't have been there. To have worn it back then would have been not only in poor taste but offensive. Roman Catholics wore a cross; Methodists didn't—I probably should change that to therefore Methodists didn't and emphasize the word therefore. But today one of the most influential and admired Methodist ministers in the city does. It's around his neck for everyone to see because, as he has written, it speaks of Christ's love for the world and of a Church that sacrificially gives itself to the world.

"I and many others who today think like Reverend Cobern would say your commitment, Mattie, in this new world all of us are being thrust into, is not ultimately to a Board, or to an arbitrarily set period of time, but to God. You need to go where he is sending you. As he has called you into Deaconess work, he can call you out of it, and can call you out of it at any time, to be his answer to someone's cry for help or to someone who will be crying for help."

"So the question then is not what the Board will or will not permit but where does God want me to be."

"That, in the end, is always the question."

"I do long to play baseball. I am sure of that. But what I am not sure of is where this desire comes from and what it means. Is it a summons that will take me closer to God, or is it a temptation that will turn me away from God? I just don't know, Sister Emma."

"Don't chastise yourself for this indecision, but welcome it, embrace it. It will keep you alert, attentive, and in prayer. Wait upon God, and the answer will come, one way or another."

* * *

Hurrying up the street, I told myself if I went faster I would be on time for my meeting with Mr. Tucker but I would also arrive dripping with sweat. Would it be better to be punctual or fragrant? I had no trouble deciding what to do. Since he was or would soon be used to the girls on his team perspiring, I started to run. I still had trouble, though, a whole lot of trouble, deciding what to do about his offer. I hadn't heard anything from God. Once again he was silent, which I didn't find too surprising. Nothing unusual had happened. Really the only incident of any interest was the dream of a seven year old. Last week when Sadie came to the gymnasium at the Halsted Street Church for playtime, she told me she had dreamed of me standing in a field. All of a sudden the wind had started to blow so hard it had turned me around, and then it had started to rain. When I asked what came next, she replied with the loveliest smile, she didn't know. She woke up. I was so captivated by that smile—it was so angelic—I found myself telling her I didn't want to get rained on, and so, even if the sun was shining, I'd take my umbrella with me wherever I went.

Mr. Tucker had attractive features and a winning smile. Well-spoken and obviously intelligent, he, with his self-confidence and easy charm, was one others would readily follow. He undoubtedly would be as successful with his baseball team as he had been in business, and those who played for him would prosper as well. He listened, with unusual attentiveness, to me describe my work, asking several questions about the churches and especially their gymnasiums, and then talked about the team and its summer tour.

Finally he turned to the question I knew was coming. What did I intend to do? I didn't answer right away. I was still waiting for something from God. But he apparently had nothing to say. It suddenly occurred to me no sign was actually the sign I had been looking for. Realizing now it had been God's way of telling me to stay where I was, I thanked Mr. Tucker for his offer. The terms were more than generous; the opportunity to play baseball again and to coach the team that he was going to put together was intoxicating. I, however, had to decline the offer. He asked if there was a possibility I might later change my mind. Shaking my head, I said no. I was quite sure my place was here serving Jesus as a Deaconess. Saying he understood, he was Episcopalian and they, too, had Deaconesses, he got up and started to leave. He then stopped and turning around said that he was curious. On such a bright sunny day, why was I carrying an umbrella? I replied that I had taken it with me this morning to please a young friend. Smiling, he said good-bye and with a wave of his hand once more started to go. But again he stopped and said that the umbrella had just reminded him of something. He had forgotten to mention the name of the team. It was going to be called the Cyclones. I stared at him, unable to speak, unable to move. In that moment, fear, wonder, joy, all of them at the same time, swept over me like the wind in Sadie's dream, which had been powerful enough to turn me around. I was standing on holy ground, I finally said to myself. Then I laughed. He couldn't have known why, but I did. I had once again laughed at the devil.

Two months later when I returned to the Deaconess Home after a long day at the Halsted Street Church, I was told there was a package for me in the office. I picked it up and went to my room. Opening it, I first saw the bloomers. Taking them out of the box, I next saw the matching blouse with the word Cyclones in large letters across the front, and underneath it was a copy of the contract I had signed and had then dated October 15, 1908.

IV

RANDALL

The Grandfather

1

LATE AFTERNOON

"That's the last page, Henri. I've finished it," Randall said, slowly closing the memoir, which was the word he was now using for Mattie's journal. "Walter was right. What we have here is huge. So tell me, old girl, what do you think about Mattie? I guess I should say Aunt Mattie." Henri, their fourteen-year-old dog, had been taking her late afternoon nap on an oversized pillow next to Randall's chair. She opened her eyes and looked up at him. Whatever Henri did think about Mattie or about anything else for that matter, she kept to herself. So Randall said, "Well, I'll tell you what I think. As a college graduate, a professional baseball player, and a Deaconess, she was, to use the term that the press of her day made popular, a New Woman. These ladies were independent souls who had the ability and the gumption to go their own way.

"But I also think I see in her, and this I find most intriguing, a little bit of Soren Kierkegaard. I'm sure you haven't forgotten him, old girl. Over the years, I have talked about Kierkegaard often enough. Why, I even wanted to name you after him. If I had my way, you would have been called Sorenina, so we could have shortened your name to Soren, but Emily didn't like the idea. No dog of ours, she said, was going to be named after a nineteenth century Danish philosopher and particularly that Danish philosopher. I pointed out he always thought of himself as a poet not a philosopher or even a theologian, but she wasn't listening. He was weird, she went on. He offended people and looked funny. He combed his hair in a strange way; he wore clothes that didn't fit, his pant legs were never the same length; he walked like a crab and always carried an umbrella even when there wasn't a cloud in the sky. But all of this was intentional, I countered. He wanted to stir things up; he wanted to get people to think in new ways. But, old girl, you know Emily. Once she has made up her mind nothing is going to change it short of a directive from God. So we named you Henrietta, which became Henri. I am, though, still of the opinion Soren would have fit you nicely. It does seem to fit Mattie nicely as well, not his name, of course, but his thought, although rather loosely, I admit.

"Think of the similarities. The two of them sought their own truth regardless of the cost. Kierkegaard told himself when he was twenty-two, 'The thing is to find a truth which is true for me, to find the idea for which I can live and die.' Mattie could have said those very same words to herself, or to anyone else who might have been interested, without thinking twice. Both were influenced in their search for truth by the attention one person in particular had received. Behind Mattie's pursuit of truth was Aristarchus, whom no one had listened to, although they should have, for he was right. Everyone was listening to the philosopher W. F. Hegel's understanding of truth, and Kierkegaard was convinced they shouldn't be, for he was certain Hegel was wrong. Both eventually believed the truth they needed was of God, and since it was, it could only be received in faith. Both insisted faith could not be derived from someone else. What they believed had to be their own decision, and that decision had to come from their own thought and from their own experience.

"Now, Henri, I have a question for you. Did Mattie run across Kierkegaard at Vassar or the Training School? His thought, especially his emphasis on the individual, might have been discussed in one of her classes or in a conversation with a professor. Maybe Sister Emma, or Mrs. Meyer, who apparently was relentless in her pursuit of truth, or even Samuel talked to her about Kierkegaard. Of course, the possibility exists no one did. A kindred spirit might have brought their lives together. Or, to be entirely forthcoming, I might have. Maybe I see a connection because I want them to be connected. But, as you well know, that doesn't mean they are. Well, old girl, what do you think happened?"

All Randall heard was a wheezing sound. "Henri," he said, grinning, "you are snoring again."

* * *

Thinking about Mattie over the next several days, Randall kept coming back to a question Jesus asked in the eighteenth chapter of Luke: "When the Son of man comes, will he find faith on earth?" That Jesus even asked the question implied he wasn't too hopeful. This pessimism caused Randall to ask a question of his own. How constant is faith? Although Mattie believed, would she always believe, would he always believe? Looking for an answer, he turned to a statement that was never far from his mind. In the ninth chapter of Mark, a man asked the disciples to heal his son, but they couldn't. The man then said to Jesus, who had just joined them, "If you can do anything, have pity on us and help us." Jesus replied, "All things are possible to those who believe." The man responded, "I believe; help my unbelief." Randall said those words "I believe; help my unbelief" slowly to himself and then said them again. As he did, he all at once realized he, and he imagined a lot of other pastors as well, had always put belief alongside of unbelief when he talked about this passage. Looked at this way, the passage was about doubt. But it had suddenly occurred to him the two possibilities could also be put end to end. First there was belief and then at some point because too much was required or too much was forgone belief gave way to unbelief. Arrange the two possibilities like this and the conversation shifted from some faith to no faith; it shifted to faithlessness.

Belief alongside of unbelief made faith weaker but limitless. It was unbounded. Belief ending in unbelief made faith stronger but limited. It was bounded by a circumstance or a condition that faith could not go beyond. Randall regularly prayed that no matter what happened he would always say without hesitation, without equivocation, I believe. But he couldn't be sure, absolutely sure, he always would. Since Mattie's memoir ended shortly after she had started to believe, he couldn't say she always did. But what about someone else's faith? He thought for a moment and then said to himself what about Lucy Rider Meyer's faith? It was strong when Mattie was at the Training School. But did it remain strong later? He didn't know, but, he told himself, he was going to find out.

He did. The information Randall gathered was abundantly clear. If Mrs. Meyer's faith came from what she had, if it, therefore, came from a belief in God's goodness, then she had more than enough reason to stop believing in God, for much of what she had she lost. She lost her health. Mrs. Meyer suffered often intensely and for prolonged periods of time from recurring vertigo, chronic fatigue, debilitating headaches, heart failure, Bright's disease, and severe inflammation of the nerves.

She lost the Training School. It reached a high point in 1910 with an enrollment of 256 students and a graduating class of 84, and then the numbers fell, and as they did, financial difficulties that had always been present became increasingly more serious. Changes were made. Men were admitted to the Training School and facilities and resources were shared with the Presbyterian Training

School. But these steps were not enough. Although feeling herself, as she said, still "fit for the task," yet fully aware she did not possess the insight and the ability needed to turn the school around, she resigned as principal in 1918. Stepping aside broke her heart, but she knew it had to be done. There was no other way to save the school she had built over the last thirty-two years.

She lost her marriage. Although the marriage itself held together, the happiness it had brought vanished and so the marriage in a very real sense did too. Differences that before had united her and Mr. Meyer now divided them causing a painful rupture that could not be mended. Both were too strong-willed, or, to use another word, too stubborn to find a middle way, so time and again, after harsh words had been spoken, after feelings had been hurt, they took their own way.

She was searching; Mr. Meyer was dogmatic. She embraced the new, especially the new scientific discoveries and the knowledge coming out of new historical research; he held onto the old, insisting it contained all that was necessary. She was open; she listened to others. He was closed; he listened to himself. She was straightforward; he, at times, was opportunistic. They clashed over the Bible, how it should be interpreted and taught; over the kind and amount of education needed for work with the poor and suffering; over the answer to the Training School's decline; over the gender of the new principal. They even clashed over Mrs. Meyer's health. She, at one point, was sure she had recovered from an attack of vertigo and was ready to go back to work. He was certain she had not and ordered her to remain in bed. She defied the order, got dressed, and, on her way to her office, stopped to speak to a secretary. As they were talking, she heard someone say Mr. Meyer was coming. He entered the room and after picking up his mail left. Although she was only a few feet away, he never saw her. She had hidden underneath a table and didn't come out until after he was gone.

Mrs. Meyer once wrote in a confidential letter to her dear friend, Belle James, that she was in some ways a sad and broken woman and thought she always would be. She didn't explain why she felt this way. The reasons, though, were obvious. Elsewhere she spoke of her regret that she hadn't been a better wife; of her grief when her mother died which did not lessen as the years went by; of her periods of intense loneliness; of her critics who relentlessly attacked her beliefs and her management of the Training School; of her antagonist the Woman's Home Missionary Society that in a bitter struggle lasting more than three decades tried to take control of the Deaconesses and the Training School.

She could have easily said I don't believe. But Mrs. Meyer never did. Instead, as she wrote in her diary, she said, "My life seems destined to be always a storm center. Blow after blow falls. I plod blindly and doggedly on, doing my heavy day's work. That's the way to hoe corn. Keep steadily at it and don't stop to look around much." She never did stop hoeing corn, right up to the very end. When she went to the hospital for the last time, two weeks before her death, she took with her a pen and lots of paper. A sedative was used to ease her pain. She worked as best she could on an article that was due for a Sunday School periodical. A doctor came into her room to give her more of the drug. Realizing she was close to finishing the article, she asked him to delay the medication for a few hours. Continuing to write although the pain became almost unbearable, she completed the article before he returned. Satisfied the deadline had been met, she put away her pen, this time for good. Periods of unconsciousness followed. In- between them, she talked of heaven, of knowing God better and more intimately, of work needing to be done.

Her faith remained strong. Randall was now sure of that and thought he knew why. She was, as Sister Emma had said, one of those few who had been chosen. Belief for everyone else, for those who had been called, was a voluntary act; for those few, for her, though, it was involuntary. Believing for them was like breathing. It wasn't something they decided to do, but something they just did. It was a blessing they had been given.

But then it occurred to him there might be another blessing that explained Mrs. Meyer's tenacity even in the darkest times. "Blessed are those who hunger and thirst for righteousness," Jesus said in the Sermon on the Mount, "for they shall be satisfied." For those who were called, this longing for righteousness was a blessing to be attained through grace and effort. It was what they wanted to have. But, Randall asked himself, didn't the chosen few, didn't Mrs. Meyer, already have this blessing? Wasn't it what they were given when they were chosen? If so, then it was this relentless and insatiable drive to be righteous, to be right with God through being right with others, and not faith that kept moving them on, that had kept Mrs. Meyer moving on, without, as she had written in her diary, stopping much to look around.

A poem Mrs. Meyer had written confirmed, at least for him, this understanding of her resolve.

> *"These sick and sad, these blind and orphan, yea, and those that sin*
> *Drag at my heart. For them I serve and groan.*
> *Why is it? Let me rest, Lord. I have tried"—*
> *He turned and looked at me:*
> *"But I have died!"*
> *"But Lord, this ceaseless travail of my soul!*
> *This stress! This often fruitless toil*
> *These souls to win!*
> *They are not mine. I brought not forth this host*
> *Of needy creatures, struggling, tempest-tossed—*
> *They are not mine."*
> *He looked at them—the look of One divine;*
> *He turned and looked at me. "But they are mine!"*
> *"O God," I said, "I understand at last.*

Forgive! And henceforth I will bond-slave be'
To thy least, weakest, vilest ones;
I would not more be free."

She called the poem "The Burden." It, he realized, spoke of an exchange that had been made. She had replaced the burden she carried with the burden others were carrying. It was an exchange she made willingly, that she made gladly, because they who suffered so were His. She would always give all of herself to making that burden lighter and if possible to making it go away altogether. Hungering and thirsting for righteousness, she could not do otherwise.

Randall gathered together his notes and after going through them a final time wrote at the bottom of the last page, "mighty fine corn and a whole lot of it." Right above these words and a large part of the reason for them was an account of the Founder's Day celebration held three years after Mrs. Meyer's death and forty years after the school had opened. That evening began with a festive meal in the dining hall. Congratulatory speeches were heard; hymns were sung; prayers of thanksgiving were offered. Everyone then moved to the chapel with some because of the limited seating having to view the proceedings from the hallways. On a table that had been placed in front of the altar there was a tall, white candle. As the room darkened, conversations ended, and then when there was complete silence Mr. Meyer came forward. After lighting the candle, he spoke of the school's beginning. The house he and Mrs. Meyer had acquired, he said, was old, gloomy, and in disrepair. Once the necessary improvements had been made and their four students had arrived, they set a time to celebrate the school's opening. Guests were invited but instead of the dozens expected only three people came. After they left and the students had gone to their rooms, he and Mrs. Meyer, looking at the chairs that had not been used and all the food that had not been eaten, wondered if the Training School would ever amount to anything.

Mr. Meyer sat down. Then a woman approached the table, and from the candle on it, she lit the candle she was holding. She turned around and, raising the candle, briefly presented the accomplishments and disappointments of that first year. Another woman, holding high her lighted candle, in the same way summarized the second year. One after another, many from the classes they represented, many of them Deaconesses, all of them serving others in Jesus' name, spoke until all forty years of the School's history had been lifted up and celebrated.

Then the room became quiet. The flickering light from the candles beating back the darkness told of victories won in the midst of adversity. The light overcoming the darkness spoke of the triumph, at great cost, of good over evil, of love over sin and death. A minute went by silently, and then another, and another. Then a woman came forward carrying a candle. After lighting it, she said that she was a missionary in Africa home on furlough. Although she was here by herself, she was not alone. Others in nearby and faraway places stood with her. For in this hour they, too, held candles lit in tribute to the Meyers and in thanksgiving for their school. These candles, she went on, have been lit from one end of this country to the other; they have been lit in Hawaii and in the Philippines; they have been lit in Japan, and Korea, and China; they have been lit in Africa, and India, and Europe. The light from this hallowed ground, she said, has gone forth not only into the world; it has gone forth around the world.

2

SUNDAY MORNING

Randall put the memoir and his notes in a folder and placed it on a shelf in a closet. Although he was through with them, at least for the time being, he knew he wasn't finished with the story they told. There was too much he still wanted to know. How long had Mattie played for the Cyclones? What was her batting average? Did she and Samuel eventually get married? If they did, where did they live and what did they do with their lives? Did they have children, and perhaps the most pressing question, who were the descendants of that marriage and where were they now living? Although he searched for answers in various historical records, especially in newspapers covering the years 1910 to 1920, he couldn't find anything that was helpful. There was, however, one exception. While visiting family in Chicago, he spent a day at the courthouse on Washington Street going through its records and came across a marriage certificate for Matilda Welsh and Samuel Bingham and a birth certificate for their daughter Mira. So he knew Mattie did become a Bingham, and they had at least one child. But since that was all he knew, his search for the Bingham family and its descendants ended at the courthouse.

There might have been more information elsewhere, but he didn't know where or even how to look for it, so he reluctantly stopped looking altogether.

The story, therefore, remained incomplete. Randall realized, though, that for him the ultimate importance of a life lived so long ago lay not in what was done, but in what God was saying through what was done. What was God saying to him through the lives in this story? That, he knew, was a question he needed to answer. He also knew the answer would come in its own time and in its own way.

As he considered these words, it occurred to him Sister Emma's riddle might be a part, a large part, of that way. She had asked Mattie what exchange was made that released and yet at the same time bound her? There was nothing in her memoir to suggest she had tried to solve the riddle. What she hadn't done he knew he had to do, and he had to do it, as Sister Emma had made clear, using only the Bible. Resources like a concordance or a Bible Dictionary were not allowed. In the search for the solution or in the solution itself, and most likely in both, there was something he needed to understand. His first thought was of Mrs. Meyer's poem "The Burden." In it she spoke of assuming the sorrow of others. Here was an exchange of sorts: her agony had given way to their pain. But instead of this exchange releasing her, instead of it setting her free, it took away her freedom. It made her, to use her words, "the bond-slave" of the weak and the depraved. This obviously wasn't the exchange in the riddle.

Randall next considered Sister Emma's hint. The answer wouldn't be where Mattie thought it was. Knowing where it wasn't, he reasoned, would help him know where it was. So, he asked himself, where would Mattie have looked for that answer? Being a conscientious student, she would have looked where her teacher would have wanted her to look. Since her teacher was Mrs. Meyer, he knew she would have gone at once to the sixth chapter of Romans. After all, Mrs. Meyer had said that chapter was worth living for. Turning to it, he immediately came to an exchange and the freedom that exchange brought and didn't bring. In baptism one died with Christ. As one rose from this death, rose from the waters of baptism, the old body that had been sinful became a new body, became a new creation, that had now been set free from sin. Slavery to sin, however, in this act of redemption had given way to slavery to a new master, it had given way to slavery to righteousness. Here was the exchange that released and yet didn't release. Here was the answer to the riddle. But precisely because Mattie would have said, "yes, it was," because he would have said, "yes, it was," because anyone who knew the Bible would have said, "yes, it was," it wasn't. It was too well-known; it was, as Mattie had said to Sister Emma, too familiar.

Wondering where to go next, Randall all at once saw something he hadn't noticed before. He realized Sister Emma had given Mattie a riddle within a riddle. There was the outer riddle having to do with releasing. It, though, couldn't be solved until he had an answer to an inner riddle having to do with binding. Throughout the day, he kept thinking about that inner riddle, about what it was that took freedom away, but at the end of the day, he still didn't know what to do with it. I'll get it tomorrow, he told himself, although not with a whole lot of confidence.

Randall, however, didn't have to wait that long. Early the next morning, he woke up from a deep sleep. According to the clock on the night stand, it was a quarter after four. He turned over and started to close his eyes. Then, suddenly, he opened them and sat up, fully awake. He knew where he had gone wrong. To bind was to restrict; it was to restrain. But that was only one definition of binding. Binding also meant to cover. What was covered was concealed. What was concealed was hidden. That inner riddle was not about freedom. It was about what couldn't be seen; it was about hiding. He didn't know where this insight had come from. Maybe he had dreamt it; maybe his mind had worked it out while he was sleeping; maybe God had worked it out for him. He only knew that although he had a way to go, probably a long way to go, he at least was now headed in the right direction. Closing his eyes, he quietly said thank you and fell at once into an even deeper sleep than before.

Over the next several days, Randall kept asking himself why did we hide? Why did God hide? No matter where his thinking took him, he always came back to an obvious explanation. At first it seemed too simple, but the more he considered it, the better he liked it. We hid, he told himself, because we didn't want to be found or because we did want to be found. We didn't want to be found because of something we had done, or had failed to do, or because of something someone else wanted to do to us. We did want to be found because of someone we wanted to attract. We wanted to be found because of a desire to be pursued. Take for instance a young lady whose interest in a young man was not returned. To attract him, she could be either more attentive or less attentive. She could recede into indifference, into ambiguity, into mystery. She, in other words, could hide. This was done and done so often there was even a word that described the strategy. The young lady, it was said, was coy.

Wasn't God also coy? Wanting to be pursued, wanting, as the psalmist declared, to be sought, God disappeared so that left on our own we saw we couldn't be on our own. Thinking we could was an illusion devious enough and destructive enough to put us into a hell of our own making and to keep us there. Out of the need to be delivered and the desire to be blessed, we turned to God. We began a search for God that went beyond finding God to knowing God, which was the greatest good, for it, as Jesus said in the seventeenth chapter of John, was eternal life.

The explanation pleased him. It made sense, and because of it, God was a little less mystifying. But it didn't satisfy him. Something was missing, something important. Then he happened to read in Mark the passage where Jesus healed a man who was deaf and mute, and it all became clear. The cure was intriguing. Jesus first put his fingers in the man's ears and then, after spitting on his fingers, placed them on his tongue. Immediately the man could hear and speak. What came next, though, was even more intriguing. No one, Jesus insisted, was to say anything about what he had just done. Why not? Shouldn't Jesus have wanted everyone to know about the healing? Wasn't it a sign, and even more than this, wasn't it a confirmation of his power, of his authority, of his love? Suddenly, though, it occurred to him Jesus was concealing the healing; he was, at this point, hiding it. He was hiding it because the healing did not stand on its own. It was part of something else, something of greater importance, and whatever it was, its time had not yet come or at least had not yet come in its fullness. Hiding here was not about being found or not found; it was about something more needing to happen. It was, he realized, about the passage of time.

Here was what Randall had been looking for. There had to be a connection between this understanding of time and an exchange of some sort. Although he didn't know what that connection might be or what that exchange was, he was convinced the two were linked together. Figure out how they were, and he would be only a step or two away from the answer to Sister Emma's riddle. I'm getting there, he told himself. But because of a phone call that evening from his brother, he didn't come any closer. His father was dying.

* * *

Taking a morning flight, he was at his father's bedside the next day. His father was comatose and by then receiving only fluids intravenously. When they had been together, Randall had mostly listened to his father talk. No matter what his father had been saying, he usually returned to one of his two favorite topics and often to both of them: his assessment of a particular situation and his insight into the intricacies of life. Randall had only vague memories of when his father had asked him what he was thinking or what he had learned. Now, as his father succumbed to death, Randall, sitting beside him, was at times silent and at other times talked at length about his family, his years as a minister, his faith.

Occasionally, a nurse came in to check a monitor or to adjust a drip feed. As the days and the nights went by, the nurses unexpectedly brought Randall a bag of potato chips, a package of cheese crackers, a cup of tea. Once, as a nurse went past him to care for his father, she touched him gently on the shoulder. Another, for a moment, held his hand. It wasn't only the nurses who were so thoughtful. One morning Randall had breakfast in the cafeteria of the Care Center. When he tried to pay for his food, the woman at the cash register told him he needed a meal ticket. The office selling the ticket, though, wouldn't open for another hour. A resident sitting at a nearby table walked over to the checkout counter and taking a meal ticket out of his wallet handed it to the woman. After thanking him, Randall said that he wanted to pay for the ticket. "You might want to," the man replied, "but I won't take it," and he went back to his table. Returning to his father's room after breakfast, Randall felt overwhelmed by these acts of kindness. They were in themselves small gestures, yet each one had touched him deeply. Each one, he believed, was a moment of grace. They spoke beautifully of God's presence, of God's love. Those potato chips and crackers, that cup of tea, that gentle touch and hand to hold, that meal ticket were all as ordinary as the day was long. Though unblessed, though unconsecrated, as they were given in love, and Randal was sure they had been, they were for him as sacramental as the bread and cup of Holy Communion and the water of Baptism.

The following afternoon his father died. He had left with Randall specific instructions for the funeral service. Only the family was to attend. The service was to be held at the grave site. He was to officiate using the words from the Episcopal *Book of Common Prayer* adding nothing to them and removing nothing from them. His father had been adamant about this instruction. Randall remembered him saying although we came into the world unequal, with that service, since it was always the same no matter who died, we left it equal. The equality he had sought in life was to be his in death.

A half hour before the funeral, Randall got into the rental car he had been driving. Thinking about the service, he somehow managed to stick the ignition key into the buckle of the seat belt. He pulled on the key but couldn't get it out of the buckle. Fortunately there was another key on the ring. All he had to do was slide the key off the ring. But the ring wouldn't open. The thought of not being able to get the car started made him try harder. This time the ring opened, and he quickly took off the second key. His relief, though, was short-lived. It vanished when he realized the other key was still in the buckle. He would get to the cemetery and not be able to release the seat belt. He saw himself driving up to the grave site, rolling down the window of the car, and telling the family he would be doing the service from the car.

But that didn't happen. The ruts in the road and a pothole that couldn't be avoided jarred the key loose. He got to the cemetery on time and went directly to the grave site. There, as his father had insisted, he went through the Episcopal service from beginning to end without changing a word. When he finished, he then said that having done what Father had wanted, there was now something he wanted to do. Taking a sheet of paper from the pocket of his jacket, he asked the family to listen to a few lines from a letter William James had written to his father four days before his father's death. The words seemed right for us. "What my debt to you is," he read, "goes beyond all my power of estimating, so early, so penetrating, and so constant has been the influence. It comes strangely over me in bidding you good-bye how a life is but a day and expresses mainly but a single note. It is so much like the act of bidding an ordinary good-night. Good-night, my sacred old Father. Farewell. A blessed farewell." As he lightly touched the casket, Randall said, "Farewell, Father. A blessed farewell."

After returning home, Randall found himself thinking about his father's death. At times he had struggled with God's love. Paul's words in Romans were especially troubling. How could Paul say nothing in all creation could ever separate us from the love of God when there was so much suffering in all of God's creation? Didn't this suffering and the agony it brought, agony that could become so acute it consumed us, refute love's presence? If it somehow didn't, this suffering certainly did refute love's power. But since his father died, Paul's words, somewhat surprisingly, had comforted him. Where, he wondered, had this peace come from? Other than the death, nothing had really changed in his life, nothing except for Mattie's memoir and, of course, Sister Emma's riddle. Had Sister Emma been telling Mattie something about God, something about God's love, in that riddle he also needed to hear? Trying to figure it out, had he, without realizing what was happening, started to grasp whatever that was? He had to get back to the riddle. He had to solve it.

That evening Randall asked Emily for help. After he had told her the riddle and what he had done with it, she said, "What are you looking for?"

"The answer," he replied.

"I would look instead for the key piece. That's what I had my math students do when I gave them puzzles to solve."

"Those puzzles that had them attempting to do the impossible?"

"Like sliding rings though spaces that weren't there or balls around obstructions that couldn't be moved, yes. The key piece made those spaces appear and those obstructions disappear. Once that piece was located and used correctly everything else sooner or later fell into place."

"That could explain it."

"Explain what?" Emily asked.

"Why I can't get the connection out of my mind."

"What connection, Randall?"

"The connection that links hiding, the hiding having to do with the passage of time, to an exchange that sets a person free. I think that connection is the key piece you want me to find. It just might be the piece that is going to make everything else fall into place. There is a problem, though. I don't know what that connection is, or where it is, or how it works. I'm stuck, Emily, and I don't know where to go next."

But the following Sunday Randall quite unexpectedly did know where to go next. Richard mentioned in his sermon the empty tomb. It was only a casual remark that undoubtedly went right past most of the congregation. Randall almost missed it too. Up late the night before, he had been drifting off to sleep. Suddenly, though, he jerked forward. Now fully awake, he said in a booming voice as he grabbed Emily's arm, "The empty tomb." Richard seemed to welcome the outburst. He thanked Randall for his response, asked him if there was anything else he wanted to say, and when Randall sheepishly shook his head, he went on with his message. Peeling his fingers away, Emily looked at Randall with the expression she had used to silence a disruptive student in midsentence. Randall sank back into the pew and almost immediately fell asleep. Although his eyes were open and he was smiling, she knew he was sleeping. His father had once told them he had learned in the navy how to sleep with his eyes open while standing at attention for long periods of time. Because of the seemingly endless meetings Randall had sometimes been required to attend, especially those held in the summer in large auditoriums without air conditioning, it was a skill he had also mastered. Here he was, Emily said to herself, sound asleep with his eyes open and a smile on his face. Now that, she had to admit, was impressive.

Leaving the church after the service was over, Randall, as he shook hands with Richard, apologized for his untimely enthusiasm and thanked him for the helpful sermon. Emily, standing next to him, just rolled her eyes. Entering the parking lot, he almost ran to the car. Emily did have to run to keep up with him. After buckling his seat belt, he turned toward her and bringing his arm down in a sharp jab with his index finger extended, he cried, "The empty tomb."

"That's the connection. Randall, now you know what it is. You really shouldn't, though. Richard paused before saying those words. They were just a stray thought that suddenly came to him. If he had stayed with his text, he wouldn't have said them then or later."

"Emily, the connection isn't the empty tomb."

"It isn't?"

"No, it's the tomb that isn't empty."

"It's not Easter Sunday then," Emily said.

"No, and it isn't Good Friday either. It's what is in-between the two."

"The key piece is Saturday?" she replied, not at all sure she had the right answer.

"Yes," Randall replied. He thought for a moment and then said, "Yes, it's Blessed Saturday." The words, as though a floodgate had been opened, now rushed out of him. "Emily, I've solved the riddle. I know what the exchange is, and, what is probably more important, where the exchange is made that sets us free and yet keeps us hidden. It doesn't take place on the cross but in the tomb because that is where the end, in all of its hideous and yet ironically in all of its glorious finality, comes for Jesus: the end of his teaching, the end of his praying, the end of his miracles, the end of his love, the end of his life. He is dead, buried, and the stone is rolled in front of the tomb to seal his end forever. The death happens on the cross on Friday, but that death is consummated in the tomb on Saturday. Saturday belongs to death. On that day, death has its way; on that day, death has its victory. But on that day, in that tomb, whose death is it? It is our death, for Jesus has taken upon himself our sin, our suffering, our forsakenness, our death so that the end does not come to us. Here then is the exchange that frees us. He has become us in our life and in our death so that, as he is raised, we can become him in his death and in his new life, in his resurrected life."

"Slow down, Randall. You are getting way ahead of me. I understand the concept: one turns into the other." Emily stopped and for the longest moment was silent. Knowing she always tried to think a matter through before saying anything about it, Randall waited patiently for her to continue. At last she went on, "There is something T. S. Eliot says in his poem "East Coker" I keep hearing. If I remember correctly, the poem opens with the idea the end is in the beginning and then turning that idea around, the poem closes with the statement the beginning is in the end. Isn't the exchange in your riddle about that reversal? Isn't it about the end in the beginning becoming the beginning in the end?"

"It is, Emily."

"What I don't get is how this happens."

"Why don't we figure that out over lunch," Randall replied, backing out of the parking space. "Is Charlie's all right?"

"Of course. Their Caesar salad is wonderful. But it will take us a good forty-five minutes to get there."

"That should give me enough time to put the pieces of the riddle together in a way that makes sense to both of us."

* * *

After settling into a booth at the restaurant and ordering their food, Emily said, "What have you come up with?"

"I think we need to begin with something I've just discovered. You probably noticed I disappeared during the fellowship time after the worship service."

"You were talking to David Sterns about storm windows and the next moment you weren't." Emily said. "Where did you go?"

"To the church library. There were several passages in the New Testament I wanted to look at. One was those verses in John where Jesus talks about being the good shepherd who lays down his life for the sheep. As many times as I have read those words, I have never paid attention to how the passage ends. But this time I did. It was like discovering treasure in our backyard. For there, right in front of me, in one sentence, in sixteen words, was exactly what I was hoping to find. Jesus says, 'I have power to lay it down,' by it he means his life, 'and I have power to take it again.' Here is Sister Emma's exchange. Laying his life down, Jesus in the tomb dies our death. Taking his life up, he gives us his risen life. The death we are to die is exchanged for the life he now lives. The power that enables him to do this, to lay down his life and to take it back up, is God's love that creates, that makes new. In the tomb where this exchange takes place, sin and death preside, but love prevails. Godlessness is neither cast aside in the tomb nor driven out but is overcome by this love of God, the grieving love of the Father for the forsaken and dead Son and the sacrificial love of the Son for the world, for us, for all of us."

"What does this exchange lead to?"

"Paul, I think, says it best. 'I have been crucified with Christ;' he writes in Galatians, 'it is no longer I who live, but Christ who lives in me; and the life I now live in the flesh I live by faith in the Son of God, who loved me and gave himself for me.' As we believe, the risen

Christ, his new life, is in us. Out of the end has come T. S. Eliot's new beginning, a beginning that is free from sin and death, a beginning that belongs to God's future, to the end of time, when all that has been created will be brought to completion. This new life that is within us, therefore, is irrepressible, it is directed, it is hidden."

"That's Sister Emma's riddle: released and yet bound, set free and yet hidden."

"Yes, Emily. It's hidden because it is within us but only in part. In Colossians, Paul says, 'Set your minds on things that are above, not on things that are on earth. For you have died, and your life is hid with Christ in God. When Christ who is our life appears, then you also will appear with him in glory.' This is what Sister Emma wanted Mattie to understand, and perhaps it's also what God wanted me to hear. A life of faith will always be at its very core a life that is hidden because more of it is to come."

"That God wants you to hear this I don't doubt. But why does God want you to hear this now? You haven't been the pastor of a church for more than a decade?"

"I'm retired from the church, Emily, but not from the ministry. Samuel left teaching to write a book. I think that's what God wants me to do."

"You are going to write a book?"

"Yes," Randall replied.

"What will you call it?"

"What do you think about *Sister Emma's Riddle*?"

"That's fine. But from my reading of Mattie's memoir and after listening to you now, I'd say an even better title is *The Perfect Swing*."

"I like it." Randall thought for a moment and then said, "I like it very much. The word *perfect* is just right. Subtly and yet at the same time pointedly, perfection, perfection that is linked to the swing of a baseball bat, speaks of God who initiates, maybe a better word here might be who woos, and who, in mysterious and even cunning ways, also hides."

"Himself and, according to Colossians, us as well." Emily said.

"In order to be found," Randall replied.

As they were driving home, Randall began to wonder if he had it only half right. Certainly Sister Emma, before she said anything else, would have said that the life of faith was to be seen. What could possibly be more conspicuous than a Deaconess? In her distinctive dress, she walked down back streets of Chicago by herself serving the needy in the name of Jesus. She was doing what Jesus had told the disciples they must do. She was letting her light shine so that others seeing her good works gave glory to God in heaven. But she was also telling Mattie this life was, at the same time, hidden in Christ. It was completely out in the open so all could see it and completely hidden away so no one except for God could see it. Randall had another thought. The visible and the hidden not only belonged to each other. They came out of each other. The visible gave rise to the hidden; the hidden, in turn, gave rise to the visible. He had one more thought. Here was an entanglement Kierkegaard, who favored the complex, would have appreciated.

3

CHRISTMAS EVE

Christmas Eve Randall and Emily were eating dinner when the phone rang. Both got up from the table. Emily went into the kitchen to get the dessert. Randall answered the phone. Hearing Randall say, "I almost fell on a patch of ice shoveling the driveway this morning," and a moment later, "Of course I will, Jim, I'll be happy to," Emily thought she knew who was calling. Jim Wilson, the chair of the church council, was telling Randall that because of a bad fall Richard was going to miss the Candlelight service that evening. She was right. A half hour ago, their pastor had been taken to the Emergency Room at St. Michael's with what looked like a broken arm. The members of the worship committee would handle the readings, the prayer, and the benediction. Jim needed Randall to preach.

When he retired, Randall had decided to keep his sermons, not with the intention of ever using them again, he had never repeated a sermon in twenty-five years of ministry, but with the thought that maybe the grandchildren or the great-grandchildren, because they were searching for answers or were just curious, might one day like to go through some of them. What he had always done before he knew he couldn't do now. There wasn't enough time, there wasn't any time, to write a sermon. Opening the drawer of the filing cabinet where the sermons were stored, he saw a thick folder labeled Christmas. Removing a sermon from the folder, Randall read it through twice, and after quickly finishing his dinner, went upstairs to get ready for the service.

An unexpected detour and the delays it caused added twenty minutes to their drive to the church. Randall had wanted to put his sermon on the shelf beneath the pulpit before the service began. But when they entered the sanctuary, the choir was already in place and the prelude, a festive arrangement of late nineteenth century Christmas songs, had started. They immediately sat down, thankful there was enough space in a side pew for them to sit together. First carols were sung that were introduced by related scripture readings. A prayer followed. The congregation then sang "Love Came Down at Christmas" in preparation for the sermon. When the music ended, Randall, taking his sermon from four years ago out of his jacket pocket, walked to the pulpit. Once there, as he turned to face the congregation, he noticed the Christmas tree that had been placed in a corner to the right of the pulpit. It was a large tree full of beautiful ornaments announcing in their glorious shapes and colors the birth of the child born in a manger. After admiring it for the briefest moment, he turned away from the tree, but then stopped and looked back at it. In the midst of all those decorations, something wasn't quite right. Going to the tree, he immediately saw what it was. A crudely made cardboard angel about five to seven inches high was wedged between two of the lower branches. Covered with yellow and green streaks, it had to be the work of a child, most likely a very young child. Perhaps one of the children from the nursery had secretly put it there, or a parent had placed it there to please a child hoping it wouldn't be noticed.

It wasn't the shape of the angel that Randall found himself staring at or its color. It was one of the angel's wings. The wing was bent back and torn. Startled, he told himself in astonishment this was the angel with a broken wing, not Sister Emma's angel, of course, but definitely one like it. Sister Emma's angel had spoken to her of the brokenness in the world. The angel he was looking at, in that moment, spoke to him as well. It wasn't of brokenness, though. Carefully he removed the angel from the tree, and with it in one hand and his sermon in the other, he went back to the pulpit. There, so everyone could see it, Randall hung the angel from the base of a small light attached to the pulpit. Then he put the sermon away. His words this Christmas Eve were not going to come from a sheet of paper. He began

Angels that first Christmas had a very specific purpose. They were messengers entrusted with directives from God. Joseph was thinking about divorcing Mary. She was pregnant, and it wasn't by him. One night in a dream, an angel came to him with a message. "Take her for your wife," the angel said, "for she is with child by the Holy Spirit." Mary was well into her pregnancy when an angel came to her with a message. The angel told her she was favored by God. These words frightened her. The angel said, "Don't be afraid. You will have a son, and you are to name him Jesus. He'll be great, and will be called the Son of the Most High." When Jesus was born, shepherds were out in the field taking care of their sheep. An angel came to them with a message. The angel said, "To you is born this day a Savior, who is Christ the Lord. And this will be a sign for you: you will find a babe wrapped in swaddling cloths and lying in a manger." This Christmas I believe an angel has come to us with a message. Because of its broken wing, this angel that you see hanging from the light on the pulpit has been stripped of its strength. Unable to go where it wants to, unable to do what it needs to, it cannot help itself; it has lost its power. This angel with its broken wing is saying to us, "The birth of the child in a manger, the child who has been conceived by the Holy Spirit, who is to be called the Son of the Most High, who is the Savior, Christ the Lord, is about weakness."

Randall abruptly stopped. He looked at the congregation, his gaze moving slowly from one side of the sanctuary to the other. He then noticed there were some who were not looking at him. Their heads were down. Perhaps they were studying their bulletins, or inspecting their fingernails, or even looking for flaws in the weave of the carpet. They and many others as well, he knew, wouldn't be back the next Sunday. *Some of you,* he continued, *really don't want to be here. You've come because you have been bribed. You'll be getting a second helping of apple pie tomorrow with an extra scoop of vanilla ice cream on top. Or you are here because you have been threatened. If you had stayed home, you would be having a peanut butter and jelly sandwich tomorrow while everyone else is eating roast beef. You, though, should have stood your ground. For you are right to have wanted to be somewhere else. There are days when I don't want to be here either. Why should we? Before this child is finished, he is going to expect too much of us.* Some, Randall saw, whose heads had been down were now looking at him. Maybe they were wondering where he was headed, or, and this was more likely, they were expecting someone to remove him physically from the pulpit. *He is going to want us to seek first the kingdom of God; to be last of all and servant of all; to love our enemies; to do good to those who detest us, to those who curse us; to deny ourselves, take up our cross every day, and follow him to the least, the last, the lost. He is going to want way too much. And way too much of what he does want has got to be wrong, for in the end, forsaken by God and by everyone else, he is nailed to a cross.*

I'd go if I were you, even if it means a peanut butter and jelly sandwich for dinner tomorrow. I hope, though, you'll stay long enough for a story I'd like to tell you. It's about a man named Cleopas. He followed Jesus. Although he wasn't one of the twelve disciples, like them, he listened to Jesus, he believed in him, he traveled the countryside with him. In this story, the years have gone by, and Cleopas is now an old man. It is a chilly evening. Dinner is over, and he and his wife, Ruth, are in their home sitting before a fire warming themselves. Beside them is their seven-year-old granddaughter, Leah, who, after finishing her nightly chores, has stopped by to visit them. For a moment there is silence as they listen to the crackling fire. Then Leah says, "Grandpa, what did you do when you were young like daddy?" "I've always been a fisherman," Cleopas replies. "Not always," Ruth corrects him. "Oh yes," he says, "a long time ago, I followed a man who talked about God. He kept saying the Kingdom of God is here. He healed the sick, brought a little girl who had died back to life, and, I was told, one day he walked on water." "What happened to him?" Leah asks. "He said God was his Father. He even said he and God were one. People didn't like that. They told him to stop, and when he didn't, they became so angry they nailed him to a cross." "He died there?" "Yes, Leah, he did." "Did you cry?" "We all did." "What was his name?" "His name, my child, was . . . It was . . . It . . . Why, I don't remember his name."

The story could end this way. Cleopas is old. There are lots of names he doesn't remember now. The man's name is just one of those he has forgotten. And there is something else. The man is easy to forget. He had his moment. It came, and then as happened to so many others, it went, and in a seemingly endless procession, someone else who claimed to speak for God took his place. Names that are no longer spoken because others are being talked about are soon forgotten.

The story, though, doesn't end this way. After the crucifixion, Cleopas had dinner with a stranger. As the stranger broke the bread they were to about to eat, his eyes were opened. He didn't open his eyes, his eyes were opened, and he saw Jesus sitting across from him. He saw that the one who had died was now alive. When Leah asks, "What was his name?" Cleopas answers, "His name was Jesus. As long as I remember my name, and I suspect even longer than that, I will remember his."

The eyes of others, countless others, through the centuries have been opened in all kinds of ways, some of them mundane, some of them astonishing, and they have seen Jesus. It could happen to us tonight in this holy place. Something here—a Christmas hymn, the decorations on the tree, a scripture reading, a prayer—one or all of them might open our eyes and we see . . . What would we see tonight? We'd see a baby. We'd hear a baby's cry, a cry of helplessness. Randall paused. He looked for a moment at the cardboard angel hanging from the pulpit and then said, *We might hear another cry. It, too, is a cry of helplessness, of utter helplessness. It comes from a cross. And if we are absolutely still, we might hear yet another cry. It, though, is different from the other two. It doesn't come out of helplessness. It instead comes out of joy, out of an unrestrained joy, that like the birth has to be announced to all the world. It is the joy of Mary Magdalene who after the crucifixion thinks she is talking to a gardener. But her eyes are opened, and she realizes he is not a gardener. To the disciples, to all who will hear and to all who won't hear, she cries, "I have seen the Lord."*

He died and yet is alive. Love has bested death. And because it has, this is a love that can never be taken away from us; this is a love that will never leave us, no matter where we go, no matter how far we fall. Wherever we are, however painful it may be, however hopeless it may appear, this is a love that in its weakness has already entered into our darkness and in its power has already overcome it to give us peace. It is a peace we can't comprehend fully, but we can comprehend it in part. It is a peace that comes out of time: the time we need to forgive; the time we need to heal; the time we need to learn how to love; the time we need to discover joy; the time we need to become faithful; the time we need to grow in grace.

There is a word we can't get away from, try as we might. Sometimes it is a piercing scream in the middle of the night; other times it is a faint whisper we can barely hear. Loud or soft or even for awhile silent it never leaves us. It is the word *maybe*. Maybe our phone will ring at two o'clock in the morning; maybe the department head will summon us to his office; maybe we will feel a lump; maybe the car coming toward us will cross over the center line; maybe a tree limb we are walking under will fall; maybe the company we work for will fail; maybe the stocks we have invested in will be worthless. Maybe, we are stuck with this word. It is how we are made; it is the human condition.

Randall noticed a young family sitting toward the front of the sanctuary. Their daughter, who was probably three or four years old, was wearing pajamas covered with baseballs, bats, and mitts. The pajamas made him think of the photograph of Mattie in her baseball uniform and then of another baseball player. *Satchel Paige was an extraordinary pitcher. He played for years in the Negro Leagues quickly becoming one of its most celebrated and one of its most flamboyant stars. His pitch came in fast, and with uncanny consistency, it went exactly where he wanted it to go. The Cleveland Indians signed him to a contract when he was forty-two years old, making him the oldest rookie in the history of major league baseball. He played the next year for the Indians and then three more years for the St. Louis Browns. In 1971, he was inducted into the Hall of Fame in Cooperstown, New York. Satchel Paige once set down rules for staying young. There was the rule about avoiding fried meats because they angry up the blood, the rule about keeping the juices flowing by jangling around gently as you moved, and the rule about not looking back because something might be gaining on you.*

Something is gaining on us, something is always gaining on us. We can react to this fact of life in one of three ways. We can follow Satchel Paige's advice and not look back. Do this and we are denying the inevitable. Or we can look back trusting in ourselves. Do this and we are declaring before the inevitable we are strong. Or we can look back trusting in the one who is overtaken by all that takes life away and yet rises above it. Do this and we are declaring before the inevitable we are weak. It is this weakness, or, to use the words that appear in the Psalms time and again, it is this admission that we are poor and needy, that allows us to rise above all that takes life away from us.

It is a statement that brings us here tonight: "Be not afraid; for behold, I bring you good news of a great joy which will come to all the people; for to you is born this day in the city of David a Savior, who is Christ the Lord." It is a question, though, that we leave with. Are we going to have our lives shaped by maybe or are they going to be shaped by this Savior who is born in weakness and who dies in weakness for our sake? If we answer by this Savior, we will hear the hard words he speaks; we will hear them and make them the words we speak. For we will know they set before us the way we must take to bring to others the good news of his love that will set them free from being trapped all their days in maybe. It is a way that begins in weakness, and yet ends in power. It is a way that begins in death, and yet ends in life, in life that is eternal.

Randall picked up the angel with the broken wing and walking slowly forward he placed it on the altar. He bowed his head in prayer, thanking God for that holy night when love came down at Christmas, for that love that had come down to suffer and to die for all, to suffer and to die for him. He turned around and said, with tears welling up in his eyes, "Amen," and heard its echo in the soft "Amen" of the congregation.

V

CORY

The Grandson

On their way back to the airport at the end of the week, Meg said, "Did you finish your grandfather's book?"

"I did," Cory answered.

"What is it about?"

"Digging."

"As in excavation?" Meg said.

"Grandfather does dig down. But it is also about exploration."

"So he digs around too."

"Yes, in history, in his soul, in his understanding of God," Cory replied.

"What did you dig up?"

"Faith."

"How far down did you have to go?"

"Not very far," Cory answered. "What Grandfather is getting at is pretty much there in the titles of his book."

"How many titles does it have?"

"Only one, but there are two other possibilities. Grandmother wants *The Perfect Swing*. That's about Mattie coming to faith. She needs to be certain about something that is by its very nature uncertain. Faith here is always in question. I want *The Angel with a Broken Wing*. That's about Lucy Rider Meyer who doesn't have to come to faith. She already has it. She always will. Faith here is never in question. Grandfather wants *Sister Emma's Riddle*. That's about his understanding of faith, what it brings and doesn't bring. Faith here is itself the question. Actually there is another possibility. I also want *Passed Over*. That's about Grandfather's faith. He writes about others but is writing, at least in part, about himself. He makes it clear he is called not chosen. Although he doesn't say this, what this means is he, in effect, has been passed over and, therefore, his faith is at risk, which he fully recognizes. So he writes about keeping the faith he's got even when God is absent, even when God is hiding."

"He thinks God hides?" Meg asked.

"He does, so we seek God. I dug up something else. The headings of the book all have something to do with times of the day. Grandfather does this to make us think about time, about the past, the present, and the future. The past, I can hear him saying, contains what has been of God and this needs to be brought forward into the present. The future contains what is to be of God and the promise of what this is needs to be brought back into the present. So the present is the intersection of the past and the future, and since this intersection is of God, it directs and sustains faith. The present, though, contains more than an intersection, he would say. It also consists of those times when something important happens, those times that mark critical points in the unfolding of what follows. Without them what does happen wouldn't have."

"Do you think these critical points occur or are they made to occur?"

"Are they a coincidence or are they arranged? I'd have to say they are arranged because so often there is a fine line between something happening and not happening. Because a perfect pitch is thrown, a swing is perfect. If a boy's pitch had been thrown a fraction of an inch higher or a fraction of an inch lower, a girl's swing wouldn't have been perfect and Mattie would have rejected God, or at least wouldn't have accepted God when she did. Because a boy running down a street bumps into Mattie causing her to drop a wooden angel, she meets Sister Emma. If the boy had run down another street or had started running ten seconds earlier or ten seconds later, Mattie never would have met Sister Emma, never would have enrolled in the Training School, never would have married Samuel."

"Think about us, Cory. There certainly was a fine line between us meeting that second time and not meeting. When we first met at the homecoming game, I was interested in someone else. So there was no second meeting then, even though we did feel drawn to each other. Three months later we did meet again. I was starting to get into the elevator you had just gotten out of. You could have been on another elevator, or your elevator could have come a minute earlier or a minute later. Either way we never would have met that second time, and we would not be married now."

"So you think that second meeting was arranged."

"I've always thought it was arranged," Meg said.

"If it was arranged, there must have been someone doing the arranging."

"There must have been. Do you think these critical points cause what happens next?"

"I think it's more they are necessary for what comes next. They give impetus and substance to what emerges."

"What else did you dig up?"

"Aristarchus. No one listened to him for seventeen hundred years," Cory said.

"Should they have?"

"What he said was right. Mattie, after listening to what happened to him, decided to look for her own truth."

"Where did that decision take her?" Meg asked.

"To William James, a philosopher; Mr. Weber, the owner of the bookstore she worked for when she wasn't playing baseball; and Lucy Rider Meyer, the principal of the training school she attended when she stopped playing baseball. For Professor James, truth is inside us. It comes from the experiences we have. For Mr. Weber, truth is above us. It comes from what we believe. For Mrs. Meyer, truth is in front of us. It comes from what we believe and pursue."

"What does your grandfather say?"

"He sides with Mrs. Meyer but adds the pursuit of truth sooner or later, depending upon the question, leads to mystery," Cory replied.

"Because he is unsure of himself?"

"Because he is humble and wants to make sure he stays that way."

"So he is saying when it comes to God what we end up with is mystery not knowledge?"

"Mystery and surprise, yes. I dug up something else. It, too, is mysterious and surprising, very surprising. Our family is much larger than we think it is."

"Because of births we haven't been aware of?"

"No, because of a whole side of the family we haven't known anything about."

"That's shocking, Cory." Meg was silent for a moment and then said, "Where did they come from?"

"From an affair my great-great-grandfather, I think I've got that right, had with a married woman whose last name was Welsh. Their child Mattie never knew who her biological father was."

"Did his own children know about Mattie?"

"Eventually, but they decided they wouldn't look for her or her family. My grandfather did. The Welsh name, though, disappeared from local records early in his search. He found in Chicago, in the records of the downtown courthouse, a marriage license for Mattie and her husband, Samuel Bingham, and a birth certificate for their daughter, but because only one child was born in Chicago and that child was a girl, his search for Bingham descendants ended there.

Since Grandfather couldn't go any further, my parents apparently thought they wouldn't be able to either and so didn't try."

"What are you going to do?"

"Mother told me," Cory replied, "if I read the book, I would know Grandfather better: who he was, what he thought, why he thought that way. She was right. I can hear him saying, 'God is constantly working out ways to bring all of us together. That is what God is doing, and that is what God wants us to be doing.' Just in case I haven't been paying close enough attention, I hear him saying in an even louder voice, 'That means all of us in the family.' I am going to find Mattie's family, which for generations now has been a part of our family."

"Do you think you'll be able to do this?"

"I do. If Mattie can find a missing house, I can find a missing family. Undoubtedly Grandfather would add, 'Along the way, God just might find you.'"

"What in the world happened to the house?"

"It was stolen."

"Cory, you have to tell me all about Mattie, the house, and also Aristarchus. For all I know that could be the name of a high-end clothing store."

"Not a clothing store, Meg, but a Greek astronomer. He is a good place to start. But since our flight won't be leaving until 1:30, let's go into the life, to use Grandfather's words, of this New Woman over lunch in the Tail Wind Cafe that has just opened at the airport."

NOTES

Much of the book is fiction: Cory and Meg, Randall and his family, Mattie and her family, Sister Emma, Samuel, the Clippers, Mattie's classmates at Vassar and the students at the Training School.

Much of the book is also fact: Vassar at the turn of the century, the train wreck outside Atlantic City, bloomer girls baseball, the Training School, the Deaconess Order, Lucy Rider Meyer, the University of Chicago, Lazarus Averbuch, Chicago in the early 1900s, the Maxwell Street Settlement, Maud Nelson.

The source for the statements about Blessed Saturday is *Between Cross and Resurrection: A Theology of Holy Saturday* by Alan E. Lewis.

Scripture passages in Mattie's journal are taken from the King James Version of the Bible. Passages in other parts of the book come from the Revised Standard Version of the Bible.

ABOUT THE AUTHOR

THOMAS LENHART, a pastor in the United Methodist Church for twenty-two years, has a PhD from Northwestern University in History of Christianity. He has written articles about the Methodist Episcopal Church that have appeared in historical journals. He and his wife, Lynne, live in Holland, Michigan.

Made in the USA
Lexington, KY
11 June 2019